the case of the
missing boyfriend

Nick Alexander was born in Margate, and has lived and worked in the UK, the USA and France. He is the author of the five-part '50 Reasons' series of novels, featuring lovelorn Mark, and when he isn't writing, he is the editor of the gay literature site BIGfib.com. *The Case of the Missing Boyfriend* was an eBook bestseller in early 2011, netting sixty thousand downloads and reaching Number 1 on Amazon. Nick lives in the southern French Alps with two mogs, a couple of goldfish and a complete set of Pedro Almodovar films.

Visit his website at **www.nick-alexander.com**

the case of the missing boyfriend

nick alexander

CORVUS

First published in Great Britain in 2011 by BIGfib Books.

This edition first published in Great Britain in 2012
by Corvus, an imprint of Atlantic Books Ltd.

Copyright © Nick Alexander, 2011

9 8 7 6 5 4 3 2

A CIP catalogue record for this book is available from the British Library.

ISBN: 978-0-85789-631-5 (eBook)
ISBN: 978-0-85789-630-8 (Trade paperback)

Printed and bound by CPI Group (UK) Ltd, Croydon, CR0 4YY

Corvus
An imprint of Atlantic Books Ltd
Ormond House
26-27 Boswell Street
London WC1N 3JZ

www.corvus-books.co.uk

ACKNOWLEDGMENTS

Thanks to Fay Weldon for encouraging me when it most counted. Thanks to Rosemary, Adrian, Giovanni, and Allan for all their help and support.

PART ONE

....

Dead Chuffed

When I open my front door, the bouquet of flowers that greets me is so vast, so dense, that I can't actually see who is holding it. The bouquet comprises roses – which I hate – and deep, green sprigs that look like they might have come from the Leylandii in Mrs Pilchard's garden.

My first thought is, *God, how dreadful!* And then, in case He, or She, or whoever, or *whatever*, is listening, I try to think graceful, grateful thoughts instead. For, truth be told, it's been a stunningly long time since anyone sent me flowers – even awful flowers – and *Thinking Your Way to Happiness* says one has to work harder on one's automatic thought patterns, so working harder, one is.

The voice that springs from behind though, is easily identifiable. 'Hi, babe,' it chirrups: Mark, my neighbour from upstairs.

In fact, as Mark both lives in the flat above mine, *and* works one floor up from me at Spot On advertising he is pretty much 'upstairs' in one form or another twenty-four/seven.

I'm feeling somewhat disappointed that the flowers are not the long dreamt of *Eureka!* moment where gorgeous-unknown-secret-admirer reveals that he has in fact been in love with me for years. And then again I'm also feeling somewhat relieved that I will not have to house the horrid bouquet for long.

I squash myself against the wall and let Mark squeeze past. 'They're not for you I'm afraid,' he confirms, 'they're for Ian's mother.'

'I thought you two split up,' I comment, frowning and following him through to the kitchen. '*And* I thought she was dead.' My gay friends have such a constant stream of boyfriends, confusion is always a distinct possibility.

With me, of course, it's easier – there is nothing *to* remember. *What we need here*, I think for the umpteenth time, *is a little redistribution of boyfriend material.* I hope He/She/It is listening.

'Well, yes, they're for her funeral,' Mark explains, propping the bouquet up in my kitchen sink and turning to face me.

The world is divided into those who dare to address me by my horrific first name, and friends who know better. Mark knows better. 'So how *is* my little CC?' he asks, stepping forward and kissing me on both cheeks.

'OK,' I say, vaguely.

'These are nice,' he adds, tapping one of my earrings. 'I haven't seen you for *days*! Have you been away or something?'

Still thinking about the earrings, I shake my head a little more vigorously than I would otherwise. 'No,' I say. 'I've been stuck down in Media all week trying to sort out the magazine space for those Hi Five ads. Actually, these are props from that shabby/chic photo shoot we did for their autumn collection.' I tap my right ear with my index finger. '. . .last worn by Angelica Wayne I'll have you know!'

Mark nods, impressed. 'Well, they suit you brilliantly,' he says. 'They look even better on you than on her.'

'If only the rest of me looked like her, eh?' I laugh, picturing Wayne's nano-waist and involuntarily pulling my tummy in.

'I told you, she's too thin,' Mark says. 'She's ill.'

'. . . no such thing as *too thin* in this business,' I say. 'Anyway, enough of work . . . So are you telling me that Ian has now invited you to his mother's *funeral*?'

Mark grins and runs his fingers through his tiny Tin-Tin quiff. 'I know,' he says enthusiastically. 'I'm dead chuffed . . .' He pulls a face: thoughtful, confused. 'Must remember not to say that to Ian . . . *dead chuffed.* It's not ideal, is it? But yes, we're back together.'

I shrug and shake my head. 'But how? I mean the last time you mentioned Ian . . .'

Mark shakes his head and pushes his lips out. 'I don't know

really,' he interrupts. 'I mean, I was just getting used to the idea of being single again and then his old mama goes and dies, and within hours he was knocking on my door and weeping all over me. He stayed the night, and then we woke up together and, tada . . . we're an item again. Nothing like a bit of grief to put an argument into perspective eh?'

I shake my head. 'Apparently not,' I say. 'I must remember that one next time someone dumps me. Murdering one of their parents is the answer, it would seem.'

'But I do think it's a sign at least,' Mark says. 'It demonstrates a certain level of trust and intimacy, inviting your boyfriend to a funeral, don't you think?' He looks at me and wrinkles his brow. 'What's up? Am I burbling? Or is it that you're jealous?'

'Erm, *no*!' I laugh, turning away to pull mugs from the cupboard. 'Do you want tea?'

But *of course* I'm jealous. I'm jealous but quick enough to realise that being sorry because I don't have a boyfriend to invite me to his mother's *funeral* is a tad on the sick side of *sad* and best not admitted to. Ever.

'A cuppa would be lovely,' Mark says, rubbing his nose and then hauling himself up onto the counter top.

'So are the burbling and that jiggly foot there a sign of too much coffee?' I ask, pointing the kettle accusingly at him. 'Or have you been . . . you know . . .?'

Checking the screen of his mobile, Mark replies, 'Sweetie – it's six p.m. on a Thursday night!'

Mark is developing quite a cocaine habit, and I have to say, I am beginning to get a bit concerned about it. But then again, it often seems that half of London is taking the stuff these days. I push the bouquet to one side and fill the kettle. 'That's not an answer,' I say. 'And well you know it.'

Mark shrugs, rubs his nose again, and grins coyly, confirming my doubts. 'Maybe a bit,' he admits. 'But it was only a booster shot – we had to finish the visuals for Hi Five and I had a hangover. Plus I'm off tomorrow for this funeral thing, so . . . Anyway, I'll be calm now.' He takes a deep breath, then says with theatrical poise, 'So how are you?'

I lean back against a cupboard and smile weakly. 'Me?' I say with a mini-shrug. 'Oh, I'm fine.'

Mark nods thoughtfully. 'You look a bit bluesy,' he says.

I shrug again.

'So is this need-a-man blues?' he asks. 'Or empty-weekend blues?'

I laugh. 'You know me so well,' I say. 'Though really I think it's just plain old *February* blues.'

Mark chews the side of his mouth. 'I could probably get you an invite to the funeral,' he offers with mock seriousness. 'If you want.'

I shake my head. 'Not quite *that* desperate,' I say.

'No,' he says. 'I guess not. You should call Darren. He's going to some fabulous pervert view on Saturday. Didn't he tell you?'

I shake my head. 'I haven't seen him all week. As I say, I've been stuck down in Media. A private view, you say?'

Mark laughs. 'No, this one really is a pervert view,' he says. 'Some Colombian bondage photographer called Ricardo something or other. It should be fabulous. Apparently the waiters are all going to be dressed up in gimp outfits. It could be a hoot.'

'And you're *missing* this?' I ask incredulously.

Mark wrinkles his nose and nods sadly. 'Yeah. Dead in-laws in Glasgow take precedence,' he says.

'She's from Glasgow?' I say.

'Yeah,' Mark says. 'Though I think you'll find that *was* from Glasgow is the correct tense. Anyway, call Darren. He split up with Peter again, so I'm sure he would love you to go.'

'I take it Ricardo Thingamajig is gay,' I say, '. . . the photographer?'

Mark nods and wrinkles his nose. 'Probably,' he says, pushing his lips out. 'Bisexual at worst, I would think. Or from your point of view, I suppose, bisexual at best.'

I grimace.

'I'm sure there will be some straight arty types there though,' Mark says raising one shoulder. 'And it has to be better than sitting here feeling sorry for yourself in the dinge all weekend,' he adds, nodding out of the kitchen window at the mass of green shadow beyond.

'I'll think about it,' I say.

Once Mark has drunk his tea and swooped off with his flowers, I sit and stare out of the window at the base of the Leylandii and think about the invitation. A year ago I would have jumped at it. But that was before I started worrying about The Missing Boyfriend.

Of course, in a way, I have always worried about The Missing Boyfriend – I have worried about him, or his absence, so frequently that I have had to shorten it to TMB just to save brain energy. Even when I was dating someone, even when I was married to Ronan, or living with Brian, I still worried about TMB, for the person sitting opposite never quite fulfilled the image I had in my mind's eye about how TMB would/should/could be.

It's not that I am particularly demanding, honestly it isn't. It's just that the men I have ended up with have been so spectacularly lacklustre. And ever since Brian . . .

A gloomy image of my life with Brian appears at the periphery of my mind's eye, like a storm on the horizon threatening devastation. I pause and sigh before swallowing hard and pushing it away.

God it's still there! Three years on, and Brian is still lurking around the edges of my brain ready to pop up at any moment. Break-ups are survivable. It's the aftershocks that get you.

Suffice to say that ever since that bastard Brian, finding a man, finding the *right man*, has started to feel urgent, because of my age. Well, my age and the baby thing.

So Darren and Mark and their boyfriends *du jour* may be fabulous fun, but I am increasingly aware that they are not the correct route through the maze that is my life – they will not lead me to the TMB.

And so I make a compromise with myself: I will go to the

dreaded speed-dating thing again and as a reward I will let myself go to Ricardo Whatsit's bondage exhibition. And you don't need to be Mystic Meg to predict which is going to be the most fun.

I reach for my mobile and dial Darren's number.

Carpenter Pants

Fridays! They're always the worst. Days stuffed with itsy-bitsy multicoloured tasks that fill every second of the day, but like M&Ms fail to nourish in any way.

I make a phone call here, send a couple of emails there, courier a DVD to the printer.

These days – and in advertising there are many of them – drive me insane. Because though I run around barely pausing for breath, schmoozing here, smoothing ruffled feathers over there, chivvying along and calming down as required, no single task is ever consequential enough to give any kind of character to the day. These *days*, and they fall often, though not exclusively, on Fridays, leave little or no sense of achievement. They are the kind of day that, when Ronan or Brian would ask me what I had done that day, (usually in response to my state of evident exhaustion) I was hard pressed to think of a single thing I had achieved.

Nowadays no one asks of course – perhaps the only advantage I can think of in being single.

Though painfully vacuous, these days are, however, essential. For without schmoozing, clients look elsewhere, and without smoothing, ruffled feathers fly away. And without chivvying, neither Media nor Creative do anything at all.

It's four p.m. I put down the phone and sigh. It's the first time since eight this morning I have had time to think about the ADD nature of the day.

I look over towards the coffee room to see if the dreaded Victoria Barclay is lurking, waiting to assail me with one of her complex look/sigh combinations – a raised eyebrow here, a pouty mouth there. Though the meaning is never explicit, I am always left feeling guilty. Just as with my mother, any look other than a smile leaves me feeling as though I am somehow a disappointment, if not to the partners (of which she is one), then to womanhood, or perhaps even to the entire human race.

And then I think about the chivvying thing again, and realise that Creative haven't given me anything whatsoever for my Monday morning pitch to Grunge! Street-Wear, so I grab the phone. When the boys fail to pick up their extension I literally jog across the room and throw myself through the closing doors into the lift.

Gotcha! Victoria Barclay, lying in wait, spider-like, gives me the once over, raises an eyebrow and then screws the end of her nose as if I am perhaps smeared in dog shit. 'Running *late* for a change?' she asks.

I smile at her. 'Not at all,' I say.

I turn to face the doors and wait for my chance to escape.

Of course, not getting anything from Creative – *The Gay Team* as I call them – is pretty par for the course really. As far as I can see they just sit around all day talking about their sexual conquests and smoking until half an hour before the deadline, whereupon they somehow miraculously defy gravity or time or something by slinging together some irritatingly fabulous idea.

Whether this ability to do nothing and then come up with the goods at the last possible moment is a sign of their brilliance, or a severe failing on their part, I can never really decide. I often wonder how good the campaign would be if they spent, say, a whole *afternoon* on one. But with Mark away, and with Jude famously refusing to work weekends (nothing must get in the way of his cycling) this is cutting things even finer than usual.

Sure enough I catch Jude and Darren leaning out of the window smoking. They drop their cigarettes into an old Marmite jar on the window-sill and spin to face me. 'Oh it's only you,' Jude says. 'Damn! Waste of a good ciggy.'

'Thank God you're still here!' I reply. 'Where are the visuals for the Grunge! pitch? I just realised, I haven't had anything.' I note a slightly hysterical tremor in my voice and decide to get a handle on that.

'What? For the pervy jeans?' Darren asks, frowning.

'*German carpenter pants*, I think you'll find,' I say calmly.

Carpenter pants are in fact black jeans, only with two zips for the fly, one to the right and one to the left of the normal opening. Quite why German carpenters, or anyone else for that matter, should need two zips for peeing is beyond me, but the Grunge! designers are convinced that it's the next big thing. It is up to us at *Spot On* to make it so.

Thinking that it's a bit late in the day for me still not to know this stuff, I ask, 'Anyway, why *do* German carpenters need a double fly? Are they, like, really big or something?'

Darren giggles. 'Maybe. Or just into general perviness.'

I sigh. 'Come on then,' I say, 'spit it out.'

Jude shrugs cutely, and blushes slightly. 'Well, that's the real point, isn't it?'

I frown. I think I'm being naive, one of my specialities – though when you're surrounded by gay men, it's often hard to appear anything else. 'OK,' I say. 'I have to sell the damn things. Explain.'

'It's so boys can get their tackle out,' Jude, now seated at his Mac says, matter-of-factly. 'For you know . . . *shagging*. Quickly.'

'Is it?' I ask, grimacing at the overload of mental imagery this concept is producing. 'And they can't do that with a normal fly?'

'Well no, dear. Not without considerable risk of rubbing it up and down the zip,' Jude laughs.

'Not to mention the risk of getting it caught in the zip,' Darren adds.

I grimace. 'Is that *really* the point?' I say. 'Or are you winding me up? Surely button flies . . .'

'No one can get in or out of a button fly in a rush, hon, even *you* know that,' Jude says.

Darren nods sadly. 'That's why leather-men have had double zips on their gear for years.'

'But how does having two zips help?' I ask, picking up a sample pair of the jeans and unfastening one zip and then the other. The rectangle of tissue between the two zips flaps downwards. 'Ahh!' I laugh. 'You undo both zips *at once.*'

Jude rolls his eyes at my apparent slowness.

'So I take it you do have an idea to sell this to the general public,' I say, 'because dungeon masters are *sooo* not our target market here.'

Jude beckons me over and Darren squeezes in beside me. 'I just did this mock-up,' he says. 'There are two campaigns – we run the gay one first, in *Gay Times*, *Têtu* in France . . . what-have-you.'

He clicks and the screen fills with an image. A guy (beautiful, skinny, photoshopped to perfection) is standing in a pub surrounded by white-toothed, earnest-looking colleagues in business suits. He's wearing carpenter pants and a sweatshirt, and around his neck is a sketched-in dog collar with a vast long lead which runs out of the door, up into the night sky, and across town before dropping into the hand of a guy who strikes me as a very Village People leather-man in breeches, boots, and one of those peaked military hats. He is heading into the door of another, much dingier looking bar with a neon sign. Across the top of the ad the copy reads, 'For guys who like to get ∧ out.' Above the ∧ is a hand-written '*it.*'

'Jesus!' I say. 'That's a bit full-on isn't it?'

Jude shrugs. '*I'd* buy a pair,' he says.

'Me too,' Darren says. 'That's brilliant.'

I shoot him a look and turn back to Jude. 'When you say you have just done this, you really mean, *just*, don't you?'

He shrugs.

'So what's the pitch?' I ask.

Jude grins disarmingly. 'Gay culture is all about invisible signs that only those in the know can spot,' he explains. 'Leather wrist-bands, handkerchiefs in pockets, key chains . . . So here we see a gay guy, by day, in a work environment, and all those suits he's with have no idea that by night he's a dirty little bugger.'

'Truly brilliant,' Darren says.

'Whereas, of course, any other gay man will have seen "carpenter pants" (he raises his fingers to make the speech marks) or at the very least this advert and will know exactly what's going on.'

'But the target market isn't only gay men,' I point out.

'No,' he says, clicking on the mouse. 'It's not quite finished yet, but . . .'

The screen fills with a soviet-propaganda-style image of a couple. The guy has cheekbones you could hang washing on and biceps the size of my thighs, whilst his girl has an Angelica Wayne nano-waist and a tied-back, blond bob. They are standing with their backs to a scene of urban desolation – London, kind-of after the earthquake – whilst before them is a vast, open vista of green fields, cows and daisies. Along the top is a similar tag line. 'For men who like to get out of the Grunge!' The guy is, of course, wearing carpenter pants.

'So here,' Jude explains, 'we're showing a Germanic alpha-male who lives the hard life in the city, but spends his free time enjoying nature. He is the touchy-feely nature-lover/muscle-man women want.'

'Is he?' I ask, briefly trying to imagine myself with the touchy-feely, Germanic, alpha-male.

'Yes,' Jude says, 'and he's leading his girl away from the grunge of the city for a lovely day out.'

My focus has shifted to the bulge behind the alpha-male's double-zip combination, and I decide that Jude is indeed right. He is exactly what women want.

'But what is the double zip gonna do for *this* guy?' Darren asks.

I frown at him. 'Have you worked on this project *at all*?' I ask.

Jude shrugs. 'He hasn't. But he's finishing off the visuals this weekend, aren't you? And the answer is that double-zips aren't going to do anything for him. It's fashion, sweetie. But once the trendy straight boys see us gay boys running around in carpenter pants they will want them too. This second ad creates a parallel message about it being to do with the great outdoors – it's an enabler – it creates a second narrative to let them buy something that they would otherwise identify as gay.'

I nod. 'OK,' I say, doubtfully. 'But heterosexuals do actually have sex, you know.' I wait for one of them to say, *'Do you?'* But no one does, which is a relief. Because if I were being truthful, I would have to admit that not *all* of us do.

'Yeah, but not in an impromptu whip-it-out kind of way,' Darren says.

I shrug. 'It has been known,' I say, affecting my best wise-woman-of-the-world expression. 'There are certainly plenty of couples who like to shag in the great outdoors.'

'Well, then the image is perfect,' Jude says. 'You can read it either way.'

'If he buys a pair for his girlfriend too then that would certainly speed things up, wouldn't it?' Darren says.

'As long as the zips don't get stuck together . . .' Jude giggles.

'So that's it?' I ask, forcing a serious tone to interrupt the chatter. 'This is what I'm pitching on Monday to Clarissa Bowles and company?'

Jude shrugs. 'What do you think?'

'I think it's awesome,' Darren says. 'I wish I had made more input, I would have been really proud of that one.'

I shake my head. 'Jesus, Mary,' I say. If my childhood priest knew the things I have to sell these days he'd . . . Truth be told, I do remember a bit of a fuss. He would probably want a pair. He probably *has* a pair. In leather.

Jude rubs my arm. 'You'll breeze through,' he says. 'You always do.'

And it's true. Every material aspect of my life is proof that I can sell anything, even a semi-obscene advertising campaign for completely pointless, outrageously overpriced, double-zipped jeans. I have no idea where this gift-of-the-gab came from, but I've been doing it long enough to know that I have it. I just wish I were as good at selling other things, like myself.

'OK,' I say, with a nod. 'I just have to work out how to pitch this without scaring them off. And don't be late with the story-board on Monday. You know what Clarissa is like about punctuality.'

'Do we still have a date for the private view?' Darren asks, as I turn to the door.

I nod. 'You bet,' I say, glancing back.

'Can I borrow a pair of these? They'd be perfect,' he asks, picking up a pair of the jeans.

I shake my head. 'Absolutely not.'

Knowing Where You're Going

In this age of virtual-everything, there is something almost old-fashioned, archaic even, about the concept of speed dating. The idea of going to meet ten guys, face to face, in just over an hour, is not only nerve-racking but also somehow a bit quaint. But as *virtual*-dating on the internet seems to bring nothing more than *virtual* boyfriends (rare is the man who turns up to a date, in my experience) – and because my social life in London seems to produce nothing but opportunities for meeting an ever-larger selection of gay men, speed dating it is.

I have to say at this point that I honestly never intended to become such a fag hag. It just somehow happened. I expect a psychotherapist searching for causes would point rather obviously at my brother Waiine's death, but I honestly don't think that that's the reason. It's simply that I meet a lot of gay guys through work, and, having nothing whatsoever against them, it would be really stupid of me to refuse all the invitations I get to tag along. Because the events they take me to are, almost without exception, more fun than I get in any other area of my life. But tonight isn't about fun. Not one bit.

When I have fun out with Mark or Darren or my best friend Sarah-Jane, it's precisely because there are no expectations. Even surfing Meetic can give me *some* hope because the most obsessive-*repulsive* of fuck-ups generally describe themselves as *happy-go-lucky, good-looking*, etc. At least we *both* get to pretend that they really are the way they say they are.

Speed dating, however, generally leaves me feeling suicidal. The guys here sadly *aren't* hiding behind twenty-year-old photos of Daniel Day-Lewis. They are sitting there, leering at you, in all their revolting splendour.

So by the time I have sat talking to six guys who look like they needed a crane to get out of bed that morning, three who sound like they may have had lobotomies, and generally one, funny, witty hunk who, at the end of the session, inexplicably fails to ask for my phone number, I'm ready for the mortuary. Which is why, whenever I can, I arrange to meet Sarah-Jane for a post-mortem afterwards.

SJ is perfect for this because a) she lives in Brixton, just around the corner from The Office – the bar where the speed dating is held – and, b) has been in the same relationship since fish first crawled onto land and so, like all such people, thrives vicariously on my dating nightmares. She also has what personality profiles call a *sunny disposition*, and, more essentially, *remains* sunnily disposed after a bottle and a half of Chardonnay.

I arrive at The Office about a minute late.

Speed dating, appealing to people with busy schedules and being organised by Nazis with stopwatches, clearly isn't something one should turn up late to. Everyone glares at me to make sure that I am aware of this.

Thomas, the organiser, sighs and points me to the end of the row. 'And *you*! You can pay afterwards,' he says in his best school-teacher voice.

At the rear of the bar ten tables are lined up. Backs to the wall, facing me, are ten guys. They pretty much fit the previously described mix, only tonight perhaps only five are clinically obese – though on second thoughts, the sixth is definitely border-line. Half of them have beards too, which I'm afraid is a no-go area for me. I don't spend half my life waxing to end up kissing a bunch of pubes.

I scurry by, trying to discreetly check out the guys *and* the competition, for the most part a similarly comfortable bunch of lassies with their backs to me.

The boys stare at me, some with distaste (presumably at my unspeakable lateness), some with slight leers of interest. All these eyes following me around make me awkward and that awkwardness makes me feel as if I am on a catwalk, which in turn makes the business of putting one foot in front of another seem suddenly terribly complex. This is not helped by the fact that I am wearing my new Jimmy Choos.

And then, two from the end, I see him: dark brown eyes, stubble, neither skinny nor fat, just sort of chunky and sporty, balding . . . Balding is a plus actually – some kind of daddy-complex, I expect. I must go see a shrink one day to find out.

Brown Eyes is wearing a blue, crew-neck jumper over a white shirt, and he's smiling at me. A good smile, slightly amused.

The smile of course tips the balance and my already floundering feet finally fail, catapulting me forwards. I collapse against an empty chair, pushing it and the table hard into the amply padded tummy of another chunky chappy, who turns out to be my first sparring partner.

I apologise profusely to Barry (yes, *Barry* – I kid you not) and then Thomas shouts, 'Are we finally ready?' and the stopwatch starts.

Whilst wiggling my foot under the table in an attempt at untwisting it, I listen to Barry drone on excitedly about how interested he is in computers and how he prefers Windows Vista even though it got a *really* bad press. He talks about Windows for two and a half of his allotted three minutes, and then somehow cleverly links to how much he appreciates *punctuality* in a woman. I spend my own three minutes wishing I were anywhere else whilst trying to sound like a total bitch who is trying really hard *not* to sound like one, but can't *quite* avoid letting her true total-bitch-nature slip out. I think I manage this pretty well because Barry wrinkles first one, then both of his hairy nostrils at me.

I am also thoroughly satisfied by my display of self control: I manage to glance at Brown Eyes only twice.

• • •

When I arrive, Sarah-Jane is frying slices of tofu in her tiny kitchen.

'They always disintegrate when I do that,' I tell her as I hang up my coat and cross the room to kiss her on the cheek.

'You have to get the pan really bloody hot,' she explains. 'burn the buggers before they realise what you're trying to do to them. So how was dating-hell this week?'

'Oh, not bad,' I say. 'Actually it was bloody awful. But there was *one* potential, at least.'

Sarah-Jane nods. 'There's some Chardonnay in the fridge,' she says in response to my own bottle of shop-warm Bordeaux. 'So tell me, what was it like?'

'As I say. They were all revolting except this one guy.'

'What's his name? And what does he look like? Did you get his phone number?'

'Well he's got brown eyes,' I say, ignoring the first question, 'balding, sort of chunky, a bit rugby-player-ish. Potentially cuddly.'

I pull the wine from the fridge, a glass from the shelf and pour myself a hefty slosh.

'Sounds good,' Sarah-Jane says, fishing strips of browned tofu from the pan and pouring in a bag of stir-fry veg. 'No beard then?'

'No beard.'

'So, shaggable?'

'Trust you get straight to the point,' I laugh.

But really it's what I love about Sarah-Jane. Well, one of the many things I love about her. I take a gulp of wine. 'Yeah,' I say. 'Given the chance . . . definitely.'

She takes a sip from her own glass. 'What did you say his name was?'

I wrinkle my nose. 'I didn't,' I say.

'INS?' she asks.

What with her being a chavvy Essex-girl called Sarah-Jane and my being an equally misnamed daughter of a lawyer from Surrey, we have invented an abbreviation for such situations: INS, or, Inappropriate Name Syndrome.

'Yes,' I say. 'Definitely INS.'

'Come on then,' she prompts. 'What is it? Dwayne? Barry? Don't tell me . . . *Winston?*'

I laugh. 'There *was* a Barry,' I say. 'But no. This one's a Norman.'

She pulls a face. 'Eeek!' she says. 'Norman Bates! Doesn't live with his mum, does he?'

I nod. 'I know,' I say. 'Personally I kept thinking about that *Spitting Image* puppet of Norman Tebbit.'

'Fucking hell,' she says. 'Norman! That's not good. That's really not good.'

'No,' I say. 'I blame the parents personally. But if there's anyone who can ignore a bad first name, well, it's gonna be me really, isn't it?'

'Yeah,' Sarah-Jane says. 'I s'pose. What's his surname?'

I shrug. 'We don't get that information. Just a phone number.'

'. . . course. But you got it?'

'I did,' I say. 'There was a Dustin too . . .'

Sarah-Jane winks at me. 'Now yer talking,' she says. 'Always had a thing for Dustins.'

'Yeah, I thought of you. He was about thirty,' I say. 'About thirty *stone.*'

'You're such a fattist,' she laughs. 'Does that exist? Fattist?'

I shrug. 'I know . . .' I say. 'I'm not in any other area of my life, honest. I mean, if I have to *work* with a porker, I don't even think about it. But having been on a diet since 1971, I don't expect to then have to sleep with someone who needs industrial liposuction. Does that make me *horribly* shallow, do you think?'

Sarah-Jane shrugs. 'Nah, love,' she says. 'It's just, well, I like a bit of padding myself. Anyway, you were *born* in 1971.'

'Exactly,' I laugh. 'But seriously, you didn't see them – you honestly have no idea. Dustin looked like Ricky Gervais. A *fat* version of Ricky Gervais. Talked a bit like him too.'

'Now, you see . . . I *like* Ricky Gervais,' Sarah-Jane says, adding the contents of a sachet of sweet and sour sauce to her mix. 'I think he's funny.'

'Yeah, but not in your bed,' I laugh.

'No,' she agrees. 'No, I suppose not. Anyway tell me about *Norman*.' She pulls a face as she says the name.

I shrug. 'You don't get a great deal in three minutes, but he does something in mental health, something to do with half way houses.'

'Probably lives in one,' Sarah-Jane laughs.

'Don't,' I say. 'I thought that already . . . He has two brothers, lives in Clapham, likes walking and reading and classical music and rugby.'

'I suppose books and music makes up for rugby,' Sarah Jane says doubtfully.

'Well, any more touchy-feely and he'd be gay, and lord knows that's not what we're after here.'

'No,' Sarah Jane laughs. 'So when are you seeing him?'

I shrug. 'When he calls.'

'And if he doesn't?'

'In a week if he hasn't phoned I suppose I'll call him.'

Sarah-Jane hands me a plate of food and a fork. 'Yeah, best not to seem over-keen,' she says.

'Exactly.'

'Though this being a heterosexual man, best not leave it too long either, or he won't remember who you are. Goldfish memory and all that. Did I tell you that George forgot my birthday again?'

• • •

In my taxi home to Primrose Hill, I think somewhat tipsily about SJ and George, and then, as if allowing myself a square of chocolate, I let myself think about Brown Eyes.

I have little fantasies about the two of us living a perfect love affair that worryingly resembles a carbon copy of SJ's life, for Sarah-Jane, who I have known since college, has it all. Such people really do exist.

She has George (who I believe to be the last of the New Men to be churned out before they gave up and switched back to producing Old Men again). She has lovely supportive parents, a great job promoting Macmillan Cancer Trust, Timotei hair, an overactive thyroid gland (it keeps her weight in check, you see), and utter faith that everything always turns out for the best.

She met George at eighteen and has loved him to bits ever since. I'm not jealous of her – I love her far too much for that. No, SJ's wonderful life warms me up on an almost daily basis, gives me the hope that comes from seeing that happiness does really exist, that people really do manage it, that relationships really *can* last.

It's just her certainty in the future I envy. For nothing bad has ever happened to Sarah-Jane, and her belief in life is unruffled. Next year she and George will have saved enough to move, and for George to stop travelling, and for her to stop work and start a family. She *knows* that, unlike Brian, George will stand by her and remain faithful and be a wonderful father, and I think that despite the odds, despite the bastardly men I seem to meet, and despite the relationships I see crashing and burning left, right and centre around me, she's probably right.

And I can't help but think that being so contented about where you have been and being so certain of where you are going, well, that must feel wonderful.

SAD Syndrome

When I wake up on Saturday morning, I can hear rain crashing against the plastic roof of the conservatory. I lie in bed as long as possible until hunger forces me from my pit – it's just after ten. For as much as rain-when-in-bed is cosy and lovely, rain-once-up depresses the hell out of me. I often wonder if I don't suffer from that SAD syndrome, though everyone I know wonders that, and if everyone has the same syndrome, isn't that just called *normal life*?

Aware that in my *best*-case-scenario I will have to undress in front of Brown Eyes (I don't seem to be able to use the Norman appellation *just* yet), I resist a two-thousand calorie cooked breakfast and make do with a yogurt and a coffee.

I sit at the kitchen table and make it last as long as possible by simultaneously reading the *Guardian* and staring out at the rain plummeting onto the lawn, but in the end there's nothing for it: on a cold, rainy, February Saturday, yogurt does not a soul nourish.

I dig some thick-sliced, white, pappy bread from the freezer and toast it and smother it with butter and marmalade and make myself a fresh coffee, this time a frothy cappuccino. I'll just have to consume nothing for the rest of the weekend to make up for it. I wonder, not for the first time, if it wouldn't be easier to just vomit everything up like Angelica Wayne does.

The toast soothes and I drift into a much nicer reverie involving my cooking a wonderful healthy lunch for Brown Eyes. I see myself chopping vegetables, and grilling fish like some modern version of a Stepford Wife and then hubby comes in and says, 'Hello, gorgeous!' Then, 'Oh, sorry, love, I don't think I can handle fish. Not with this hangover.'

Quite why my daydreams always end up so badly I have no idea. Well, I *do*. That scene is an act-for-act representation of my life with Ronan. He was an alcoholic, and being drunk, or having a hangover, were his excuse for just about anything he didn't want to do. Or anything he *did* want to do for that matter.

I try another scenario. Brown Eyes and I are shagging away this rainy Saturday. The bed feels warm and wonderful. He rolls on top of me, slips his way in, and then pauses, looks into my eyes and says, 'You are still on the pill, aren't you? You know how I feel about kids.'

You guessed it. Brian.

As a distraction, I spend a leisurely hour and a half plucking and peeling away any evidence that I too might be descended from an ape. Beauty magazines call this pampering, but there's nothing pampering about it. It hurts. It's hell.

I dress in my favourite tattered jeans and a paint-stained sweatshirt and head back through to the kitchen, half thinking about food again, half realising that I could have missed a phone call whilst I was washing my hair. When careful checks of the BlackBerry and landline reveal that I haven't, I turn inevitably back to food and cook two sausages to make an evil thigh-expanding sausage sandwich. I then get a grip and bin one of the sausages and one of the slices of bread. When I have eaten the remaining half-a-sandwich, I shamefully peer into the bin to see where the rejected sausage and bread have landed, but they are in a splodge of dried up cat food which means of course that for now I am saved.

Humm, I think. *Cat.*

I frown and look around the kitchen. I call Guinness, but he doesn't appear. I check the office and the bedroom.

I peer out of the kitchen window and spot him at the bottom of the garden sheltering under the Leylandii, and then I see what I have been waiting for for months: a flash of yellow behind the fence.

I open the back door, grab an umbrella from the hall and run outside. Guinness screams his own catty version of reproach at me and bounds inside in a soggy blur.

At the bottom of the garden, I stand on tiptoe and finally catch Mrs Pilchard beneath the Leylandii. Quite what the old bag is doing weeding in the pissing rain I have no idea.

'Oooh!' I call out.

Mrs Pilchard visibly jumps. 'Oh, you made me jump,' she confirms. 'Creeping up on people like that! Honestly!'

'I didn't,' I say. 'Anyway, I'm sorry I made you jump.'

'Sorry, dear?' she asks, straightening her back and wiping her hands on her pinny.

'Nothing,' I shout. 'It's about your tree.'

'I'm just doing a bit of weeding,' she says. 'Lovely day. Such bright sounds.'

I pause to listen, but other than the white noise of the rain and the swish of cars drifting from the main road beyond the roofs I can hear nothing. 'Yes,' I say. 'Lovely. Now I need to talk to you about this thing.'

'What thing?' she asks.

'This thing!' I say, pointing above our heads. 'It's getting out of hand. It *is* out of hand.'

'Beautiful, isn't it?' she says, smiling up at the tree.

'Well . . . beauty is in the eye and all that,' I say. 'But it's too big. It's cut virtually all of the sun out. My lawn is dying because of the shadow. I can't even grow herbs in the kitchen any more. Actually I feel like *I'm* dying because of the shadow. You have to get it pruned or something.'

'Pruned?' she laughs. 'You can't prune a tree, dear.'

I think you probably can, but she has gained an advantage, because what I know about trees you could write on . . . well, on something really really tiny. 'Well, you need to do something,' I say. 'Maybe get it thinned, or perhaps . . .' I cough. 'Cut it down?'

'Now why would I want to do that?' she says. 'A lovely tree like . . .'

'Because otherwise I shall phone the council,' I say, forcefully. 'I'm sure there are rules about this sort of thing.'

Remaining on my toes to peer over the fence is making my feet hurt, which in turn is adding to my general irritation about the Leylandii, and my dingy kitchen, and the rain dripping down my back, and not ever being able to eat enough food to actually not feel hungry, and not having a boyfriend and the many, many disappointments of life in general.

At this point she places one hand on each hip and smiles at me, and I wonder, not for the first time, if she isn't a little doolally.

Demonstrating that she definitely *isn't*, she says, 'Well phone them then, dear. They just started a *plant-a-tree-and-save-the-planet* campaign. Did you see the posters?'

As it happens, I did. They're everywhere.

'I'm sure they would love to talk to you about trees,' she continues.

I shake my head and sigh as she gives me a little wave, chucks a, 'Ta-ta!' over her shoulder and struts off into her house.

I return to my kitchen, feeling irritated about the tree, and to be honest, somewhat disappointed that our argument didn't last longer. It felt like shouting at her was kind of helping my mood. Plus now I still have six hours to kill before I am supposed to meet Darren.

I move through to the lounge and glance at the TV: anaesthetic on demand. I resist it for a few more minutes by pressing my nose against the bay window.

I watch a mother run to her absurdly sized 4x4 whilst sheltering her child with her coat. I see the postman push a trolley of soaked letters past and think that it is somewhat irresponsible of him not to flap the lid back over to protect the letters and that if he delivers a piece of soggy pap through my letterbox, I shall tell him so. In a friendly manner, of course. I don't want to be invited onto *Grumpy Old Women*! But he just walks straight on to number forty-eight, denying me the pleasure.

With no further action on the street, I settle onto the sofa nursing the Sky remote. Guinness, who knows that my lap is warmer than the cushion, jumps onto me immediately. He's still pretty damp, but because it's my fault he's so wet, and because his presence, even soaked, is comforting, I let him stay.

My finger hesitates over the button for an instant, and then I realise that I have not one, but two recorded episodes of *Desperate Housewives* on the hard disk. Watching how those Yankee bitches deal with their problem neighbours is the perfect balm, because, of course, being American, the solution generally involves murder.

I click the button to fast-forward through the commercial break. I suppose that as I depend on advertising for a living, this is somewhat contradictory, but I figure that as the monster that is advertising devours my working week there's no reason to feed it my weekends as well.

Just as I hit *play* in order to find out which of the residents of Wisteria Lane have died in the freak tornado that has devoured their homes and ripped up all of the trees (now there's something to dream about), the phone rings.

As the number is hidden, I hesitate. My first thought is that it could be Brown Eyes, so I should really pick up.

But if it *is* Brown Eyes and he asks me out tonight I will have to miss the photography party thing, *or* refuse the date which would seem terribly ungrateful.

Then again, if it *is* him and he *doesn't* leave a message then I shall never know that it *was* him which would be awful.

And if I *do* answer and it *isn't* him then I might have to listen to one of those new hyper-aggressive double-glazing callers and have to be rude, which always leaves me feeling bad in a *you-horrible-person-she-was-only-trying-to-earn-a-living* kind of way.

Finally I decide that if it *is* him and I *do* tell him I'm too busy tonight because I have an invitation to an art exhibition then I shall just appear to be a jolly hip groovy chick with a seductively exciting lifestyle. In the final millisecond before it switches to voicemail I stab the answer button.

The voice that greets me, though, is not the soulful baritone of Brown Eyes, but the hyperactive twitter of my mother. 'Oh you *are* there!' she says. 'I didn't think that you were going to answer and I was just about to hang up myself.'

'I thought you—' I start, but she interrupts me.

'And then I thought, of course, she'll be out gallivanting around with all her London friends, or shopping or at work, but no! You are actually in.'

'Yes, But I thought—'

'I'm so glad I caught you though, dear. I tried to call you yesterday but . . .'

'I was at work, Mum.'

'Yes, and then I realised I had the days mixed up. That happens as you get older, you'll see, and even more when you're on holiday. The days all just seem to slip into each other. It is Saturday, isn't it?'

'Yes, Mum. But aren't you supposed to be in—'

'Well I am dear. I'm phoning you from the hotel.'

'OK . . .' I say vaguely. 'It's just that you always say that it costs too much to call from the hotel and—'

'Yes, but this chap I met bought me this calling card thingy,' she says. 'It's terribly complicated, you have to dial a number and then another number, and then a pin code, and then the number for England, and then your number.'

'Right,' I say. 'What chap?'

My mother doesn't meet 'chaps'. In fact even the word *"chap"* isn't something she's particularly comfortable with. She believes that any word invented since nineteen-fifty needs to be quarantined from the rest of the sentence by surrounding it with visual speech-marks. *'Disco'*, *'DJ'*, *'gay'*, *'laptop'*, *'mobile'* and, yes, *'chap'* all require inverted commas. I imagine that, on the other end of the line, she has just used her free hand to make them.

'Honestly, love, it's like a hundred numbers all together, and it took me three attempts just to get them all right, which is why I'm glad I caught you as I don't think I would have had the courage to try again. But apparently it's cheap as chips.'

'Great,' I say. 'What chap?'

'Oh, he's just this local lad I met in the souk. He's been showing me around.'

'What, like a guide?' I ask.

'Humm,' she says. 'Anyway, how are you, my love?'

Now my mother virtually never asks me about myself, and when she does she certainly *never* pauses long enough for me to reply. I am surprised and more than suspicious. 'I'm . . . fine,' I say. 'But who is this guy?'

'Which guy?' she asks, suddenly senile.

'The guy who bought you the calling card,' I say.

'Oh him. He's lovely, darling. I'm sure you two would get on like a house on fire. Anyway, I'm glad you're OK. I suppose I had better hang up though. If I save some of the card I can give you another call next week, though to be honest, I haven't the foggiest how many minutes I get with this thing anyway.'

'Mum!' I say. 'Who—'

'Anyway, have a lovely weekend. Toodle-pip.'

And with that she hangs up.

I sit and stare at the handset for a moment, for everything about the call is wrong, starting with the fact that she called me *at all*.

Mum has spent the last three winters in Morocco. She stays in a cheap hotel in Agadir with full board from December to March. It would seem that there are lots of oldies doing this now, and she claims that it is cheaper to stay in a hotel there than feed herself and pay the heating bill in England. The way gas prices have been rising she's probably right. But it remains the case that, until today, not once has she phoned me during these sojourns.

Also, although the form of the call, her inimitable, uninterruptible monologue, is entirely normal, the fact that she sounded so upbeat, didn't mention her sciatica or her migraines or even her recurrent sinusitis, is literally a first, for her calls are generally more monologue-of-pain than anything else.

And yet the obvious conclusion – that my sixty-seven-year-old mother is having a holiday romance – is unthinkable. Isn't it?

Or is that just me, doing a classic, my mother-can't-possibly-have-a-sex-life, thing? My mother-can't possibly-have-a-sex-life-*if-I-don't*, thing . . .

I put the handset back on the base-station and stare blankly at the frozen image on the TV screen: Teri Hatcher is holding a gun and looking nervous. Her arms look uncomfortably thin to me.

The Right Words

When I get out of the taxi in Shoreditch, Darren is already standing outside Old Street station – our arranged meeting place. The rain has stopped and the street is glistening with reflected light from neon signs and passing cars. People are streaming in and out of the station, but it's not hard to spot Darren: he's the only person wearing carpenter pants.

As I reach him, I laugh and shake my head. 'You rat!' I say. 'I mean, what's the point of asking me if you then just ignore what I say?'

Darren grins sheepishly and pecks me on the cheek. 'I knew you wouldn't really mind,' he says. 'And they're so perfect for tonight's event, I couldn't resist it.' He grabs my arm and we head off towards Hoxton Square.

'Only I did mean it,' I tell him. 'We're under contract not to reveal the product before the launch in March. If anyone sees you . . .' I shake my head.

'Oops,' he laughs.

'Oops indeed. If anyone asks you where you got them . . .' I lean back and check his bum.

'No, there's no brand on this pair,' he confirms.

'If anyone asks, say you bought them in a street market in Spain. That's where they get all their stuff made and there are always strays and rejects popping up.'

'Sorry,' Darren says. 'If it's really important I can go back and change.'

I sigh. 'No. It's fine,' I say. 'But don't make a habit of it.'

'Hey, I'm so glad you came,' he says, steering me across the road. 'I hate going to these things on my own.'

'Yeah, what happened to Pete?' I ask. 'I thought you were in love.'

'Oh, you know me,' Darren says. 'There's always something wrong. It just takes a few days to find out what.'

'Like?'

He shrugs. 'We don't like the same things, or we don't have the same view of relationships, or we both want to bottom.'

'Bottom?'

'Yeah, we both want to be, you know . . .' He whispers the final word. '*Fucked.*'

'Oh, right,' I say. 'Sorry. Of course. And with Pete?'

'Oh, Pete? I found out he wore brown socks,' Darren says nodding sadly. 'I couldn't possibly date a guy who wears brown socks, could you? And they were nylon. Yes, there's always a brown-sock moment, sadly.'

I steal a glance to see if he is winding me up but he looks deadly serious. 'I could probably put up with that,' I say. 'If everything else was OK.'

A rough-looking girl with a cigarette, coming the other way, barges into my arm and knocks me into Darren's side. 'Hey!' I say, turning to look at her as she heads on down the street. 'Just, you know . . . look where . . .'

She stops in her tracks and turns back to face me. 'You got a fuckin' problem?' she asks. She looks drunk.

Darren seizes my arm tightly and forces me on along the road. 'Don't engage,' he says. 'Come on.'

I glance behind to check that the chavvy serial killer isn't following us, and say, 'Is it me or is London getting more and more aggressive?'

'No, it's terrible,' Darren agrees. 'One word out of place and you could get stabbed.'

'So you're not joking? About the socks?'

Darren shakes his head. 'They were horrible,' he says. 'The ultimate turn-off.'

'Right,' I say. 'Fair enough.'

We turn down a side street and then into Boot Street. 'I'm loving these jeans though,' he says. 'They're ever so comfortable.'

'They look great on you too,' I say. 'They really make your arse look good.' I pause and pull a face. 'I mean, of course, that they really *show off* your arse. Your already fabulous arse!'

Darren gives me a circumspect look and raises an eyebrow. 'I've been doing squats at the gym all week,' he says. 'My arse better be looking good. You're looking pretty smooth too, by the way. That outfit makes you look almost attractive.' He grins at me cheekily.

I'm wearing my favourite D&G little black dress, a black cashmere coat and my Christian Louboutin Robot Boots. 'Yes, I thought black was safest,' I say.

'The boots are perfect,' Darren says with a nod. 'I'd quite like a pair of those myself. So what did you get up to last night?'

'Oh I went to speed dating,' I say. 'I hate it, but . . .'

'I can't think of anything worse,' Darren says. 'I do all my shopping online these days.'

'Do they do *gay* speed dating?' I ask.

Darren wrinkles his nose. 'I don't think so,' he says. 'Then again, I suppose that's all our bars and pubs ever are. Speed dating, speed shagging, speed splitting up. So not good then?'

'No,' I say. 'Same as you really. There's always something wrong. There's always a brown-sock moment when you realise that they have some terrible structural flaw. A terrifying number of them are really badly overweight these days. It's scary.'

'Not so much a problem with our lot,' Darren says. 'But I do know what you mean. I notice it when I go out to straight pubs. We're turning into American burger-eaters. But I suppose if you're in it for the long haul, you could always choose one and then put him on a diet.'

'Yeah,' I say. 'If you get that far . . . I suppose. But then, couldn't you just have bought Pete some new socks?'

Darren laughs. 'It wasn't that *really*!' he says. 'God, I love that you're so gullible.'

'Oh,' I say. 'Well, you're jolly convincing.'

'No, it turned out Pete had a boyfriend up in Leeds.'

'I thought he went there for work,' I say.

'Yeah, me too,' Darren says sadly. 'But no. They've been together for fourteen years.'

'How did you find out?'

'I logged into my email and his came up instead. He had been using my laptop and forgot to log out. And more fool me, I took a peep. And there were, like, three messages a day from this Lee guy.'

'God, how awful.'

'Pete made out that it didn't matter because *of course* they have an open relationship, blah, blah . . . But I asked him, "Do I look like a side-dish for bored couples?"'

I giggle. 'Great line,' I say. 'I never think of things like that until after the event. And?'

'He said that, yes, I did. Look like one, that is.'

'Oh!'

'Well, it wasn't so bad really. He said, yes, I did, and a very appetising one at that.'

'Smarmy bugger.'

'Exactly.'

'And you weren't having any of it? Good for you.'

Darren wrinkles his nose. 'No,' he says. 'I'm thirty-five in October. I always promised myself that if I wasn't married by thirty-five I would kill myself, so I don't have time for any pissing around.'

'I know the feeling,' I say.

He pulls me to a halt, and looks up at the blanked-out windows of the gallery. 'Looks like we're here,' he says. He pulls an invitation card from his pocket and flashes it at me. It says, 'White Box Gallery – Hoxton Square. Ricardo Escobar – Perverted Justice. Private Viewing.'

'Shall we?' Darren asks, gesturing towards the door.

I squeeze his arm. 'Sure, but first . . .' I say. 'You wouldn't, would you?'

'What?' he asks.

'You wouldn't think about . . . you know . . .'

Darren laughs. 'Oh, hon,' he says. 'Of course not. These days I don't even get watery-eyed over them. I've had six-inch steel plating fitted all around my heart.'

'Good,' I say. 'Because I really like having you around.'

'Come on then,' he says. 'This is gonna be good.'

As the windows and doors have been blanked out, the interior of the gallery is a complete surprise. The single, vast, white-walled room already contains about thirty people, mainly rather attractive thirty-something men. They are milling around appraising the huge black and white photos on the walls, or circling the giant installation in the centre. A few are chatting around the drinks table at the far end. Everyone of course is dressed in black.

I feel suddenly nervous. Art exhibitions do this to me. I'm always terrified that someone will ask me for an opinion. For though I generally have the gift of the gab in most social situations, I have never been able to master that weird brand of art-speak people use at exhibitions. My opinions on visual art rarely extend much further than liking or not liking whatever is in front of me.

'Jees! Will you look at that!' Darren mutters, moving into the room towards the centrepiece.

'I know . . .' I say. 'Amazing.'

In the middle of the room are four life-sized figures. The first, a bare-chested, steroid-pumped, black-leather version of a gladiator, is standing on a sledge. He is holding the reins of three . . . how to describe them . . . virtual *husky dogs* I suppose you could say. These three 'dogs' are actually men though: men on all fours, in harnesses. They are wearing nothing but big labourers' boots and leather shorts. They have little pretend puppy-tails and rather unnerving doggy masks hiding their faces.

'That's incredible,' Darren says.

'And so realisti—' I say. But as I say it one of the reins twitches ever so slightly. 'Oh my God!' I laugh, stepping forwards until

I am a yard away from the main centurion figure. 'They're real!' I gasp, peering into the centurion's face, which twitches with a restrained smile.

'Awesome,' Darren says.

I walk around the figures, shaking my head. At least ten other people are doing the same. It crosses my mind that we look like a tribal circle surrounding these man-dogs. And as we are all dressed in black, we almost look like we are part of the exhibit – it's quite unnerving. 'Ouch,' I murmur. 'Are those pretend tails . . .'

But then I realise that Darren is no longer beside me. He has crossed the room to the drinks table, where a heavy-set yet attractively swarthy guy in a black suit is talking to him. I clomp my way across the marble floor to rejoin him.

'So you like my installation?' Swarthy asks, his Latin accent thick. He picks up a glass of champagne and hands it to me.

'Oh, incredible,' I say. 'You're the artist?'

He nods.

'Well, I'm speechless.' It strikes me as I say it, that being speechless provides excellent cover for having nothing intelligent to say. I must remember it for future exhibitions.

'And my photos?' he asks.

'I haven't had a chance to look yet,' I reply.

'OK, well do come tell me what you are thinking when you have finish,' he says. 'And you . . .' He directs this at Darren. 'Don't go before you have give me your phone number.'

As he moves away, I say to Darren, 'Wow, that was quick!'

Darren shrugs and leans in towards my ear. 'He seems really nice, but he's not really my type, to be honest,' he murmurs.

Darren and I follow the general direction and move clockwise around the room, pausing in front of the first photograph: a vast black and white macro-shot. The photos are taken at such close proximity and cropped so heavily, that it's hard at first to work out what many of the images are of. This makes the whole viewing process a bit like one of those game shows on TV where you have to identify the object. Only the answers here are ruder, of course.

'Wristband?' I venture, studying the crisp image of shiny leather, flesh and chrome before us.

'Yeah,' Darren agrees, tipping his head to one side. 'Wrist restraint, and a padlock.'

'They're amazingly crisp for such big photos,' I say, wondering if that is technical enough to be repeated to the artist. I figure that it probably isn't.

'They're rather beautiful,' Darren says.

'Oh, is that . . .?' I murmur, moving onto the next picture.

'I think so, yes,' Darren says. 'Isn't it?'

I move close enough to read the little card to the right: *Chrome ring and balls – Ricardo Escobar.*

As we move around the room playing our I-spy game, I also get time to check out the wondrous selection of men present. I'm sure that they are all gay, but who cares: it is a visual feast. And I'm shocked, yet again (for this happens every time), just how fit and good looking most gay men seem to be compared to the porkers I meet at speed dating. Of course they aren't all model material: there are a couple of men in their late fifties, perhaps even early sixties. And there are far too many beards for my liking: sadly the gay community seems to be having a bit of a beard fetish at the moment. But I understand entirely when Darren whispers in my ear, 'Cute guys! Honestly, I'd *do* any of them!'

'Well that's why Mark calls you *Super Tramp*,' I say.

'It is indeed,' he laughs. 'And see the little guy with the red hair over there . . . He keeps smiling at me. Could be my lucky night.'

I glance across the room. 'He's a bit small for you, isn't he?'

Darren shakes his head. 'Uh-huh!' he says. 'I love the pocket-monsters.'

I shrug. 'Well, I suppose someone has to.'

'As long as they aren't too up themselves,' he says. 'I find the little ones often seem to over-compensate for their lack of stature by being complete twats.'

'Hitler syndrome?' I say.

'Exactly.'

We are now level with the first of the three dog-men, and I make the most of the opportunity to have a good stare. 'That floor must be very hard on their knees,' I say, thinking as I say it that it's a terribly old-lady kind of a comment to make, the sort of thing my mother might say. 'And are those tail things actually . . .'

'Yeah,' Darren says. 'They are.'

'Ouch,' I say.

'They sell those all over the place now. The masks too. Dog-training is very big at the moment.'

I push my lips out and nod knowledgeably. 'I'm sure,' I say, thinking that I will have to get Darren to explain about *dog-training* to me another time.

'Talk to me about something else,' Darren says as we position ourselves in front of the next photograph. 'These pictures are giving me a bit of a . . . Huh-um.'

'Let's hope the carpenter zips are well made,' I laugh. 'Wouldn't want you breaking out.'

'Don't!' Darren says.

I resist glancing at Darren's zips and turn to face the next picture. 'I understand though,' I say. 'They are incredibly erotic.'

And it's true. Though I have never had any kind of leather fetish, and nothing but the most fleeting of S&M fantasies, the exhibition, the semi-naked men in the middle of the room, the pretty guys all around us . . . it is all conspiring to make me feel dreadfully horny.

'I'm serious,' Darren says. 'Change the subject.'

'It's not easy when you've got a yard-wide cock in front of you,' I whisper, laughing. 'That *is* what we're looking at here, isn't it?'

'Yeah,' Darren says, pulling off his leather jacket and flopping it over his arm.

'Oh, poor you!' I giggle. 'OK, erm, think about work . . . Did you finish the storyboard for Grunge!?'

'Yeah, I did. It looks great,' Darren says. 'Oh, look . . .' He grabs my arm and pulls me to the centre of the room.

'What?' I ask.

'The shorts,' he says, nodding. 'Look at the shorts they're wearing. Check out the zips.'

I look left and right to check that no one is watching me and lean down to peer at the crutch of the men's bondage shorts. I somehow sense that the guy behind the mask is grinning at my close inspection. Sure enough the shorts have double zips.

I straighten up. 'You're right,' I say.

'You see. Nothing new under the sun,' Darren laughs. 'God, I think I need another drink, don't you?'

'I'll go,' I say. 'You stay there and think calming thoughts.'

Amazingly, in the thirty seconds it takes me to fetch two fresh glasses of champagne, Darren has become ensconced in a conversation with the ginger pocket-monster who would be quite beautiful were it not for his size and shocking red beard. But *les goûts et les couleurs . . .* as the French say: there's no accounting for taste.

I linger beside Darren for a moment waiting for red-beard to notice me and include me in their conversation, which, I can't help but notice involves him regularly touching Darren's chest. When he eventually does glance at me, he simply raises his half-full glass and says, 'No, I'm fine, thanks.'

It takes me an instant to realise that he thinks I'm serving drinks. 'Sorry, no,' I say, wondering as I say it why I'm apologising. 'I'm with Darren.'

Darren turns and breaks into a huge grin. He rubs my shoulder with his free hand – a soothing gesture – before taking the glass from my grasp. 'CC, Dave, Dave, CC.'

Darren leans towards my ear and says very quietly, so that only I can hear him, 'He's gorgeous.'

'Oh sorry,' Dave says. 'It's just that you're dressed the same as . . . Sorry.'

I glance around the room. The crowd has swollen to about fifty people. I now notice that of the five other women in the room two of them are indeed wearing little black dresses and big boots. They also happen to be serving drinks. I feel myself blush.

'So, CC,' Dave says. 'How do you spell that?'

'Just "C" – the letter "C",' I say. 'Twice. It's an abbreviation.'

'What for?'

'It doesn't matter,' I say, smiling superficially and looking around the room.

'Oh, but it *does*,' Dave says.

'Don't,' Darren tells him.

'Oh,' Dave says. 'OK. Secrets, secrets!'

Darren goes red and bites his lip. Dave glances at his feet. And then, thankfully, Ricardo joins our momentarily paralysed ensemble.

'So, you have a chance to look?' he asks, nodding and wiggling his eyebrows funnily at me.

Darren nods and raises his glass. 'It's stunning,' he says. 'If I were richer I'd buy one.'

Ricardo nods and grins. 'Maybe we can think of a way for you to earn one,' he says, saucily. He turns to me. 'And you? What are your thoughts? Give me the woman perspective.'

I swallow. *Oh God!*

'They're really nice,' I say. I think, *Oh, get a grip girl: Nice? Really Noyce?*

But my mind remains a desert. 'I love them,' I add.

The only other thing I can think to say is that they have left me feeling horny, but that hardly seems appropriate. Why oh why can I never think of witty things to say at the right time?

Dave wrinkles his nose and half-laughs, half sneers at me. 'Personally,' he says, turning to face Ricardo, 'I feel that the exaggerated objectification of the human body as sex-toy is terribly exciting, and I am left wondering, is there not a note of intentional humour, or perhaps even, dare I say it, social comment in your work?' He raises an eyebrow at me.

Ricardo seems unimpressed though. He frowns at him and shakes his head. 'No,' he says. 'There isn't.'

'Oh,' Dave says, looking suddenly less smug. He turns back to me, clearly having decided that I am far easier prey. 'So what do *you* do, my dear? You're clearly not an art critic.' He laughs here at his own joke.

'No, I'm in advertising,' I say.

'Oh *advertising*,' he says with a definite sneer.

'I take it you don't like advertising,' Darren says quietly.

'Well, what's to like?' Dave laughs, clearly unaware that he is blowing his chances with Darren. 'It's really just a form of prostitution, isn't it?'

'Prostitution?' I repeat.

'Yes,' the gnome says. I have already stopped thinking of him as Dave.

'Wouldn't you agree that selling products you don't believe in, to people who don't *need* them, living on a planet that can't *afford* the sheer environmental cost of them, is a form of prostitution?' he asks.

I shrug. Again words fail me. Under different circumstances I would agree with him – it's actually pretty close to what I think about advertising myself. But the rudeness and brutality of his public attack have shocked me. The first phrase that comes to mind is, *Piss off, you opinionated little prick*, but I restrain myself.

Darren turns towards me. 'Oh,' he says, pulling a face. 'Brown-sock moment.'

'Yes . . .' I say. 'Indeed! Nylon, methinks.'

'Sorry?' the evil-one asks.

'So what do you do, Dave?' I ask him, my voice over-sugary in an attempt at hiding my gathering anger.

'Oh, this . . .' he says, gesticulating to the four guys in the middle of the room. 'I'm responsible for this.'

'Oh, sorry,' I say. I turn from Dave to Ricardo. 'I thought this was all your work.'

'It is,' Ricardo says. 'Dave is a . . . a sort of fixer for events, aren't you? He found these beautiful men for me.'

Dave nods proudly.

'Right,' I say. 'Well, that can't have been easy.'

Dave shrugs. 'Well, they're just escorts,' he says, somewhat dismissively I feel, considering that said escorts are all within earshot.

I try to think of a really good put-down, but of course, nothing comes to mind. And truth be told, if I did think of something really good I wouldn't have the nerve to say it to him anyway. Being bitchy on demand requires training and dedication and sadly, I just haven't put in the hours.

Ricardo grabs my arm, links it through his, and literally yanks me away. 'Come and look at some of the *bigger* works,' he says loudly.

I bite my lip, unsure if he is having a dig at Dave's size or not, but I'm grateful to have been saved.

As we walk away, he murmurs into my ear, 'Such a nasty little queen, don't you think? In Colombia we say that they smell funny.'

'Who?'

'The red ones.'

'Oh, gingers?' I restrain a snigger because of the un-PC nature of the remark.

'But he's a great organiser,' Ricardo continues. 'He has all the good contacts. He had no problem finding four prostitutes to pose naked for selling *my* stuff. What does he think this is if it isn't advertising, huh? Now come on, tell me what you really think.'

'Oh, I'm useless when it comes to art,' I say, suddenly feeling that I could quite like this man.

'That's because you're nervous,' Ricardo says. 'You think you have to say things like, what was it? *Exaggerated objectification of human body blah blah . . .*'

'Yes,' I laugh. 'But honestly. Other than the fact that I think your photos are beautiful, and very arousing . . .'

'Ah! So they make you feel hot, huh? This is what I want to know.'

I nod and smile at him. 'Well, yes, they do,' I say.

'And you know how I get that . . . how do you say it? *Erotic*, into my art?'

'Eroticism,' I say.

'Yes. Of course. Eroticism. But you know how I get it to communicate?'

I shake my head.

'I have to be very horny, and very frustrate.'

I nod.

'So no sex, just, lots of temptation. And then it work. It's funny, huh?'

'So you really do have to suffer for your art,' I laugh.

He nods. 'Oh yes,' he says.

'There's something very powerful about them, quite . . . I don't know . . .'

'Primeval?' Ricardo prompts.

'Maybe, yes,' I say. 'I was thinking how tribal the centrepiece looks with all those people walking in a circle around them. Almost like a sacrificial offering or a witch-burning or . . . Oh, honestly, I don't know what I'm talking about when it comes to art.'

Ricardo freezes and then unlinks himself from my arm, then turns to face me and takes hold of my shoulders. He looks like he's maybe going to give me a good shaking.

He stares madly into my eyes. His own have tears in them. 'The tribal circle!' he says crazily. 'You see it! It is the reason they are there! And you are the only person who see that! I think I love you!'

I slip into a grin. 'Well, thank you!' I say. I nod across the room and see Darren crossing to join us. 'And thanks for saving me from the red dwarf.'

I say this last part discreetly, but Ricardo roars with laughter, and repeats *very* loudly, 'The *red dwarf*! I *love* this woman!'

House of Cards

In the nightmare – a scene lifted straight from the French film I watched on Film 4 on Thursday – I am the crazed Betty and my boyfriend is smothering me with a pillow.

I awaken with a jolt to find that I am lying on my front and my mouth is indeed full of pillow. No prizes for interpreting *that* dream then.

I roll over and take a deep breath and wait for my brain to assimilate the fact that *that* was a dream, and this is reality.

Grey light is leaking through a gap in the curtains. My mouth is gloopy and disgusting, and the pain above my left eye is really quite stunning. I groan and rub my eyebrow. 'Jesus!' I mutter. 'What a night!' Though in truth, for the moment, I can't remember much of it.

In the bathroom I listen as what I assume to be a litre of pure rum gushes out: *Rum. Mojitos . . .* memories are surfacing.

Whilst I wait for two Alka-Seltzer to dissolve (they seem to take forever) I feed Guinness. The smell of the cat food makes me retch. The noise of the Alka-Seltzer fizzing hurts my head.

I eventually down them but have to remain poised for a few minutes over the kitchen sink as I'm not entirely sure they won't be coming straight back up.

I look out at the twilight of the garden. It's just before eleven a.m. but the cloud cover is so thick that it looks like evening already. What light *is* dribbling through is of course being double-filtered by the Leylandii.

As I stare into the middle distance waiting for the Alka-Seltzer to do its stuff, it starts to drizzle.

I switch the kitchen light on and fill the kettle and slump at the table and try to remember how I got home. For some reason it's always the first thing I try to remember. There's something particularly unnerving about not knowing how you got to where you are.

But I soon give up on working my way backwards, and start at the beginning: I remember the exhibition, my sudden friendship with the crazy artist, the endless drinks of Champagne as the crowd dwindled ... I remember Ricardo saying that the Champagne was all paid for and that we had better drink it. And I remember doing precisely that.

I recall six of us in a taxi to Brixton, to a Colombian bar – Amazonica, I think – and drinking mojitos, lots of mojitos, and ... oh God! ... dancing sexy salsa with ... I'm thinking ... V? *Victor*, perhaps?

I pinch the bridge of my nose and struggle to remember.

I make a giant cup of tea and take it through to the lounge. My body aches and the big purple sofa is beckoning to me.

On the coffee table I find a beer mat from Bar Code, and this prompts another memory: a different taxi, this time just Darren and Ricardo and, yes, Victor, the three of them snorting white lines in the back of the taxi ... me being terrified in case the taxi driver noticed. I didn't partake, thank God, or my hangover would be even worse. Which is, of course, precisely why I don't: the only effect cocaine seems to have on me is to enable me to drink far more than my body can handle, and I could never really see the point in that. Indeed I seem to be able to achieve that perfectly well *without* chemical help.

I glance at the beer mat. Yes, Bar Code: stuffed with men – stuffed of course with *gay* men. Darren and Ricardo went to the bar and were absorbed by the crowd leaving only Victor sweetly chatting to me, the only one of the three to worry that I might be feeling left out. I remember feeling too drunk and having to sit down and looking at everyone's waists around me – an impenetrable wall of jeans between me and the exit. It reminded me of being a little girl and looking up at all the adults, only this time no one was there to hold my hand, no voice coming over the tannoy to save me.

Darren and Ricardo never did make it back from the bar, and for a while it was fine, Victor and I had the loveliest chat about music and life and the importance of friends and the need to escape to the country and I thought for a moment that he might kiss me, but he introduced me to a *friend* instead whose name I really don't recall, and I felt stupid because, of course, Victor, like the rest of the world, was gay, and I felt sick and lousy and had no idea what the fuck I was doing there anyway.

And then I somehow stumbled through the crowd and out into the rain and fell into a taxi. And here I am. The gaps have been filled. Phew!

I sip my tea and snort sadly. The thing about a *gay night out* really *is* knowing when to stop – when to stop and go home. And I'm afraid I never seem to get that right. There is always a terrible moment of drunken solitude when I realise that whoever I was with has gone off, or is kissing someone . . . There is always a moment when I realise that I have become surplus to requirements, and that ultimately I'm an intruder in someone else's space, a voyeur whose alibi has vanished.

I sip my tea and think, not for the first time, that though I love my nights out with Mark and Darren, this isn't healthy – really it isn't.

It's a bit like watching TV – a useful distraction but ultimately unproductive. I need to reorganise my life. I need to spend more time with straight friends. I need a boyfriend of my own.

And then I remember Brown Eyes and wonder if he has phoned.

I stand and cross the room for the handset. For a second I think I might throw up again. I have to steady myself by holding on to the mantelpiece as I dial voicemail.

There is an instant of hope when the computerised woman – she of the erratic intonation – announces that I have *one . . . new, message . . . yesterday . . . at . . . ten, oh, five . . . p.m.*

I hold my breath for a moment, but then groan as Cynthia's nasal twang says, 'Hi pumpkin. Cyn here. As I'm *sure* you remembered it's Carl's birthday on Thursday, so of course we're having the traditional "do" on Friday. Hope you can come. The usual crowd. Let me know if you're bringing anyone. Oh, and no need to worry about food. Just bring lashings of Champagne. It's the big four-oh!'

Oh God! The *traditional* 'do'! The *usual* crowd! *Lashings* of Champagne!

I slump back onto the sofa, feeling not only sicker but thoroughly, irrecoverably depressed.

After the break-up, when all the possessions and friends got divided up, I somehow ended up with Cynthia and Carl. That doesn't sound very appreciative, and I guess that it isn't really fair – it's just my hangover doing my thinking for me.

Fact is, that Cynthia and Carl couldn't forgive Brian for what he had done to Yours Truly, so when everyone had to choose sides, they chose mine. Which is lovely, really, seeing as they had previously been Brian's friends rather than mine.

So I'm not ungrateful . . . it's just that the *traditional 'do'* means a sit-down dinner at their house, and the *usual crowd* means Cyn and Carl, Pete and Betina and Martin and Cheryl. Don't get me wrong . . . they're all perfectly nice couples. But the truth is that now I'm a single girl, I fit into happy-couple-hell (New! With added children!) about as well as I fit into single-homo-hell . . .

In fact, I probably fit in slightly better with the gay crowd, for at least they understand that lives and loves are tenuous at best. We at least have that shared knowledge to bitch about.

The happily-marrieds really seem to have no idea. They don't understand yet just how fragile their relationships are. They don't realise how reliant they are on their partners remaining sane, and stable, and truthful, and, long-term, how improbable that is.

We: the single, the dumped, the lied-to, have learnt that relationships are a house of cards, and that with the slightest jog of the table everything comes tumbling down.

And it occurs to me that far from the loss of the relationship itself, the most profound thing Brian did to me was to give me that knowledge: that you can be the happiest, luckiest girl around. You can be in love, confident in your future and overjoyed to be pregnant. And then someone (Brian) nudges the table, and *wham!* you're a single, childless spare, casting desperately around to try to find someone, *anyone* to fit in with.

It can happen anytime. And it can happen to anyone. And it happened to me.

And now I think I need to throw up. And then I need to go back to bed.

An Arse-Slapping Success

By the time Monday morning arrives, the worst of my hangover is past and I am feeling almost human again. And yet, as is always the case with these things, a shadow of my self-inflicted abuse remains, specifically a vague blurring of my thought processes, an inability to concentrate on a single thought for long enough to get anywhere with it.

This is not good news for the Grunge! pitch and I am only too aware of it.

When I get to the impressive offices within the far bigger, but less sexy sounding, Bowles, Richards and Parkinson Group, or BRP as they are known in the trade (Darren calls them Burp most of the time), I am well known enough to be able to make my own way to the boardroom where the presentation is to be held. I am half an hour early – half an hour which I hope is going to enable me to organise my thoughts.

In the otherwise empty boardroom I find Darren spreading glossy posters out on the giant oval table.

'Hey,' he says, as I close the door. 'Have a look at *this* and tell me what you think.'

He sounds sharp and confident, and stunningly awake, and I wonder for a moment why dealing with hangovers gets so much harder as you get older. Then again, I never remember having felt like that after a weekend on the razzle at any age.

Darren reveals his secret, though, before I can ask. 'Shit, you look rough,' he says. 'You look like me when I got up. Do you want a line? Because I've got a bit left.'

I roll my eyes.

'I know you don't and everything,' Darren says, 'but it is sort of exceptional circumstances. Anyway, the offer's there.'

But a single glance at the posters on the table provides the jolt of adrenalin required to get my brain on the move. No drugs required. 'What the *fuck* is that?' I say, rotating one of the glossy sheets towards me.

The image is a total reworking of the concept I was presented with on Friday. In fact, the image, a man on a sledge in carpenter pants holding a three man-dog husky team looks more like a poster for Ricardo Escobar's exhibition than an ad for jeans.

'You don't like it?' Darren asks incredulously.

'I . . .' I say, momentary speechless.

It's a beautiful poster but it's not what we agreed. And it's not what Grunge! will want to see. I leaf through the other posters on the table. They are all slight variations on the same theme.

A voice behind us says, 'Like what?'

We both swivel to see Jude enter the room, lean his bag against the glass partition, and circle the table to join us.

I shake my head and swallow and put my now trembling hands into the pockets of my D&G trousers. The three cups of espresso plus the quickly mounting stress have pushed me from comatose to panic attack in a single leap.

Jude rounds the table. 'Huh!' he laughs. 'Cool. Were these taken at that exhibition you two went to?'

'The next day,' Darren says. 'You see, *Jude* likes it.'

'Yes,' Jude laughs again. 'Excellent. Anyway . . . Show me the visuals for today. We haven't got long.'

Darren frowns at him.

'The storyboard,' Jude says. 'Show me the finished storyboard.'

'I thought this . . .' Darren says, his voice tailing off.

'You did *do* the storyboard?' Jude says. 'The original one. The one we *agreed*.'

Darren coughs. 'I thought this was . . . better,' he murmurs.

Jude wrinkles his brow and looks from Darren to me.

I say nothing, but combine a raised-eyebrow look which expresses, *You see what I'm dealing with here* . . . with a, *Your problem not mine, you fix it*, shrug.

Jude turns back to Darren, then grabs his arm and bustles him into a corner.

As head of Creative, Jude has never let me down, but even so . . . this is cutting it fine, even for them.

In an attempt at remaining calm I stare out of the window at the London skyline and repeatedly sing ten little Indians in my head. In Italian. *Uno, due, tre indiani, quattro, cinque, sei indiani* . . . Ridiculous, I know . . . but it has always worked for me.

I try not to listen to their discussion, but occasional phrases slip through my filter: *Where the fuck . . . don't care if the fucking Queen took the fucking photos* . . . so you *do* have them . . . Go! Now!'

Darren grabs his laptop bag and turns to leave.

'And take this shit with you!' Jude bellows.

Darren swivels back, gathers the posters, rolls them, and then, red as a beetroot from his dressing-down, runs for the door.

Jude turns to me, smiles, and slides into a seat.

'And?' I say.

'Don't worry,' Jude replies calmly. 'He'll be back.'

'With the boards?'

Jude nods. 'I think he just got carried away. A case of less is more, I'm afraid.'

I shake my head. 'Incredible!' I say.

'I'll sack him if you want . . .' Jude says. 'He would have asked for it.'

'Shit!' I say. I shake my head and sigh. 'Well . . . we can talk about that afterwards. If any of us are still alive.'

At precisely ten I take my place beside the empty whiteboard and begin my pitch.

I smile confidently at the assembled people: Clarissa Bowles, Peter Bowles (her father), four people from the Grunge! marketing department, the Grunge! marketing director Simon Savage, and Peter Stanford, our own grey-haired, impeccably suited, sixty-something, Romeo/Director of Marketing.

Three words are bouncing around my head: *How the fuck?*

I take a deep breath and try to shout myself down. 'Hello everyone!' I boom. 'We're here today, as you know, to present our campaign for the new Grunge! Street-Wear range of unisex carpenter pants.'

I cough and clear my throat and Jude winks at me, egging me on.

'It's a well-known fact that gay fashion typically precedes the mainstream by anything between six months and two years, and for this product, because our market research has revealed instant appeal within the trend-setting gay market, our strategy evolves . . . sorry, *re-volves* around exploiting this fact for maximum advantage.

'We intend, in a nutshell, to specifically target the gay market a full six months to a year early with a stunning tailored campaign to . . .'

I manage to keep this up for a full twenty-two minutes, whilst silently praying for Darren's return. And, even if I do say so myself, I sound bloody convincing.

But at ten-twenty-two, Peter Bowles interrupts me in typically blunt fashion with, 'OK, OK . . . Enough of the blah, blah, my lovely. Show me the bloody visuals . . .'

No further stalling possible.

I cough. I glance at Jude. He shrugs discreetly.

'I'm sorry,' I say, 'but . . .'

And at that second, I see Darren press his nose against the glass partition.

I force a smile, and beckon for him to come in.

'I'm sorry,' I say again, 'but . . . I didn't want to show you the visuals until I had explained about the specific market targeting we have planned. The first ad . . .'

Without looking at Darren, I put a hand out to take the sheet from him. If he doesn't have them, or if these are still the wrong ones, then this pitch will now crash, and I want to make sure that everyone realises that this is not my fault.

To my great relief, like a marathon runner passing the baton, Darren places something, still rolled, into my hand.

I unroll the poster-sized sheet, turn it right way up, clip it to the whiteboard, and then for an instant words fail me. Just for a few seconds, I am so stunned that I could burst into tears there and then.

Because the photo before us – Darren's reworking of the original concept Jude showed me on Friday, a man in a bar with a sketched-in dog collar, is so – and there's really only one word for it – *beautiful*, it takes my breath away.

The original pub location has been replaced by a glitzy London bar with multicoloured neon strip lights behind the bar, and everything about the photo is so lush, so rich, so gorgeously vibrant . . . every expression on every person in the shot, every suit, every drink . . . everything . . . everything about this shot is *perfect*.

I suddenly remember that this is the moment which makes advertising worthwhile; this is the moment when, sometimes, just occasionally, what we produce is more than advertising. Sometimes advertising meets art. And I'm overwhelmed with pride to be the one presenting it.

'We . . .' I stammer, turning back to the group.

I see Jude consciously close his own mouth.

'We used an incredibly famous gay photographer for the location shots,' Darren says, nervously filling in. 'His name is Ricardo Escobar and he's terribly well known in the gay community and I think it shows: you can really see that this is a photographer at the peak of his creativity.'

'So . . .' I say, catching my breath. 'As you can see, the image shows a fashionable man wearing carpenter pants surrounded by work colleagues . . .'

• • •

An hour later, as we spill onto the pavement outside, Peter Stanton, says, 'Brilliant show, guys. Spot On, as they say!' He guffaws at this regularly repeated joke.

I nod. 'Erm, thanks.'

'I thought the anticipation before revealing the visuals was particularly effective,' he continues. 'So well done for that. We should use that more often, I think.'

'Yes . . .' I say vaguely, raising an eyebrow at Darren who is beaming at me like a six-year-old who just got given a remote control fire engine.

'Anyway, gotta go . . . busy day and all that,' Stanton says.

And then, he, Peter Stanton, our director, slaps my arse, and strides away.

We all stand in silence for a moment, until Jude says, 'Did I dream that, or did Stanton just slap your arse?'

I shake my head slowly. 'No,' I say. 'That really happened. That all really happened.'

• • •

On Thursday morning, I am called into Stanton's office.

This makes me a little nervous because of the arse-slapping incident.

Though I realise, of course, that this event could be useful in case of future redundancy negotiations (there were, after all, two witnesses to this particular act of sexual harassment), flirtation at Spot On is a tight-rope to be navigated with extreme care.

Stanton, like all four male partners in fact, has always been an outrageous flirt, and fact is, most of the women who have done well at Spot On (as well as a few who have been fired) got where they are today by sleeping with one of them. Or in a few cases, *all* of them.

That I have managed to climb the corporate ladder whilst avoiding this particular fate is, I think, what annoys Victoria

Barclay the most. And if it *is* this that upsets her so much, then of course one is left wondering what she had to do to get to *her* top-bitch position.

When I get to the third floor, Stanton's door is open so I peer in.

He's generally pretty dapper in a slightly stuffy upper-crust kind of way, and today is no exception: he's wearing the trousers and waistcoat of a three-piece grey silky number over a very *Apprentice* pink shirt/tie combination.

'Ah!' he exclaims, looking up. 'Our star player! Come! Come!'

As he says *come, come*, he pats the desk, as if perhaps hoping I will perch myself on the edge of it. I choose the chair on the other side of the desk instead.

'Hello,' I say, sitting down and pulling my skirt as low as it will go.

'Stunning performance the other day Ch . . . Sorry! CC.'

'Thank you, sir.'

'Bloody good campaign the boys came up with, but your pitch was really quite outstanding.'

I smile and try to look relaxed. But the fact is that being in Stanton's office is rarely anodyne. It always leads to *something*, whether that be promotion, demotion, sacking, or, in the case of many, a blow job.

So far I have navigated the pitfalls of my relationship with Stanton like a true professional by being just flirty enough to get on with him, and just cold enough to keep his hands off me. It's a bit like doing an arm's-length tango . . . he steps forward, I step back; he steps back, I move in.

'The thing is,' Stanton continues, somewhat unnervingly standing and moving around to *my* side of the desk, 'that, I have to tell you, Bowles *loved* the campaign.'

'Clarissa or Peter?' I ask.

'Er . . . both really, but Clarissa particularly.'

Stanton is now perching on the edge of his desk in front of me – which is difficult as I have to strain my neck just to look up at him.

I could stand myself, but that would put me inches from his face . . . Or give in and just look at his crotch, which, I'm surprised to admit, I'm finding almost appealing today, lurking as it does beneath grey silky folds. I have always had a bit of a thing for men in expensive suits.

I slouch back as far as I can in my seat as this makes it easier to look him in the eye and increases the distance between my nose and his genitals. 'That's great news,' I say.

'Yes, only, here's the thing,' he says, scratching the inside of his thigh. 'And it's a bit . . . I suppose you would say, *political*.'

'Political,' I repeat.

'Yes,' he says. 'Political. You see, they have spoken to the Americans about the brilliant campaign we're putting together.'

'To *Levi's*?' I ask, incredulously.

'Yes. To Levi's.'

'But I thought, that was just a project . . . I mean, I didn't know . . .'

Stanton shakes his head. 'All done and dusted, my dear. They have sold US rights for the entire range to Levi's for two years. It's a big old deal.'

'I'll bet,' I say. 'Well that's great news, isn't it?'

'Sort of,' Stanton says. 'Only, of course, Levi's have their own marketing people . . .'

'Harper & Baker?'

'Harper & Baker.'

'So no crumbs for us.'

'No. And if Harper & Baker do well on the US account . . .'

'We could lose Grunge! here in the UK.'

'Well, yes. Except, as I was saying, for the fact that, Bowles, *Peter*, he spoke to someone or other over there, and they now want to see *our* stuff. They want to see our pitch. So, to cut a long story short, I want you to go over and flog it to them.'

'Levi's wants to see it? In New York?' I ask, starting to feel a flush of excitement and stress.

'Yes,' he says. 'If anyone can pull this off, you can. And if we could get a foot in that particular door . . .'

'It could be big,' I say.

'Very big,' Stanton says, I hope *coincidentally*, running a hand across his crotch. 'Of course, this is where the politics comes in,' he adds.

'Yes?'

'Yes. Because of course Victoria has overall responsibility for America.'

'But we don't have any American clients.'

'Well, no. But if we did, they would fall under her remit.'

'I see.'

'So I was thinking maybe if I gave it all to her to organise, and then she could take you along for the actual pitch.'

I swallow. A film of sharing a transatlantic flight with VB plays in my mind. It's a horror film. I wonder if I can get away with a blindfold and an iPod for the entire flight without provoking her anger.

But I am clever enough to spot when I have no choice. And so I slip into my best, chocolatey sales smile.

The trick about smiling when you don't really want to is to scrunch your eyes up as if there's too much sun. Sarah-Jane taught me that years ago – she saw it on telly, and I must say, it's been incredibly useful.

'Sounds like a plan,' I say. 'Sounds like an excellent plan.'

Peter beams back at me. 'Well then,' he says. 'I'll get Victoria to sort it all out.'

Two for the Price of None

I arrive in Clapham at the tail-end of the seven-to-nine invitation that Cynthia, understanding my work schedule, generously conceded.

It's always a bit hard, as a single, to fit in to these evenings anyway, but arriving late, when people are already on a G&T roll really doesn't help.

Cynthia takes my coat and leads me into the dining room where everyone is already seated. 'Tada!' she declares, as she leads me in.

Multiple conversations around the table cease and I'm met with a hubbub of, '*Hiya.*'

'Sorry about the hour,' I say. 'Hellish at work at the moment.'

'Still working you into the ground then?' Carl, Cyn's husband asks.

'Yes,' I say, taking my seat. 'I'm afraid so.'

'Are you still with whatsits – the ad agency?' Betina asks.

'Yes,' I say. 'Still there. Still at Spot On.'

'Spot On – that's the one,' she laughs. 'I always forget it. Always sounds like an acne cream to me.'

'I think there is an acne creme called Spot On,' her husband Pete says, as if this is an original revelation – as if we haven't had this conversation a thousand times.

'Indeed, there is,' I say. 'And there's also an advertising agency.'

'Still working with a load of poofs then?' Martin, ever boorish, asks.

'Yes,' I say. 'Everything is exactly the same.' I'm hoping that this will head off the next, inevitable question, but of course it doesn't.

'And still no chap in tow?' he asks.

I look around as if I might have mislaid the boyfriend. 'No,' I say. 'Apparently not.'

'So what's that all about?' he asks.

'I'm damned if I know,' I reply, holding out my glass so that Betina can fill it. I take a large gulp.

'I expect you single girls get more, you know, than we married folks do these days, anyway, don't you?' Martin asks, a distinct lecherous tone to his voice. He sounds slightly drunk already. 'I mean, it's all OK now, isn't it? It's all anything goes these days, isn't it?'

'Actually, I forgot to wash my hands,' I say, standing. 'I won't be a tick.'

Quite why my sex life is considered public domain just because I'm single, I can never really work out. But experience has taught me that by the time I return the conversation will have moved on. Apparently their *need* is far more to do with asking the questions, than having any answers.

Indeed, when I return everyone is talking about house prices, and *are they artificially high or can they continue to rise?* Pete, who works in some big City brokerage firm, is explaining that one of their top analysts has been sacked for warning that the housing bubble is about to burst and drag the western world as we know it, down with it.

'It's all very worrying,' Cynthia says, sipping her wine and shaking her head.

'Yes,' Pete agrees. 'For those of us who remember the eighties,' and here, he winks at me, 'it's most worrying. Most worrying indeed.'

Why me? I think. *We're all the same age here.*

'I think all of us remember the eighties in some form or another,' I say.

'I don't,' Carl laughs. 'I blew all my brain cells out with E.'

'Carl!' Cynthia admonishes.

He winks at me and shrugs. 'Well, I did. All I remember from the eighties is the strobe lights.'

'Anyway,' Pete says. 'According to this guy at work, it could be even worse this time around.'

'Well, we all survived,' I say. 'No one actually died because of the recession . . . I mean, it was awful for some people, but let's be honest, not really for people like us. That's what was so unfair about the Thatcher years. But my dad made a mint during the eighties.'

'Well, they may have been *unfair*,' Peter says. 'But where would we be now without old Thatch? Lord, we'd be like France, walking around in wellies and growing our own cheese.'

Cynthia leans over my shoulder and hands me a plate. As she moves on around the table, I say, 'Ooh! What's this? Looks lovely.'

'Red-pepper crostini,' she says. 'It's Jamie Oliver.'

'Well I still think it could happen,' Martin says. 'And if house prices crash, we'll all be stuck in negative equity. And that's a nightmare. You wait and see.'

'Well, I'm not worried,' I say. 'Honestly, I refuse to worry about the value of my house . . . As long as I can live in it, I really don't give a damn.'

'Good for you,' Carl says.

'Your place is all paid for anyway, isn't it?' Pete asks.

I wrinkle my nose. Apparently, tonight, *everything* about me is public domain. 'Nearly,' I say. 'I paid most of it off when my grandmother died.'

'Well that's one thing you got right, at least,' Martin says. 'Because people don't realise it, but debt will cripple us all in the end.'

'Says the man who just bought a new car on credit,' Cheryl, his wife, says, holding her pregnant belly and laughing.

'What about yours, Pete?' Carl asks, winking at me again. 'How much do *you* owe on that bloody mansion of yours?'

'I don't think I want to tell you,' Pete answers.

'No,' Carl says with a grin. 'No, I thought not.'

I sit and eat my crostini, which turns out to be a delicious type of cheese on toast, and let the conversation drift around me, and wonder what the 'one thing you got right,' was supposed to mean. I suppose it's something to do with the fact that I'm single, and that being a sign of ultimate failure on my part. But you would have to have one hell of an imagination to decide that my separation from Brian, for example, was my fault, was an error of *my* judgement . . .

And then I slip into my own little bubble, and imagine how different my life would be if I had met a different guy instead, different *guys* . . . And I wonder why Brown Eyes hasn't phoned, and then what it would be like if he were here tonight. Would I suddenly feel at ease with these people? Or would they suddenly feel more at ease with me? Perhaps a single girl is a threat . . . perhaps that's why I always sense so much latent aggression in these get-togethers. I look around the table at Cynthia, mother of two, and her witty fashion-obsessed husband Carl. I look at smug banker Pete and his dull Surrey-wife Betina, who looks somehow not from my generation at all, but from my mother's instead. I bet she even listens to Radio Two. Of course, we all listen to Radio Two these days. They play Oasis and Blur. I wonder what station people of my mother's generation *do* listen to.

I look at lecherous, drunken Martin with his pretty air-head wife Cheryl, and wonder if Brown Eyes would fit in with these people, and if he did, would I like him *at all*? For, in the end, though they are supposedly my friends, I wouldn't want to be any of the women present, and other than Carl, I doubt I could tolerate any of their husbands for a weekend, let alone a life.

And all of this leaves me wondering if this dream of mine – that out there, somewhere, hiding, there exists a guy who is cultured and calm, and smiley and faithful, who wants to escape the rat-race with me and, apparently like the French, wear wellies and make cheese . . . Well, I wonder if it can possibly exist.

I don't want much . . . just someone who would lie flat on his stomach next to me in the garden watching ants carrying crumbs through the jungle of blades of grass. I wonder if that can *ever* exist, anywhere, for anyone.

Personally, I blame *The Good Life*. My father was obsessed with it, which is strange really, as it bore so little resemblance to our own lives. Perhaps that was the appeal. My brain developed in a white, aseptic box in deepest most comfortable Surrey, filled – by TV – with images and dreams of something different, something better: pigs and chickens, greenhouses and piglets.

My family life *was* Margo and Jerry, only with two extra kids and a TV showing *The Good Life*. And all I ever really wanted was to move next door to live with Tom and Barbara.

I refocus on the room and realise that some time has passed and that our numbers have dwindled.

'Go and chivvy them along would you?' Betina, who is somewhat trapped in the corner, asks. 'I would go myself, but . . .'

I smile at her and feel a little guilty that in my dreaming I have failed to notice the departure of Cheryl and Cynthia, and that Betina is now encircled by men – men apparently discussing *Top Gear*.

Here, I can only agree with my gay friends: heterosexual men truly do have the strangest conversations. Right now they are arguing about whether Jeremy Clarkson is a tosser or, according to Martin, a *very cool dude*.

I mean, *hello?*

In the kitchen, I find Cynthia and Cheryl blowing smoke out of the back door. As I enter, Cheryl is saying, 'Since September last year!? Oh you poor thing!'

When she catches sight of me she jumps. 'Oh! Hello.'

'Hiya,' I say. 'I have been sent to find out where you have vanished to. Poor Betina is being ambushed by the Jeremy Clarkson fan club.'

'Sorry,' Cynthia says, glancing furtively along the corridor. 'You know how it is. We were talking about sex.'

Cheryl pulls a face. 'Can you believe Cyn and Carl haven't had a bonk since . . .' she says.

' Cheryl!' Cynthia protests. '*Don't* . . . you know . . .'

From this I deduce that though my sex life is public domain, for the married women amongst us, it's clearly a private club.

Cheryl pulls a face and stubs out her cigarette on the side of the doorstep.

'Sorry,' Cynthia says. 'Anyway, let's get this show on the road. If you can carry the plates through, and you the sauce there, and I'll get the *gougère* from the oven.'

'So what have you done with the kids?' I ask as we head through to the other room. Carl's previous birthday dinner had suffered a constant stream of interruptions as Chloe and Lilly found a never-ending series of reasons to come downstairs.

'Oh, they're at my sister's,' Cynthia laughs. 'Never again! Not after last time.'

This leads inevitably to a round of kiddy conversation, another constant in our dinner parties. It's not that I don't like kids, it's not that at all. It's just that there's only so much you can say about them before it all goes around again. I mean, I like sunflowers. But I'm not going to talk about them *every* time I see anyone.

And so I listen, and smile, and nod as we hear about how *well* Chloe and Lilly are doing *academically* at the new school (I mean, they're five and seven, for Christ's sake) and how well Thomas, Pete and Betina's little lad, is doing at toddler group, and finally a round of baby advice for pregnant Cheryl which includes the charming dinner-table advice that Pampers are worth the extra cash because Tesco's own-brand leak (shit presumably) all over the shop.

I struggle to remain present in the conversation. I know I want kids myself, but I can't help but remember fondly the conversations we used to have in the old days about ecology and politics and books.

After dessert we give Carl our birthday gifts. Most of these are generic items from Habitat – candleholders and paper-weights which I know for a fact Carl bins as soon as no one is looking. He must do, otherwise there would be no visible surfaces left in the place.

I give him a Deelish wallet, a freebie from work which he of course loves. Carl is the only heterosexual man I have ever been able to buy for. I just look at what my gay friends have and buy him the same thing. Mark met him once, and unforgettably described him as a *poor wee gay man trapped in a big strapping hetty body.*

Finally, Carl gets out the port, and Cynthia and Cheryl drift outside for another cigarette and, I presume, a fresh round of analysis of Cynthia's and Carl's missing sex life. It's a shame I'm being excluded from that one, as really I'm quite the expert.

And then Carl goes to the toilet, and Pete follows him, and I am left, uncomfortably with Betina and Martin.

Within a group of seven people there are a myriad of combinations possible. Some of these work like clockwork, and others are about as comfortable as a weekend at Guantanamo Bay.

For reasons unknown to me, though I get on OK with Pete and Betina, and can tolerate Martin when he's with Cheryl quite efficiently, this particular threesome has always felt like walking on glass. I say for reasons unknown . . . actually, I have my suspicions that Martin and Betina are having an affair. Or at the very least, have had one in the past. I think I'm the only person to whom this has occurred, and guess that they somehow sense that I have picked up on it. I also suspect that Martin was, and probably still *is*, closer to Brian than he lets on.

Whatever the reason, today is no exception: silence falls across the table, and I am just thinking up excuses why I might have to leave the table myself when Martin asks, somewhat drunkenly, 'So, you ever see anything of old Brian?'

I stare at him for a moment, composing myself.

Brian has never been a subject of dinner conversation here, and, I'm pretty sure, everyone knows why.

'No,' I eventually say. 'No, I don't.'

'Of course she doesn't,' Betina chips in, bless her.

Martin shrugs and runs his tongue across his front teeth. 'Hey,' he says. 'I'm just asking . . .'

'Anyway, I really have to nip to the . . .'

'So how come you two never had kids?' he continues. He's definitely sozzled.

'Martin!' Betina protests.

I think, *Such a shame . . . things were going so well . . .* 'Hey,' Martin says. 'Just because it didn't work out in the end . . . I mean you guys were together for . . . how long was it?'

'Five years,' I say through gritted teeth.

'Yeah, five years. So, in five years, I mean, it could have happened.'

'Martin, really!' Betina says. 'I don't think this is appropriate . . .'

'Chazza doesn't mind, do you?' Martin asks.

Before I can formulate a polite way of saying that, *'Yes, I do mind . . . And don't ever call me Chazza,'* he continues, 'I mean, did you always know it wasn't gonna work out . . . sort of woman's intuition or something . . . or didn't you want kids at all?'

'I—' I say.

'Because, of course, it's obvious enough that Brian did.'

'I have to . . .' I say. And then I pause. 'What does that mean?' I ask.

'Please!' Betina exclaims, now looking wide-eyed and shocked.

'What?' Martin asks. 'What did I say?'

'Why is it obvious that Brian wanted kids?'

'Martin! *Shut up,*' Betina whines.

'Don't tell me to shut up!' he mutters, slopping more port into his glass.

'She doesn't *know,*' Betina whispers, as if this is somehow going to prevent me from hearing.

I laugh sourly. 'OK, whatever this is, that's enough. What don't I know?'

'Oh!' Martin says, nodding exaggeratedly. 'Oh, sorry.' He raises a finger to his lips and says, 'Shhh!'

'Betina,' I spit. 'If you don't tell me what you're talking about, I swear . . .'

She licks her lips. 'I'm sorry,' she says. 'It's just that . . . well, it's just that, Brian, you see . . .'

'Oh, for God's sake,' Martin says. 'He's got kids. I can't believe you don't know that. Surely, you know that, right? I mean, it's been two fucking years . . . it's hardly news.'

'What do you mean, *kids*?' I ask, performing a quick bit of mental arithmetic. 'How can he have kids? Plural? And what do you mean, *two years*?'

Betina nods slowly, then says, terribly, terribly quietly, 'Twins. They had *twins*.'

Martin swigs at his port. 'Did you really not know that?' he asks.

'Betina's right,' I say, standing. 'Shut up! Just, shut up!'

As I leave, Betina scoots around the table sliding chairs underneath as she does so, but I'm too quick for her.

I run upstairs, and barge into the bathroom.

Pete and Carl look up at me. They are kneeling in front of the toilet. The seat-cover is down, and Pete is rubbing his nose.

Carl is holding a rolled banknote. He smiles at me and raises a finger to his lips. 'Not a word to the missus,' he says. 'Cyn might find this a bit sordid. You want some?'

I back out of the room, pulling the door closed behind me. I hear Carl say, 'I thought you locked the door.'

'I thought I did, *sorry,* old chum,' Pete replies. 'You don't think she'll tell Betina, do you?'

I am trembling with shock, and though I never really blub these days, my eyes are watery enough to be blurry. I need somewhere to be alone.

I cross the landing and take the first door I find – a bad choice, because, of course, this is one of the children's bedrooms.

And there, seated on a Barbie quilt cover, surrounded by paraphernalia which could have belonged to my own little girl, I sit and gnaw my knuckle and mutter, *Fuck Brian! Fuck him,* and wait for my heart to slow.

When I finally make it back downstairs, word has clearly spread. Everyone looks up at me wide-eyed.

I wave a hand at them as if batting a cloud away. 'It's fine,' I say. 'Whatever.'

But of course it isn't fine. My shock is subsiding, but now I'm being assailed by waves of mounting anger. I'm just hoping to keep it bottled until I can get away.

'Sorry,' Martin says, incongruously raising his glass at me, as if in a toast. 'Bad choice of subject.'

'Yes,' I say. 'Well, at least now I know, eh?'

'So stupid!' Cynthia mutters. I'm not quite sure who she means. Brian? Martin? *Me?*

'How old are they?' I ask. 'Did you say they're *two*?'

'It really doesn't matter,' Cynthia says.

'How *old* are Brian's kids?' I ask, my voice quivering.

'They're two,' Carl answers, provoking a glare from Cynthia. 'I think she needs to know,' Carl tells her, with a shrug, then to me, softly, 'They're just two, a week ago. They were two last Thursday. I'm sorry, CC.'

'I couldn't know she'd be upset,' Martin says. 'I mean . . . it was just a bad choice of subject. But I couldn't know.'

I take a deep breath and grasp the edge of the table. 'Yes,' I say, with artificial poise. 'Bad choice. Never mind, eh?'

'I'm sorry,' Cynthia says. 'Let me get you a coffee or something.'

'In fact, Martin,' I continue. 'You'll probably want to remember never to bring that subject up again. With anyone.'

He wrinkles his nose at me and nods. 'Right,' he says. 'If you say so.'

'I do,' I say. 'Because, when you ask a woman of my age, a woman who is forty this year, why she hasn't had kids, the answer will usually be either that she hates the fuckers – which will make *you* feel uncomfortable, or that she loves them, but her boyfriend doesn't, or didn't, which will make *her* feel bad, or that she can't have kids, which will make *everyone* feel bad.'

'Yes,' Martin says. 'Sorry.'

'Or in *my* case, seeing as you're so keen to fucking know, it's because the guy she was with, your friend Brian, felt that it wasn't *quite the right time* for them to have kids, and convinced her, against every instinct she ever had, to have an abortion. Whereupon, he dumped her.'

'Oh,' Martin says.

'Yes, *Oh!*' I spit. 'And then, *apparently*, he fathered another child, *sorry* . . . make that *two* children with another woman. And seeing as it takes nine months to make a baby, and seeing as these kids are now just two, that would mean that he did this magical deed, that his sperm entered . . . *whoever's* vagina, a mere two months after he dumped me, that is to say, a mere *two months and two days* after he brought me home from the abortion clinic.'

'Golly,' Pete says.

'Yes, *golly.*'

Cynthia reaches for my hand, but I pull it away.

'You knew,' I say simply.

'I thought it best, if . . .' she says.

'I'm sorry,' I say. 'But I really need to go home now. I really, really do.'

Numb

I sit and stare at the steam rising from my cup of coffee.

It's a beautiful day outside, possibly the first spring day of the year, and I remember how years ago, when I bought this place, the low sun used to stream in through the kitchen window. I even still have a pair of old sunglasses in the kitchen drawer – I used to wear them when sunny mornings coincided with a hangover.

That whole era had been full of optimism. I had a new flat and a new boyfriend (Brian) and a new life.

And then there is today: I just feel tired and empty.

After Martin's dinner party revelations I had expected an anxious, sleepless night, but in fact I slept like a dead woman. But despite nine hours of uninterrupted, apparently dreamless sleep, I have woken up feeling exhausted.

I watch tiny white clouds skimming across the triangle of visible blue sky that the Leylandii hasn't yet seen fit to steal, and think that I should probably go out – that sunshine and fresh air would probably do me good.

But I know that I won't.

I sip my tea and run a finger around the edge of the mug, as if maybe I am expecting it to sing like a wine-glass.

My brain is entirely paralysed by this new information about Brian. Who would have thought that he still had the power to hurt me?

It's not that I'm thinking about it in any way – the thought is somehow too vast for that . . . No, I'm just sitting here, taking in the enormity of it. It's as if someone has dumped so much rubble around my house that I can't get through it, and I can't get over it, and, for the moment, I can't even begin to imagine a strategy for moving it out of the way.

And so I sit with a slowly cooling mug of coffee and watch clouds incongruously skipping by and I think . . . well . . . nothing really.

About eleven, a grain of self-awareness appears, and I see myself sitting in the kitchen, still in my pyjamas, and somehow vaguely realise that no useful conclusion is going to manifest today, and that I might as well just get on with the mechanical motions of a normal day. And so, despite the surprising amount of willpower required, I heave myself to standing position and head for the bathroom.

After a shower and with my weekend face a little more heavily slapped on than usual, I decide that at least I look human again. Maybe my brain will catch up if I just give it time.

As I leave the bathroom, wondering what to do with the day, and, in a way, answering that question by wondering which recordings I have waiting on the Sky box, a silhouette appears beyond the frosted window of the front door, and I remember, belatedly, and with some irritation, that I have arranged to spend the day with Sarah-Jane.

For a moment I consider hiding from her, but knowing from experience that she too can probably see *my* vague form moving beyond the glass, I sigh heavily and walk the length of the hall, bracing myself for SJ's fabulous (but occasionally hard to bear) brand of irrepressible optimism.

The Sarah-Jane I find on the doorstep, however, looks as sullen as myself.

'Hiya,' she says, managing to make the word sound like a sigh.

She kisses me perfunctorily on the cheek and heads straight through to the kitchen. I frown, close the front door, and follow her.

By the time I reach the kitchen she has already slumped into a chair, and I realise that this isn't me communicating stress, or even projecting my own angst onto her: something is seriously awry.

'Are you OK?' I ask her. 'Because you look the way I feel. And I'm more used to you looking the way *you* feel.'

Sarah-Jane rests her head on one hand and looks up at me dolefully. 'You too, huh? And there was me thinking you were gonna cheer me up.'

I pull another mug from the cupboard and glance over my shoulder at her. 'Sorry, babe,' I say. 'We're all out of cheer here. I can probably manage tea and sympathy but that's about as far as it goes.'

'So what's up with you?' she asks, as I make the tea. 'Whatever it is, I bet mine's better.'

'You first then,' I say with a little, sour laugh. 'If you're going to get all competitive.'

'Nah, go on – I'm bored with mine.'

'Me too,' I reply.

'Work? Men? Life? That bloody tree?'

'Brian,' I say.

SJ rolls her eyes at me. 'You *are* joking?' she says. 'Don't you think it's time you got over bloody Brian?'

'I went to dinner at Cynthia and Carl's,' I say. 'You know, the usual birthday thing.'

Sarah-Jane nods. 'No wonder then. You always come back miserable as sin from those.'

I laugh sourly. 'That's actually pretty good,' I say. 'Miserable as sin . . . miserable as Cyn . . . get it?'

Sarah-Jane frowns at me in a way that leaves me unsure if she 'gets it' or not. 'So what is it this time? That wanker . . . *Martin* is it? Did he say something?'

I shake my head in amazement. 'You should get one of those little huts on Brighton Pier,' I say. 'Sarah-Jane Dennis, fortune-teller extraordinaire.'

She nods, her expression still blank. 'So?' she prompts.

'It seems that Brian has kids,' I say. 'Two of them.'

SJ rubs an eye and pulls a confused expression. '*Your* Brian? I mean . . .'

'I know what you mean,' I say. 'Yeah. *My* Brian.'

'And *kid-z* with a z, as in more than one?'

I shrug. 'Apparently so. Twins. So lovely Martin says.'

'Wow,' Sarah-Jane says. 'That was quick going.'

'And the best bit,' I add, 'is that they have just had their second birthdays.'

Sarah-Jane scrunches her brow and rolls her eyes to the ceiling, clearly performing mental arithmetic, then says, 'Oh, do the maths for me, will you? I'm too tired to work it out.'

'Estimated insemination: about two months after he picked me up from the clinic.'

SJ's mouth drops. 'God!' she says. 'What a fucking cheek. That guy is such a worm.'

'He is,' I agree, adding milk and handing her a mug of tea.

'Someone needs to just stop him, you know what I mean?'

'I do,' I say.

'Someone should just shoot him and put him out of his misery.'

'Put everyone else out of his misery, more like.'

'God you must be devastated,' she says.

I shrug. 'I guess . . .' I say, then, 'no, not really. Just sort of in shock.'

'Did you weep all over their dinner party? I bet Cyn loved that.'

I pout and shake my head.

'No, of course,' she says. 'You never do really, do you? Though I still think a good blubber every now and then would do you good.'

'If the tears aren't there . . .' I say.

'I s'pose not,' Sarah-Jane says. 'You should listen to Ben Harper more. Always does it for me.'

'I tried,' I say, 'the last time you gave me that advice. I watched *The English Patient*, too, on your recommendation. Nothing.'

'Ice queen,' she says.

'That's me.'

'God, what a prick! Do we know who she is? Poor girl.'

'Nope,' I reply. 'And we don't want to.'

'No,' she says.

'Anyway, enough of shit-face. What's up with you?'

SJ blows through pursed lips. 'Oh, just stuff,' she says, vaguely.

'Let's go through to the lounge,' I say. 'You can tell me all about it.'

'Sure,' she says, standing. 'Though I'm not sure I want to.'

But of course, I know she will.

Once seated in the lounge, Sarah-Jane sips her tea and waits for me to prompt her.

'So?' I say, after a respectful pause.

She shrugs. 'I went to see a gynaecologist,' she replies.

'A gynaecologist,' I repeat.

'Yeah. A doctor who . . .'

I shake my head. 'I *know* what a gynaecologist is . . .' Sometimes SJ scares me. 'Why though?'

'My period was late,' she says. 'Last couple of months.'

'Right.'

'And we're trying for a baby now. We finally both think it's time.'

I stare at her. In fact, in truth, I am staring *through* her. Shamefully, I'm having trouble concentrating on anything she's saying. For the Brian business is still occupying my mind, stealing the oxygen from every other possible thought.

'Well, that's good, isn't it?' I say, vaguely aware that I sound like I do when I talk to my mother and read my email at the same time.

Sarah-Jane nods. 'But it's maybe more than time,' she says, incomprehensibly.

I frown and shake my head. 'I don't . . .' I say. But something in her voice – the tiniest of tremors perhaps – snaps my brain out of its self-absorbed lethargy. My eyes refocus on her mouth and I notice that her top lip is trembling, Sue-Ellen style.

'*SJ?*' I say, putting down my mug and joining her on the sofa. I rub her back. 'What's happened?'

'Well my period was late,' she explains, quivery-voiced, for some reason starting back at the beginning. 'So I went to see

71

the doctor, and *he* sent me to the gynaecologist . . .'

'And?'

'He's ever so pretty,' she says, somewhat obtusely.

'Right. But what did this pretty gynaecologist *say*?'

'They did some tests. So we're not sure yet.'

'Tests . . .' I repeat, solemnly.

'Oestrogen levels and stuff.'

I nod.

'It doesn't look good,' she says. 'He thinks it might be too late.'

'Too late for what?'

'For babies,' she says. 'They think I might be . . .' She raises a clenched fist and presses it against her mouth. A tear slides out of the corner of her eye and down her cheek.

'Come on,' I say. 'You can tell me.'

'Menopausal,' she says. The word comes out in a gasp.

'*Menopausal?*' I repeat.

'They think I may have premature menopause.'

'But you're only . . .'

'Thirty-seven,' she says. 'Yeah. Sometimes it happens early, he says.'

And then, with a shudder, she collapses into me and I sit and shake my head and hold her as she silently sobs into my shoulder.

'George is going to be so upset,' she murmurs at one point.

'You haven't told him then?'

'He's in Germany,' she sobs.

After maybe ten minutes like this, her tears abate, and she pulls away from me looking puffy-eyed but somehow rather beautifully, profoundly . . . *human.*

Not for the first time, I feel jealous at her ability to simply cry and let it all out.

'I need to go wash my face . . .' she says, standing and leaving the room.

When she returns, visibly recomposed, she says, with determined brightness, 'Even if the tests do show I'm premenopausal, there's still a chance. There might still be a window of opportunity of a couple of years.'

I nod. 'Well,' I say. 'There you go. You'll be fine. I'm sure you will. And this doctor . . . you trust him?'

She nods. 'He seems to know his stuff. And if the diag . . .'

'Diagnosis.'

'Yeah. Diagnosis and Diagnostics . . . I always get them mixed up. If the diagnosis is confirmed then he'll send me to a fertility specialist.'

'God!' I say. 'So that is quite serious then.'

And here, Sarah-Jane's famed resilience shines through. She smiles weakly at me, slyly even.

'What?' I ask her, bemused by the sudden change.

'He *is* bloody gorgeous though,' she says. 'Honestly, you should see him.'

I pull a face. 'I think I'd rather see a woman myself. For that, anyway.'

'Oh me too,' she says. 'But he is bloody lovely. It weirded me out a bit. Having him fiddling about down below. He's single too. Well, no wedding ring anyway.'

'Jesus!' I exclaim. 'What are you like?'

'Well I was thinking about you, actually,' she says. 'He'd be right up your street.'

I pull a face. 'Except that he's a gynaecologist,' I say.

'Well yeah. There is that.'

'I couldn't . . . I mean . . . could *you* date a guy who spends all day . . .?'

'No,' says Sarah-Jane. 'I don't think I could.'

I pull a face again and shake my head. 'Imagine,' I say. 'You'd be wondering all the time who he'd had his hands up.'

'Nice day at the office, dear?' Sarah-Jane laughs.

'Exactly,' I say. 'So what happens next?'

She shrugs. 'We wait. We wait for the test results. Hopefully I'll have them by the time George gets back.'

I sigh. 'Well, if you need me to go with you or anything . . .'

SJ grins dirtily at me and winks.

'No!' I say. 'Not for that. I told you. I don't do gynaecologists.'

'As far as I can see you don't do anyone any more.'

'Well quite,' I say.

'Though just being serious for a minute . . .'

'Yeah?'

'Well, if you want kids – because, like, I know you *do* want kids . . .'

'Then I should get a move on? Is that it?'

'Well, yeah . . . Don't wait too long. Not like me.'

I snort. 'I would have to find the right bloke first.'

'Well, for that you may have to stop being so picky,' she says.

'Picky?'

'Yeah, like ruling out entire professions.'

'Right,' I say.

'And you need to stop hanging out with the fudge monkeys. You'll never find a boyfriend with them. Well, not a straight one.'

I pull a horrified face. 'Fudge monkeys? That's *horrible.*'

She shrugs. 'Sorry. I picked it up from Jenna. And she's a lezza. That makes it OK, doesn't it? Anyway, you see my point. Plus, what if the right guy turns up too late? You need to work out what your priorities are . . . I mean, if it's important to you . . .'

The implications of this comment – that even my best friend isn't convinced that I will find the right guy in time to have kids – stings me to the core. But I blank the thought for now. My mind just can't deal with any more on that subject.

'So what's the plan? For today?' I ask. *'Fudge monkeys indeed!'*

'Oh, I dunno . . . I brought some films,' she says, fishing two DVDs from her bag. *'Slumdog Millionaire . . .'*

'Ooh, I missed that when it was at the cinema,' I say. 'It's supposed to be great.'

'Yeah, I thought it would cheer me . . . us . . . up,' she says, putting the DVD on the coffee table and studying the second one. 'And *The Boy in the Striped Pyjamas.'*

'Which definitely won't cheer us up.'

'No?' she says.

'No! That's the one about a boy in a concentration camp . . . *Dying.'*

'Oh,' she says.

'Plus, I've seen it.'

'*Slumdog* then?'

'*Slumdog*.'

The Apprentice

On Monday morning, I share the lift to the third floor with Victoria Barclay. She says, apparently with genuine (and uncharacteristic) enthusiasm, 'So we're going to New York together. What fun!'

I actually start to feel hopeful that the trip might be bearable after all.

Perhaps, I figure, the fact that it is my own success, my own stunning pitch, which has made this trip possible, means that she will even be nice to me for once.

Down in Creative I explain my theory to The Gay Team. With VB being a partner, no one is going to say anything outrageous against her, but Jude pulls a strange, tight-lipped face and turns back to his Mac whilst Mark and Darren both wiggle their eyebrows expressively at me, unanimously communicating that they suspect me of engaging in wishful thinking.

'You don't think that's going to happen then?' I prompt.

Darren shrugs. 'I've read a lot of fairy tales, but evil witches rarely turn into fairy godmothers,' he says. 'That's all I'm saying.'

We briefly discuss their proposals for the US version of the campaign and then I leave them to (hopefully) get on with it.

Back at my desk I think about New York, and, of course, about Brian. Perfect husbands can, as we all know, turn into devils.

I'm still unable to formulate any specific feelings about Brian's new life as a daddy, except maybe that it never ceases to amaze me just how mean human beings can be to each other. To me.

Of course, I tell myself, knowing a little about human

history, knowing for instance what the Spanish (men) did during the inquisition, or, say, what the Germans (men) did during the Second World War, or hey, closer to home, what Tony Blair and George Bush have been up to recently . . . well, one could hardly claim not to have been forewarned about the nature of the male of the species. Trying to force a note of optimism into my thoughts, I forcibly remind myself that not all men are this way. Just apparently the ones who run countries. And the ones I date.

• • •

Midweek, I am summoned to VB's office.

Gone is the girlish enthusiasm for our 'fun' trip together: she has clearly decided to prove that men do not have a monopoly on bad behaviour.

'So,' she says, lounging and swivelling in her chair as if she is the new Alan Sugar. 'I've been thinking, and I want to see your pitch.'

I haven't even sat down yet. 'May I?' I ask, gesturing, with hypocritical meekness, towards the chair.

'Sure,' she says, then, 'No, actually don't. I want to see the full pitch, so can you go and get the props?'

I smile at her and then, as I head from the room, I somewhat childishly pull a face.

On my return, what ensues is a comedy version of *The Apprentice*.

She makes me stand and pretend to pitch to a room full of people. A room full of people represented by herself: the slouching, swivelling, VB.

I attempt to remind her that the pitch has already been successful. Successful enough, in fact, to generate an invitation to repeat it in New York. But, of course, VB is having none of it. Having lived in the States for nearly a whole year, she is the unchallengeable expert on all things American.

'Stop stop stop!' she whines, banging the flat of her hand on the desk like a toddler in a high chair. 'This lead-in is far too long! Everyone will be asleep by the time you get wherever it is you're going.'

'No one fell asleep at BRP,' I point out.

'But these are Americans, dear. They're far zippier. Lucky you have me here to help you tighten things up.'

I nod and smile and scrunch my eyes up. 'It is!' I reply. 'So are they really that different? I don't think I've ever met any in the flesh.'

'Just listen and learn,' VB tells me. 'Delete all that pap about market enablers and then take it from the top again.'

'With pleasure,' I say, wondering if it is humanly possible to get through this without dragging her to the ground by her hair.

'And don't let me forget to discuss wardrobe with you,' VB says. 'We don't want to turn up looking like a couple of country bumpkins, now, do we?'

I mentally compare VB's outfit: green roll-neck and plaid skirt, with my own Agnes B trouser-suit. If anyone is flirting with country bumpkin here, it isn't me.

I truly can't think of a polite reply, so I ignore the comment and strike a red line through half a page of my script and start the presentation over again. 'Hello, everyone! We're here today, as you know, to present our campaign for the new Grunge! Street-Wear range of unisex carpenter pants.'

'Stop,' VB says. 'You're right. They *do* already know that. Delete it.'

The only good thing about all of this is that by the end of the week, my hatred for Victoria Barclay and my stress about the trip have reached such a fever pitch that I am spending entire half-days without thinking about Brian – entire half-days without even picturing him pushing a double pram down the street.

It rains all weekend, so I sit and stare at the remains of my ravaged pitch and try to invent strategies for making it presentable without obviously ignoring everything Victoria

Barclay has said. At one point, in despair, I dial Peter Stanton's number, but then hang up. I know that he can't do anything to help me here.

By Sunday evening when the landline rings, I can honestly say that not only have I stopped thinking about Brian, but I have stopped thinking about anything else, or anyone else, whatsoever.

'Hello?' a deep voice says. 'Can I speak to the sexy lady who goes to speed dating?'

'I'm sorry?' I reply, still staring at a page from my pitch.

'Oh shit. This isn't . . . I thought I was speaking to . . . Sorry. Can I speak to CC, please?'

Brown Eyes!

'Is that *Norman*?' I ask in astonishment.

'Yeah,' he says. 'Sorry, I thought it was someone else for a moment.'

'No . . . It's me . . . Long time no hear,' I say.

'No, yeah . . . sorry about that. I was up in Newcastle. On a course. So I couldn't. Sorry.'

'Wow, now there's an unexplored market niche,' I say, unable to resist.

'I'm sorry?'

'Selling telephones to the north of England. I think they'd really love them, don't you?' I grimace at my abrasive sarcasm, then add, 'Sorry. I'm being a bitch today. Bad week.'

'OK . . .' Norman says, quietly. 'You did have my mobile number too.'

'You're right,' I say. 'Again. Sorry. I'm kind of stressed about work. How are you?'

'Good. Yeah. Really good actually.'

Despite my attempts at convincing him that I am a praying mantis, Norman still invites me to dinner.

I roll my eyes at destiny's fabulous sense of timing. 'I'm touched,' I say. 'But I can't. I'm off to New York tomorrow. I won't be back until Thursday.'

'OK, well, maybe at the weekend then,' Norman replies. 'I'll give you a call on Friday.'

'That'd be great. I'm sorry, but . . . well . . . that's the way it goes.'

'No problem. Talk to you Friday then,' he says. Then with laughter in his voice, he adds, 'Unless you call me before. Oh . . . Do they *have* phones in New York?'

Hotline

It is the first time I have been to Heathrow Terminal Five. At first glance (from outside) the place looks modern and impressive. Indeed, even inside, the white discs of light which cover the ceiling give the place a certain Star-Trekky air. It would be easy to imagine that they are teleport machines and that simply standing beneath them will whisk you off to another place. If only.

Sadly, the décor is where modernity ends, for experientially Terminal Five is like any other airport terminal: a confusing mess.

At eleven a.m., when I arrive, the hall is literally a sea of people. It looks like the rabble outside IKEA on the opening day of the January sales, and, pushing through the crowd, it is virtually impossible to gain any idea of where you are heading, let alone which direction you *should* be heading.

Still, forewarned, as they say, is forearmed. Everyone at work warned me about Terminal Five (most memorably Mark, who said, '*Terminal* being the operative word,') so I have three full hours before my flight.

Victoria, who told me specifically to wait for her before check-in, but also refused to authorise business-class tickets (they have their own special tiny queue) clearly didn't realise that we would be meeting in the equivalent of a Madonna concert at the O2 Arena.

As I shuffle my way left, and right, and then left again along the absurd snake, which, I hope, leads to the correct check-in desk, I shamefully pray that VB won't turn up at all. 'Please let her cab have crashed,' I chant, silently.

Of course I'm only joking. I'm sure if there is a great power somewhere clever enough to tune in specifically to *my* thoughts, He/She/It will also be clever enough to realise this.

It takes a full forty minutes of this absurd conga line for me to near the front of the queue. I finally weaken and try VB's mobile, but there is no answer – just her sharp, 'Victoria's mobile. Leave a message.'

'It's CC,' I say. 'I'm wondering where you are. I'm going to have to check in. Meet you at the departure gate.'

As I press the end-call button, I restrain a smile. For the first time I am seriously considering the possibility that I won't have to travel with her after all. It's such a lovely idea, I hardly dare believe it.

With a final smug glance back at the crowds, I step up to the desk and dump my bag onto the scales.

A second conga line takes me to passport control, and a third, the longest of all, through security. They steal my nail file, of course. I know they do this, but I always think it's worth a try. I somehow think that the day I can fly again with my nail-file will be the day the world has returned to sanity. I mean, I've certainly never heard of anyone hijacking a plane with a nail file. Have you?

In the departure lounge the electronic signs are already directing me to gate seven-thousand-nine hundred-and-seventy-six, so I head off down the world's longest corridor. It looks like the optical illusion you get when you put one mirror in front of another . . . regular, repetitive, endless.

At the gate, when there is still no sign of VB, my mood shifts from optimism to unease. *Oh God!* I think. *Please don't let her have really had an accident. I was joking!* Then, despite the fact that it could mean she still turns up in time for the pitch tomorrow, I generously add, *Let it just be . . . I don't know . . . a breakdown or something.*

Just before boarding the shuttle train to the plane, I give her number one last try and then call the office.

Sheena, Victoria's long-suffering secretary sounds as surprised as I am. 'God, I hope something hasn't happened,' she says, in what I can't help but interpret as a velvety tone of anticipation.

She puts me through to Peter Stanton who says that he has no idea where VB is either, and asks, without apparent sarcasm, if I think I can manage on my own.

It is with a confusing mix of feelings that I board flight BA177.

It never ceases to amaze me how the different companies continue to have such clichéd identities for their cabin crew. They must have very specific processes to choose their new staff.

Air France girls all look like failed top models who might spit in your drink if you don't pronounce *Bonjour* in exactly the right way. EasyJet hostesses all look like they have a bottle of WKD Blue and a packet of condoms hidden down their orange blouses for break-time. And the BA women all look like Sarah-Jane's mum: homely and reassuring – like they know how to make a *lovely* cup of tea.

As the flight progresses, my guilt builds.

As the old saying goes, you can take the girl out of the church, but you can't take the church out of the girl. At least, you can never take away the Catholic capacity for guilt. Or the desire for a priest to absolve.

Though my mother is staunchly atheist, my father, who was Irish, dragged me *religiously* to Sunday mass. Waiine, for his part, always preferred to help Mum with the Sunday roast.

As a child, of course, I enjoyed it. It was a special thing that only Dad and I did and, lord knows, kids love exclusive clubs. But once I reached adolescence, well, I could think of a million better things to be doing of a Sunday morning.

Following a certain fuss about inappropriate use of choir boys, Father Rowlings vanished and was replaced by the fiery Father Gleeson. I think from then on we both found his tales of fire and brimstone somewhat less appealing than Rowlings' cuddly (in more ways than one) vision of God. It took less than a year before we were both regularly missing services.

These days I struggle to convince myself that I'm no longer Catholic.

I can't bear the Pope, and the idea that he somehow has a hotline to God always strikes me as profoundly stupid.

Then again, despite my best efforts, I have trouble looking at, say, the beauty of a flower, or the miracle of conception, and still imagine that it all comes down to a chance bumping together of molecules in some distant chemical soup.

Agnostic is my preferred label these days, and in an attempt at convincing myself, at shaking off my Catholic shackles, I always try to force myself to think of the unknown power as *He/She/It*.

But of course without anyone to absolve me, the only thing that I can do during my flight is sit and drown in the guilty secret that I actually prayed for VB to have a car accident, and that, just perhaps, as a direct result, the seat beside me is now empty.

Well, half empty. As it happens it is half-occupied by a rather voluptuous chap in the end seat. Were Victoria here, no doubt I would be squashed into the remaining space.

As Chunky snores his way across the Atlantic, and as BA hostess Shirley serves me with, you guessed it, a lovely cup of tea, the only thing I can do is to repeat a corrective mantra. *Please let her be OK. Please don't let her have had an accident. Let it just be a breakdown or something.*

It's not until I'm sitting in a yellow cab whizzing along a surprisingly empty road towards Manhattan that my mobile beeps to tell me that I have a voice-message.

It's from Peter Stanton: 'Hello, CC, Peter here. It's a bit embarrassing but it appears that VB has had some sort of a breakdown and so she won't be joining you in New York. It looks like you'll have to go it alone. Call me if you need anything. Good Luck.'

I'm confused as to why a simple breakdown might mean that she isn't coming at all. But I cannot deny that my overriding emotion is one of sheer joy. I run my tongue across my teeth and let myself slip into a broad grin – broad enough, it would seem, for the driver to spot it in his rear-view mirror.

'First time you are visiting New York?' he asks in a thick Italian accent.

I shake my head and lean forward. 'No, third time. But I haven't been back for years.'

'Well, you are looking happy about it,' he says.

I nod. 'Well, yeah, I love New York. And anyway, it's not where you are, is it? It's who you're with.' *Or not with*, I think.

He nods, seemingly having understood something – presumably that I am meeting the love of my life here.

Which strikes me, after all, as not such a bad idea.

Seeing as the hotline to whoever, or whatever, today, for the first time in my life, appears open, I close my eyes and have one more try.

'Thanks for the breakdown,' I think. 'But now, if you could just set me up with a really successful pitch, that would be great . . . Oh, and a lovely bloke.'

I open my eyes and nod in satisfaction. This is going to be a great trip.

And then I close them for one last wish. 'Make that a lovely bloke with brown eyes. Oh, no beard please. And a farm.'

That's probably pushing things a bit far, but well . . . as my father used to say, if you go around asking for cheese sandwiches, you can't then start complaining when you don't get steak.

Men Only

The most that I see of New York that first evening is the stretch of pavement between the door of the cab and the Park Lane hotel – such are the disappointing realities of business travel.

Still, I cheer myself up by reminding myself that I have all day Wednesday to explore.

The room itself is clean, well-furnished and fairly generous in terms of size. Like most hotels these days it's also pretty generic. Once inside I could be staying in just about any major city really, which, for tonight, is fine. I need to work on my pitch and the fewer distractions the better.

I hang up my grey Vivienne Westwood chambray suit which I note with satisfaction has survived the trip remarkably unwrinkled, and order a tuna melt and a single beer from room service, and sit down to work.

Irritatingly, the original, pre-Victoria version of the pitch is missing from my laptop, so I take a pen and a pad, and start to jot down what I remember.

As each deletion had been so painful, it's not so hard to recall what to put back.

By ten p.m. it looks about right, so I pack everything away and attempt to sleep. It being four a.m. back home, this should be easy, but despite the double glazing, the sound of New York – mainly horns and sirens – still reaches my ears.

I am incredibly psyched up about the pitch and the only alternative subjects I seem able to think about are Brian's kids, Sarah-Jane's menopause, Victoria Barclay's absence, or my weekend date with Brown Eyes. Clearly none of these is going to send me to sleep.

I zip through a hundred or so TV channels until I hit the hotel's pay-to-view channel which is offering the latest *Star Wars* movie. I puff up the pillows, ready for a night's viewing.

When I wake up in the morning I will have no memory of even the opening minutes of the film, or for that matter of having turned the TV off. Good old *Star Wars*. For me, at any rate, it's the perfect sleeping pill.

. . .

It's a cold crisp morning, and the walk across town enlivens me. I have travelled lots, mainly with work, and though some of the Asian cities I have visited are literally throbbing with life, nowhere ever strikes me as quite as 'alive' as New York. It has a busy sophistication which is quite unique. I think it's something to do with having seen images of New York in so many films. The second I hit the sidewalk (not the pavement, you see) I feel instantly infused with star quality.

The Harper & Baker building on Madison Avenue is stunning. The interior looks so much like Ugly Betty's office that I wonder if they didn't simply hand the DVD to their designers and say, 'We want that.'

Indeed, everyone working at Harper & Baker also fits the *Ugly Betty* mould. Which of course means that everyone except Ugly Betty is beautiful: clear complexions, high-fashion outfits, shiny suits and white teeth abound. And how come all Americans have those teeth? I have asked my dentist and the best he could offer is a polish and bleach, and the result is sooo not the same thing.

Tom, from the Harper & Baker creative team, comes down to reception to greet me and leads me through security into the building.

He, too, is square-jawed with short blond hair, big blue eyes and, of course, long white, almost rabbity teeth. He is exquisitely dressed in a black pin-stripe suit over a white-collared blue shirt and a grey tie.

Those shirts always make me think of my father. My mother bought him one once in the eighties, and he complained that it looked like he was too poor to afford a collar that matched. He never once wore the thing. I have always rather liked them myself.

Tom smiles and asks me about my trip in that unique American way that combines banal conversation with a voice which gives the impression that this is the most interesting chat he's ever had.

He takes me first to the in-house café which is considerably bigger than your average Starbucks. Over excellent cappuccinos Tom tells me, somewhat nerve-rackingly, that they are all very excited to hear my pitch. 'It's not that often we get to work with people from the smaller independents,' he says. 'And that's usually where the best talent is.'

The guided tour of the offices takes about half an hour. Everyone is wonderfully polite, and I remember again how this is always my overall impression of America. Whatever their politicians get up to, and no matter what people in Utah would like to do to my gay friends, the overriding impression you come away with is always that Americans are among the friendliest, most polite, most welcoming people on the planet.

The overall layout of their operation is identical to the one back home, with the difference that everything is super-sized. Super-sized and spanking new. The whole thing simply oozes wealth.

At twelve on the dot, Tom hands me over to Cindy who, as far as I can ascertain, works on the Levi's account.

Cindy is a female version of Tom – in fact they could be twins: same hair, same eyes, same teeth. Compared with Tom's openness, though, Cindy plays a guarded game, apparently trying to get as much information from me about Grunge! and our campaign whilst giving as little away as possible about Harper & Baker or Levi's.

This reticence on her side provokes a similar distrust in myself, and so we are reduced to superficial, non specific chit-chat.

Cindy tells me that working at Harper & Baker is *awesome*, so I reply in kind, telling her that Spot On is also a really nice company to work for. *Really nice*, I reckon, is about as close as we ever get to *awesome* over our side of the pond.

After a salmon sandwich and another cappuccino, Cindy announces that she will show me the boardroom.

I'm somewhat shocked, on arrival in said boardroom, to see that all the people I am to pitch to are already sitting there waiting: sixteen people in all.

'So, this is CC from Spot In,' Cindy says, by way of introduction.

'Spot On,' I correct her.

'Yes, sorry, isn't that what I said?'

'It doesn't matter,' I say, turning to face the seated men. 'Hi!'

'Good, so, I'll leave you to it,' she says, backing somewhat nervously from the room.

One could hardly blame her. Sixteen men in a semicircle is hardly the easiest audience to face. Spot On is pretty male dominated, but even I am surprised to find that not a single woman will be present for my pitch. Harper & Baker's glass ceilings are evidently shiny and intact.

I swallow hard and scan the faces. Tom, the only person I have met before, smiles at me encouragingly.

'So, hi there,' I say again, for some reason. 'I'm CC Kelly from Spot On.' I realise that there's a slight Irish lilt to my accent today. This sometimes happens in moments of stress. I decide not to try to contain it. Americans famously love that stuff.

'Oh, my bag,' I say, suddenly realising that it and the rolled visuals have remained at reception.

But Tom raises a hand to get my attention, and then points towards the corner of the room where my stuff has magically materialised.

After a little undignified scrabbling on the floor, I stand back up with my notes and face the men who are all silently watching me with glassy expressions.

I lick my lips and start again. 'Sorry, so, as I was saying, I'm

CC Kelly from Spot On.' As I say it, I realise that this is now my third introduction and start to sweat.

Tom raises the palm of his hand and grins at me. 'Tom Parker,' he says. 'Creative director here at Harper & Baker.'

Oh God! He's the creative *director*. He didn't tell me that. I trawl through our conversation in case I have said anything I shouldn't. But his introduction thankfully starts a round-the-table chain reaction.

'Craig Peterson, marketing director at Levi's.'

'Michael James, Media. Levi's also.'

This feels like a different kind of meeting. I keep expecting them to clap, or add, '. . . and I am an alcoholic.'

By the time the introductions are over, I have learnt that I am pitching to some of the top brass from both Harper & Baker, America's second largest advertising agency, and of course from Levi's. Thankfully I have also had the time to get a grip on myself. I take a deep breath, swallow hard, and throw myself off the edge of the cliff.

'As you know, we're here today . . .'

It's incredibly hard to know how the presentation is being received as once the initial smiles fade (and even Americans can't keep it up forever) the expressions facing me become waxy and hermetic. Having been to a few of these meetings myself, I would guess that many of those present are thinking about whatever they were working on before they were forced to stop and come to this meeting. A few will be thinking about sex, and a couple about what to eat tonight.

Certainly, the (very) occasional nods and, *ums* and *ahhs* bear little relation to anything I'm saying.

When I unroll the first visual, everyone momentarily wakes up, but even then the only comment anyone makes is Tom's, 'Looks like a photo of this place.'

Which, the white-walled, neon lit bar in the photo undeniably does.

'Well spotted,' I say with a wink. 'Great minds think alike.'

But everyone else looks bored, or lobotomised or dead. It's the most uncomfortable pitch of my entire career.

By the time it's over, I have only one desire. To run from the building and lock the door to my hotel room and have a good scream.

'So! Any questions?' I ask.

Silence.

'Any comments? First impressions?'

Silence.

I feel like a schoolteacher trying to chivvy a bunch of adolescents into talking about geography.

'I have one,' Craig Peterson finally asks, flicking my business card over in his fingers like a card sharp doing a trick.

I brace myself to defend our decision to tackle the gay market first. Surely, if there is to be only one comment, then that's what it's going to be about. But no.

'What does CC stand for?' he asks.

I lick my lips and sense the first flush of heat that signals the beginning of a blush. 'Oh, it's just an abbreviation,' I say.

'Yes, but for what?'

'It's, um, an abbreviation . . . of my first name. I don't like my first name, so I prefer to use CC.'

'OK,' he says, flatly. 'So what *is* your first name?'

Anywhere else, I would say, *As I say, I don't like to use it. So I'm not going to tell you!* But this is the marketing director of Levi's here. And the stress around the table, is palpable.

'It's Chelsea,' I say, quietly.

'Chelsea,' he repeats. 'And you don't like that, *because . . .*'

I blink at him. I shrug. 'I have no idea,' I say. 'I don't like certain things. Who knows why? For instance, I don't like . . .' I'm about to say beards, but I realise that three of the men in the room have them. 'Marmite,' I finally say. It's a lie, but it's the first alternative which came to mind.

'Marmite?'

'It's a British thing,' Tom says. 'A savoury spread.'

'OK,' Craig says.

'My niece is called Chelsea,' Tom offers.

'Damn fine name,' Craig comments.

I nod and open my mouth to speak, but nothing comes out.

'OK,' I eventually say. 'So, are there any other comments about the pitch?'

Silence.

'Well, in that case, I think we're done here,' I say.

At this everyone starts to stand, chatter, and file from the room. It's as much as I can do to resist shouting, 'Ding ding. Class dismissed.'

I retain a fixed, benevolent expression until the room is empty, then let my face fall into a grimace befitting my state of tired, irritated disappointment.

Tom sticks his head back in the door. 'Ooh!' he says, catching a glance of my grotesque snarl. 'The mask falls!'

I switch back to *smile*. 'Sorry, it's been a hard day.'

'I bet,' he says. 'You're at the Park Lane, right?'

I nod. 'I am,' I say.

'OK, I'll pick you up about seven. OK?'

I shake my head in bewilderment. 'For . . . *what* exactly?'

'Sorry, didn't Cindy tell you? I'm officially charged with showing you a good time tonight.' Here he wiggles his eyebrows suggestively.

'I'm not sure . . .' I say.

Tom winks at me. 'Sure you're sure,' he says. 'See you at seven in the lobby.'

And with that he is gone.

This time, I cross the room and close the door before I let my face collapse. I sit in a chair at the empty table and rest my forehead on one hand and sigh.

Half an hour later, back at the hotel, I drop my bag inside the door and hurl myself despondently onto the bed.

'Mary, mother of Jesus!' I mutter.

Funny really, how adversity always seems to bring out the Irish in me.

Funny, Awful and Ironic

I hesitate long and hard over what to wear for my 'date' with Tom. It's always difficult with these hybrid professional/social events. If Tom is going to turn up in his suit and spend the evening discussing work, then my best bet is to recycle the Westwood suit. Then again, if he turns up in casual clothes and takes me to a drinking den, I would be better off in jeans and a pullover.

I change four times, but in the end I simply can't face the suit again. Whatever tonight turns out to be, I don't want it to be a continuation of today. I settle for a compromise. Black trousers and a heavy, grey, belted cardigan. I get to the lobby at five to seven and find Tom already waiting for me, changed, I note with satisfaction, into grey combat trousers, sweatshirt, and a leather jacket.

Dressed differently, I suddenly see him in a different light. Sneaking a peek at his pert bum – what my gay friends would call his bubble butt – it suddenly crosses my mind that tonight may not be so bad after all. I always was a sucker for a pretty bum.

'Hello!' he says. 'You look more relaxed.'

I smile. 'Is this too relaxed?' I ask. 'I wasn't sure where we were going so . . .'

'It's perfect,' Tom says, then nodding towards the door, 'Shall we?'

Outside the hotel we jump into one of the waiting cabs. The temperature is dropping fast and I'm glad not to be wearing a dress. 'West Village,' he tells the driver. 'I'll tell you where when we've decided.'

'So,' he asks me, 'what do you want to eat? Sushi? Italian? Chinese?'

I shrug. 'I'm pretty easily pleased when it comes to food. As long as I don't have to cook it's all fine.'

Tom shrugs. 'Well it's your choice,' he says.

'Sushi?' I say, simply because it was the first on his list.

'Sushi it is,' he laughs. He leans back towards the driver. 'That'll be the junction of Thompson and West Houston then,' he tells him.

The cab lurches away in that unique New York way. I seem to recall that it's something to do with V8 engines and automatic gearboxes and then remember geeky car-fan Ronan telling me exactly that on our trip here twelve years ago. Funny the random bits of information the brain retains.

'You were great today,' Tom says.

I laugh lightly.

'You don't think so?' Tom says flatly.

I roll my eyes and shake my head.

Tom frowns at me. '*Really?*' he asks.

I laugh a little louder. 'Oh come on, Tom,' I say. 'Half the people there fell asleep. The other half committed suicide shortly after I left the building.'

Tom laughs. 'You're hard on yourself,' he says. 'Women in business are. Cindy is the same.'

I shake off the comment and look out of the window but wonder if this is true. I suppose we have to be tougher on ourselves than men do . . . we know about the invisible ceilings we're trying to break through.

The cab slows to squeeze through a crowd spilling off the pavement.

'They're queueing for tickets,' Tom tells me. 'Actually, if you want to go to a show or something after dinner, then . . .'

I shake my head and look back at him. 'I went to see *Cats* when I was here in ninety-six. It put me off musicals for life.'

Tom nods. 'That good, huh? I haven't seen it myself.'

'I fell asleep in the first fifteen minutes. Let's say I enjoyed it as much as you enjoyed my presentation,' I say.

Tom laughs. 'Now there you go again. I really don't see—'

'Tom,' I interrupt. 'Stop pretending. I'm not blind. Or deaf. No one smiled, no one laughed at the jokes, no one had a question at the end.'

Tom shrugs. 'That's normal,' he says.

'It is?'

'Sure. It's big-client paralysis,' he says with a shrug.

I turn towards him and rest one arm along the back of the seat. 'Big-client paralysis?' I say. 'Sounds like an official diagnosis.'

'It's what we call it,' Tom says.

'When . . . ?'

'When . . . OK, so . . . Levi's is our second-biggest client, right? So without Levi's, half of us get redundancy.'

'Right,' I say.

'So everyone is scared.'

'OK . . .'

'So no one from HB can react until the client does. I mean, if Craig had laughed, then everyone would have laughed.'

'I see.'

'And if Craig had said he loved the pitch, then *everyone* would have loved the pitch.'

'Right,' I say. 'Only he didn't.'

Tom pouts and wrinkles his nose. 'He never does. He never expresses a view in public.'

'Great,' I say.

'He will go back to his office and sit down with, say, Michael James and Rowan Askey, and say vaguely that he enjoyed it, or didn't, and depending on how they react they will all whip themselves into a frenzy about this being the best thing they ever saw or . . .'

'Or the worst.'

'Well, there's always that possibility, but having been there today, I'd honestly say you have nothing to worry about.'

'Right.'

'And I'm sure they loved that Irish accent you put on.'

I open my mouth in mock outrage. 'I did not put it on,' I say.

'Ooh! It's back!' Tom laughs.

'My father was Irish,' I say. 'It comes and goes.'

'Well, it came at the right moment,' Tom says. 'Craig Peterson's grandmother is Irish. Well, she *was*. He's very proud of his Irish heritage.'

'And if, despite my lovely accent, he hated it?'

Tom shrugs. 'You're dead in the water. Me too, probably, for setting it up.'

'Great,' I say again.

'But it'll be fine. You'll see.'

I'm not entirely convinced. This could just be Tom trying to make sure I have a good evening, but, for the moment at least, I decide to suspend judgement. For now, I decide to enjoy a night out in New York with a very good-looking man.

When we get to the restaurant, Tomoe Sushi, at least twenty people are queueing outside.

'It looks a bit busy,' I say. 'If you want to go somewhere else we can . . .'

Tom shakes his head and grabs my arm, pulling me towards the door. 'If you're eating raw fish, never go to an empty restaurant,' he says.

Just as in films (for this clearly never happens to me) the Japanese guy on the door spots Tom and beckons him forward. As he leads us past the front of the queue, he apologises to those now behind us. 'Sorry, but he's my brother,' he says.

Once we are seated, I lean towards Tom. 'He seems really sweet but I'm assuming that he isn't really your *blother*.'

'No,' Tom laughs. 'But he is kind of framily.'

'Family?'

'No, *framily*. Don't you Brits use *framily*?' Tom asks. 'It's, you know, friends who you've known so long that they're like family.'

I smile. 'No, I never heard that,' I say. 'But I like it.' I think of Mark and Darren and wonder if they are my framily. 'I like it a lot,' I say.

'Yes, I've known Tamotsa for . . . yikes! Maybe twenty years.'

'Schoolfriend?' I ask, looking around at the restaurant. It's a far less chic choice than I thought Tom would have chosen, but it's clearly incredibly popular. A couple of tables are occupied by gay couples, but then we are on the edge of The Village here.

'No,' Tom says. 'Not really.'

Apparently switching from a subject he doesn't want to talk about to one that I don't want to talk about, he says, 'Sooo. What's all this CC business? Everyone's intrigued about that.'

I roll my eyes. 'Do we have to?'

'Not at all. So, what are you eating?'

'I don't know yet . . . Sorry. Look. It's Chelsea,' I say. 'I said so in the meeting.'

'Fine,' Tom says. 'It's just that no one can see why you wouldn't like that. But anyway, it doesn't matter. What are you eating?'

'It's a bit chavvy, that's all. It's no big deal. I fancy some kind of soup and then some fish. Preferably cooked.'

'They do a mixed fish grill,' Tom says. 'It's excellent. A bit what?'

'I'm sorry?'

'Your name. You said it's a bit . . .'

'Oh! *Chavvy.*'

Tom shakes his head.

'Never mind,' I say.

Tom puts down the menu and puts both elbows on the table and leans his square chin on both hands. He looks hopelessly cute. 'I did teach you *framily*,' he says.

I sigh. 'Oh Lord,' I say. 'Chavs . . . chavvy . . . how to explain it? Chavs are, you know, a certain kind of girl. Well, or boy. But usually girls.'

'A certain kind?'

'They wear pink hoodies and low-waist jeans and wander around in winter with their pierced belly-buttons showing.'

Tom looks at me wide-eyed. 'And they're called Chelsea?'

'Lots of them are, sadly for me. Plus my mum didn't even spell mine properly,' I tell him. 'But that's a whole different story.'

'The pink hoodie thing ... sounds like you're describing Britney Spears,' Tom comments.

'Well those that aren't called Chelsea often *are* called Britney,' I laugh. 'Or Ashleigh. Or Tammy.'

'So anything ending in an *ee* sound,' Tom laughs.

'Mostly,' I say. 'I never really thought about it. Or Jordan. Or Chantelle.'

'Right,' Tom says. 'So chav means kind of the same thing as trailer-trash?'

I laugh. 'I love that. Trailer-trash. Always makes me laugh.'

'Trailer-trash names would be, um, let me see, um ... Doreen, or Joleen, or, no wait, *Turleen*. Turleen is an excellent trailer-trash name.'

'Turleen?' I repeat. 'Is that really a name?'

'It is if you come from Texas.'

'Well there you go. I'm sure if you were called Turleen, you'd reduce it to *T* on your business cards.'

Tom raises an eyebrow. 'I think I would change it to Tom, Turleen being a girl's name and all.'

'Of course,' I laugh.

'So that's it. Chav equals trailer-trash. You see. This is educational.'

'I suppose so. It supposedly stands for Council House And Violent.'

'Council house and violent,' Tom repeats. 'Meaning?'

'Council houses are special low-rent houses.'

'Like the projects.'

'Yes, like your housing projects.'

'But violent.'

'Exactly. Sometimes.'

'Nice.'

'Exactly.'

'And CC? What's the other C? The second C?'

'It's a nickname. From my younger years. When I still thought it was funny. When everyone thought it was funny. Chelsea Chav.'

Tom laughs loudly and slaps his thigh. 'I love that. That way you Brits have of laughing at yourselves. Well, it's special, that's all. Chelsea Chav. I love that.'

I smile and lower my gaze. 'Good. Now we have that out of the way . . .'

'Sure,' Tom says, still smirking. 'So what do you want to eat?'

An hour later, after a wonderful bowl of clam soup, some excellent grilled mixed fish, and four glasses of sake, Tom bundles me into another cab, this time to show me his favourite neighbourhood bar.

As the alcohol takes effect, I'm finding Tom increasingly attractive.

Of course, it's not difficult: he *is* attractive. He may not have brown eyes, and he may not be dark and swarthy, and he may not have a farm either, but he is a very good-looking man, and he is open and funny and charming. As the taxi hurls us around the corners, I am feeling increasingly drawn to the flesh beneath the cotton of his combat trousers. Drawn enough to accidentally let my leg bump against his.

I sit and calculate exactly how much thigh to thigh contact can be allowed to 'accidentally' occur, and ponder the fact that he has chosen his favourite neighbourhood bar. It's likely, of course, to be near his flat.

The fact that tonight might turn out to be more than a simple drink with a work colleague seems increasingly evident. And I really need to get a grip on how I feel about that before we get to the point of no return.

I glance at Tom who is texting on his iPhone, and he looks up and smiles at me. 'Is this OK?' he asks, 'because if you want something more memorable I can take you to Bar Centrale . . . we might even spot some New York celebs. Actually, we can do that after if you wish. The night is young.'

I shake my head. 'No, this is fine,' I reassure him. 'Much nicer to have a genuine experience of New York . . . to see where you would normally go.'

Tom snorts as if this is somehow cute or funny and returns to his texting operation. I, for my part, turn back to the window and watch New York spinning by, and calculate the pros and cons of letting myself have a business trip fling.

Pros: He's fit. He's funny. He's good looking.

Cons: He's a client. He's a client. He's a client.

For, of course, that's the biggy. I have known many a contract crumble to dust because someone, somewhere, shagged the wrong person.

But then, if, as Tom says, it's really Levi's running the show . . .

But even then, one-off business-trip sex is pretty slutty. Do I really want to live up to my chavvy name? But do I really want my vagina to heal over through lack of use either?

'Hey,' Tom says, squeezing my shoulder to get my attention. 'We're here.'

That squeeze somehow shifts the balance in Tom's favour. It's been a long time, too long in fact, since anyone squeezed any part of me.

The Excelsior is exactly as a New York bar should be. Lots of dark wood and low suspended lights. A big jukebox in the corner . . . Big slatted wooden blinds fill the large windows, making the place feel intimate and private.

There are only perhaps twenty people here for now, mostly men, all very casual/chic, very Abercrombie and Fitch.

'This OK?' Tom asks, returning from the bar with a bottle of beer and my white wine spritzer.

'Perfect,' I tell him. 'Lovely.'

'So do you go out much in London?' he asks. 'I had such a great time when I was there three . . . no, four years ago.'

'Yes,' I say. 'Quite a bit. Probably not as much as I should. You know what it's like when you live somewhere.'

'Sure,' Tom says. 'And is there a Mister Chav or do you go out on your own?'

I laugh, shake my hair, and notice that I am being outrageously flirtatious. 'Not now,' I say. 'There was once. Now I just go out with friends.'

Tom nods. 'The city is better when you're single,' he says.

I take a sip of my wine and Tom smiles at me, and then slips into an amused grin. I assume that it's because he has noticed that I'm flirting with him.

And then he glances behind me, as if lost in thought, smiles broadly and slides along the bench seat until he's only a few inches away.

I'm a little surprised that the moves are coming so fast, and wonder, as if I am watching someone else, how I will react.

I suppose it depends on what happens next. And how it feels once it happens.

What does happen next is that a very tall, thin, dark-haired man looms over our table. 'Hello,' he says, looking at Tom, and then me.

'Hello!' Tom says. 'CC, meet Ron. Ron, CC.'

'Oh!' I exclaim, holding out my hand and freezing my face before it can form a frown. 'Hello!'

Ron shakes my hand but looks at Tom as he says, 'You're so lucky. I was just about to jump in a cab over to Avenue C when I got your text.' He looks at me and adds, 'Mister Last-minute-invitation here!'

I look from Ron to Tom. Tom shrugs. 'I just wanted you to meet CC here,' he says. 'I thought you would really enjoy each other.'

I can't help it any longer. I start to frown. Either Tom here is setting me up with Ron. Which, seeing as we were getting on so well, looks more like *fobbing me off* on Ron. Which despite Ron's ideal dark, swarthy looks, would have to be classed as somewhat insulting. Or this is some dastardly piece of industrial espionage on behalf of one of Grunge!'s competitors whom Ron works for. Or Tom is hoping for some weird kind of threesome – which would be really exciting and of course completely impossible to go along with, and which would *really* upset the apple cart in terms of our business relationship.

As Ron heads off to the bar for a drink, I try not to look too wide-eyed and wait to see what's going to happen next.

He returns almost immediately and grabs a spare chair from a nearby table. He seats himself opposite at which point Tom slithers back along the bench to his original (distant) position.

'Sorry,' Ron says. 'I didn't catch your name.'

'CC,' Tom volunteers. 'She doesn't like her name so she just goes by CC, don't you?'

I nod. 'That's right,' I say.

'It's actually Chelsea, which in England is a real trailer-trash name, which is why she prefers CC. Isn't that right?'

I cringe at this brutal explanation and wonder if my mother would be as devastated as I suspect if I changed my name by deed poll.

Ron nods. 'I see,' he says, sounding like he doesn't see at all.

'So what do you do, Ron?' I ask, trying to move away from a subject which is starting to seriously irritate me, and at the same time determined to find out why Tom has brought him here.

'Oh!' Ron says. 'That's a bit like your name. I try not to talk about it.'

'Right,' I say. 'Because?' No one is sparing my feelings here. I don't see why I should start wearing kid gloves.

'It's a bit of a cliché,' Ron says.

I nod. 'I see,' I say, using exactly the same tone of voice as Ron just did.

'Ron is a hairdresser,' Tom volunteers. 'He has some very famous clients.'

I nod. I think that I must have drunk too much. It seems as if everyone is speaking in tongues.

'And that's a cliché because . . .?'

Ron frowns at me, and then stands. 'I'm going to put some music on,' he says, then to Tom, 'Explain to your friend, would you?'

I watch Ron cross the bar and turn my frown upon Tom. 'I'm sorry,' I say. 'Call me stupid, but . . .'

'We're partners,' Tom says.

I nod. 'In his hairdressing business?'

At the very moment I say this three things happen.

The first is that the intro to 'Enough is Enough' by Donna Summer and Barbra Streisand starts to drift from the Jukebox, apparently chosen by Ron.

The second is that a big bearded biker at the bar, behind Tom's head, kisses the little Asian guy sitting on the bar stool opposite him. On the mouth.

And the third is that I manifest what I'm pretty sure must be the brightest, reddest blush my face has produced since Nigel Perry kissed me in the middle of the netball court.

'I . . . I'm sorry,' I say. 'I scare myself sometimes.'

'No. He's my *partner*,' Tom says. 'We're a couple.'

'Yes, yes, I get it,' I say. 'Doh! Gosh. Sorry.'

Tom shakes his head in confusion and glances over at Ron, beckoning him with a nod back to the table, but Ron rolls his eyes and turns back to the jukebox.

'Is that OK?' Tom asks. 'I mean, if you're not cool with that . . .'

I shake my head. 'Oh, I'm very cool with that, Tom,' I say. 'Nearly all my London friends are gay. I'm probably London's biggest fag hag. I don't know why my gaydar is so dodgy tonight.'

Tom nods and grins. 'Cool,' he says. 'I knew you'd be cool. I can usually tell. Ron! Come over here!'

I take a heavy swig of my drink and exhale slowly.

'This is awful, sweetheart,' Tom says when Ron returns. 'Why did you put this on?'

'It's funny,' Ron says. 'And ironic.'

'No, it's not. It's just awful,' Tom says.

Ron looks at me and shrugs, a little camply, I now see. 'You choose,' he says. 'Ironic, or awful?'

I bite my lip and shake my head. 'I think it's exactly like life,' I say. 'Awful and funny and ironic. All three at the same time.'

If It's Fun, It's a Sin

The next morning I wake up feeling good, almost joyous in fact. My hangover is surprisingly lightweight.

I yawn and stretch luxuriously on the hotel bed. The sheets, which up until now I have been too stressed to notice, feel crisp and fresh.

I lie and reflect on my successful night out on the town. Once my fag-hag credentials had been established, things had become much, much more fun with Tom and Ron. After a couple of drinks in the Excelsior, they whisked me further across town to Club 40c.

Here, I felt immediately at home amidst the fifty/fifty straight/gay mix. I even had a dance with Ron at one point which was nice in a make-believe kind of a way.

Today being, for them at least, a work day, the evening had wound up just before one a.m. when they dropped me off at the hotel. This probably explains the lack of anything seriously resembling a hangover.

All in all, other than Ron's not being straight and not having a farm, I couldn't have hoped for a better night. My working relationship with Tom is now forged in steel, and I have a couple of new clubbing friends if I have to come back to New York for work, as I hope I might.

Showered and dressed in simple jeans and a pullover, I head out into the sunshine. It's a beautiful spring day and my only agenda is to find the three coffee shops Tom listed for me and have a walk in Central Park. I'm sure the girls from work will all be asking me what shopping I have done, but strangely for someone in my field, shopping has never really done it for me. Though I do spend a fair bit on clothes (many of my clients pretty much expect this of me), in fact, I tend to shop like a man:

1: In.
2: That'll do.
3: Out again.

I often feel a bit of a failure as a tourist because of my lack of any kind of ambitious agenda. I know people, indeed, have dated men, who arrive in each new city with an alphabetic list of museums to be visited.

I never want to do much more than sit quietly in a café or coffee shop and watch the locals being themselves. That's what, bizarrely, interests me about other places.

Right now I am heading for Union Square where Tom has told me I can get a perfect American breakfast.

My day goes exactly to plan, which is, after all, the advantage of non-ambitious plans. The Coffee Shop is perfect, with bar-stools and long swoopy counters and a gum-chewing waitress with a notepad clipped to her belt. I overdose on calories by ordering the special: pancakes with eggs, bacon, strawberries, maple syrup, and cream. Only in America!

I head down as far as Wall Street and watch the city traders (*all* wearing blue shirts with white collars) dosing on caffeine. I stand and wave at people on the departing Staten Island ferry which feels silly but rather lovely.

A couple of times I think that it would all be nicer if I had someone to share it with, but I remind myself that this is a business trip and that even if I did have a boyfriend at home, the feeling would be the same.

On my way back up to Central Park, I walk along Fifth Avenue (Audrey Hepburn requires this of me) and I even find five minutes to pop in and buy a pair of Marithé + François

Girbaud trousers and a jacket. The exchange rate, I calculate, makes this a good enough deal for me to momentarily consider forgetting Central Park in exchange for more shopping time. But thankfully I resist – feeding the birds at the John Lennon memorial is the perfect end to my perfect blip-visit of a day.

Then it's back to the hotel, and off to the airport.

By eight p.m. when I arrive at JFK I feel like I have had not one day, but one week's holiday.

There are moments in life – and I would have to admit that I don't have them as often as I would like – when everything just comes together, and when, even being single, I feel happy, relaxed and confident. Some days, like today, I feel, as the French would say, so comfortable in my skin, that I could almost cry with the joy of being alive.

On top of my great night out and my perfect New York day, two more things happen at the airport which lock me definitively into my happy zone.

The first is that Peter Stanton phones to congratulate me because Levi's, apparently, loved our campaign and will be coming over to London shortly to discuss possibilities for collaboration.

The second (and this one is a bit shallow, but does nevertheless make me giggle with joy), is that I get bumped up from economy to business class, no doubt because of my new Girbaud outfit and oozing smile.

As our plane swoops out over the Atlantic, and as the squares of sunshine from the windows sweep through the cabin, I take my first sip of complimentary champagne.

'This is more like it,' the man beside me – an elegant fifty-year old – declares.

'Yes,' I say, smiling. 'It is.'

'Business wasn't so good for a while,' he says. 'So I had to plump for economy. It's good to be back.'

I grin at him and raise my glass. 'To business class!' I toast.

'Charles,' he says, raising his own glass and then proffering a hand.

'C . . . Charlotte,' I reply.

• • •

Air travel is such a strange experience. It's such an intimate thing, to travel alongside a stranger for so many hours, to eat together, take in a film, snooze side by side. In economy I think that it's so intimate, that like neighbours on the same landing, most of us consider that it's better not to take the risk of ever getting to know them. In business class, there's just enough room – as elbows don't actually touch – to take that chance.

He is, he tells me, South African, but left when he was twenty. 'I could never stand apartheid,' he says, 'which is why I left. Ironically, my parents, most would say, deservedly, lost pretty much everything when apartheid ended, so there's not much point going back. Of course, I visit them, but . . .'

Charles tells me that he is 'in rubber'. He's a specialised commodities trader. There's lots of money in rubber, it would appear.

For a slightly older man, he's pretty attractive. Salt and pepper hair, rounded friendly features, a fit trim body. He has a slightly wicked sense of humour, and keeps me regaled with funny stories about his many business trips.

We chat and drink and chat and eat and chat some more until they dim the cabin lights, and then, as air travel dictates, we snooze side by side. His presence beside me feels somehow reassuring.

As we start our descent to Heathrow, Charles asks me if I'm travelling on anywhere else today.

'No, just home,' I say. 'To London. I had a really successful trip to New York, so my boss has given me tomorrow off to recover. So it's just back home to a lovely long weekend.'

'Well I hope you have someone lovely waiting for you,' he says.

I laugh. 'Yes. Guinness will be waiting.'

'Guinness?' He pulls a face. 'Funny name.'

'Indeed,' I say. 'He's my cat. And you?'

'Oh, I'm single. And no cat.'

I bite my lip. 'Sorry, that sounded . . . I meant where are you *going*?'

'Oh. Sorry. I'm flying on to Nice. In France. I have a meeting on Saturday, but other than that I just intend to kick back.'

'Nice is nice,' I say, unable to resist the cliché comment.

'It is,' he says. 'I suspect that the Niçois themselves are more friendly if you can speak the language, but the town itself is lovely.'

'You don't speak any French then?'

'Oh, I can say, "*Bonjour*," he laughs. 'And, "*Je ne parle pas Française*."'

'*Français*,' I say with a grin. '*Je ne parle pas Français*.'

Charles frowns. 'I was told it was feminine. Because languages are all feminine or something.'

'Ah, yes,' I laugh. 'If you say, "*Je ne parle pas la langue française*," then that would be feminine. But the name of the *langue française* is just *Français*. It's completely crazy of course.'

Charles grins at me, apparently impressed.

'A level French,' I say. 'It was my best subject. I spent a year on exchange in Aix en Provence too, for my degree.'

'Clever, pretty . . . where does it all end?' Charles laughs.

I laugh too and do my hair flicking thing. 'Oh, not so clever . . .' I say. 'I just have a good memory.'

'I don't suppose you want to come and translate for me?' he asks.

I laugh. 'Thanks, but . . .'

Charles shrugs. 'Oh well, it was just a thought. And then on Monday night I'm off to Dusseldorf.'

'Eeek,' I say. 'I think I prefer Nice.'

'Yes,' Charles laughs. 'Better food too. I know some lovely restaurants in the old town. And a great one on the port in Villefranche.'

'Sounds lovely,' I say.

'You could come,' Charles says. 'I mean, seriously, I would love to spend the weekend . . .'

I laugh lightly to cover my embarrassment. 'I don't think so,'

I say as lightly as I can manage. 'Really.'

Charles turns to look out of the window. 'Raining,' he says. 'Can't see a thing.'

'It always is,' I say.

Charles turns back to face me. 'Look, Charlotte. I know this sounds weird . . .'

I laugh. 'Please don't,' I say. 'You're embarrassing me.'

'You'll get over it,' Charles says. 'But I won't if I don't say this.'

I shrug and stare at my lap. 'OK,' I say.

'I don't know if you *could* come to Nice with me, I mean, I don't know how your life is organised . . .'

'I really—' I start.

'Hear me out,' he says. 'Please.'

'Sure,' I say.

'I travel on my own all year round. I see beautiful places and eat in beautiful restaurants *all year round*. And it's fine. I enjoy it. But there's always this moment when I feel a bit sad because I don't have someone with me. Someone to say, "isn't this lovely". So I'm not being heavy here at all . . . at least I hope not. I'm just saying that I've enjoyed your company today and if you did want to spend your bonus long-weekend in Nice with me, well, I would think that was absolutely lovely. I would obviously get you your own room at the hotel. I'm staying at the Negresco, by the way. And I would promise to be the perfect gentleman at all times. There. It's said.'

To disguise my embarrassment, I laugh lightly. 'It's very sweet,' I say. 'Really it is. But I can't. I . . . I have to get home. I have obligations.'

'Such as?'

'Well, for starters, I have Guinness to feed. You wouldn't want to be responsible for the death of a cat, would you?'

Charles grins and shrugs. 'Absolutely not,' he says. 'Oh well. Life, huh?'

I nod sadly. 'Life!' I say.

The weather at Heathrow is truly atrocious. It's nine-thirty by the time we reach passport control but outside it still looks like midnight.

'It's sunny in Nice,' Charles declares, pointing his iPhone at me. The display shows seven little suns with smiles.

'Lucky you!' I say.

'So I can't convince you?' he asks. 'Because this is where the paths split.'

He points at the queue for immigration and I realise that he now has to go to the tiny 'Non EU' side whilst I have to snake my way along the mega 'UK Citizens' queue.

I shake my head. 'I'm so sorry,' I say. 'It's been lovely meeting you, but . . .'

Charles shrugs and holds out a hand. 'Well, have a lovely weekend,' he says.

'You too!' I say, shaking it vigorously.

As he heads off, I add my body to the end of the snake and watch him as he queues for the desk, then hands over his passport, and then, with the tiniest wave, vanishes from sight.

I feel a pang of regret, but, well, no one could deny that it was an absurd proposition, could they? Surely any sane person would have done the same thing . . .

And anyway, I now remember, I have a date with Brown Eyes this weekend. I'm a little shocked at myself for forgetting.

I switch on my BlackBerry which instantly beeps with a text message. A text message from Brown Eyes, no less.

SOZ HAD GO NEW CASTLE AGAIN NEXT WEEKEND?

I roll my eyes. 'Men!' I mutter.

The second text is from Darren: CALL ME WHEN YOU GET IN. QUESTION ABOUT GRUNGE!

I delay until I am through immigration and waiting for the baggage carousel then phone the office. The receptionist answers the phone with, 'Congratulations! I hear you were brilliant. The whole place is abuzz.'

'Thanks!' I tell her. 'Can I speak to Darren?'

Darren also congratulates me. His query is simple enough – whom specifically to address the final versions of the visuals to at BRP. I tell him that he should mark them for the attention of Clarissa Bowles. 'Even if she just gives them to someone else, she likes to feel that she's being kept in the loop.'

'Great,' Darren says. 'Well, I'll get those off today. I hear the pitch went well.'

'Yes,' I say. 'Apparently so.'

'And New York?'

'Great,' I say. 'Like London. Full of poofs.'

'Brilliant. Well, you'll have to tell me about that. I hope the weather was better than here.'

'It was,' I say. 'I just had someone trying to convince me to go to Nice for a dirty weekend. When I saw the weather I was sorely tempted.'

'Who's that then?' Darren asks. 'That bloke from speed dating?'

I laugh. 'Nope! *He* just cancelled our date for this weekend, so I'm Johnny-no-dates again. No, it was just the guy next to me on the plane. Wanted a translator. And a shag probably.'

'Brown Eyes cancelled?' Darren asks. 'Amazing. What's wrong with these guys?'

Even though he can't see me, I shrug. 'I have no idea,' I say.

'So why aren't you off to Nice?'

'What, with a stranger I met on a plane? Oh come on.'

'Was he *bad*?'

'No, he was pretty cute. But I can't just go swanning off with the first person who happens to chat me up.'

'Lord no,' Darren laughs.

I'm glad he understands.

'Heaven forbid,' he continues. 'You might actually have had some fun. Anyway, Mark's here. He wants to talk to you.'

Feeling a little slapped down by his *heaven forbid*, I say, flatly, 'OK, bye.'

'Hello, beautiful,' Mark says.

Behind him I can hear Darren telling the story, presumably to Jude. '*She's only been stood up by that bloke from speed dating, and now some other geezer has invited her to Nice for the weekend, but she'd rather sit at home with her cat. I can't work out if she's lazy or crazy...'*

'Hello,' I say.

'Your cat's moved out on you,' Mark says.

'Moved out?'

'Yeah. He's fine though. He's up in my flat. He tried to follow me on Monday when I went in to feed him, and he's been up in my place ever since.'

'Oh, OK.'

'Just go and get him. You still have a key, don't you?'

'I do. Thanks for that.'

'So what's this about a bloke?'

'Oh I really don't want to go through it all again.'

'OK.'

'Just a guy on the plane. Asked me to go to Nice for the weekend.'

'Are you going? Because don't worry about Guinness... I can—'

'No, I'm not,' I say.

'What's wrong with him then?'

I laugh. 'I don't know really... I only met him a few hours ago. He seems nice enough.'

'But?'

'But nothing. I don't jump on planes with people I just met, that's all.'

'Why not?' Mark sounds genuinely confused.

Darren's voice comes from behind again. 'Tell her to go!'

'Darren says you should go,' Mark says.

'I heard.'

Then Jude's voice: 'Me too!'

'Thanks,' I say. 'Lucky I have my own brain for deciding these things then, isn't it.'

'You Catholic girls,' Mark says. 'You just can't do it, can you?'

'Do what?'

'Let go.'

'It's got nothing to do with being Catholic. Or letting go.

Anyway, I've told you a million times, I'm not Catholic.'

'OK...'

'Don't OK me like that,' I say.

'All I'm saying is that you act like you are. Catholic that is. Jeez. Don't go home and sit in the gloom. Go to Nice. Have a proper pizza. I would.'

'Pizza is Italy, sweetie,' I say. 'Nice is in France.'

'I know. I've been there. And they make the best pizzas on the planet,' Mark says. 'Thin and crispy and mmmm.'

'I'm not going to Nice, Mark. Anyway, he's gone now.'

'OK. Well, I'll call in and see you on my way home. We can have a cup of tea together in your kitchen. It's not quite a glass of rosé on the Cours Saleya, is it? But there you go.'

'Right. See you later.'

'Laters.'

As I stand and watch the baggage carousel, I reflect on all these different definitions of reasonable behaviour. My gay friends clearly all err on the side of what I would call recklessness. My own value system, if I'm being honest, clearly is rooted in religion. In the end, it all does come down to what a priest would consider a sin, and what he would think to be OK.

And running off to Nice with a stranger, could lead to sin. And going home to Guinness, tea and my kitchen, clearly won't.

It always amazes me how all of the fun options are denoted as 'bad' by all the major religions. And I wonder if I shouldn't do more to break free. Maybe I should go to some kind of personal development course that teaches how to be reckless.

My bag eventually arrives, and, feeling somewhat despondent, I traipse through customs and out into the main hall. Beyond the vast glass windows, it now looks even darker than before. The rivulets of water streaming down the windows make them look like water-features. I scan the walls for signs to the Tube station, and head, tiredly, off.

I only get a few feet, though, before someone grabs my arm. I turn to find Charles gripping my sleeve.

'I didn't get your email address,' he says. 'Can I at least have that?'

'Have you been waiting here all this time?' I ask.

He shrugs. 'The Nice flight isn't for another three hours, so I was having a coffee. Having a coffee and regretting not getting your email address. I want to spend the weekend sending you photos from Nice so that you can regret not coming.'

I smile and flick my hair. 'Well, that's very sweet,' I say.

'I'm a very sweet guy,' Charles says, smiling beautifully and pulling his iPhone from his pocket. 'So?'

'OK, it's, erm . . .'

For a second, I'm not sure that I want to give him my email address. And then I think, *Why not?* And then I think of an even better idea.

'It's Charlotte . . .'

I stand and do battle with my entire upbringing as I watch him type the letters. *After all,* I reason, *I am a grown woman.* I can defend myself. I have credit cards and enough French to book my own taxis. I can find alternative accommodation if need be. It's not like anything would be out of my control.

'At,' I dictate.

'Yes?'

'T-A-K-E,' I spell. 'M-E . . .'

'Yes.'

'T-O.'

'Right.'

'N-I-C-E. Dot. Com.'

'So,' Charles repeats. 'Charlotte @ take me to mice dot com ?'

'Not *mice*,' I laugh. 'It's an N.'

'OK . . .' he says, positioning his cursor to make the correction. 'So take me to nice . . . Oh! Nice!' He looks up at me with a wry grin. 'Really?' he says.

I shrug. 'You're only young twice, huh?'

'Gosh!' he says. 'Wow. Um. Excellent. OK. Um. Really?'

I nod. 'But no funny business.'

'Oh no,' he says. 'No funny business at all.'

Baroque Dreams

On the way to the BA desk, Charles insists that he wants to pay for the ticket.

Initially, at least, I'm glad about this.

It's not that I can't afford it myself, or the fact that I approve particularly of chivalry ... No, it's simply that, as game-breakers go, after my dislike of beards, tightness comes a close second.

In fact, I'm of a very generous nature myself: in our family everyone has always argued about who will pay. To be the one being paid *for* was the shameful role.

The problem is that I also detest being taken for a ride. So if I find myself in the presence of some thrifty Timothy, I have to stop being generous in order to avoid being used as a walking credit card. And it's that very fact of having to change my own nature that irritates me so much.

So, South Africa, *six points* ...

When we get to the British Airways counter, of course, I suddenly realise that for Charles to book my flight I will have to reveal my real name. So at the not inconsiderable risk of looking like a hysterical bitch, I freeze and stare him straight in the eye. 'You know what?' I say.

'Oh please don't pull out,' he says. 'Not now. I've got you to the desk, for Christ's sake.'

'Humm ...' I say. 'Well, OK. But you have to let me pay. My self-esteem requires it.'

'But ...'

'No buts.'

'Can I at least pay for the hotel then?' Charles asks.

I stifle a huge sigh of relief. 'Yes,' I say. 'It's a deal. Now you go sit down over there and let me do this. You're on the 13:55 flight, right?'

'That's the one.'

'So go sit down.'

'But I'm—'

I give him my raised-eyebrow serious-schoolteacher look, and, bless him, he complies.

I turn to face the girl behind the counter. 'Hello, I'd like to book a flight to Nice. On the 13:55 flight. Or at least I think I would.'

'You *think* you would?' she repeats unsmilingly.

'Joking,' I say.

The girl frowns at me.

'I do,' I say.

'On today's 13:55 flight?'

'Yes,' I say. 'If that's possible . . .'

'OK.' She taps at her computer screen. 'It's not going to be cheap, but it should still be possible as long as there are some seats.'

As she clicks her way through seemingly endless screens, I glance over at Charles, now obediently seated, and wonder if I'm not making a mistake.

This of course is the problem with snap, reckless decisions. They have to be made, and remade, every step of the way – as I buy the outrageously overpriced tickets, as we head for passport control, as we wait for the gate.

Charles, I'm guessing aware of my internal struggle, switches to charm overdrive, and he's very good at it. Good enough, in fact, to keep me on track until take-off. And let's face it, by the time he has got me that far he has pretty much won.

But I never manage to silence the nagging voice telling me that I'm completely crazy, that the weekend will be horrible, that he's a rapist or a serial killer . . .

Indeed, like a Met officer hunting terrorists, my finger is

constantly trembling on the trigger: the eject-and-run-away-quickly trigger.

Amazingly, though, we make it as far as Nice. I can see from the slow descent along the beautiful coastline that the weather is exactly as predicted by Charles' iPhone.

We're quickly out of the lovely bright airport and whizzing down the palm-tree-lined Promenade des Anglais in a taxi.

The Negresco hotel is stunning: it's a vast white building with a huge pink dome on the top. The overall effect is that the place looks like a luxury wedding cake. Of course I have seen the Negresco from the outside before – it's something of a landmark on the Promenade des Anglais. Nothing, however, has prepared me for the palatial interior.

'Jesus! Do you stay here often?' I whisper as we cross the cavernous white lobby.

'No,' Charles says. 'Not lately. The last time I stayed here was 2003, I think. It was out of my price range for a while. Lovely though, don't you think? Again, it's good to be back.'

He follows my gaze and looks up at the enormous chandelier above our heads. 'That was commissioned for Nicolas the second, the Russian Czar,' he tells me. 'He had to cancel his order because of the revolution so they had to find another buyer. That's what it says in the hotel brochure, anyway.'

At the check-in desk, Charles asks, without prompting, for a second room, and then, in answer to the clerk's question, replies, 'No, not adjoining.'

South Africa, *huit points*...

Charles quickly asks for the second room to be added to his bill (I don't even get to see the cost this time, but the mind boggles), and then the porters head off with our baggage.

I start to follow them, but Charles grabs my elbow. 'Just let me show you something first,' he says. 'It's my favourite room here, and that way we can meet there later.'

He takes me through a round, white, museum-scale central hall, and on to an incredible lounge which the plaque says is the Salon Versailles.

The Salon Versailles is totally breathtaking. It has blood red walls, adorned with giant renaissance oil paintings, and theatre-like drapes either side of the doors and windows. The floor is a beautiful giant marble mosaic, the ceiling is comprised of stunning *trompe-l'oeil* framed squares each containing a painting, and the furniture is an orgy of velvet and gold baroque excess. But most stunning of all, set in the middle of the longest wall, is a huge, floor-to-ceiling window, open onto a view of the blue sky, sea and the swaying palm trees of the Promenade des Anglais.

'Absolutely gorgeous,' I say in a whisper, not wanting to disturb the old lady in the corner. She's snoozing with a novel on her chest.

'Isn't it lush?' Charles murmurs. He nods towards the old lady. 'There are quite a few rich widows living here full time.'

'How the other half lives,' I say. 'Or rather, lived.'

'How this half lives,' Charles laughs. 'For the next two days, at any rate.'

'It's beautiful,' I say.

'Now, I hope you don't mind, but I'm feeling somewhat shattered – jet lag and everything. I think I need a shower and a snooze.'

I nod and follow him from the room. 'Good idea,' I say.

As we head up in the lift, Charles says, 'Don't expect too much of the room. I went for the most basic option. I tried the expensive rooms before, but it never felt worth it. Not when you can go and sit in that wonderful red lounge.'

'I'm sure it will be lovely,' I say.

'Shall we meet at, say, seven?' he asks.

'OK,' I say vaguely.

Seven is later than I had figured, and I'm kind of wanting to make the most of my time in Nice. Foreign places do that to me. I rarely feel able to rest on arrival, no matter how tired I am.

'Or is that too early?' Charles asks, flashing his watch at me.

'Oh, is that the time *here*?' I ask. His watch says five, and I was convinced it was more like three.

'Yes, we're another hour ahead here.'

'Of course. My internal clock is way out. So in the crazy red room at seven?'

'Perfect.'

The lift door opens but Charles doesn't budge. He just smiles at me. When I glance out of the door, he says, 'I think that this is your stop.'

I check my room key. 'Oh, yes, of course, thanks.' I had momentarily forgotten that we weren't staying in the same room, which strikes me as most peculiar on my part, especially considering all the implications that that would have. I put it down to tiredness.

'See you at seven then,' I say, giving him a little wave as I leave the lift.

My room, of course, is fine. It doesn't have a sea view which is a tiny disappointment. It looks out instead onto a broad side-road.

It also has a few quirky features that one wouldn't expect in a luxury palace.

The most notable of these is the fact that the electrical cable for the bedside lamp has been clipped around the top of the baroque golden bed-head with white plastic cable clips. But this actually makes me smile. It all somehow adds to the crazy charm of the place.

If only I had a camera, I think. I could send a photo to Mark. He'd be so impressed at such a stunning outcome to my new-found recklessness.

I open the window and lean out and look at the unbelievable blue of the sea at the end of the road. Then I sniff the various lotions in the bathroom, and finally I throw myself onto the springy mattress and stare at the painted clouds on the light-blue ceiling and think that if ever I have a baby, this is how I will paint the ceiling of his or her bedroom.

Within seconds, I'm asleep.

I sense a warm presence against my back. I yawn and stretch and roll over to find a brown-eyed man smiling at me. Even though his features are Ron's, I somehow know that this is in fact Norman.

'I thought you might fancy a shag,' he says with shocking straightforwardness.

'Hum,' I murmur.

The room is deepest red, like a womb, and beyond the huge window I can see the twin towers. 'I thought they were—' I say, but Brown Eyes raises a finger to my lips. 'Shhh!' he says. 'No one knows they're here.'

He wriggles across the bed towards me. I can feel his dick pressing against me. It feels bigger than I remember dicks generally being, but, well, it's been a while.

He fidgets around and then reaches down and positions himself. He's pressing at the gate, now, slipping past security. Now he's in.

He rolls with me so that I am on my back and he's on top of, and inside me. I try to focus on his face but he's somehow too close, it remains a blur. He lifts my arms above my shoulders and slips my hands through the loops of cable along the top of the bed-head. 'What are you doing?' I ask. But for some reason, though I try, I can't move the muscles to resist. I wonder if I have been drugged.

And then he's writhing against me, and then slamming into me and the bed-head is bashing against the wall, and something is falling around me. I look up and see that the bed is knocking lumps of red plaster from the wall. Blood is oozing from the holes.

'Brian!' I exclaim. 'You're damaging the . . .'

And then, surprised at my own utterance, I look back at his face and it's no longer Ron masquerading as Brown Eyes. *Brian* is on top of me.

'Brian, stop,' I say.

'But I want a baby,' he says, breathlessly. With each thrust he adds another word: 'You. Will. Give. Me. A. Baby.'

I struggle but I can't get my hands out from the loops of wire. The bed-head continues to slam into the wall. I can feel the blood oozing up through the bed. *Bang. Bang. Bang.*

'Brian, stop,' I cry. 'Brian, please stop.'

'I'm coming,' he says. 'I'm going to . . .'

'No!' I shout. 'Stop!'

I close my eyes and then feel Brian's body spasm and collapse against me, and then his weight vanishes.

I gasp and open my eyes.

Above me is a beautiful baby-blue ceiling with clouds.

I lift my hands just to prove that I can. I glance above my head to see the wall intact. Only the banging sound continues.

And then a voice: 'Charlotte? Are you there?'

I slide to the side of the bed and sit and rub my eyes. 'Jesus!' I mutter.

'Charlotte?'

'I'll be there in a second,' I call.

I shake my head vigorously as if this will help put extra distance between reality and the dream. And then, with a final check that I am still dressed, I cross the room and open the door.

Charles smiles at me and then slips into a frown. 'You OK?' he asks.

'Sorry, yes, I went out like a light.'

'I waited for a while, but then I thought I should come and find you,' he says.

'Umh. I had a weird dream. Jet-lag sleep. What time is it?' I'm sure I've been asleep for minutes, not hours.

'Eight o'clock.'

'In the evening?'

'Yes.'

'Just checking. OK, can you give me another fifteen minutes, just to have a shower?'

'If you'd rather just sleep through . . .' Charles offers.

I think for a moment. The bed does seem incredibly appealing.

'I'm only going for a glass of rosé and a bite to eat in the old town,' Charles says. 'So you wouldn't be missing much.'

I run a hand over my face. 'No,' I say. 'I'll come. There's no point coming to Nice and then just sleeping, is there?'

'Let's say eight-thirty then?' Charles says.

I nod. 'OK, that's perfect.'

'I would say take as long as you wish, but this being France they can declare the working day over and stop serving at any point.'

'No, it's fine. Make it eight-fifteen after all. I'll do my quick-change routine.'

'OK. You better get going then,' Charles says, glancing at his watch again and turning away. 'See you downstairs in a tick.'

A Near Miss

The evening is so strange, it feels quite surreal. There is always a brain-lag effect with modern air travel – it always takes a while for the mind to understand where the body has been transported to. But this: the fact that I was in New York, and then London, and now, unexpectedly, the south of France, is all compounded by the fact that I'm now spending what looks like being the most romantic evening of the past four or five years with a complete stranger.

We walk along the Promenade des Anglais together; the temperature is dropping fast now, and I'm glad I plumped for jeans.

Charles chats quietly as we walk, telling me about his recent trip to Barcelona. 'I love these Mediterranean towns,' he tells me. 'Though I think I'm probably too old to survive the Spanish lifestyle. As far as I can see they simply never sleep.'

When we arrive at the end of the Prom we turn left through a couple of arches and find ourselves on the huge Cours Saleya which I recall Mark having mentioned.

It's a vast *rectangular* square, if that makes any sense, surrounded by red and ochre buildings with slatted shutters. Charles takes us straight to a fish restaurant – Le Grand Bleu. They have those external gas-heater things which always strike me as environmentally outrageous – but I have to admit that getting to sit outside in March is wonderful.

We pick at a plate of complimentary olives and sip at our rosé and I watch the locals – pretty, skinny, dark skinned, French – wandering past.

'You know,' I say. 'Whenever I end up somewhere like this, I always think the same thing.'

'Yes?' Charles asks. 'What's that then?'

'Why, oh why do I live in England?'

Charles laughs. 'I know what you mean, but roots are powerful things.'

I shrug. 'I wouldn't say I really have any roots in England. I was born in Waterford in Ireland. But we moved when I was five.'

'To London?'

'No, to Camberley. It's in Surrey. About an hour and a half west of London.'

'And you've been in London since?'

'Since I was twenty-two,' I answer. 'I got my first job in London and never looked back really. Surrey never really did it for me anyway. It always felt sort of comfortable, but not me. A bit like a hotel room.'

Charles nods. 'I know exactly what you mean,' he says. 'So, you moved out when you were twenty-two.'

'Oh no, I moved out when I went to college. At eighteen.'

Charles nods thoughtfully.

'I suppose you're trying to work out how long ago this all was,' I laugh. 'I'm thirty-nine.'

Charles nods slowly again. 'I wasn't actually, but anyway . . . Thirty-nine. That's young. I'm fifty-five.'

I swallow. I had assumed he was a bit younger.

'You think that's old, I expect,' Charles says.

I shrug. 'Not at all. What's old? When I was twenty I thought forty was ancient.'

'Right,' Charles says. 'So you presumably like living in London. If you've been there for twenty years.'

I wobble my head in a half-hearted nod. 'London's great. Honestly, these days I think it's one of the world's great capitals.'

'These days?'

'It wasn't so hot during the eighties,' I explain. 'It all got pretty grimy during the Thatcher years. But now, I think it's an amazingly vibrant place to live. It's just that, in a way, I always think of it as a single person's place. I have never been able to imagine being old there.'

Charles nods. 'And you think you could live here though? I suppose at least you speak the language.'

'Maybe,' I say. 'That was sort of my plan. When I was in my twenties. I really liked Aix en Provence.' I laugh at this, causing Charles to frown at me.

'Oh, it's just that, ironically, I had the worst time in Aix,' I say.

'What happened in Aix?'

'Nothing really. That was the problem. I was living in a big friendly shared house in Birmingham, and I swapped with this French girl from Aix – who, incidentally, I never even met . . . The thing was that she had her own flat. So it was pretty luxurious.'

'But lonely . . .'

'Exactly. And the people at the college weren't as friendly as I had hoped . . . You sort of expect people to be interested in you because you're foreign and exotic or something, but the French aren't really like that. They all pretty much ignored me. It was a bad time.'

'I bet,' says Charles. 'You poor thing.'

'I used to phone my mum all the time, reverse the charges, so that I could cry down the phone. That girl – Véronique – had a brilliant time with all *my* friends though.'

Charles laughs. 'I would have thought that would put you off France,' he says.

I lean in conspiratorially. 'To be honest,' I whisper. 'It did put me off the French a bit. I mean – I thought they were the bee's knees before I lived here.'

Charles nods. 'Well every country has a cliché . . . the Brits are all alcoholics, the Spaniards never sleep, the Italians are loud and emotional, and . . .' he leans in to my ear and continues, 'the French are superior and arrogant. There's always a reason why a cliché is a cliché. It's always rooted in truth somewhere along the way.'

'It's such a beautiful country though,' I say. 'There's so much variety compared with England. And so much space. Not to mention the weather.'

Charles nods. 'Yes,' he says. 'There's a terrible Italian joke about that. It's not very politically correct I'm afraid.'

'Yes?'

'They say that when God created all the countries, all France's neighbours were jealous. So Spain cried out, "Why do they have these magnificent forests?" And Italy cried out, "Why do they have all the beautiful beaches?" And Germany said, "Why did you give France the wonderful Mediterranean sea?"'

'And God, woken from his slumber by all the complaints, said, "OK, OK, don't worry, I have a plan to even things up."'

'Yes?'

'So he created the French.'

I snort and almost have to spit my wine back in the glass. I glance around nervously in case anyone has overheard. 'That's terrible,' I say.

'Yes,' Charles smirks. 'Indeed. Not my fault though. It's an Italian joke.'

I smile and roll my eyes and then glance around the square. 'It's not even just the country though,' I say. 'It's the buildings too. I've always thought that the French have a built in sense of aesthetics. Or maybe, at least, of the importance of aesthetics. Do you know what I mean?'

Charles shrugs. 'I suppose all the designers and stuff are French, aren't they?'

'It's as if the Germans worry about how efficiently things will *work*. And the French worry about how they will *look*.'

'And the Brits?'

'Sadly, I think we mainly worry about how much they will cost.'

'Yes,' Charles says. 'Yes, your big projects are always a bit on the cheap. Nothing ever seems to quite work properly.'

'I don't think it was always like that . . . in fact, I don't think it was like that really until the Second World War . . . maybe we just ran out of money then. Maybe we made a culture of getting by. I mean, if you look around, there are plenty of magnificent things from before . . . Buckingham Palace, Saint Paul's Cathedral . . .

but the French *still* build stuff like that. Even that big bridge they opened a few years ago . . . in Millau, I think it is . . . even that's beautiful.'

And so the evening passes. I don't know what has got into me, but I talk and talk and then talk some more. Perhaps it's the rosé, or perhaps it's the Mediterranean ambience. Then again, perhaps it's simply that no one seems to have been this interested in anything I have to say for a long time. Well, not outside work at any rate.

By eleven p.m. when we leave the restaurant, I feel like I have been engaged in a talking marathon. And when I stop, I suddenly feel terribly, terribly tired.

'I'm not surprised,' Charles says when I tell him. 'It is five a.m. in New York.'

'Actually, it isn't,' I say. 'New York is *behind.*'

'Oh yes. Well, the change is still confusing!'

After a short taxi-ride back to the hotel, Charles thanks me for a lovely evening, and I say, 'No! Thank you for a lovely evening.'

And just for a second, oiled by rosé and chatter and a long lovely meal, I think that Charles deserves a kiss. I'm stepping out of the lift when this thought occurs to me, so I turn back to peck him on the cheek.

I'm fully aware that this peck may lead to something else, but am, as yet, confused about whether this is what I want or not.

Charles though, has turned away and remains totally unaware of my hesitation. He is far too busy looking for the 'close door' button of the lift.

And then the moment is past, and as I turn away, he now notices, and says, 'Yes?' but the doors are already closing.

'Nothing,' I call through the diminishing gap. 'See you tomorrow.'

I'm not sure if this is a missed opportunity or a lucky escape.

Romance by Design

The next morning – partly from habit but mainly due to a strip of sunlight sneaking through a chink in the curtains – I'm awake at seven-thirty a.m.

As Charles and I haven't agreed any particular plan for this morning, I shower, drink a glass of water and head straight outside, determined to make the most of my mini-break.

The air is still cool, but the sky is a pure cloudless blue, the sea a crazy turquoise colour and the air fresh with salt and iodine.

I cross the road and stare at the sea for a while, and then, inspired by all the joggers, start to walk briskly westwards.

After fifteen minutes, I take a break in one of the little blue chairs the town authorities have thoughtfully strewn around. I note that they are painted exactly the same blue as the sea. More confirmation of my theory about French aesthetic instinct.

After another ten minutes watching the waves, I turn and walk slowly back towards the hotel. When I come level with the pedestrian crossing, I spot Charles, also seated on one of the chairs, staring out at the horizon. He looks serious, mournful even, and I hesitate a moment before crossing the pavement to talk to him. 'You look pensive,' I say.

Charles physically judders at the shock of being spoken to from such close proximity. 'Gee. You made me jump!'

'Sorry,' I say.

'It's fine. You OK?'

I nod. 'I went for a morning walk. What a glorious day, huh?'

'Yes, isn't it?'

'You looked very thoughtful,' I say again.

'Me? No. Not really. I was just watching those gulls. I know they only have a brain the size of a pea or something, but I can't help but think that they look like they're enjoying themselves. I was just thinking that maybe their brains only have that one function. It wouldn't be so bad.'

I pull a chair over and take a seat beside him. 'You're right,' I say. 'They do look like they're loving it.'

We sit like this for a while watching the birds sweeping and swooping apparently pointlessly, apparently, as Charles says, just for the fun of it, and then Charles' stomach rumbles loudly.

He laughs. 'Did you hear that?'

'Time for breakfast?'

'Yes, I think so too.'

'Back in the hotel, or . . .?'

Charles wrinkles his nose. 'I didn't find breakfast to be very good there. And it's terribly expensive. Don't get me wrong, I mean, if you want . . .'

I shake my head. 'I have no preference at all,' I say. 'As long as I get some caffeine and a few calories.'

'I usually just have a coffee and a croissant in the first place I find.'

'Sounds perfect,' I say, following his lead and standing. 'Sounds like a proper authentic French breakfast. It's just a shame I don't smoke.'

'Smoke?'

'Well, yes. That's the real French breakfast, isn't it? Coffee and a cigarette.'

'Yes,' Charles laughs. 'Yes, of course. I suppose it is. Now, if I remember correctly, we just need to go down that little side road . . .'

The day is perfect.

We have fresh buttery croissants and microscopic doses of caffeine.

'When caffeine tastes this good . . .' I joke, swapping the decaf coffee slogan around, '. . .who needs coffee?'

We amble through the winding streets of the old town, and I get Charles to take a photo of me in the middle of the brightly coloured vegetable market to prove to Mark that I was really here.

For lunch we both have perfect Niçoise salads on Place Rossetti before wandering around the port to look at the boats. Charles points at a big sleek number he tells me is a forty-footer and says that he used to have the same one.

'Why did you get rid of it?'

He shrugs. 'Money mainly. The mooring cost a fortune, and after the first summer, I never really used it. Boats are a bit like second homes. It's better really just to decide where you want to go and rent something.'

'Where is your first home? I mean I know you move around all the time, but . . .'

Charles shrugs. 'Most of my stuff is in Chicago these days. And the kids. And the ex-wife, of course. But I honestly don't spend much time there.'

'It must be strange. Not having a proper home. How many kids have you got?'

'Two,' Charles says. 'They're adolescents now. I don't see much of them either, of course. Not with them being in Chicago and me being mostly anywhere else. *Everywhere* else.'

'No, I suppose not.'

That evening, we take another taxi to a small nearby town – Villefranche sur Mer. Here we eat in a swanky fish restaurant overlooking the twinkling lights of the port.

As Charles says, all clichés exist for a reason, and the candlelit dinner overlooking the sea predictably breaks through any remaining barriers I might have about feeling romantic. The food is beautiful, the bottle of white crisp and fruity, the table linen white and starched, the windows spotless, the music soothing.

Indeed, Charles himself looks tanned and appealing in the flickering candlelight. What girl could fail to be wooed under such circumstances?

Guys, listen and learn: it's a cliché because it works!

The only sour note of the entire evening is provided by our somewhat overbearing waiter. He keeps appearing to top up our glasses. When our glasses don't need topping up, he makes little visits to brush crumbs off the table with a sort of handheld carpet sweeper.

I know that this is the way five-star service is meant to be, but the truth is that I have never liked it. Trying to have an intimate conversation under these circumstances is like trying to work while someone is hoovering under your feet.

Charles leans on the table, and rests his chin in his hands. 'You know . . .' he says.

I smile at him gently. 'Yes?'

'At risk of . . .'

And of course, at that second, our obsessive-compulsive crumb-cleaner returns for his third table sweep. Clearly, it's getting to Charles too. 'I'm sorry, but can you just wait?' he asks the waiter.

'Pardon?' the guy asks, hovering over the table with his silver carpet-sweeper thing.

'Don't do that crumb thing. We don't *care* about the crumbs,' Charles says.

'I'm sorry,' the man says in a thick accent. 'You have a problem?'

'Sorry, Charlotte. Can you explain before I . . .' Charles mutters, turning to look out of the window.

'Nous essayons . . .' – *We're trying to talk*, I tell him in my best French.

'*Vous* pouvez *parler*,' he replies with typical French nonchalance. – You *can* talk.

'We would *rather* you cleaned the table *after* the meal,' I say.

'But this is how we do it in France,' he says.

'Not tonight,' I tell him. I see Charles watching me, looking impressed, and decide that I need to win here.

'But—' the waiter says.

'Look,' I interrupt, 'we're paying for all of this, so can you just let us eat the way we want to?'

'*Comme des chochons?*' he says, which I think, but am not sure, means, 'Like pigs?'

'I'm sorry?'

'You want me to leave your table dirty?'

'We do.'

'Would you perhaps like me to bring back what I already took?'

'I'm sorry?'

'Seeing as you like crumbs, would you like me to return those that I collected before?' He shakes his little crumb sweeper at me and a few fall out. 'They are yours, after all. You *paid* for them as you so rightly pointed out.'

I want to say, '*How dare you!*' but my French fails me and so I just say, 'No!' and stare at him, mouth ajar.

He then smiles a horrid, contrite little smile at me, gives a perfect Gallic shrug, and sweeps away from the table.

Charles turns back to face me. 'I take it from your expression that that didn't go well,' he says.

I shake my head. 'What can I say?' I laugh. 'He's French. Outrageous!'

'Well there goes his tip,' Charles says.

'I bet he wonders why foreigners never tip him. You were about to say something?'

'It doesn't matter,' Charles says. 'Shall we get out of here? I could do with stretching my legs.'

We walk aimlessly along the edge of the port. A number of other couples are doing the same. It's a lovely feeling to fit into that scene for once, instead of feeling like a spare wheel. I notice how the people walking past smile at me, as if we are all complicit in sharing this beautiful evening.

When you're alone people look at you differently – with suspicion, or desire, or concern.

It's not yet cold, but it's getting cooler fast. A gentle breeze is rocking the small fishing boats moored along the dockside.

'That was perfect,' I say. 'Thanks.'

'Nearly perfect,' Charles says.

'Oh that's nothing,' I laugh. 'When I went to Paris with . . . when I went to Paris . . . everyone was so mean. And we used to say, shall we go and eat at Mr Grumpy's, or at Mr Nasty's?'

'It's strange that it never changes. I mean with all the international travel going on. You'd think they'd realise.'

'It is strange,' I agree. 'Though to be honest, I do think it's getting a bit better. Slowly.'

'You'd be sacked on the spot for showing off like that in the States.'

'I don't think they *can* sack people in France. I think that's the whole problem. But anyway. Let's not think about Mr Grumpy any more. The fish was delicious.'

'Yes. That vegetable thing too.'

'The terrine?'

'Yes. Absolutely gorgeous.'

'It's been a lovely day all round,' I say.

'It has,' Charles says, softly, stopping and leaning against the guard rail. 'I don't know quite how to say this. Not without ruining everything . . .'

'No?' I reply. 'Just say it. However it comes out will be fine.'

'I've had a lovely day,' he says.

'Yes,' I agree. 'So have I. I'm so glad I came.'

'And I'm fighting the desire to kiss you.'

I turn to face him and smile. 'Then kiss me,' I say, with a shrug.

He slips into the widest grin and then leans in towards me. 'You're sure it's OK?' he asks.

'Do I look like it might not be?'

We both lean in and he rests his lips against mine. A slow, chaste, peck. And then he straightens and smiles at me again.

'Is that it?' I ask, using humour to disguise my request for more. 'I mean, it was nice, but . . .'

Charles winks at me. 'I'm not very public,' he says, glancing around. 'What do you say we go back to the hotel?'

I raise one shoulder in a half-shrug. 'Sure. Why not?'

'I just need to make a quick call,' he says, pulling his phone from his pocket. 'You will excuse me?'

'Sure,' I say again.

As Charles wanders away, I hike myself up onto the railings and stare out at the lights rippling on the surface of the sea.

Inside, I'm trembling.

I feel nervous, and a little afraid. But also excited and joyous and reckless and brilliant. Of course, I wonder for a moment if I'm doing the right thing, for it's clear as day that we're going to have sex, and fairly likely that we won't see each other again, or at least, not until his next trip this way.

Maybe it's the wine and the moonlight, or maybe it's that it's just been too long and the animal in me is not asking, but *demanding* physical comfort ... Perhaps it is simply that it is the right decision after all. But whatever the reason, I order my internal voice to stop criticising. 'This is happening,' I tell it quietly. 'So shut it!'

The Wrong Kind of Rubber

In the taxi on our way back to Nice, Charles rests one arm along the back of the seat rest; his hand drapes gently over my shoulder, and our thighs bump together as the car swings around the many bends in the coast road.

It all feels lovely, and, for the moment at any rate, I'm suffering from nothing more than normal, first-time-with-a-new-partner nerves. If anything, I'm feeling quite pleased with my bravery.

My only negative emotion is a niggling sadness that whatever this is, it won't last. Charles doesn't live in London. In fact, as far as I can tell, Charles doesn't live anywhere. Q: How can you have a relationship with someone who never stands still? A: You can't.

Back at the hotel, there is a brief moment of confusion in the lift again. Charles hits button three, clearly thinking that we're going to *my* room.

For reasons I would rather not have to explain, I prefer to go to his. 'Let's go to yours,' I say with a smile, certain that he will politely comply.

Charles, though, has other ideas. 'No,' he says, firmly. 'I would rather go to yours. I haven't seen your room anyway.'

'I haven't seen yours,' I counter.

God! Why is it always so hard to talk about sex? Of course, it is the fact of verbally acknowledging what we *are* about to have sex that is the problem here. Sex isn't, for some reason, supposed to be planned. It's just, somehow, meant to happen. I know what is likely to transpire in my room, and Charles knows it too, but discussing it before it happens is quite another thing. Discussing it means that it is, as they say in murder cases, premeditated. And, for me at any rate, there is something profoundly uncomfortable about that.

When the door opens, I hesitate. 'No, really,' I say. 'Let's go to yours.'

'Why?'

'My room's a mess.'

'How can your room be a mess?'

'Oh, you know girls. Make-up and dresses all over the place ...'

Charles frowns and holds the 'door open' button as the door lurches back and forth, as undecided as ourselves.

'Maybe mine's a mess too,' he offers.

'Is it?'

'No, but it could be.'

I roll my eyes. This is getting even more uncomfortable than simply confronting the truth. 'Look,' I say, steeling myself. 'I don't have any contraceptives in my room. Have you, in yours?'

'Oh!' Charles exclaims, blushing. 'Condoms – of course. Sorry. I'll nip up to mine. I'll be right back.'

As the lift doors close behind me, I let myself frown. *What was all that about?* I wonder.

When I open the door to my room it becomes clear though that Charles' room really would have been the better option. Due to God knows what mix-up, my room has been filled with pink balloons. They cover almost every inch of the floor and bed.

'Jesus!' I exclaim, stamping on a couple to make enough room to be able to move into the room. *And there was I worrying about a lack of rubbers*, I think, laughing and shaking my head in disbelief.

I pick up the phone and call the front desk. '*Allo?*' I say. '*Je viens de rentrer et j'ai plein de ...*'

But it's no good. I don't know the word for balloons in French. '*Oui?*'

'I'm sorry, do you speak English?'

'Of course, madam.'

'Well there are loads of balloons in my room.'

'Yes?'

'Erm, I don't want loads of balloons in my room.'

'No. What would you like me to do?'

'I don't know. Get rid of them? Deliver them to whoever *does* want a room full of balloons?'

'I will send someone up immediately,' the man says.

For the second time today, I wish I had a camera. I pick up the phone to ask Charles to bring his, but then realise that this might sound a bit kinky. He might want to take photos of a different kind.

I laugh and kick a balloon, and then remember that Charles is on his way, and wonder if I have time for a shower, and if I *do* have a shower, would it be slutty not to get dressed again before he arrives?

But before I can decide, it's already too late. There is a sharp rat-a-tat-tat.

I wade through the pink sea and open the door. Charles looks into the room, smiles, and raises an eyebrow. '*Nice*,' he says.

'Yes,' I laugh. 'How crazy is that? There's been a mix-up and some idiot has filled my room with balloons.'

Charles steps into the room, picks one up and throws it across onto the bed. 'I rather like them,' he says, apparently unfazed.

I kick a few out of the way and follow him into the bedroom. 'Some five-year-old somewhere will be weeping,' I say.

'Don't you like them?' he asks, in mock concern.

'I did when I was five,' I laugh.

'I think it's rather fun,' he says, reaching out to stroke my arm. 'So are you still up for more kissing?' he asks. 'Or have the balloons put you off?'

I laugh. 'I'm not so easily put off,' I say.

'Good,' he says, stepping forward, sliding one arm around my waist and reeling me in. He repeats the chaste kiss of before, only this time he follows it with a series of mini-pecks. And then, I open my mouth and let myself melt against him.

I can feel his erection pressing through our clothes, which, momentarily, unnervingly, reminds me of my nightmare. But

I push this thought away and run a hand over his chest, which feels surprisingly muscular. 'Someone's been working out,' I say.

'Not much else to do when you live in hotels,' Charles says. 'At least they all have a gym.'

'Can I?' I ask, fingering the top button of his shirt.

'Oh yes,' he laughs.

But the second I have undone the top button there is a second, more formal, knock on the door.

'Oh, sorry,' I say, letting go and crossing the room. 'It'll be room service. I'll just get rid of them.'

I open the door a quarter of the way and see a teenager in hotel uniform grinning and brandishing a huge hat pin.

'That's perfect,' I tell him, taking the pin from his grasp. 'I can manage myself. Thanks so much.'

I close the door and turn back to face Charles.

'I'll just pop a couple of these – make some room,' I say, showing him the pin.

'Humm,' Charles murmurs, pointing at a balloon. 'Pop this one!'

As soon as I pop it, he points to another. 'And this one.'

'Actually,' I say, glancing at my watch. 'It's a bit late for popping balloons. I'll wake the whole hotel up.'

I glance up at him and see that not only has he removed his shirt, but his erection is now so pronounced that it truly does look like . . .

'Is that a gun in your pocket?' I laugh.

'No,' he says, running his own hand over it. 'Just pleased to see you.'

'Well, I think we have better things to do than pop balloons, don't you?'

'I suppose we do,' he says.

And so, surrounded by pink, squealing balloons, we make love. It's all very slow, very sensual, to start with. And then, just as the doctor would have ordered, it builds to a sweaty, back-arching climax. I worry that in spite of leaving the balloons intact, I may be waking a few neighbours anyway.

Afterwards, I doze in Charles' arms for a while. I'm surprised to see that his erection though, doesn't go away – I suspect that he has taken Viagra.

Brian used to pop a Viagra sometimes for fun, and there was always something a little artificial, a little larger-than-life, or, more particularly, longer-lasting-than-life about the erections the drug produced. I always felt afterwards that I had somehow had sex with an artificial appendage rather than with him. And I always struggled against the feeling that if he needed Viagra, then there was something wrong with our sexual chemistry.

Charles goes to the toilet, declares that he can't pee, scoops a load of balloons off the floor and throws them at me, and then dives back onto the bed, squashing them between his body and mine.

By the time I fall asleep, the orgasm score is: Charles, three; CC, two. Which is more, let's face it, than any girl dare hope for on a first date with a fifty-five-year-old.

When I wake up the next morning, I wonder for a moment if the whole thing wasn't a dream. A single glance at the balloons covering the floor though proves that it all really happened. Charles, though, has vanished.

I stretch luxuriously in the bed, and reflect that this feeling, this desire to stretch, and purr like a cat, means that the sex, also, was real.

I don't mind that Charles has vanished at all. In fact, I'm glad: it gives me time to wake up at my own rhythm. And time to decide how I feel about Charles now that we have done the deadly deed.

After dozing for another hour, I finally get up and dress. Realising that I have run out of clean clothes, I recycle the least suffering of my underwear and dress again in my jeans and pullover. It looks like I will have to do some shopping today.

I phone Charles' room, but there is no answer, so, realising that I still don't have his mobile number, I repeat yesterday's schedule and head out for a walk, almost certain that I will find him sitting on one of the blue chairs.

As I pass the reception, the desk clerk calls me over. 'Madame Kelly?' he asks, waving a baby blue envelope at me.

'Yes,' I say.

'Monsieur Van Heerden left this for you.'

'Thanks,' I say, taking the envelope between finger and thumb. 'Is he in?'

'I'm sorry, madam, I have no idea.'

I'm pretty certain the clerk knows exactly who is in and who isn't, but I understand his tact. I smile and start to turn away, but then pause. 'Oh, and no need to worry about the balloons,' I say. 'I popped them myself.'

'Popped?' he repeats, frowning.

'Pop!' I explain, making a pin motion.

He remains stoic and simply raises one eyebrow.

'But you might want to find out who was supposed to have the balloons in the first place,' I tell him. 'Because some child somewhere is probably not too happy.'

The clerk frowns deeply at me.

'The balloons . . . If *I* got them, then someone else didn't.'

The clerk shakes his head. 'But Monsieur Van Heerden ordered the balloons for you, madam.'

I laugh and shake my head. 'No,' I say. 'That's what I'm telling you. It was a mistake. They must have been meant for someone else.'

The clerk frowns at me and raises the eyebrow again. I decide that he has the most mobile eyebrow that I have ever seen. I wonder if the other one moves as well. I get a fit of giggles at the crazy conversation I'm having. It's like something from a Carry On movie . . . 'Never mind,' I say. 'It doesn't matter. Not to me.' The clerk shrugs and looks back down at his register, which I take as my cue to leave.

Outside, as I wait for the traffic lights to change so that I can cross the road, I read Charles' note.

Dear Charlotte

Sorry to disappear like a thief in the night, but, as I explained, I have meetings all day today. Will be back about seven for dinner. Meet you in the red room. Have a lovely day. And enjoy the balloons!

Charles xx

Deflation

It's closer to eight p.m. when Charles and I finally meet up in the red room. He kisses me lightly on the lips – not a sexual kiss, but not chaste either. 'How did your meetings go?' I ask, as we cross the lobby and step back out into the evening.

'Great,' he tells me. 'I think I have a new contract with Rawling International. They supply Pirelli, amongst others.'

'So you're supplying Pirelli with rubber for their tyres?' I ask, impressed.

Charles laughs. 'Well, on paper.'

'On paper.'

'Do you know anything about options trading?' he asks.

I shake my head. 'Sorry,' I say.

'Well, it is kind of complicated. There are markets, the same as stock markets, but these are options markets. People trade options . . . the option to buy things at a fixed price. So, suppose you think the price of petrol is going to go up, you could buy an option to buy it at today's price. Does that make any sense?'

I nod. 'Yes,' I say. In fact it doesn't really, but the truth is that for some reason, I find myself completely devoid of interest in the subject.

'So I'm an options trader. Specialised in rubber, copper, and zinc.'

I nod. 'Great!' I say.

'Anyway, how was *your* day?'

'Fine. Nice. I walked back into town, had breakfast on the Cours Saleya, phoned some friends, just to reassure them that

I'm still alive. I bought a few bits, had a peep in the Museum of Modern Art . . . well, just in the shop to be honest . . . it's been a perfect lazy day in a foreign city.'

'Nice,' Charles says. 'I envy you.'

We automatically head east – back towards the old town again, before Charles asks, 'So what do you fancy eating tonight? We had fish again at lunchtime, so if I can avoid fish this evening, that would be good.'

'Actually,' I laugh, 'I phoned a friend in England. He knows Nice quite well, and he told me about a little local place where they supposedly do the best pizza on the planet.'

'Pizza sounds perfect,' Charles laughs.

'OK. Well, I think it's pretty close to the Cours Saleya. It's sort of a few streets behind it according to the map.'

As we wander back through these streets, by now starting to feel familiar, I become hyper-aware that this is our last evening here. In fact, it's very possibly our last evening anywhere together. I desperately want to broach the subject and see if, like me, Charles has any desire to take this further. Or indeed, any plausible strategy for meeting again somewhere so that we can take this further. The idea of simply jumping on a plane and arriving back in London as a single girl is heartbreaking. But I can't help but think that a wrong answer will only spoil our last evening together. It's clearly wiser to save that discussion for tomorrow.

The restaurant Mark suggested – Le Gesu – is probably a little lower key than Charles is used to, but he doesn't say a word.

Though the chairs are plastic, and the prices as low as I have seen for some time, the pizza is as good as Mark said. The base is thin and crisp and somehow vaguely caramelised, whilst the topping is oozing in garlic, olive oil, and beautiful rich mozzarella. In fact, I can only agree with Mark's verdict: it is probably the best pizza I have ever eaten.

The only real downside to the place is the gigantic Catholic church overlooking the restaurant. I sit with my back to the open door and between conversations I chant a mantra : that I'm not a Catholic, and therefore whatever I do, it *isn't* a sin . . .

By eleven-thirty, we're back at the hotel. I'm fully expecting a repeat performance of last night. When I open the door to my room, though, Charles looks momentarily flummoxed.

'What's wrong?'

'The balloons,' Charles says. 'They are all gone.'

'Yes,' I laugh. 'I couldn't move!'

'You got rid of them?' he asks, flatly.

'I did. It was great fun popping them. There were thirty-seven of them. I counted.'

'Thirty-seven?'

'Yes. Thirty-seven.'

'Right,' Charles says. 'You could have waited.'

'Waited?'

'Never mind.'

'It was a shame really. I quite fancied a photo of them to send to Mark. He'll never believe me now of course.'

'We could get some more?' Charles offers.

I laugh. 'No,' I say. 'I think I've had quite enough balloons for one day.' I step closer and stroke his chest. He looks around the room as though the absence of the balloons has left him disoriented.

'Don't look so sad,' I say. 'I'm still here.'

But Charles looks suddenly deflated. When I pull him against me, I can feel that, indeed, compared with last night, he *is* thoroughly deflated.

'You know,' I say, stroking his wrinkled brow, 'the man on reception thought that *you* ordered them. The balloons, that is. He said you ordered them specially for me.'

'Really?'

'Yes.'

Charles shrugs and glances away.

'You didn't did you?' I ask.

Charles shrugs again.

I laugh. 'You funny man,' I say, laughing genuinely. 'You did!'

'There were thirty-nine,' he says. 'One for each year.'

'Of course. I popped two yesterday. Yes, thirty-nine.'

'But you didn't like them,' he says, sticking his bottom lip out. He sounds about two. He sounds like a toddler about to throw a hissy fit.

'Sure I did,' I say. 'It was funny. They were very . . . memorable.'

Charles smiles weakly at me and we kiss again. I run a hand over the front of his chinos but this only confirms that, if yesterday's raging erection *was* Viagra-induced, he clearly hasn't taken the drug today. Maybe, I figure, it's dangerous to take it two days in a row. I try to remember what I was wearing yesterday, anything I might have done to excite him, but as far as I can recall he pretty much arrived with a raging hard-on.

'You look sad,' I say, for some reason in a slightly mocking baby voice I instantly regret. 'What's the matter?'

Charles shrugs. 'It's just a shame you popped all of them,' he says. 'You could have saved one or two.'

I screw my nose up. I wonder, *What's happening here?*

For I can feel the evening slipping out of control and I have no idea why. But I'm sure that this is what is happening. I know this feeling only too well. It's what used to happen with Ronan all the time when he was drunk. Everything would be going fine, and then, suddenly, as if a cloud had drifted in front of the sun, the light would vanish. And there was no way out.

'Charles. I think we can manage without balloons, don't you? They were funny and lovely, and I'm grateful. Now let's not spoil our last evening here over a bunch of pink balloons, huh?'

Charles sighs. 'I suppose,' he says.

We kiss again. He runs a hand down over my buttocks and pulls me roughly against him. And then, suddenly, from nowhere, the storm is upon us: he pulls away. His features are dark and brooding, his brow creased. 'I'm sorry,' he says. 'This isn't going to work. Not tonight.'

'Oh,' I say, now holding onto his arm in an attempt at stopping him from pulling away. 'It doesn't matter. Just spend the night with me.'

'No,' he says, quite literally shaking me off. 'No, I don't think so.'

'Oh come on, Charles. It's our last night here. Don't . . .'

But Charles is already heading for the door. 'No, I have a long day tomorrow. It's better this way.'

He spins back, crosses the room, and pecks me coldly on the cheek. 'Sorry,' he says. 'But we oldies. We can't just perform on demand.'

I shake my head in disbelief. 'It's fine. Stay. I don't mind . . .'

I watch the bedroom door close behind him and sink onto my bed, and try to work out what just happened.

After five minutes, the only theory I have managed to come up with is that his male pride was injured. Men are famously sensitive about their ability to get a stiffy. Or not.

But then I'm famously sensitive about my ability to give my men stiffies. Or not. And *I* haven't stormed off.

I think about phoning his room to talk about it but remind myself that I don't know him well enough to know the best course of action. Nothing, for instance, ever made Ronan more angry, more violent even, than following him once he had gone off in a huff. And even if that doesn't happen, I'm not sure I want to hear what Charles might have to say – for it's of course entirely possible that he simply doesn't fancy me that much.

I walk through to the bathroom and turn from side to side and look at myself in the mirror. I look OK. But I have looked better. Perhaps I looked better yesterday.

In my experience, most men can get a hard-on the first time – with pretty much anyone. It's whether they *maintain* their sexual interest that counts. Maybe Charles only fancied me enough for a one-off.

Yes, best not to explore the subject any further tonight. Far better, whichever way you look at it, to let sleeping dicks lie and salvage whatever can be salvaged in the morning.

But of course I don't feel at all sleepy now.

I take a trip down to reception for a newspaper to read. The desk is still being manned by the clerk from this morning.

'Wow!' I exclaim. '*Encore vous*!'

'*Oui*,' he repeats drily. '*Encore moi*.'

I remember, belatedly that '*encore vous*' is 'you again,' whilst, 'still you,' which is what I had wanted to say, is '*toujours vous*'. His expression is enough to tell me that they aren't the same thing at all.

'*Désolé* . . .' I explain grovelingly. 'Sorry but I mean, you're *still* here. You must have had a very long day.'

He nods with appropriate tiredness. 'The other guy is sick,' he tells me. 'So, yes. A long day. What can I do for you?'

'Do you have a paper? Something in English?'

'American,' he says, glancing half-heartedly behind him. '*Herald Tribune*.'

'That would be perfect,' I answer.

He fetches me the newspaper and forces a smile as he hands it to me. 'Here you are,' he says switching to excellent English.

'Oh, and I'm sorry,' I say. 'I owe you an apology.'

'An apology?'

'Yes, the balloons. Charles *did* order them. For me, that is.' The clerk frowns, so I elaborate. 'This morning, I thought it was a mistake, but it wasn't.'

He shakes his head. 'No mistake,' he says.

'No. So I'm sorry. Oh, how do you say balloon in French?' I ask.

'Balloon?'

'Yes. Balloon.'

'*Ballon*,' he says.

'Oh, OK. Of course. I thought that was a ball, that's all.'

'It's both,' he says. 'They are same thing.'

I briefly imagine what football would be like on TV if this were true. Wimbledon would probably be worth a watch too.

'OK, thanks,' I say, smiling.

He crinkles his mouth sideways in a sort of wry, suppressed smile. 'As long as you *enjoyed* them,' he says. It sounded, for some reason, like he put emphasis on *enjoyed*, but it's probably just his foreign accent.

I give a tiny, confused shake of my head, lift the paper from the counter, and sweep away. 'Anyway, thanks for the paper,' I say.

Just as I am leaving the lobby, I hear him talking to someone else, and glance back. I can't hear the conversation, but they are both leaning low behind the counter and looking up at me. Whatever he says, both he and the bell boy smile with what I can only describe as smutty schoolboy smirks. And something about those smirks sets my brain racing.

Back in my room, I cast the newspaper aside. Instead I sit and run the evening across the cinema screen of my mind. Frame by frame I analyse it.

I remember Charles raising an eyebrow and smirking in that same way when he saw the balloons. I remember him throwing them at me on the bed and jumping on top.

As I brush my teeth, I remember him reaching down whilst we were bonking and scooping balloons back onto the bed. I start to be convinced that this new theory slowly formulating, is, however bizarre, the right one.

Propped up on pillows, I open my laptop, select Google, and type 'balloon fetish'.

Already feeling a little sick, I click on the first of 1,400,000 search results. 'Damn you,' I mutter. 'It wasn't Viagra at all, was it?'

The site is called 'Looner Vision'. And as the screen fills with images of women blowing up balloons, women popping balloons, women sitting on really big balloons, and one in particular, a busty blonde lying on a hotel bed surrounded by pink balloons, I almost heave.

I click on a couple more links and then close the browser and lie back on my bed.

God! I think. *When he said he was 'in rubber' I thought he meant professionally.*

For a moment, I feel a little better. If Charles' issue is the lack of balloons then at least his lack of performance isn't any failing on my part. At least I haven't somehow become less sexy than yesterday.

And then I realise that if it was all about balloons, then maybe it was nothing to do with me *at all*. Perhaps any woman in a room full of balloons would have done the trick. Perhaps just a room full of balloons would have done the trick. Perhaps without the balloons he wouldn't have found me sexy yesterday either.

I have a feeling that tonight the baby blue sky is going to be no solace. It's going to be a long one.

Early Exit

I hardly sleep at all that night. I stare at the ceiling until about four a.m. and then doze until seven, whereupon, in a fit of activity, I leap from the bed and start packing.

My flight isn't until five this afternoon, but it's simple and instinctive: I just don't want to be here any more.

Down in reception, though, a problem arises. 'I need Monsieur Van Heerden here for checkout,' the desk clerk tells me. 'The room is on his bill.'

'I'll pay,' I say. 'Really, it's fine. I would rather pay for myself anyway.'

'But I am obliged to phone Monsieur Van Heerden. If that's OK . . . He did reserve the room.'

'Well, I would rather you didn't.'

'Madame, I understand . . .'

I am just about to launch myself into a manufactured explosion which will be so loud and so embarrassing that the clerk will have no choice but to let me have my way, when a hand touches me on the shoulder.

'It's fine,' Charles says. 'I'm here.'

I shrug the hand off and turn to face him. 'I'm sorry, but I need to get away now . . . I'm perfectly happy to pay for my own room.'

He laughs. 'I doubt that,' he says. 'Do you have any idea how exp—'

'Don't you dare patronise me!' I say. 'I'm perfectly capable of paying my own way.'

'I'm sure,' he says, raising his hands in submission. 'But really.

Please. Let me. To make up for last night.'

I shake my head, but, as often is the case, the two men in the room have decided, with a wink and a nod, to sort this out between themselves.

'So I'll just add it to your bill, monsieur?'

'Yes,' Charles answers.

The clerk smiles at him, raises the magic eyebrow at me, and slips the manila sleeve back into the drawer.

'Could you look after my friend's bag whilst we have a coffee?'

'Certainly, sir.'

'I haven't agreed to coffee or anything else,' I point out.

'I know,' Charles says. 'But you can't just leave like this. The weekend hasn't been *that* bad, has it? At least have a coffee with me.'

I sigh. I am, I realise, being a bit rude. And maybe a bit hysterical. 'Coffee,' I say, flatly.

'Coffee. Where's the harm?'

I stare at him. I stare through him. I try to make up my mind. 'OK,' I say after a calculated pause.

'Can we have two coffees in the red room?' he asks the clerk.

'The red room,' the man repeats.

'The salon Vuitton or whatever,' Charles says.

'Versailles,' I correct.

'Yes, of course,' the clerk says. 'I'll send a waiter. Please . . .'

I hand over my suitcase and follow Charles to the Salon Versailles. It's as stunning as ever, and we take our seats in front of the big bay window, this morning, closed.

I look out over the sea at what is clearly going to be another beautiful day and wonder what it must be like to live somewhere where it's always sunny. It certainly must make planning picnics easier.

'I *am* sorry,' Charles says earnestly. 'About last night.'

'Yes,' I say. 'Well . . .' It's the best I can manage for the moment.

'Still, we had some fun though, didn't we?'

I nod vaguely. It's undeniable that, overall, the weekend has been lovely. Last night was a blip. A profound blip, but a blip nonetheless.

I'm struggling to maintain my hardened features. The resulting expression is the one that, when my mother does it, I call '*sucking lemons*'. And I wonder why we still do this as adults. For there's clearly something very childish about pretending to be miserable when you aren't, just to make a point. '*Cutting off your nose to spite your face*,' my father called it.

'It's fine,' I say, my voice softer than I had intended.

A waiter arrives and takes our order, and we sit silently watching the sun rising in the empty sky until he returns with the drinks.

'So back to London for you,' Charles says finally.

'Yes. Back to my long-suffering cat.'

'Will he be OK?'

I nod. 'Yeah. Apparently he's moved into my neighbour's place. They have no loyalty, cats.'

'It's good to have good neighbours,' Charles says. 'Useful.'

'Yes,' I say. 'Mark's an old friend. And a work colleague too. In America they say that people like that – people you know so well they're like family – they call them framily.'

'Framily?'

'Yes. I really liked that.'

'So Mark is your framily?'

'Yes. I suppose so.'

'Were you and he ever . . . you know . . . together?'

In spite of my desire to remain stony-faced, I smile. 'No! Mark is gay.'

Charles nods. 'I see,' he says. 'And you . . . I mean . . . that isn't a problem for you?'

'No,' I say, frowning now. 'Why would it be?'

Charles shrugs and sips his coffee. 'I'm not sure what I think about that sort of thing, I suppose. But then I'm older than you.'

'You just have to let other people be the way they are,' I say. 'There's really no other choice.'

'Yes, I suppose so,' Charles says.

'I know so,' I say.

'I always think that there need to be *some* limits though . . .

to what's acceptable . . . I mean, don't get me wrong, I'm sure your friend is very nice . . . but . . . well, I'm sure you know what I mean.'

So, homophobic! I sigh and shake my head gently. I wonder, if we sat here all day, how many other things would fall out of Charles' closet? How many other 'brown sock' moments would we have? Plenty, I'm guessing. 'When's your flight to Dusseldorf?' I ask.

'Half-three,' Charles says. 'And then tomorrow night, to Berlin. And then on to St Petersburg.'

'In Russia?'

'Yes.'

'Don't you get tired of all that moving around?'

Charles shakes his head. 'Not really,' he says. 'I used to. When I had stuff to get home for. Nowadays I don't mind so much.'

'Sure,' I say, finishing my coffee and putting the cup down decisively. If he carries on like this I shall start feeling sorry for him, and that isn't what I want at all. 'Well, thanks, Charles. It's . . . it's been fun. And you've been very generous.'

He smiles and nods vaguely. 'My pleasure. And you've been wonderful company. And I am truly sorry about last night. These things happen at my age, sadly . . . it's . . . unpredictable. I'm sorry to have disappointed you.'

I run a finger across my brow. I had been about to leave, but this is suddenly sounding like he thinks I'm upset because he couldn't *get it up*. And that's not the problem. That's not the problem at all.

'It wasn't that,' I say, settling back into my seat for a moment longer. 'It was the balloon thing.'

'The balloon thing?' Charles repeats.

I wrinkle my nose and lean in. 'Yes. You have a bit of a balloon thing, don't you?'

Charles swallows and straightens his back and turns to look out of the window.

'It's fine, Charles,' I say, suddenly wondering if I have got this wrong. 'But it's not for me.'

'Right,' he says, still looking away. 'Not for you . . . Why?'

I shrug. 'I suppose, erm, when I sleep with someone, I like to think that it's about them finding *me* attractive, really . . . rather than about the, um, *accessories*.'

'Oh, but I do find you attractive,' Charles says.

'Yes,' I say. *But only in a room full of balloons*, I think.

'Anyway, it's like you said,' I continue. 'There have to be limits. And everyone's limits are different. You're not comfortable with gays . . . I'm not that comfortable with off-the-wall fetishes.'

Charles nods, thoughtfully taking this in. 'It's not really the same thing though, is it,' he says.

'No,' I agree. 'It isn't.'

'Just so you know,' Charles says, 'it's actually quite common.'

'Right,' I say.

'I'm not . . . you know . . . some kind of freak.'

I take a deep breath and place my feet beneath me ready to stand again. 'No,' I say. 'OK.'

'I'm in a club. On the internet. And there are over ten thousand other members who like . . . well . . . the same things.'

'Right,' I say, nodding, pulling my handbag towards me and standing. 'Well, this is where we say goodbye.'

Charles, too, stands and rounds the table to my side. I try not to cringe as I accept his hug, but when he pecks me on the cheek, it's too much, and I pull away.

'Bye then,' he says sadly.

'Bye,' I answer.

And then I walk out of that room as fast as I can without running.

Back in the lobby, as he hands me my bag, the desk clerk says, 'Goodbye, and we hope to see you at the Negresco again soon.'

'Thanks,' I reply, already whizzing my noisy case towards the door. 'But I doubt it. I really do.'

It takes only minutes, of course, seconds perhaps, for me to realise that not leaving my case at the hotel was a mistake. But I am feeling lucky. For Charles hasn't asked me – by design or accident, I'm not sure – for a phone number, or an email address for the photos he took, or any other contact information.

I dare not go back now. And so I trundle my case, suddenly as un-steerable as a shopping trolley, down the street, beneath my old window, and then turn right down the first side street that will take me out of sight.

I soon come to a pedestrian precinct I haven't seen before, and here I find a secluded café where I park my case and order croissants and tea. Any more coffee and I shall blow a fuse.

And it's here that I spend the most part of the day. I'm really just too tired to bother moving my case again. Plus, sitting and watching the pretty people wandering by, and wondering if *they* ever failed to give their partners hard-ons, is, I think, all my brain can cope with today.

A little before three, calculating that it's late enough to be certain of missing Charles, and that they might have some kind of seat I can doze in at the airport, I walk back to the seafront and jump in a cab.

At the airport, I send Mark a text to tell him that I'm on my way home. This initiates a rapid-fire exchange of messages.

'GOOD! LOVE?'

'NOT!'

'WHY?'

'REASONS'

'REASONS?'

'PLURAL OF REASON'

'HA! WHAT REASONS?'

'NOT NOW'

'OK SEE U TONIGHT. LOVE U LOTS.'

And suddenly, I feel so lucky to have framily to return to, I could cry.

Man Poisoning

By the time I get back to Primrose Hill, it's seven p.m.

I'm in a state of complete exhaustion, and feeling a little depressed. I'm not that sure I feel up to a kiss-and-tell gossip evening with Mark after all.

When I go upstairs to fetch my furry bed-warmer, Mark, however, is having none of it. 'I looked after Moggins here for a whole week,' he protests, 'the least I deserve is a bit of gossip.'

And so, lured by home-made prawn curry, I agree to stay. Mark is an excellent cook, and my own fridge is in a state of post-absence emptiness.

We proceed to down two bottles of nicely chilled Pinot Gris. As we slurp the evening away, I tell him first about the meetings in New York, and then about Tom and Ron. 'Poor you!' he laughs. 'Water water everywhere but not a drop to drink.'

'Well exactly,' I say.

'You should have sent me – *I* might have got a shag.'

'Except that you're married,' I point out.

'Well so are they,' he argues, as if this makes some logical point. 'Anyway, of course, you did get a shag, didn't you?'

So I tell him about being bumped into business class, about sharing a bottle (yes, in the new version, the glass becomes a bottle) of Champagne with Charles.

I exaggerate how good the service was, and how good-looking Charles was, and as the story advances, I start to feel better about the whole thing.

And this, I realise, is how we human beings deal with pain.

This is how we heal. We turn our hurts and failures into stories. Into *funny* stories for the most part. And with each telling, with each exaggeration, the line between fact and fiction becomes a little more blurred. And at some point along the way, the memory of the event itself is lost – only the memory of the story of the event remains. And when we're no longer quite sure which part of it was truth, and which part fiction – at that point, the power of the original event to hurt us is gone. For it has become just a story. A story which we tell friends and family. And framily. A story in which we have become the hero.

By the time I stumblingly carry my complaining Guinness back downstairs, I am feeling not only a little sloshed, but a whole lot better.

. . .

My meeting with Peter Stanton on Monday goes, of course, like a dream. 'I don't know whether to kiss you or give you a pay rise,' he declares.

'No offence, but I'll plump for the pay rise,' I say with a flirtatious giggle designed specifically to avoid offence.

'Well, we can discuss it in April,' he says, 'when we do the year-end reviews.'

'Great,' I reply, thinking, *I bet that if I had chosen the kiss, he wouldn't have needed to wait till April.*

I give him a blow-by-blow account of the meetings with Levi's and Harper & Baker, and, as I now know the outcome, I'm able to exaggerate my role there too. 'They all behaved like ice-statues,' I tell him, 'but I could tell by the twinkle in Craig Peterson's eye that we had them hooked.'

Stanton is duly impressed, and I am just about to float out of his office on my own little cloud when we have the following comedy exchange:

'Oh, and CC? While Victoria is away, can you liaise with Sheena and make sure that nothing urgent gets overlooked?'

'I didn't know VB *was* away,' I retort, lingering in the doorway.

'Well, yes, of course she is.'

'How long for?'

'Well, one never knows with these things, does one?'

Aware that I'm missing something important here, I frown. 'Where is she?'

'Well, still at the clinic I would think.'

'At the clinic?'

'Yes.'

'I'm sorry, I, erm, didn't know. I mean, I knew she had a breakdown on the way to the airport, but that's where it ends.'

'I don't think she was on her way to the *airport*.'

'So what's wrong with her?'

'Who knows. Stress, I suppose. That's what everyone puts things down to these days isn't it?'

'Stress? Because of a *breakdown*?'

'Rather the other way around I should think.'

'I'm sorry?'

'I would think that it was more the stress which caused the breakdown. If stress *was* the cause.'

'Yes, of course,' I say, licking my lips and grinding my teeth. 'Sorry, but which clinic is she in? I might send her some flowers.' I'm having the first inkling of understanding but I dare not say it in case I've got the wrong end of the stick.

'Check with Sheena, but I think they took her to Saint George's.'

I nod slowly and stifle a smile. 'Saint George's. Right. OK. Well, I better go. Lots to do.'

'Indeed,' Stanton says. 'And maybe you could send the flowers from all of us . . . I'm sure she'd appreciate that.'

'I'll do that,' I say.

'Thanks, CC. And again – congratulations.'

As the door swings closed behind me I slip into a wry smile. It's a rather *unkind* wry smile, of course . . . but the fact that VB is in Saint George's not only is rather amusing, but it also means that I get a VB-free break of unspecified duration. If she had been nicer to me then I'm sure my thoughts would have been more charitable.

On my way back to my desk, I can't resist popping my head around the door of Creative. All three men, Jude, Darren and Mark, are slouched in their office chairs with their feet on their desks, and Darren is screwing up balls of paper and lobbing them across the room *at*, but not for the most part *into*, the wastepaper bin.

As soon as he sees me, Darren breaks into a broad grin. 'Got any balloons?' he asks.

'Enough of that, you,' I say. 'I want no more mention of balloons or anything round, or anything pink, or I'll be having nightmares.'

'Prisoner style,' Darren laughs. 'Big pink balloons chasing you around.'

'Indeed. Hey, I just found out about VB. How come you didn't tell me, Mark?'

Mark shrugs. 'I assumed you knew.'

'I thought she'd had a *breakdown*,' I say. 'I mean the other kind of breakdown . . . I thought her car had broken down. Or her taxi, or something.'

Mark bites his lip and snorts. 'You dippy cow,' he says. 'No, she lost the plot in the middle of Tesco and started shrieking or something. They reckon it was the stress of having to go to New York with *you*. Which I can understand. Sheena says she's been sectioned in Saint George's, the old home for loose women, and now for complete and utter loons.'

'Don't say that,' Jude says. 'My mum went there for a while.'

'Sorry,' Mark says, pulling a guilty face.

'Do you know what you're doing at the weekend yet?' Darren asks me.

I shrug. 'Absolutely nothing, I should think. Why?'

'Oh, it's just that we're all going to that place in Brixton again with Ricardo.'

'The salsa place . . . Amazonia?'

'Amazonica, I think, yeah. Jude's coming too, aren't you? And Victor needs a dancing partner. He was somewhat smitten by your fancy footwork it seems.'

'Right.'

'So, you up for it?'

'Sorry no . . . No, definitely not. I've been away, and, you know how it is . . . I just need a weekend at home.'

'Sure thing. You just tuck yourself up. I hope you have slippers.'

'Hey, I followed your advice this weekend, and you know the result,' I say with a sour laugh. 'So give me a break.'

'Sure,' Darren says with a smirk. And then he starts to sing a pink version of Nena's hit, 'Ninety-nine red balloons'.

Of course the double workload from my absence, added to VB's (unsurprisingly lightweight) tasks, means that my week goes by in a blur. I work late, buy takeouts on the way home, and collapse straight into my bed.

A couple of nights I'm so tired I even forget to feed poor Guinness.

By Friday night I'm in a state of near-exhaustion.

As I leave the office, at the moment I pass through reception, I hear Cheryl, our rather abrupt temporary receptionist say, 'No, I'm sorry, I'm absolutely certain, mister. We don't have a single Charlotte here . . . No . . . Sorry . . . No . . . None . . .'

I freeze and listen to the conversation. *Please don't let it be Charles*, I think, feeling the blood drain from my face.

'That's right. As in, *not one*. No. Goodbye!'

Cheryl looks at me and frowns. 'Are you OK?' she asks.

'Sure,' I say, swallowing hard.

She wrinkles her nose at me and nods vaguely at the switchboard. 'Some bloke wanted to speak to Charlotte . . .' she says. 'No surname or anything, just Charlotte. He called yesterday too.'

I pull a face. 'Oh . . .' I say.

'We don't have a Charlotte, do we?'

'No,' I say. 'No we don't. And you wanna watch him. I think he's a weirdo. I got him a couple of weeks ago when the regular girl was at lunch. Next time, just hang up on him. That's my advice.'

Cheryl pulls a face. 'I thought he sounded creepy,' she says. 'So, yeah, I will. Anyway, have a good weekend.'

I then perform a feat of mental yoga and manage to squeeze Charles back out of my mind.

The next morning, however, when I switch on my mobile to a text message from Brown Eyes, I'm forced to think about him again.

For the sad fact of the matter is that although Charles, other than being a male of the species, clearly has nothing whatsoever to do with Norman, just as a bad batch of seafood can put you off *all* seafood for months, Charles, the loony looner as Darren has now nicknamed him, has put me off *all* men. I'm suffering from a bad case of man-poisoning. Let's just hope that it's temporary.

I finger the phone for a while, trying to convince myself to send a reply, but in the end I have no choice but to give in to irresistible instinct and delete the SMS.

My phone starts to chirrup, and, convinced that I am now going to have to deal with Norman on the landline, I cross the room and peer at the screen, but the caller ID reveals that it's in fact my mother's home number. I don't think I have ever been so relieved to talk to her.

'You're back!' I exclaim.

'Yes, darling. I got back last night but I was too shattered to move.'

'I bet.'

'It's terribly tiring travelling.'

'Tell me about it! I got back from Ni . . . from New York on Monday.'

'Yes?'

'Yeah, I was . . .'

'Look, I was thinking of coming into town tomorrow.'

I grimace at the phone. My mother has visited me in London precisely three times in fifteen years. 'Really?'

'Yes, why not?'

'Sure. But well, why now?'

'Well, we never really get the chance to talk, do we?'

'We're talking now.'

'Yes, I suppose we are. So what about lunch?'

'Lunch.'

'It's a meal between breakfast and—'

'Ha! Sure, Mum, lunch. It's just you never come into London. Is there a specific—'

'I'll leave the car in Richmond and come in on the Tube.'

'OK . . .'

'So maybe we could meet in that restaurant in the museum again. That was nice.'

'It was also years ago, Mum. I don't know what it's like now.'

'I'm sure it'll be fine.'

'Well . . . no, it probably won't be.'

'Well I liked it, dear.'

'I know you did, but—'

'So let's just go there.'

'I think it would be nicer if—'

'So if I meet you there about—'

'Mum! Tomorrow is Sunday. The Tate Britain will be chocka!'

'I'm sure it won't be that bad. I'm sure you're exaggerating.'

'Mum, listen to me. It won't be fine.'

'Gosh, everything's so complicated with you, isn't it?'

'Why don't you just come here?'

'What about Kew?'

'Kew?'

'Yes, Kew Gardens. I haven't been there for years. And it's easy for me. I can park up right there.'

'Sure,' I say. 'If you want . . . I don't know what the food options are but—'

'Well, I'm sure there's some sort of café or kiosk or something. Though I still think the Tate would be nicer.'

'OK.'

'The Tate then?'

'No, Kew.'

'About midday?'

162

'Can we make that one?'

'You never change. One o'clock it is then, sleepy head. I'll meet you at the Tube stop.'

'So, Kew Gardens Tube station? One o'clock.'

'Yes.'

'Oh, Mum . . . bring your mobile OK? Just in case.'

'Yes, dear. OK. Toodle pip.'

I press the *end call* button and hold the telephone at arm's length and try to remember the last time my mother came to London. I decide that it was nine years ago. It was to tell me that she was selling the family home, something she never finally did.

And then I try to remember the time before that, and realise that it must have been when she travelled in to give me the letter Waiine had left for me.

Ominous. Ominous indeed.

Too Young to Die

When I get up on Sunday morning, I'm met with a predictable veil of grey drizzle. At ten a.m. my kitchen is so dark that I have to switch the lights on. I vaguely think of taking a bread-knife to the Leylandii but there isn't really time . . . Kew Gardens is right the other side of town, necessitating at least a couple of Tube-swaps.

In fact, the idea of trudging around Kew in the rain now strikes me as so very unappealing that I attempt to phone Mum's mobile to change the venue, but I'm too late. There is no answer – she must already be driving along the motorway – so there's no alternative but to dress up like a South Seas fisherman and head off to the rendezvous.

When I get to Kew Gardens Tube station, Mum is already there. Like me, she is dressed in a blue mac, jeans and trainers.

'Oh look at us,' she declares. 'We look like a "*pop*" group.' She surrounds the word *pop* with her trademark inverted commas.

I glance at our reflection in the window and wonder which pop group she's thinking of – we look more like a school outing to me. 'I don't think I've ever seen you in trainers before,' I comment.

'No,' she says. 'They're new. I got them on holiday – in the souk. They were a pound or something.'

'Fair enough,' I say.

'There are lots of beautiful walks in the hills above Agadir. But you can't do them in heels . . . That's why I got these.'

'Right,' I say, bracing myself for a day of surprises. For not only have I never seen my mother in trainers, not only would I never have imagined her buying a pair of twisted-seam Levi's such as she is wearing, but, now that I think about it, I have never seen her walk anywhere, ever. Not once. When I think *walk*, I remember my dad and me running along the beach whilst Mum sat in the car with *Reader's Digest* and the coffee flask.

'So what's this all about?' I ask, suddenly nervous that there is more.

'All what about?'

'Well, I'm assuming you want to talk to me about something specific?'

'Huh!' she laughs. 'If I can't even have lunch with my favourite daughter . . .'

'Your only daughter.'

'Well, you're my favourite too,' she says, linking her arm through mine. 'Shall we?'

'I can't wait,' I laugh, looking out at the rain.

In fact it's not so bad. The gentle rain means that the park is unusually empty for a weekend, and it also forces Mum and me into rare physical proximity as we squeeze beneath my umbrella. We never were a huggy family, but this feels rare and nice.

'How was the drive in?' I ask her.

'Oh, fine. Though, I have to say that I like driving less and less. Everyone is so aggressive on the roads these days.'

'You never liked driving,' I say. 'You used to say the same thing when you drove us to school.'

'Did I?'

'Yes.'

'Well, I like it even less now. Do you still not have a car?'

'No,' I say.

'I don't blame you. And I suppose they are expensive, once you count the repairs and insurance and what-have-you.'

'It's not the expense, Mum. Loads of people in London don't have cars. You just don't need one, not with Tubes and taxis and stuff. And when I do need one to come out to Surrey or whatever, I just rent one, like I did last time.'

'That was a funny little car you had last time.'

'Yes. The Nissan, wasn't it? It was sweet.'

'I might get rid of mine. Or get something smaller.'

'Well the Volvo won't go on forever, but I think you do need a car where you live. I mean, how else would you do the shopping?'

'I suppose. Apparently you can do food shopping on "*the line*" these days,' she says, wiggling her fingers to indicate quotes.

'Online? Oh, you can. You can buy pretty much anything on the internet now.'

'Yes, but I had a go and it was taking me four times as long as actually *going* to Waitrose.'

'Yeah. I found that too.'

My mother laughs at this. 'Well, that's reassuring. I thought it was just me being an oldie.'

'So how was Morocco?'

'Oh lovely. As always. The food didn't seem as good this year . . . We all kind of had the feeling that they were making cutbacks in that department. But, no, I had a lovely time. Fred and Jean were there again – the people from last winter – and they're always good fun. Though I do think Fred drinks too much.'

'A lot of people do these days,' I say.

'But we got out more this time too. We went on some lovely walks.'

'That surprises me,' I say. 'I never really think of you as a walker.'

'Well, we're all full of surprises, aren't we? I have some photos in my bag. I'll show you later. Anyway, how are you?'

'Fine,' I say. 'Same old, same old.'

'Nothing new at all then?'

I know that she's hoping for some man-news, but I side-step the question. 'I went to New York,' I say. 'That was fun.'

'On your own?'

'Yes, well, it was work, Mum.'

'Oh, right. So you couldn't really take anyone anyway.'

'Look, I know what you're getting at and, yes, I'm still single.'

'I wasn't "*getting*" at anything dear, but, seeing as you brought the subject up, I must say that I don't understand why – a lovely girl like you.'

'Well, I'm not sure I understand myself,' I tell her. 'Maybe I'm not as lovely as you and I seem to think.'

'Rubbish,' she says. 'There's someone for everyone. You just have to find the right person, that's all.'

'Well, it's not for want of looking, Mum. I can promise you that.'

'Maybe you should travel more.'

'I think there are probably as many men in London as anywhere else, don't you? It's just that all the good ones seem to be taken. Or gay.'

At the G word, she exhales sharply through her nostrils. Any mention of the subject always produces the same response. I expect it reminds her of someone she just doesn't want to think about: I expect it reminds her of Waiine.

'Anyway,' I say, moving quickly on. 'As I said, I was in New York last week. And I went to Nice recently for a weekend.'

'I'd very much like to go to New York myself,' she says.

I frown. 'You?' I say. 'You never mentioned it before.'

'Well,' she says. 'I suppose you get to a certain age and start realising that there's a whole world you haven't seen.'

Trainers, walking, travel . . . I wonder if my mother has had some kind of brain transplant. I turn my attention to the map. 'You know,' I say, 'looking at this map, the only place I can see to eat is where we came in.'

'Oh, should we turn back, do you think?' she asks, pausing to peer back down the path.

'Well, this is the Palm House on the left here . . . so . . .'

'Shall we have a peep in there first and then go back and eat?'

'Yeah,' I say. 'At least it's out of the rain.'

We turn down towards the Palm House and as we walk, I continue to study the map. 'Actually there is another one . . . oh, *and* another. The White Peaks Café and the Orangery.'

'The Orangery sounds nice,' she says.

'Yeah, it looks nicest.'

Inside the Palm House it is hot and humid. A surprising number of people are sheltering from the rain, including a large number of shrieking children. The place sounds like a public swimming pool on a Saturday morning.

'Do you remember when we brought you here?' Mum asks, predictably.

It's one of *those* stories – of which she seems to have about ten. They are so few, and so often repeated, I wonder sometimes if she was there for my childhood at all, or if someone just gave her a crib sheet. 'No, Mum, I don't. I was two or something.'

'You were *five*,' she says. 'And Waiine was seven. He put . . .'

'He put a plant in my pocket,' I say. 'I know.'

'Yes, he wanted to steal one of those carnivorous plants. And he got you to carry it home for him.'

'Yeah, I know.'

'You just said you didn't remember,' she says, tetchily.

'I don't remember coming here. But I remember the story.'

'Fine,' she says. But then, as ever, she can't resist finishing it. 'You killed it though by prising the jaws open to feed it cheese.'

'Did I?' I ask, looking away and rolling my eyes.

I watch the kids tearing around, and think, as Mum clearly is in the process of doing, about Waiine. It seems almost surreal now, the idea that I once had a brother . . . a naughty tearaway brother who stuffed stolen Venus Flytraps in my pockets. It's a bit as if the stories have been told so many times that I can't remember any of the events first-hand any more. We weren't close towards the end . . . I was at college being all studious and Waiine was working in clubs in London and going to rave parties and popping pills . . .

I don't really *miss* Waiine any more. I just sort of wonder what it would have been like. I suppose we could have been best mates, the way I am with Mark and Darren . . . then again, you can never really know. The dynamics of *family* relationships are so much more complex than with *framily*. The story of Waiine and me is as if I read half a novel and then accidentally left the book on a train. So now I shall never know how it was supposed to end. Perhaps it was just a shorter novel than I was expecting. Waiine. My brother. My novella.

'Of course there are huge palm trees in Agadir,' my mother is saying.

'I bet.'

'You should come and visit one winter. I'm sure you'd like it.'

'Right,' I say. Now I *know* something is wrong. 'You're not ill or anything, are you, Mum?' I ask, suddenly concerned.

Mum frowns at me. 'No, why? Do I *look* ill?'

'No, you look positively tanned and bouncy,' I say.

'Well there you go,' she says with a little laugh. 'You are funny sometimes!'

Mum rejects the White Peaks as a bit British Home Storesey and we plump for the Orangery. Which, in truth, were it not in such a beautiful building would look a bit like a BHS cafeteria as well. Perhaps I'm just spoilt after my weekend in Nice.

We both choose the lasagne and side salads and then by a stroke of luck a table comes free in front of one of the big windows. 'And today, through the arched window,' I laugh, as we take our seats and shuck our plastic macs.

'Gosh, *Blue Peter*,' Mum says. 'That's still going. It's not the same of course, not without John Noakes and Valerie Singleton.'

I brace myself for another cliché from my childhood. 'Do you remember when—'

'I met Valerie Singleton?' I say. 'Yes, Mum.'

'You interviewed her. Really you did. "Why are you in Brighton today? Are you enjoying it?"'

'Yes, I remember you telling me.'

'She was with a Sunshine bus of disadvantaged kids.'

'Yeah. I love big windows,' I say, glancing outside and changing the subject. 'Even when the weather's horrible, it's lovely to sit and watch.'

'Yes,' she replies, following my gaze.

'They had a huge window in the hotel I was in in Nice,' I tell her. 'Overlooking the Med. That sea is such a crazy colour. Next time I move I want huge windows that let in loads of light.'

'I know what you mean,' my mother says. 'Especially in winter . . . light is important.'

'I sometimes wonder if I don't suffer from that SAD syndrome,' I say. 'Like people in Sweden.'

'I think that as well,' she says. 'It's funny really, because everyone says the same thing these days. And everyone wants windows and light. I wonder why?'

'I think it's just natural really, isn't it?'

'But when I was a girl, we all had tiny windows – because of the cold. We didn't have double glazing then, and windows were cold and draughty. But no one ever gave a second thought to light. I wonder what happened to make us so sensitive to the light levels.'

'Maybe it's the Prozac in the tap water,' I say.

'Yes, I read about that in the *Sunday Telegraph*.'

'Though I suppose that should help really – the Prozac. My place is as dark as a coal-mine now.'

'Still that tree business?'

'Yeah,' I say. 'Mrs P's Leylandii.'

'You should get a tree surgeon to come and prune it,' she says.

'I wasn't sure if you *could* prune a tree.'

'Of course you can! Why ever not? Plus, any branches overhanging your land, you can do whatever you want. Legally, it's as if they were yours.'

'Are you sure?'

'I *was* married to a barrister for twenty years, dear.'

'Yes. Of course,' I say, unconvinced. Being married to a barrister has left my mother *believing* that, through some kind of osmosis, she has absorbed Dad's legal knowledge. In reality, her judicial opinions rarely stand close inspection. 'Anyway, I don't really want to fall out with Mrs P,' I say.

'Well,' my mother says. 'I suppose it's like everything. At some point you'll just have to choose. Mrs P, or sunlight.'

'I certainly need to do something,' I say. 'Even the lawn is dying.'

But the second I have said it, I know it's a mistake. I groan internally as she raises one eyebrow and says, 'Well, you know what I think about that.'

Paving over my tiny lawn is one of Mum's many obsessions. Why the simple fact that I don't *want* to pave my back garden isn't sufficient to end that particular discussion once and for all, I'll never know. Waiine used to say Mum was *Psycho-rigid*. I have no idea whether that is a medical term or one he made up, but it's certainly a good description.

'All that mowing and watering, and all for a bit of scrubby green,' she continues, for the hundredth time. '*And* there's a water shortage. Worldwide. They say it's going to get worse and worse too.'

'You have far more lawn than I do,' I point out.

'Yes, but my lawn is big enough to be worthwhile. Yours is just a lot of heartache for nothing.'

'I'd hardly say it gives me *heartache*,' I say.

'You know what I mean. It's a lot of work for nothing.'

'Well, I like my lawn.'

'Not that you can *call* it a lawn,' she says. 'A patch of dying grass is more like it. Now, some nice paving stones, something ochre, or limestone. It would look so much better . . .'

When we have finished eating, my mother produces her Morocco snaps. They are pretty much as expected – lots of oldies with sunburn sitting around horrible-looking hotel terraces. But I'm slightly surprised to see my mother looking so happy. It can't be easy travelling alone at sixty-seven. Hell, it isn't easy travelling alone at thirty-nine. With such concrete visual evidence of the new life she has, I'm realising, built for herself, I can't help but be impressed by her resilience.

'There seem to be lots of women,' I comment. I have been keeping an eye out for a potential love interest, but other than a couple of photos showing specific couples, the group looks resolutely feminine.

'Well, the men all die so young,' my mother says, taking one of the group photos and rotating it halfway towards me. She points a fingernail at the photo, and then lists the women. 'That's Anne – her husband had a heart attack two years ago. That's Sheila. Another heart attack, but a long time ago I think. Marian. Some sort of cancer. Jenny – she's actually divorced, but I think he's ill with something anyway. Fred and Ethel. He's still very much alive, though quite how – the way he drinks – is beyond me.'

'Eek,' I say. 'If I do find a new man I need to take him for a check-up first by the sounds of it.'

'Or go for a younger model,' Mum says. 'One that's too young to die.'

'So who are these people?' I ask, pointing at a group of adolescent locals hiding in the corner of the photo.

'They're the staff,' she says. 'Waiters, guides, what-have-you.'

'They look happy too,' I say.

My mother shrugs. 'I think they're a very happy people. And these ones obviously have jobs, so . . .'

'Who is this one with the big grin?' I ask.

'Oh, yes, he's the group guide.'

'The guy that got you the phone card?'

'Yes, that's right.'

I smirk at my own silliness.

'What?' my mother asks.

'Oh, nothing,' I say.

'No, go on?'

'Oh, just me being silly. I suspected you of having a holiday romance with him, but that's clearly ridiculous!'

'Really,' she says flatly, scooping the photos suddenly back into the sachet. 'So, shall we finish our walk?'

'We haven't had coffee yet, Mum,' I point out.

'I don't think I fancy it any more.'

'But we already paid,' I say, pushing one of the coffee tokens towards her across the table.

'No,' she says. 'No coffee. Come on.'

I lean down and peer up at her in an attempt at making eye contact. 'Mum?' I say. 'Are you sure there isn't something you wanted to talk to me about?'

'No, dear, I don't think so,' she says.

'OK . . . So can *I* get a coffee?'

'Do what you want,' she says. 'You always do.'

I shake my head. 'This is silly,' I say, standing. 'You're sure you don't want one?'

'Certain,' she says.

But when I return with my coffee my mother has vanished and a family have already squatted our table.

'I'm sorry, this table's taken,' I say.

'Yeah, by us,' the mother, who looks and sounds a bit like Tracey Emin, says.

I glance around the room looking for my mother.

'Your friend's outside,' the woman says with a nod at the window.

'Oh, thanks . . . My mum actually,' I say, putting my coffee down on the table and turning away.

'You're supposed to clear the table,' the woman says. 'It's self-service, innit.'

I grab my coat from the back of her daughter's chair and head for the door. 'Yeah, sorry about that,' I say.

When I catch up with Mum, she glances at me coldly. 'Where's the umbrella?' she asks.

'Shit,' I mutter. 'Don't move.'

When I return for the umbrella, 'Tracey' holds it out at arm's length. 'And don't worry about the plates,' she says. 'I sorted them for you.'

'Thanks,' I say. But as I turn away again, she mutters, 'Bloody cheek.'

I suppose she's right. I suppose it is a cheek. But frankly, right now, I have other things on my mind.

Back outside, I find Mum sheltering against the side of the building. It's raining quite hard now, and for this I am grateful. I suspect that otherwise she would have vanished into the distance.

I lean against the wall beside her and say, 'So come on, what happened there?'

'I don't know what you mean,' she answers crisply.

'Oh come on! One minute we're having a nice leisurely dinner, and the next we don't have time for me to drink the coffee I already paid for.'

'Yes,' she says. 'Sorry. Let's just forget it and enjoy our day, OK?'

I open my umbrella, and we link arms and walk on for a while in silence.

After a pause, I say, 'I'd much rather you just told me what I said to upset you.'

'It really doesn't matter,' she says. 'I understand.'

'What do you understand?'

'Forget it,' she says. 'It's classic Freudian angst.'

'What's classic Freudian angst?'

'Kids never want to imagine their parents as sexual beings,' she says.

'So you *did* have a holiday fling?'

'I think it's quite clear from your reaction that you would just find it amusing,' she says.

'Oh, Mum!' I admonish. 'Don't say that. It was just him. I thought you were having a fling with your guide. And then when I saw him, he was just a boy. That's the only reason I laughed.'

'He's twenty-three,' she says.

'OK, twenty-three. Whatever. So come on, who is he? What's his name?'

'The name's a bit unfortunate,' she says. 'You mustn't laugh.'

'I promise,' I say. 'I'm dead good with dodgy Christian names. I have to be with mine.' I feel her flinch when I say this.

'There's nothing whatsoever wrong with your name,' she says. 'Jenny Robinson called her daughter . . .'

'Primrose. Yes, I know.'

'So think yourself lucky.'

'I think I prefer Primrose,' I mutter. 'But anyway, that's not the subject here. So what's his name?'

'Saddam,' she says.

'Saddam?' I repeat, my voice as flat as I can manage. I turn away and blow silently through pursed lips as I restrain my smirk. 'OK,' I say. 'Well, that's a good strong name if ever I heard one. He doesn't have a big straggly beard, does he?'

'I knew you'd find the whole thing terribly amusing.'

'Oh, Mum, it's just a name. I mean, obviously, it's a bit funny. You don't meet a lot of Saddams do you . . . But it's fine. What's he like?'

'What do you mean, what's he like?'

'OK . . . What does he look like? Hopefully not like *the* Saddam.'

'You know what he looks like.'

'Do I?'

'I just showed you. He was in most of the photos.'

I frown and attempt to run the images through my mind's eye. 'I think I must have missed him,' I say. *Unless he looks like an old woman or a teenage boy*, I think.

'He was the guide,' she says.

I freeze. I unlink my arm from hers and turn to face her. This involves leaving the protection of the umbrella. 'You had a fling with the boy *in the photo*?'

'He's not a boy,' she says.

'The twenty-three-year-old, then,' I say.

'Yes, dear.'

I swallow with difficulty. I open my mouth to speak, and then, when words fail me, I close it again.

'You see,' she says. 'I knew you'd find it all terribly funny.'

But I don't. I don't find it funny at all. In fact I feel like my lunch is about to come back up. 'But he's . . . he's twenty-three,' I say.

'I know. *I* just told *you* that.'

'You had a fling with a twenty-three-year-old.'

'I did not have a fling with him. Will you stop saying that?'

I frown at her. 'Oh! So you *didn't*?' I say. 'Oh, thank God for that. I was getting completely the wrong end of the—'

'It wasn't just a fling,' she says. 'That's what I mean. It's an ongoing thing.'

I nod, and then shake my head, and then nod again. 'An ongoing thing . . .' I repeat, finally. 'So you're hoping to see him again next year? Is that what you mean?'

'Not at all, dear,' she says. 'He's coming to Camberley at the end of the month.'

On Any Other Day

The force of the rain is such that, though I have no desire whatsoever for physical proximity with my mother, I am quickly forced to return beneath the umbrella.

As we head back towards the entrance to the park (apparently there is an unspoken agreement that our lunch date is now over) I try to remain unemotional – I try to limit myself to logical, practical objections. 'But what can you possibly have in common with a twenty-three-year-old Moroccan?' I venture.

'We make each other laugh,' my mother offers, with a shrug. 'We have a good sex life. What more is there?'

'And how do you know he isn't just after your money? I mean, you said the Moroccans aren't exactly rich, right?'

'Well if he *is* after my money, he won't be getting it. So it's a bit of a non-issue, as far as I can see.'

But the truth of the matter is that my reactions aren't logical. They are visceral, and, as time passes, increasingly hysterical. I am struggling desperately to control them, to understand them, to catalogue them, because I sense that otherwise this discussion will spiral *waaay* out of control.

I'm feeling disgusted that my mother feels she can replace my beautiful clever father with a stupid twenty-year-old Moroccan boy. My brain is clever enough to divide itself into chunks, and the logical bit is informing me that this specific reaction is an absurd cliché, and as such should simply be ignored. Virtually all children, it says, feel this jealous repulsion about their parent's new partners, no matter *how* suitable they are.

Next on the list is that I'm feeling genuinely worried about my mother's mental well-being. As I listen to her rambling on about how helpful Saddam is, and about all the beautiful places he took her to around Agadir – places she would never have seen otherwise – I can only think that she has lost her grip on reality. The guy is a *tourist guide*, for Christ's sake. He is *paid* to be helpful and to show people around. It's like falling in love with the dry-cleaner because he's good at dry-cleaning.

But the biggest sensation of all is one of overriding physical disgust, and it's this that I'm having the most trouble containing. I'm trying to understand where it comes from, trying to see if it comes from jealousy, or religion, or logic, or prejudice, but in the end I can neither understand it, nor mask it.

'It just, somehow ... it doesn't seem right,' I say.

'It doesn't seem right,' my mother repeats flatly.

'It seems *wrong* then,' I say.

'Wrong?'

'He's young enough to be ... well, he's almost too young to be your son. He's young enough to be *my* son,' I say.

'Only he isn't your son.'

'Well, no, of course he isn't. But he could be.'

'That makes no sense and you know it,' my mother says, her tone increasingly terse. 'Anyway, he's too old. You would have to have had him at sixteen. And we're hardly that kind of family.'

'No,' I say. 'You're right. We're not the kind of family that has children at sixteen because that would be wrong. And going out with someone forty-four years younger than you is wrong too.'

'Having sex at sixteen, or fifteen or whatever is illegal. It's hardly the same.'

'I can see that,' I say. 'Honestly. I can. But, I don't know ...'

'What's your point then?'

'My point is that I'm worried about you.'

'Well don't be.'

'And I feel sick. This thing ... It ... I don't know. I'm sorry, Mum.'

'Sick?'

'OK, look. So where do *you* draw the line? I mean, if you were a hundred and you were dating, say, an eighteen-year-old. Would that be OK?'

My mother sighs deeply. 'This is pointless. I'm not a hundred.'

'But if you were. Would that be OK?'

'I suppose. If it was what we both wanted.'

I shake my head. I'm about to say that surely there has to be a line, an actual physical, non-negotiable line. But then I remember Charles saying it and putting my gay friends on the wrong side of it.

'I honestly never thought you would be so "*square*" about it,' my mother says, surrounding the word 'square' with visual quotes.

This comment momentarily takes my breath away. Being called 'square' by my sixty-seven-year-old mother from Camberley is a new event in my life. 'Look, I think I need to go home,' I finally say. 'I'm sorry. I . . . I don't know what to think. And I don't want to say what I *do* think until I've thought about it. If that makes any sense.'

'Why, what do you think?'

'I don't . . . please . . .'

'No, come on. It's not like you to hold back.'

I unlink my arm from hers. I can't think what to say to the woman. Or rather, the only word I can think of is one that will go down like a neutron bomb. 'Really. I don't want to . . .'

'You've said everything else.'

'OK, look. I know it isn't, technically . . . But it seems like . . .'

I swallow hard. My mother opens the palm of her hand as if to say, 'And?'

'No,' I say. 'No. This isn't a good idea. Let's just, let's go our separate ways for today and, we'll talk in a while.'

My mother shakes her head in apparent despair, then shrugs and opens her arms. We hug rigidly and then I turn and start to walk briskly to the gate, leaving my umbrella with her. I have no idea how she feels about my reaction. I don't seem to have the space in my brain to work it out.

The rain is harder now, but I don't put my hood up. The cold droplets lashing my face feel good.

Just as I pass through the gate, I glance back and see Mum still standing on the same spot watching me go. My guess is that she might be in tears, but I just give her a tiny wave and then vanish from view.

I feel sorry for her. She seems so happy about it all. I honestly don't want to ruin that for her. But if I had stayed one moment longer I would have said the word that was on the tip of my tongue. I would have told her that her relationship with a twenty-three-year-old may not technically be wrong, but that it feels, to me at least, like paedophilia. That's the word I would have used.

The call of the pub at Kew station is too much to resist. I feel trembly with pent-up emotion and so, for only the third time in my life, I head for the bar and order a double whisky. Around me, the pub is stuffed with families tucking into Sunday roasts.

I don't even like whisky, and I totally hate going to pubs on my own, but this is ritual, and in such situations, ritual is useful. My father – who rarely drank otherwise – always greeted any good news with a pint of Guinness and any bad news with a '*stiff whisky.*' When things happen that are so big you don't know what to do next, ritual, I find, is usually your best bet.

As I watch the barman pour the double measure, I think about the irony that my mother's new love interest is up there with Waiine's death and receiving my divorce papers. On my personal Richter scale of life events, this fits into the top three.

I don't know why downing this glass of burning liquid helps, but somehow it does. The scorching sensation at least makes me aware of my body again, which takes me out of my brain for a few seconds. I fish for my purse to pay the barman and momentarily consider ordering a repeat. But the thought that he will think me an alcoholic quashes that idea.

Apparently a double whisky is international sign language, for the man beside me at the bar says, in a thick French accent, 'Bad day, yes?'

I turn and look at him blankly. 'Yes,' I say, quietly. 'Yes, I suppose so.'

His expression – scrunched eyebrows, tight-lipped smile – perfectly expresses brotherly concern. 'You want to talk?' he asks.

I restrain a sigh. I try to look at him objectively. Though I can see that he's cute and well-dressed, and French (which despite everything, I rather like), the sad truth is that my brain is just in too much of a swirl to care about him today. I shake my head. 'Thanks, but no,' I say.

He nods thoughtfully. 'OK, I understand,' he says. 'No problem.'

I give him a similar tight-lipped smile to his own, and knock back the remains of my whisky.

'Another?' he asks.

I turn back to face him and he nods at my now-empty glass.

I wrinkle my nose. 'Thanks,' I say. 'You're very sweet. But I have to go home now.'

He looks thoroughly forlorn as I turn and head for the door. Poor guy. On any other day he would have been in luck.

On any other day, *I* might have been in luck.

But of course on any other day I wouldn't have been at The Railway in Kew in the first place. Such are the complex webs of chance and missed opportunity that Lady Luck weaves around our lives.

As I negotiate the Underground, I'm glad I didn't have the second whisky, because travelling slightly drunk at midday on the Tube is a strange and unnerving experience. Everything feels a little unreal, as if I'm watching a pop video with blurred visual effects and over-saturated colours.

When I finally get home, I sit at my kitchen table and stare out at the Leylandii and the rain and nurse a cup of tea, and think about my mother, and Brian, and Ronan, and Waiine and the French guy in the pub.

I seem to have been sitting at this table for years, and amazingly, nothing ever really seems to change. Summer, winter, now spring again . . . and here I sit, alone. Even the Leylandii seems to change faster than my life. Even the Leylandii is growing and broadening its horizons. That tree! It's like an inverse barometer of my life – as it constantly gets bigger and stronger my life inexorably shrinks into greyness.

I can't help but wonder if the problem is with Lady Luck – providing inappropriate opportunities at the right time, or appropriate opportunities at the wrong time, and no opportunities most of the time – or if the problem is with me. Would someone else be able to take my life and seize these moments and mould it into something different? Or am I destined to sit and wait for . . . well, for destiny, I suppose? Because it certainly feels like I do my best. And looking at the results – looking at the difference between where I am and where I want to be – I can only acknowledge that my best just doesn't seem to be good enough to get me there.

Still, surely something will change soon, won't it?

PART TWO

Autumn Blues

I sit and eat my yogurt and flip between flicking through the *Guardian* and staring out at the garden. I watch a red autumn leaf from a distant tree drift through the air and land in the lower branches of the Leylandii. Proper English trees at least have the respect to shed their leaves and let the winter light in.

But I can't complain, it's a beautiful day today – the weather people are calling it an *'Indian Summer.'* I sip my morning coffee and think that I really should get out and make the most of the weekend. As the red leaf warns: winter will be with us soon enough. If only I could bottle a little of this sunshine up and open it in January, like jam.

I hear the metallic clack of the letterbox and drag myself from my reveries to the front door where I scoop up the letters. I know it's weird, but I love getting post, even if it *is* only bills. Today provides the usual collection – Visa statements and electricity bills – plus one. A hand-written, purple envelope, which, on opening, turns out to be an invitation to Mark and Ian's housewarming in Tower Hamlets. Confirmation, if any were needed, that other people's lives really do move on. And proof that mine is about to become challengingly worse. For winter, single in this flat, without my old ally Mark living upstairs, is frankly a thought that terrifies me.

Still, I think, struggling to find the bright side, at least it shows that anything is possible. For this time a year ago, Mark would never have imagined such a happy outcome.

And at least the envelope isn't from my mother . . . for a fleeting moment I had feared that it could be an invitation to a wedding. Not that she has mentioned any plans to marry Saddam, in her 'e' mails – she always writes *email* as *'e' mail*.

But apart from these regular 'e' mails about how much Saddam has been enjoying Camberley, the only actual conversation we have had since Kew has been a single phone call. A single phone call that degenerated, almost immediately, into an argument.

She had called to ask if I had any idea how to buy a goat over the internet. She wanted, she said, to buy Saddam's mother a useful gift, and he had indicated that a goat would be most appreciated. With my usual tact, I told Mum that this was the most ridiculous thing I had ever heard and she proceeded to hang up on me. Well. A goat!

Anyway, this argument was entirely my fault, because I myself had told her, she now claims, that you can buy truly *anything* online these days.

So, no ... No marriage plans as yet ... but, well, how can I put it? Nothing she could come up with would surprise me these days. Once your mum starts dating a Moroccan adolescent, you have to get ready for anything really.

I finger Mark's invitation ... it's set for the eighteenth of October which also happens to be Darren's birthday. I'm pretty sure that Mark will have chosen this date out of kindness, but it crosses my mind that Darren – being as sensitive as I am about being single – might well feel that he is having his nose rubbed in Mark and Ian's happiness.

Still, perhaps by then Darren too will have a new boyfriend. Maybe this one will even be the right one. Maybe even *I* will have met someone by October. Maybe pigs will fly.

Mark once told me about Mona's Law, which he had seen in a film, or read in a book – I can't remember which. Anyway, Mona's Law apparently states that everyone wants three things – that happiness is made up of a three-piece jigsaw: a good relationship, a nice place to live, and a good job. And Mona's law states that it is mathematically impossible to maintain more than two out of the three. Thus, if you have a good job and a nice flat and you meet a lovely guy, bam – you lose your job. So you change jobs and find the perfect undreamt-of work opportunity, and wham, your landlord kicks you out on the street. I reckon that these days I'm *due* for a shake-up. Yes, I still love my flat, even though it's now darker than Stockholm in January. And my job is perfect, especially now I am working regularly with lovely Tom on the New York Grunge! campaign. But the truth is that I would happily live in a tent and eat out of dustbins if I could find The Missing Boyfriend.

But how to shake it up? Should I quit my job? Should I sell the flat? For as far as I recall, Mona's law never said that it's impossible to lose *all three* bits of the jigsaw. It's clear though that I have to do something, or I shall end up sixty years old, still wondering when things are going to change of their own accord.

I imagine this for a moment. In my mind's eye I'm wearing a pinny like Mrs P's, and her Leylandii has broken, Triffid-like, through my kitchen windows.

Even my mother says that it's mad that I don't have a boyfriend. But that, sadly, doesn't provide any solutions. I laugh ironically, and stand and shake my head. 'Enough!' I say out loud. As long as there's sunshine outside, I still have the force to shake it off.

I shower and dress in my new G-Star jeans and French Connection top (the advantage of a late summer – all the summer clothes are on sale!) and head out of the door determined that by the end of the day my head will be in a better place than it is now.

I kick my way through the ochre leaves as far as Camden market, and linger long enough to buy some organic goat's cheese and some tiny but incredibly tasty Niçois olives.

I continue as far as the High Street and head for Waterstone's. A deckchair in the garden, a good summer read, olives, a glass of rosé . . . that's a plan. Three days of sunshine and we all want to live like Mediterraneans.

I drift inexorably to the *Self-Help* section. This, I note, has been halved in size to provide space for their ever-burgeoning collection of *Personal Pain Memoirs*. Glancing over my shoulder to make sure that no one is watching, I pick a few of these up:

Don't Tell Mummy: a shocking tale of sexual abuse. Betrayed. Ugly. It strikes me that situating the Personal Pain Memoirs next to Self-Help isn't entirely accidental. Presumably when one is fed up with drowning in sorrow, one moves onto healing strategies. Or perhaps it's the other way around. Maybe once one has tried all the healing strategies and they have all failed, the only succour left is to read about other people's misery. Whichever way it works, I don't need anyone else's *Personal Pain* right now. I choose hope instead.

I proudly leave the store with a novel: *The Blue Bistro* (A Light, Fun and Intoxicating Summer Read), and *Depression – Be Gone!*

The Ups and Downs
of Self-Help

When I get back to the house, I'm pleasantly surprised to discover a strip of sunlight shining on the mossy remains of my once-vibrant lawn.

The patch of sunlight is only an inch wider than my deck chair, necessitating constant and precise solar-tracking manoeuvres. But a patch of sunlight is not to be sneezed at, especially when trying to create Mediterranean ambiences in London in September.

I put on shorts and a tacky old halter-top and lounge back on my stolen Regent's Park deck-chair with my stunningly pink bottle of Coteaux d'Aix, half a pound of cubed goat's cheese and my tiny but incredibly tasty olives. The deck-chair, I hasten to add, was not stolen by me – I don't, as Mum would say, come from that kind of family. The previous owner of the flat luckily did though.

I read the back cover and reviews of *The Blue Bistro* again and then start to speed-read *Depression: Be Gone!*

I don't really know how to speed read, but I have read so many of these books, I can pretty much skim the fluff. In a nutshell, you just look for anything with italics or bullet points.

I quickly learn that depression is caused by *unchallenged* mental untruths which fall into three major categories:

• Feelings of unworthiness
• Feelings of hopelessness
• Feelings of entrapment

As none of these really ring my bell, I choose the closest – *Feelings of entrapment* – and start to mentally list all the things that seem wrong with my life that I can't work out how to change. I'm supposed to do this exercise with pen and paper but paralysed by either the rosé or perhaps by my *latent depression*, I simply can't be bothered to go inside to fetch either.

So my problem areas are: not having a boyfriend, not wanting to spend my whole life in London and not wanting to spend my life in advertising (selling things to people who don't need them, as some arsehole once told me).

Three seconds' thought produces three problems. And this is the snag with depression: feeling bloody miserable leaves you feeling bloody miserable about *all* of the areas of your life.

The book says that I have to verify whether what I have written is *True* – and delete any situations which would be *acceptable*, were all the other things in the list OK.

So, number one: the lack of a boyfriend.

Problem? Yes. It's a problem. No discussion required.

Number two: London.

London's OK, if I'm being fair. I have quite a bit of fun because I live where I do. It's just that it's all somehow a bit superficial – what's *right* about London is all razzle and glitter. There's no sense of feeling centred or fulfilled in my day-to-day existence. It doesn't satisfy the *Earth Mother* in me.

At least I love my flat. Though even this, I have to admit, I am liking less now the Leylandii has turned it into a Siberian salt mine. And now that Mark is moving out.

So, on to number three: Advertising.

Advertising is the perfect way for me to earn a living within the life that I have *now*. It's a problem only when placed in the context of everything *else* I want. I'm good at it, and it pays the bills with ease. It's just that were I able to change that life for something better – say a husband and a child and The Good Life then everything that advertising represents would become an absurdity.

I sigh and slosh another quarter-bottle of rosé into my glass.

As ever, the whole equation just seems too complicated for my brain, for everything depends on everything else. My life, as set up, meshes perfectly with itself. But I have to change it. And to change any of it, I have to change all of it. And even trying to think how to begin that process makes me feel like I'm drowning.

I'm fed up with being single, fed up with being a consumer, fed up with being the resident fag hag for my gay friends and being left in the corner as soon as a man comes along. I want a child – no, *need* a child. Since the abortion I carry an emptiness around with me everywhere I go – a physical sensation of loss, that I think, hope, *know* only a baby would fill. My brother and father are dead. My mother is turning into a paedophile.

Jesus, I think. *How many REAL problems do you want?*

And so I close *Depression – Be Gone!*

Muttering, 'Depression – Be Gone! Be Gone!!' I hurl it across the garden.

Listing my feelings of entrapment has not liberated me from them. It has simply produced a whole swathe of *feelings of hopelessness*. I expect that there's another step to this process – I'm sure listing my problems was just the first stage. But sadly, right now, I just don't have the willpower for any more self-help. I barely have the energy to slosh more wine into my glass. But of course I just about manage that.

The patch of sunlight reaches the point where I can no longer sit in it (without sitting on my rose bushes) at exactly the same moment my bottle of rosé finally expires.

I scoop up my depressing book on depression and move to the lounge. Phase one has left me feeling quite dreadful.

I take a deep breath. Let's hope phase two – *Acknowledging Your Personal Power* – is more uplifting.

For each of the *real* problem areas I must now define my unsatisfactory *start point A*, an attractive *palatable outcome B*, and specific *feasible steps* to get from *A* to *B*.

As the phone pad and pen are now beside me, I really have no excuse for not doing this properly, so I write down:

A. Start point: Missing Boyfriend. B. End point : Non-missing Boyfriend.

Steps required: Find Missing Boyfriend.

Even after a bottle of rosé, this doesn't strike me as particularly constructive, but, as far as my in-depth skimming can tell, the book is a bit lightweight on actual solutions to real problems.

I shrug and try another one.

A. Start point: London. B. End point: farm.

Steps required: Sell flat. Buy farm.

It's at this point that I wonder, through my rosé haze, if maybe the book isn't onto something after all. Because I suddenly feel better.

I close the book – with respect and a little awe this time – and fetch the laptop from the kitchen.

I Google, *estate agents, farm cottage, Devon,* and after a few random clicks I am drooling over a grey stone cottage with roses around the door set in ten acres of farmland just outside Bristol. It's priced at about fifty thousand pounds less than the value of my flat. It would be so easy to set it all in motion that, momentarily, I feel quite buoyant.

But of course, every image I project of myself standing in the rose-bordered doorway requires a bloke standing beside me, or, more to the point, a bloke holding a spade, ready to dig the vegetable patch.

A bloke whose face I can't picture because *he doesn't bloody exist.*

Which pretty much brings me back to square one.

For:

- Having a baby – requires a boyfriend.
- Moving to isolated country cottage – requires a boyfriend.
- Finding a boyfriend – requires a boyfriend.

I'm not asking for the Earth here, am I?

I mean, he doesn't have to be rich, or famous, or look like, say,

Jamie Thexton . . . Hum. Now there's a thought.

Jamie Thexton does the ecology programme on Five. I wonder if he's single. He'd be perfect because he's cute and fit and beardless and knows how to grow perfectly formed veg, *and* shoot, pluck and cook a pheasant. I would probably have to convince him to ditch the dreadlocks, but, well, with time, that's feasible. If not, maybe I could even get used to them. We all have to make sacrifices.

He's probably a bit young for me in fact – he must be early thirties. Thinking about the age thing makes me think of my mother.

It's weird really, because when I was in my twenties my ideal men were thirty-year-olds. And when I was in my thirties, my ideal men were thirty-year-olds. And now I'm nearly in my forties, my ideal man is Jamie Thexton.

I Google him. The photos show that he's as gorgeous as ever.

Wikipedia reveals that he was born in 1983. Twenty-six. Ouch! I wonder briefly if paedophilia is an inherited tendency.

Jamie Thexton apparently lives in a three-thousand-foot, glass-walled loft in London's Docklands. And amazingly, he lives there with our very own, anorexic supermodel, Angelica Wayne. So much for The Good Life!

Reading on I learn that he has his own fully equipped gym within the apartment.

And there was I imagining that those muscles came from digging.

A Mug's Game

On Sunday morning when I wake up, our Indian Summer is clearly over. It is grey and rainy, yet still muggy and hot. Then again, maybe that is exactly what an Indian Summer is like. What would *I* know?

I have a vague headache this morning and feel heavy and bloated and tired. It could just be a hangover, but because I finished drinking nearly twenty hours ago, and because my period is also four days overdue (for the second time), I'm left wondering if there isn't something else going on. Surely Lady Luck wouldn't be so evil as to dump premature menopause on me along with everything else. Would she?

This reminds me that I need to phone Sarah-Jane and see how she's doing on her new hormone therapy.

Because I read in a beauty magazine (when I was nineteen) that it helps un-bloat pre-menstrual women, I drink a cup of disgusting green tea.

It has never once worked for me, but you have to live in hope.

Just before three, Darren appears on my doorstep.

'Sorry, but do you know where Mark is?' he asks the second I open the door. 'Only I'm supposed to be helping him with boxes and he's not in.'

'Hello,' I say. 'I'm another person in the world.'

Darren frowns at me and then, bless him, blushes brightly. 'Sorry. Hello, CC,' he says. 'Too much coffee and not enough sleep.'

I nod sideways inviting him in and head through to the

kitchen. '*Coffee* . . .' I say. 'Are you sure that's all?'

'For once, yes,' he says.

'So you don't *want* a coffee, I take it?' I say, gesturing at the kettle.

'Tea might be good,' Darren replies.

'And no, I have no idea where Mark is. Is he really moving today?'

'Just the boxes,' Darren says. 'The furniture goes next weekend, I think.'

I grimace. 'The end of an era,' I say. 'He's been upstairs for five years. God knows who will move in next.'

Darren tries Mark's mobile again and this time gets an answer. As Mark tells him that they are on their way, I make tea and suggest we move to the lounge. 'I can't stand how dark it is in here,' I tell Darren.

'It's that tree,' he comments, nodding out the window. 'You should poison it.'

'I know,' I say. 'If only I could.'

'Do it!'

'But she'd be able to tell, wouldn't she?'

Darren pouts and shakes his head. 'My mum did it all the time in our old place. All the trees were listed so we weren't allowed to cut them down, but Mum wanted a vegetable patch. She just sprayed five litres of Roundup on each one – at night – and then claimed ignorance when the poor things withered and died. They sent a guy from the council and even he had no idea. He said it was probably because of Chernobyl.'

'It's certainly an idea,' I say. 'That is, Roundup, not Chernobyl . . . Because the lack of light is really doing my head in and the old hag won't even discuss pruning it.'

'Just say the word and it's done,' Darren says.

'*The word,*' I laugh, handing Darren his cup.

Darren rolls his eyes at me and shakes his head.

Once we are seated in the lounge, it takes a moment for the conversation to restart. For some reason things have always been a little awkward between Darren and me when we're alone. It's probably because Darren is more junior at Spot On. I expect he feels he has to watch his words.

'Crazy weather,' he says, finally – the great British fallback subject. 'It was lovely yesterday.'

'I know,' I say. 'I spent the afternoon getting sozzled on rosé and pretending I was in Cannes.'

'Nice one,' Darren says.

'And you?'

'Me?'

'Yes, what did *you* do with our brief Indian Summer?'

Darren blushes again and stares down at his tea. 'I don't think you want to know what I got up to.'

I frown. 'Well, I *didn't*,' I say. 'But I sure do now.'

Darren snorts. 'You remember Ricardo?' he asks. 'Ricardo Escobar?'

'How could I ever forget?' I laugh.

'Well yesterday he gave me that photo I wanted.'

'He gave it to you?'

Darren licks his lips and shrugs and blushes again. 'I had to, erm, model for him.'

'Model.'

'Yeah,' he says. 'He wanted to paint me.'

'How flattering,' I say. 'In the nude, I suppose.'

Darren smirks. 'Not exactly,' he says. 'He wanted me in one of those doggy outfits.'

I bite my top lip and stifle a grin. 'No! You're having me on!'

'He's a bit weird, I think. Well, I know he is.'

'Yes. A bit of an understatement really. So you had to wear one of those scary masks?'

'Yeah, and a collar. And a leash. He tied the end to the bottom of the stairs and then spent five hours painting me. He did three canvases. They were pretty good actually.'

'Five hours? Wow. And afterwards?'

Darren shrugs. 'Nothing. I was almost disappointed. He's not really my type, but by the time it was over the truth is that I was feeling quite up for it.'

'He told me that he had to be frustrated to create. Now we know what he means.'

'Yeah. He's weird, because he's not really very sexual in the end.'

'But I would have thought that once he'd finished painting . . . I mean . . . if you were both willing.'

Darren shrugs again. 'Well, no . . . Nada. Still, I got my photo. I put it over the fireplace. It looks stunning.'

'I bet,' I say. 'Was it the one you wanted?'

'Yeah, the one with the shiny padlock.'

'That was for sale for a couple of thousand, wasn't it?'

'Five. Five grand.'

'A grand per hour. That's a good rate.'

'Well exactly. Though, of course with art . . . I mean, it didn't sell, so . . . I suppose it's hard to say what it's worth really. In a way it's just a framed photo. But I love it.'

'And you'll be the star of Ricardo's next pervy exhibition.'

'Yeah. Maybe. Only unrecognisable, of course.'

'Of course. The mask.'

'I suppose you think I'm a perv,' Darren says.

I shake my head. 'Not really. I suppose the art aspect makes it more . . . acceptable, somehow. No, I think you're quite brave. I wish I could be more like you.'

'What, you fancy being tethered at—'

'No,' I interrupt, laughing. 'No, I just mean, well, if I could be a bit more easy come, easy go . . . about sex, in particular.'

'Well, we'd all like to be a bit more easy come, easy go,' he says.

I frown at this. For the life of me, I can't see how anyone could be more relaxed about sex than Darren. But, because it would seem rude to say so, I just nod, and cross the room to look out at the street. In the distance I hear rolling thunder.

'Storm,' we both say, at exactly the same moment.

'I thought we had one coming,' Darren adds.

'I love a good storm.'

'Me too,' he agrees. 'Makes me horny. Actually most things

make me horny. Anyway. What are you reading?' He picks up *The Blue Bistro,* revealing my copy of *Depression – Be Gone!* beneath. 'Oh,' he says.

'Yes, Oh!' I laugh.

'That's shite. The only ones that are any good are the ones based on CBT.'

'CBT?'

'Cognitive Behavioural Therapy,' Darren says. 'You know that CBT also stands for . . .'

'Yes?'

'Never mind. But the CBT ones are quite useful. This one just made me feel worse though.'

'Me too,' I say. 'Though I have to admit, I only really skimmed it.'

'Don't bother with it,' Darren says. 'I'll bring you some CBT books on Monday if you want.'

'You never struck me as the self-help type,' I comment.

'Nor you.'

'I suppose not. I'm just trying to work out how to reorganise my life really.'

'Reorganise it?'

I shrug. 'Everything really. That's the problem. I kind of just feel that I have done this whole scene now. London, and jetting to New York, and . . . I want something different now. I want a farm and a veg patch, and some kids.'

'The Good Life?'

'Exactly.'

'You should go for it. According to the telly the world is about to end anyway. Once all the banks have vanished and all the shops have closed, the only survivors will be people who grow their own veg.'

'Yeah. A little bleak, but . . .'

'My problem is that I don't know *what* I want.'

'You don't fancy goats and chickens then?'

'Oh no. I can't think of anything worse. But I understand why someone else might.'

'But I don't want to do it on my own,' I tell him. 'That's my problem. I mean, a farm on Exmoor, yes. A farm on Exmoor on my own, no way.'

Darren snorts. 'Honestly, you people. I had exactly this conversation with Victor.'

'What, Twinkletoes Victor?'

'Yeah. He wants to move back to France and—'

'I thought he was Spanish,' I interrupt.

'Nah, Basque. Whatever that means. I think it basically means French with a chip on the shoulder. Anyway, he was born near Perpignan, I think. And now he wants to move back, but not on his own. But as I keep pointing out, the chances of meeting someone who wants to live in France would be a little higher if he actually went and lived in France!'

'Yes, I suppose,' I say, thinking that if I was a gay man, I'd jump at the chance to move to France with a lovely guy like Victor.

'Relationships are tough enough anyway, without throwing crazy criteria like *must want to move to France* into the mix. Waiting for other people to let you live your life is a mug's game.'

'I suppose,' I say again. 'Though of course there *are* things you *need* someone else for. There are things you *can't* do on your own.'

Darren wrinkles his top lip. 'Like?'

'Like having a baby,' I say.

'You want kids too?'

I shrug. 'Maybe, but it takes two to tango.'

Darren laughs.

'What?'

'Well . . . two to tango. You should talk to Jenna about that one.'

'Your lesbian friend?'

'Yeah.'

'Well, even she needed someone else . . .' I point out. 'Even if it was only for a few seconds.'

'Sure. And a turkey baster.'

'Is that going well? The whole motherhood thing?'

'Sure. Fred is a lovely kid. He's five, I think. They moved in with Catherine, which caused some hassles.'

'I bet.'

'Not about . . . Not because she's a woman. Kids don't give a damn about that stuff. But Catherine is pretty anal. A place for everything and everything in its place. I think they both have some adjusting to do. But anyway, Jenna didn't need a man. So you see, there's always a way. If you know what you want then just seize the day, CC. Carpe diem and all that. I just wish I knew what *I* wanted.'

'Yeah.'

'A problem is never as permanent as a solution.'

'What?'

'Dunno what it means really. My mother always says it. Usually when she wants me to see a shrink and go straight.'

'It's not *yours*, is it?'

'I'm sorry?'

'The kid.'

'It?'

I pull a face. 'Sorry. I don't know why I said that,' I say. Actually, I *do* sort of know why I said that. I was thinking about my own, potential, and so far, sexless child, and whether whoever fathered Jenna's child might want to do the same for me.

Is it an option I would consider? *A problem is never as permanent as a solution.* 'Anyway, *is* he? Yours?'

Darren laughs. 'No,' he says. 'But – and don't say I said anything – but I suspect that the dad might be Mark.'

'Really?'

'Well, he and Jenna *are* really close.'

'But he never said so.'

'No. But I mentioned it once – who the father was – and he seemed funny.'

'Funny.'

'Yeah. He just sort of changed the subject.'

'Right.'

'Anyway, don't say I said anything.'

'No,' I say.

A movement outside catches my eye, and I turn to see a van parking opposite. 'Talk of the devil,' I say. 'White Van Man is here.'

All It Takes is a Plan

I throw myself at work, and with the European Grunge! campaign going live, the stateside one hitting production (some mornings I arrive to find fifty emails from Harper & Baker in my inbox) and Victoria Barclay still off, there is easily enough work for me to lose myself in it completely.

I think that the reason that Mark's law – or rather Mona's law – appears so true is that the human brain is by nature dissatisfied. Dissatisfaction is one of the defining features of being human – if it were not the case we would still be happily living in trees and eating bananas.

The way we modern apes channel our dissatisfaction is to look at our three-piece puzzle and focus all of our capacity for dissatisfaction on the least successful third of our lives until the situation becomes, or at least *appears* to become, untenable. Equally, the human brain, unable to think about more than one problem at a time, creates a rosy pretence that the other two thirds are, for now at least, just dandy. So when we're in a bad relationship we throw ourselves with relief at our jobs. It's not that the job is perfect, it's simply that we are too busy funnelling our angst at the unsatisfactory home-life to care. We need to pretend that the job and the flat are fine just to survive. Equally, the day we fall in love, the job doesn't get any worse . . . it's simply that because we no longer need it to escape the awful ex (and because we would rather stay in bed shagging) we direct our angst at the job.

Right now, I'm loving my job. It's exhausting and exciting and satisfying and massages my ego on an hourly basis. I have a half-a-million pound international ad campaign swirling around me, and so, professionally at least, I'm right there at the hub of my life.

My job digests my days, and often my evenings and half the weekend as well. By Sunday I'm too tired to do anything or think about anything else anyway. I sit and drink (too much) wine and watch (too much) TV and wait for the Monday morning juggling to recommence.

It's not that I'm missing much outside of work anyway. Sarah-Jane is cocooning with George (read: shagging for a baby) and Mark is cocooning with Ian (read: simply shagging). As for Darren, he is on a coke-fuelled man-hunt, which *also* seems to involve vast amounts of shagging, though mainly, from what Mark tells me, with absurdly inappropriate partners.

Indeed, I seem to be the only person I know who *isn't* shagging.

But it's all fine, because, as I say, my job is brilliant. My job is my saviour. My personal life can wait.

At the end of September, the European Grunge! campaign hits full steam, and suddenly there isn't much to do except watch and wait to see if it works. Indeed, we have a bet on at the office that the first person to take a street-snap of a stranger wearing carpenter pants gets a bottle of Champagne from each of the rest of us. Liking a drop of Champagne but rarely having my hefty camera with me, I even consider lending George a pair of the trousers and getting SJ to send me a photo.

On the last day of the month, the US campaign enters what we call the eye of the storm. This is the moment when the whirlwind of preparation is over and there are a few fallow weeks before the campaign launches and causes a flurry of fresh media enquiries. Being a bit of a last-minute outfit, we rarely experience this moment of spooky calm here at Spot On, but Harper & Baker's campaigns are organised with military precision, mainly by Tom, and on the first Wednesday of October, I open my email to find no messages at all. Not one.

I stare at my screen, click on 'fetch mail' a few times, and then sigh deeply. I have been dreading this moment.

Even our other accounts seem dormant right now, and when by Thursday lunchtime I have made precisely one phone call (to a printer about an unpaid bill) and received two emails (both spam messages which have slipped through the net), I can take it no longer. I head up to Peter Stanton's office.

'You might as well take a long weekend,' he tells me when I explain my problem. 'Lord knows you've done enough hours recently.'

I send a final, hopeful, email to Tom asking if there's anything I can do to help, but when even this produces only an automated reply that he is out of the office until Monday, I steel myself against the terror of an empty October weekend – an empty *long weekend*, and shut down my computer, sling my monastically silent BlackBerry in my bag, and head for the door.

It's raining gently as I step out onto Soho Square.

I retreat and linger for a moment with the smokers as I wonder where to go. I have the whole of London surrounding me. People travel the world to come to our museums and our galleries – surely I'm not going to just go home and sit at the kitchen table. Am I?

Surely I'm going to go and visit the Tate Modern, or the National Portrait Gallery, or the V&A . . . Aren't I? On my own, all of these options just strike me as depressing.

What *is* this inability to take joy in doing things on my own, I wonder. Isn't that what they call co-dependency? I nod, suddenly decided, and head off towards Foyles. A book on co-dependency is clearly what's required.

It turns out that whatever I am suffering from isn't co-dependency. Co-dependency is another pleasure reserved for people in relationships.

Instead I pick up a copy of the best-selling *Single Blues: Beat them from the get-go*, and another: *Living Life Lightly: a guide to creating joy in your life*. I hesitate over *Living Life Lightly* because, ironically, the book (a hardcover) is so heavy I'm not sure I can be bothered lugging it around. But in the end, the bullet points all seem suitably uplifting to make the effort worthwhile.

Then, still not wanting to face my kitchen, I stop off at Nero's for a cappuccino. Sitting in Nero's with a copy of *Single Blues* on the table is a bit like walking around with a sandwich board marked '*I'm available. Please chat me up.*' At any rate, I hope it is.

I'm Available, Please Chat Me Up suddenly strikes me as a brilliant idea for a book. I reckon millions of single women would buy copies. It would be the ultimate dating aid. Maybe *I* should write it.

I decide, on further reflection, that advertising that I have the blues probably isn't the nub of a good campaign, so I hide *Single Blues* beneath *Living Life Lightly: a guide to creating joy in your life*. Figuring that advertising my need for joy isn't going to do much better, and noting that the only single guy in the place has a crazy Bin-Laden beard anyway, I give up and put both books back in my bag and resign myself to the non-judgemental sanctuary of home.

It's five when I get in. I dump my bag on the table and look around the kitchen. Winter is closing in and it's already pitch-black outside.

This was a bad decision. I don't think I can bear to spend the next hour in my flat, let alone the next three days. I need a plan.

Perhaps I should accept the invitation to help Mark and Ian paint their kitchen. I wrinkle my nose and look around. I haven't painted anywhere since Brian and I painted this room, and that was five years ago, and I didn't enjoy it much then.

And then I smile. Bugger Mark's walls! I'm going to paint *my* kitchen.

I remove the books from my bag and swipe my keys from the table.

Amazing how quickly emotions can swing from one extreme to the other. I suddenly feel energetic and elated.

All it takes is a plan.

• • •

It takes most of Friday for me to wash the walls, move the furniture out, and to tape plastic sheeting around the kitchen cabinets. I have a fleeting moment of despair when I realise that I can't manoeuvre the table out of the kitchen on my own, but then the postman unsuspectingly asks me to take in a parcel for Mark so I co-opt him into helping me with the table.

On Saturday the first coat takes considerably less time than I had hoped, but even this works out fine. The smell of paint drives me from the house and, at a loss for anything better to do, I simply go to the cinema. *Vicky Cristina Barcelona*, the latest Woody Allen film, does just the trick: it demonstrates that people in relationships are as miserable as I am.

By the time Sunday evening comes, my kitchen is looking positively perky.

To reward myself and to find a fresh victim for table-moving duties, I order a pizza from Domino's. The delivery guy is the usual spotty adolescent, but he eventually agrees (on hearing my offer of a five quid tip) to help me move the table back where it came from.

It's only once I have eaten my pizza and downed a third of a bottle of Chardonnay (my first drink for three days) that my carefully constructed optimism finally starts to disintegrate. For how much nicer it would be to have a boyfriend to help move tables! How much nicer to have a man to share the wine! How much nicer to have my boyfriend drop in unexpectedly and congratulate me on my stunning handiwork!

Just as I am wavering over whether to drink the rest of the bottle and collapse into a satisfying state of misery or put the bottle away and heroically resist, my period starts. I have to run, knock-kneed to the bathroom. I'm now nearly a week late so the relief is stunning.

I don't get that irritable with PMT, thank God, but when the dam finally breaks, there is always a weird moment of clarity – a fleeting instant of comprehension – in which I realise that at least fifty per cent of whatever emotional state I was in *was* caused by PMT after all.

A wave of calm rolls over me. Within minutes, I feel centred, composed and thoroughly relaxed: at one with everything and everyone – even with the rain outside. Even with Mrs Pilchard. Even, dare I say it, with her Leylandii.

By ten I'm tucked up in bed with *Living Life Lightly*, trying to concentrate on exercise one.

Thoughts, the book says, *become reality*. Exercise A is simply to force oneself to imagine the outcomes one desires in life.

It takes me quite a few attempts to create a mental picture of a brown-eyed man who is neither alcoholic, nor balloon fetishist, nor bastard, but in the end I manage it.

By the time I drift off to sleep, I am daydreaming, and then suddenly *dreaming*, of a man and a baby and a big farm kitchen. A big farm kitchen with freshly painted walls.

What a Waste

On Monday morning, the post-apocalyptic silence of the office continues and I wonder for the first time if there is something more to this than the usual lull of the project cycle. There doesn't, after all, seem to be much new work coming in either . . . Perhaps the doomsayers have it right. Perhaps it is going to be the eighties all over again.

The open-plan floor I work on is so quiet that people are whispering to each other. A couple of times, I pick up the phone just to check that it is still working.

At ten, out of sheer boredom, I phone Sarah-Jane.

'Hello, dear, how are you?' she says.

'Bored. It's like a morgue here. No emails, no calls . . . it's bizarre.'

'You're the only person I know who says *bizarre*,' she comments. 'It's the same here, by the way.'

'What, bizarre?'

'Yeah, scary. They reckon recessions hit charities really badly too.'

'Do you really think it's going to be that bad?'

'Do you *have* a telly?'

'Well, yeah, but I only really watch *Desperate Housewives*. And *The Apprentice*. And *Dragon's Den*. Everything else is too depressing.'

'Well the stock market crashed again this morning, and another bank almost folded too.'

'Another American one?'

'Yeah, Bear Sterns or something.'

'God, it makes you wonder.'

'George is busy moving our savings into as many banks as possible, just in case.'

'The *Guardian* said that the Nationwide is really safe. I don't remember why, but that's what they said.'

'I'll tell George. Though he probably knows already. He's pretty up on these things.'

'Anyway, how are you?'

'Bored too.' I hear her yawn as she says this.

'So how's the treatment going?'

'Good. I've been regular as clockwork since June. I'd rather be preggers, but at least the pills seem to be doing something.'

'And how are you coping with all the shagging?' I laugh. 'Must be awful.'

'Actually, we're limited to twice a week. Sundays and Wednesdays. Produces better sperm or something.'

'I didn't know sperm knew about days of the week.'

'Nah, you dap. But every three days is best, they reckon.'

'I'm aiming for every three years myself.'

'You must be due then.'

'I am. Talking of due . . . my own have been a bit hit and miss lately.'

'Could be just stress and stuff. *How* hit and miss?'

'Four days last month and then . . .'

'Four days is OK.'

'Yeah, but I'm usually regular as the atomic clock. And this month I was a whole week late. I felt like a whale by the time it finally happened.'

'God, I hate that. But you should get it checked out.'

'Yeah, if it continues.'

'Well, it's up to you. But I wouldn't hang about if I was you. Not at our age.'

'Right. Thanks for that.'

'You want Doctor Yinkchovsky's number.'

'Yinkchovsky? What sort of a name is that?'

'Dunno. He looks sort of Latino.'

'Sounds more Russian.'

'That's what I thought.'

'This is the sexy one, right?'

'Yeah. He's drop dead gorge.'

'I think I'll wait,' I say. 'Anyway, I prefer to see a woman.'

'OK, but get it checked.'

That evening, on the Underground, I see my first public pair of carpenter pants. As soon as I surface, I phone Mark to tell him.

'You're too late,' he says. 'Jude just emailed me a photo of two guys wearing them in Comptons.'

'Comptons? That sounds like a set-up.'

'I know,' Mark says. 'But he swears it's legit.'

As he says this, my BlackBerry beeps to tell me that I too have received the email.

'God, if I'd had a camera-phone I could have beaten him,' I complain, peering at the photo. 'I need a new Blackberry.'

'You need an iPhone, sweety,' Mark says. 'BlackBerries are sooo *début du siécle.*'

· · ·

Prompted by SJ's remarks about my being out of touch, I spend the evening channel-hopping. As she suggested, coverage of the financial crisis is back-to-back. House prices are crashing, banks worldwide are falling to their knees, usually-skint governments are falling over themselves to throw billions of pounds of my money at them (money I didn't know I had), and the news-readers are dribbling with excitement about the depth of the coming recession.

Whereas governments usually try to *reassure* the markets, our own useless chancellor (he of the crazy eyebrows) is jumping from studio to studio as fast as I can channel-hop in his efforts to convince everyone that this is going to be the end of civilisation as we know it. He clearly hasn't read *Living Lightly* chapter one: Belief becomes reality.

When I see him predict, for the tenth time in less than an hour, a recession that will be the *'worst in living memory'*, I give up on TV and retire to the safety of my bed, and my reassuringly weighty self-help book.

It takes less effort tonight for me to conjure up my desired image of a brown-eyed, beard-free farming chappy. I must be getting better at it.

But tonight, the second I fall asleep, he will sadly, and somewhat unnervingly morph into a Russian gynaecologist in a green-tiled clinic in Siberia.

After a couple of failed attempts at alternatives, I do, in the end, make an appointment with SJ's gynaecologist. My first choice couldn't see me for two weeks, and the second was off sick (which so doesn't work for me – I do like my medical practitioners to display perfect mastery of at least their own health).

SJ's doctor tells me that he can see me the next morning due to a cancellation, which, because I hate pre-gynaecological stress almost as much as I hate the visit itself, is perfect.

Her spelling of course, turns out to be a little wide of the mark, and by the time I get to Doctor Ynchausty's surgery I'm feeling not only my usual pre-stirrup anguish, but also a bit intrigued about the doctor himself.

The practice on Sloane Square is just flashy enough to be reassuring. One gets the impression that people are happy to pay to return here and yet the doctors haven't become millionaires through unnecessary procedures. Best of all there are no green tiles.

A nurse shows me into the examination room and then leaves me to shiveringly contemplate the cold metal of the stirrups. Behind a frosted glass door, I see the doctor washing his hands.

When he steps into the room, I see that SJ wasn't joking about his looks. I think my mouth actually drops.

If Doctor Ynchausty were in his twenties rather than his late thirties, he would – with his olive skin, jet black hair, and deep brown eyes – be perfect model material.

But just as I start to realise something more profound about the way he looks, his model smile fades and his face slips into a confused frown.

'CC?' he says.

'Victor!' I exclaim. The spell is broken.

'The salsa lady.'

'Twinkletoes! Right! Look, I'm sorry. I had no idea that you . . . well . . . that you were *you*.' I frown at the nonsense coming from my mouth.

'The last time I looked I was, yeah . . .' he says drily.

'I mean, I didn't know your surname. A friend advised me, and . . .'

'Darren?'

'No! No, not at all. No, if I'd known it was you I wouldn't have come. Obviously.'

'Thanks.'

'I didn't mean . . . but . . . no, Sarah-Jane Dennis sent me. She said she thought you were Russian.'

'Russian?'

'Yeah.'

'*Why?*'

'The name I think. But she spelt it all wrong so . . .'

'No, it's Basque. From France. The south. Or the north of Spain. Take your pick. But no, not Russian, sorry.'

'No.'

Victor smirks. 'That must be terribly disappointing for you. Russian doctors being renowned for their bedside manner and warm hands and all.'

I pull my bag towards me. 'This is sort of . . . inappropriate, isn't it?' I realise that I'm sweating with embarrassment. 'Maybe I should make an appointment elsewhere?'

Victor shakes his head as if to wake himself from a daydream and raises his hands to indicate that I should stay seated. He takes a seat at his desk. 'Look, now you're here, at least let's see if there's something I can help with, eh?'

'Don't you think it's a bit . . .' I say.

Victor shrugs. 'It's not as if we see each other every day,' he says.

'No.'

'When was it?'

'When? Oh . . . March,' I say. 'No, February. After that photography exhibition.'

'Of course,' he says. 'That was a crazy evening.'

'It was.'

'Anyway, I suppose we're not here to . . . What seems to be the problem?'

I run my tongue across my top teeth. 'I really don't think this is . . . I mean, you know Darren, and everything and . . . I don't really feel that comfortable . . .'

Victor shrugs. 'It's entirely up to you. But, well, I know lots of people. So do all doctors. But we're very good at keeping things separate. We have to be. It's up to you, of course, but seeing as you're here and I'm free . . . Wouldn't you rather just get it over and done with? I've never blabbed about a patient yet.'

I blow through my lips and glance out of the window, weighing it up. It's clearly embarrassing to be examined by Victor. And then again, at least he's a known quantity: Darren likes him, SJ trusts him. And at least he's gay – that's almost like being examined by a woman, isn't it?

'It's your call, CC. I understand entirely if . . .'

'OK,' I say, settling back into my seat. 'But I'll probably find someone else for next time, if that's OK.'

'You can see my colleague next time if you prefer. If you do need to come back.'

'I generally prefer women anyway,' I say. 'No offence.'

'None taken. And she is. A woman that is. Not Russian either though, sadly.'

'Right.'

'Scottish.'

'Right.'

Victor claps his hands together. 'So, down to business. Is this just routine or is there a specific reason you came today?'

Whether Victor feels uncomfortable about this consultation, I have no idea, but if he does, he's certainly not letting it show. Or skimping on his procedure.

He asks me a hundred questions about my lifestyle, sexual activity (lack of), and previous pregnancies (one, aborted). Though under any other circumstances these questions would be embarrassing, something about his manner puts me perfectly at ease. In a way it feels almost like talking to Sarah-Jane, which is strange and unexpected. I know that SJ would never judge me for the simple reason that we have known each other for so very long that she truly *gets* who I am by now: nothing I might say could ever change her view of me. I don't really know Victor at all, of course, but something about his calm, non-judgemental manner makes the whole thing feel no more threatening than a detailed chat with a very good friend.

Eventually, of course, he asks me if I would like to have children in the future and on what time-scale.

'Maybe in a year or two,' I say, and he vaguely raises an eyebrow and pauses.

'I'm sorry, I didn't get the impression you were in a relationship,' he says.

'No. Well. I'm not actually.'

'OK.'

'But some friends had a baby . . . some lesbian friends . . . and I wondered . . . well, it crossed my mind. You know . . .'

'I see.'

'It's not . . . it's not what I want, I mean, it's not how I would choose to . . . but . . . well . . . I don't want to wait till it's too late. And after what happened with SJ . . .'

'I see.'

'You think that sounds bizarre?'

He shrugs. 'I don't think anything anyone says to me is *bizarre*,' he says. 'It's just that the abortion was fairly recent really.'

'I know. I knew you'd think that. It sounds mad, doesn't it? But there were extenuating circumstances . . . why I had to.'

'I'm sure.'

'I was with a guy . . .'

'Is it medical?' he asks, suddenly sounding abrupt.

'I'm sorry?'

'Is the reason to do with something medical?'

'Um, no.'

'Then that's probably one thing that I *don't* need to know,' he says.

'OK,' I say, internally grimacing that I have overstepped some invisible line of what a patient should tell her gynaecologist.

'OK,' Victor says, slipping back into his professional mode. 'So let me get the nurse in, and we can give you a full check-up and then we should have some idea just how much margin you have, time-wise. Does that sound like a helpful idea?'

'It does.'

He checks my weight, blood pressure and heart rate. He gives my breasts a good squeeze, takes a blood sample, a pap smear and has a good peer and prod between my legs. The only thing I am spared is the rectal examination. *Thanks be* for small mercies.

Finally he tells me that everything seems fine, makes an appointment for me to see his colleague for the results of the blood tests and smear, and saying, 'And if you ever fancy a little salsa . . .' and miming a phone, he expels me onto the street.

The first thing I do is walk into Oriel Brasserie opposite and order myself a large glass of white wine.

I grab my BlackBerry and hit speed dial #3.

'Russian!' I say.

'What?' SJ answers.

'You said he was Russian! The gynaecologist.'

'Right. He isn't then? Did you go?'

'He's French.'

'Ah, OK. It was just the name that made me think . . . I mean he *sounds* completely English, doesn't he?'

'And the name is Ynchausty,' I say. 'Not Yinkchovzky.'

'Whatever,' SJ says. 'He's pretty though, isn't he?'

'He is.'

'I told you.'

'And gay.'

'Gay?'

'Gay!' I laugh.

'Are you sure?'

'Totally.'

'How come? I mean, I didn't get that vibe at all.'

'His name's Victor.'

'OK . . . Victor Yinkchovzky. That's quite sexy.'

'Yeah, Victor. Think about it.'

'Is that, like, a really gay name or something? Because I don't spend as much time with them as . . .'

'No!' I laugh. 'He's Victor, the guy I went dancing with.'

'Dancing?'

'Yeah, after that exhibition. With Darren. Remember? I told you about it.'

'Oh right. When they were all snorting coke in the taxi?'

'Yeah, right.'

'So Doctor Yingchovsky is Victor the gay, coke-snorting salsa-dancer? Is that what you're telling me?'

'It is. And it's pronounced *Yan-shau-stee.*'

'God! Are you sure it's him?'

'Of course I'm sure! He remembered me too.'

'Oh God, how embarrassing. But he's gay.'

'Exactly.'

'God. What a *waste.* Still, perfect for you really.'

'Because?'

'Well, you're such a fag hag, aren't you? Now you even have a gay gynaecologist.'

Dealing with the Past

As if having my bits inspected by Twinkletoes wasn't enough trauma for one day, just as I walk into Spot On, my BlackBerry beeps with a message from Darren. 'She's New, She's Improved. She's Back,' it says.

I glance around to see if he is sitting in the lobby and then shrug the message off and look up at the receptionist.

'She's back!' she says.

I shake my head in disbelief. 'Jesus. If you can't take a morning to go to the doctor's without getting a load of gyp . . . Anyway, as far as I recall you were off for four *weeks* in June, so—'

'Not you!' she says in a whisper. 'VB. She's back. And she wants to see you.'

When I enter VB's office, she stands, walks around her desk and . . . hugs me. I am so shocked by this that I remain entirely rigid, and then, rather cleverly, I grab her shoulders and force her away in the pretence of getting a better look. 'Well look at you!' I exclaim, holding her at arm's length. 'Gosh you look well.' And she does. She looks more than well: she looks like an entirely different person.

She seems to have aged about ten years in six months, but she looks better for it. Her features look softer, her skin less taut – it's as if she's had a reverse facelift.

'Oh, I don't,' she says, uncharacteristically. 'I look a mess really. But I'm not sure I care any more. I hear you've done a sterling job on the Grunge! account, by the way.'

I swallow hard and release her shoulders in the hope that she will now return to her side of the desk and stop being creepy. She does neither.

'So how are you?' she asks.

'Good thanks, yeah.'

'No, I mean, really. How *are* you?'

'Good,' I say. 'I *am* good. Really.'

'I realised that we spend more time with people here than we do with our partners.'

'Yeah,' I say. 'I suppose we do.'

'Do you have a partner, CC?'

'I, um . . . Look, did you want to see me about anything in particular?'

VB shakes her head. 'No, not really. I just wanted to catch up.'

'Would you like me to give you a report on the whole Levi's thing?'

VB shrugs. 'No. Everyone tells me that it's all going swimmingly without me, so . . . I'm just easing myself back in gently, if you know what I mean.'

'Sure,' I say.

'Everything OK? At the doctor's?'

She's really weirding me out now, and I'm having trouble keeping it out of my facial expressions. 'Yeah, just a check-up,' I say. 'Routine.'

'Good, well, if there's ever anything . . . If you ever need to talk. Well, I'm here for you.'

'Right,' I say. 'Well, I'll, erm . . .'

'It's no good bottling things up.'

'No. Well, I'll catch you later on then.' And with that, I give her a little wave and walk briskly out of her office.

On my way down I call in to Creative. Mark is on holiday, but Jude and Darren both look up from Jude's screen which is displaying an image of a yogurt pot.

'Hiya,' I say. 'Don't tell me you're actually working!'

Jude frowns at his screen, and then turns slowly to face me. 'Working?'

'That is work, I take it,' I say. 'Not some new dairy fetish?'

'Yeah,' Jude says, vaguely. And then as if his spirit snaps back into his body, he suddenly breaks free of whatever he has been thinking about. 'Sorry, yes. It's for that dairy campaign. We're just looking at what everyone else is doing.'

'Cornish Cow? But we haven't even signed them yet,' I say.

'No,' Jude says. 'But there's nothing else happening at the moment, so we were just having a look. Dairy is very dull. I hope if we do get it we can shake things up a bit.'

'Shake it up!' Darren laughs.

I frown.

'You know. Dairy. Milkshake . . . never mind.'

'No,' Jude says drily. 'Never mind.' He clicks his mouse and the screen goes blank.

Both he and Darren swivel to face me. 'What's up?' Jude asks. 'You look confused.'

'It's just bizarre here today,' I say. 'VB is being all huggy and now you're both working.'

'Ah, you met the cyborg,' Darren laughs.

'The cyborg?'

'Yeah, we think that they've replaced VB with a cyborg.'

'Right. Well she's certainly being very Stepford-Wifey.'

'Stepford what?'

'It doesn't matter. It's a cult film, but probably a bit before your time. A bit before *my* time, actually.'

'Did she hug you?' Jude asks.

'Yeah,' I say. 'She did. You too?'

Jude nods.

'She was going on at Jude about dealing with the past and not bottling things up,' Darren says.

'I got that too.'

'Personally I think they've blown her brains out with electric shock therapy,' Darren laughs.

Jude pulls a face like he's smelt something bad. 'She *is* still one of the partners,' he points out. 'I don't think we should be, you know . . .'

'Sorry,' Darren says.

'And anyway,' he adds. 'Mental illness isn't something to be joked about.'

'No. Sure. Sorry,' Darren says again.

I shrug. 'Well, I'm with Darren on this one,' I say. 'That Greenham woman out there is *not* VB.'

'Greenham?' Darren asks.

'Greenham Comm— oh, never mind. Again, a bit before your time.'

That night, unable to concentrate on my exercises, I add *Living Life Lightly* to the heap of self-help books above the bed and try to read the first chapter of *The Blue Bistro* instead. But my mind is elsewhere, and my eyes just skim the page.

My brain is occupied with a vague unfocused process of passing the day in review. It's not unlike dreaming.

I feel the cold steel of the stirrups, and see Victor's head bobbing between them . . .

I hear VB say, 'Do you have a partner, CC?' and then Jude with, 'She is, you know, a *partner*.'

I see Darren smiling at me and hear Victor saying, 'The abortion was fairly recent . . .'

I try again to read the first chapter of *The Blue Bistro* and then give up and lie and stare at the wall instead.

I hear Darren saying, 'Deal with the past'.

Victor, *Victoria*, partners and *partners*. Even before I'm asleep, the whole day feels like a riddle.

· · ·

I scream like a child in a horror film and hurl myself from the side of the bed, knocking whoever is attacking me out of the way.

It's completely dark in my bedroom, and for a moment I think my assailant has attacked me with a bat. I wonder where the nearest weapon would be, but then, as I scrabble my way across the bedroom floor towards the vague, grey light of the hall, I find

I'm walking on rubble, and think that perhaps we're having an earthquake and a lump of the wall fell on me. I'm sweating and shaking and my heart is racing.

In the hall, all is incongruously quiet. I start to wonder if this isn't a nightmare.

I stand and grab a hefty bottle of perfume from the bathroom shelf and return to the bedroom door. It's not much of a weapon, I know, but it's heavy and square, and hitting someone over the head with a glass brick has got to be better than bitch-slapping them. Plus, in films, squirting it into their eyes always seems to do the trick. I have some doubts, though, about the range of L'Eau d'Issey's squirter.

I edge to the door. Silence. I reach out and take a deep breath and simultaneously flip the light switch and leap, ninja-style back into the room.

And then I understand. No attacker. No earthquake. No dream.

Just one collapsed IKEA bookshelf.

One side of the fixture has broken free, ripping a lump of plaster from the wall, and the entire thing has hinged downwards, whacking me on the face and scattering my books across the floor. I'm lucky I'm not unconscious.

I raise a hand to my cheek – now stinging – and return to the bathroom mirror. I have a small straight cut along the top of my cheekbone.

One inch higher and it would have had my eye out. *'Fucking hell!'* I mutter.

I dab some perfume on the cut as an antiseptic, then return to the bedroom and start to scoop the books from the floor and pile them against the wall. There are a surprising number (mostly self-help manuals), and, as I build the pile, I end up surprised not that the shelf collapsed, but that it held out so long.

I shake the white chunks of plaster from the bedding and pillows (it's far too late to be vacuuming) and slip back beneath my quilt, and then fall surprisingly quickly back to sleep.

When my alarm goes off at seven on Thursday morning I'm pretty sure that I have been having nightmares all night – certainly I feel tired and irritable.

But as I lie in my bed, looking up at the damaged wall, and then over at the pile of books, thinking, *Do I really have to go to work today?* only one dream sequence remains within reach. I was lying on a slab, in a morgue. The slab was uneven because it was made of piles of books. Beyond my swollen belly, between my knees, Victor the gynaecologist was bobbing around, and then laboriously, painfully, pulling something out of me. At first I expected to see a baby, but then I realised, in anguish, that whatever he was delivering was *dead*. And *huge*.

Once it was over, Victor had looked at me and smiled and done a little salsa dance. 'Success,' he had said. 'All gone.'

I looked over to see what he had removed: a bloodied adult body. A dead body. Brian's body.

Still thinking about taking the day off, I force myself out of bed. But when I see the state of my face, it's a no-brainer: I call in sick.

The cut on my cheek is tiny, but my eye has come up in a real shiner. I am stunned. I haven't had a black eye since Ronan.

Experience tells me that four days will be enough for the bruise to fade. By Monday, Michael-Jackson quantities of foundation will suffice to hide any remaining signs of injury.

I eat breakfast, then vacuum the bedroom and momentarily consider trying to put the shelf back up. Though I have a box full of tools I have never been much cop with a screwdriver, let alone a drill. I think that I inherited my mother's '*why have a dog and bark yourself?*,' mentality as far as DIY is concerned. Which is fine, of course, as long as you have a dog. Alone, unscrewing the remaining side of the bookcase is as much as I manage.

Without the shelf, the piled books get in my way, and, in fact, begin to embarrass me. For there's clearly something not quite right about having fifty self-help books . . . Clearly there is something a little shameful about having so many and *still* not being 'sorted', as they say in the personals.

On further reflection, there's also something rather sinister about the fact that the shelf that Brian put up has combined forces with my fifty failed self-help books to try to murder me in my sleep. By the time I have had lunch, it's decided: with the exception of *Living Life Lightly,* (which, presumably was the straw that broke the IKEA shelf's back) the books have to go.

I phone SJ and ask her if she can swing by on her way home and run me to Oxfam.

It's twenty to six when I open my front door. Her face falls. 'Fucking hell,' she says. 'You have been in the wars.'

'I know,' I say. 'It looks worse than it is.'

'It looks like you're back with Ronan,' she says.

'I know.'

'You're not, are you?'

'Of course I am,' I say, rolling my eyes. I grab her hand and pull her through to the bedroom and nod at the missing lump of wall. 'Bookcase fall on lady face,' I say.

'OK. I believe you,' she laughs. 'Fuck though! And you were *asleep?*'

'Scared the shit out of me. I thought I was being attacked.' I glance at my watch. 'Can we get a move on though? They said they close just after six.'

We load the seven bags of books into her Megane. 'Are you sure you want to come with me with that face?' she says. 'Cos I can just drop 'em off and come back if you want.'

'It's fine,' I say. 'You can take them in if you want . . . I can stay with the car in case of traffic wardens and stuff. At least they won't mess with me looking like this.'

'So you were asleep,' she says again, as she pulls out onto Regent's Park Road.

'Yeah. My first reaction was to run into the bathroom for a weapon.'

'Have you got one? A weapon?'

'The only thing I could find was a big bottle of perfume.'

'Ooh,' SJ giggles. 'I've got a bottle of Paradise and I'm not afraid to use it.'

'Actually it was L'Eau d'Issey – a big bottle though. *I* wouldn't want to be whacked over the head with it.'

'You look like you *have* been,' she laughs.

'Yeah, well . . . My second thought was that it was an earthquake. The books made a hell of a noise.'

'Well, we do get a lot of earthquakes,' SJ says mockingly.

'Well, my logic circuits weren't working too well at three a.m. God, it's good to see you. It's been ages.'

She glances at me and smiles. 'Yeah, I know. Sorry about that.'

'Oh, I'm not . . . I'm just saying.'

'No. So, why are you dumping the books? Can't you just fix the shelf?'

'They make me feel a bit funny, to be honest,' I say.

'Because they attacked you in your sleep?'

'Well exactly. No, they're all personal development books . . . Yoga and crystals and . . .'

'Self-help shit?'

'Exactly.'

'I remember you doing yoga. You lasted about a week.'

'Three days. On the third day I cricked my neck and that was that.'

'I never knew you were into crystals though.'

'I was when I was eighteen. I just never threw the book away.'

'Right. What about those stupid balls that Cynthia gave you?'

'The Qui Dong balls? Yeah, they're in the boot, along with the instruction manuals.'

'I still don't see why you have to get rid of them *today*,' SJ says.

'They're just embarrassing somehow,' I say. 'And depressing. I have every self-help book ever written and my life's still a mess.'

'Well, I think we've all got a few of those kicking around. You haven't got any on dreams, have you? Cos I've been having really weird ones since they put me on oestrogen.'

'No,' I say. 'I think I need one. I've been having really freaky dreams too.'

'So the real reason you're dumping this lot is to make room for more,' SJ laughs.

'You know me so well.'

'Anyway, this is it,' she says, pulling up on double-reds. 'So, you stay here, just in case, and I'll just dump them and run away before they look at them and think that *I'm* the sad-ass?'

'Exactly.'

Back at the house, SJ offers to help me put the shelf back up, but once she inspects the damage she declares the task beyond even our combined capabilities. 'Even George can't fix that,' she says. 'You need a plasterer or something. Plus, you don't want it coming down on you again.'

And so we sit down with a cup of tea and attempt to analyse our dreams instead.

SJ's are pretty strange, involving rides along Blackpool beach on pregnant donkeys. 'And I've never even been to bloody Blackpool,' she points out.

'But nothing bad happened?'

She shakes her head. 'Nah. It was just a nice day out.'

'So it's a good omen. Because the donkeys were pregnant, right?'

'I suppose so.'

I then tell Sarah-Jane about my nightmare involving Victor and dead Brian, and then, perhaps because of my newly damaged bedroom wall, I remember the dream I had in the Negresco in Nice and tell her about Brown Eyes shagging me and then morphing into Brian.

'So what do you think?' I ask her.

SJ shrugs. 'You're right,' she says. 'They're strange. Or bizarre, as you would say.'

'Do other people really not say bizarre?'

'Not much,' she says. 'Not as much as you.'

'Maybe their lives aren't as bizarre as mine.'

'Maybe. You really need to get rid of that fucking tree, by the way.'

'I know.'

'It's out of hand. You should call the council.'

'I know. So what about my dreams? Is that *it*? Bizarre? Is that your verdict?'

'Yeah.'

I wrinkle my nose. 'I thought hard about analysing yours,' I say in a sullen voice.

Sarah-Jane sighs. 'I don't think you'd like what I think, that's all.'

'Oh come on, SJ.'

'Well they're a bit mad, really,' she says.

'Mad.'

'Yeah. And Brian keeps coming up.'

'So you're going to say that I'm still in love with Brian or something?'

'No . . .' She swallows and looks out of the window again, then turns back to face me. 'But I do think you have issues. It's not that hard to interpret, is it?'

'Isn't it?'

'You need professional help, to get rid of Brian once and for all.'

'To rip his dead corpse from my womb?'

'Well, yeah.'

I tut. 'That would be fine, except that I got rid of Brian years ago.'

'Yeah. Only you haven't. Or you wouldn't still be on about him all the time.'

'I'm not *on about him* all the time. I *never* think about Brian.'

SJ raises an eyebrow.

'OK, we're talking about him now . . . but that's just because of the dream.'

She shrugs. 'You dream about him, we're talking about him . . . I just think maybe you need to see someone, to help you deal with all that stuff better.'

I snort and shake my head.

'And now you're annoyed with me,' she says.

'I'm not. It's just that I *have* dealt with all that . . . honestly . . . ages ago.'

'You never even cried. Not when you got the abortion. Not when Brian dumped you.'

'But you know I don't cry like you do.'

'Did you cry when Waiine died?'

'No. I told you. The last time was when Dad died.'

Sarah-Jane nods thoughtfully. 'I'm not saying you're a loony or anything.'

'Well that's a relief.'

'But I do think you should talk to a counsellor or something.'

I nod. 'I understand what you're saying, but I don't know for the life of me what I would talk about.'

'About the dreams. About what Brian did to you. About how you felt. About losing Waiine. Cos I know you *think* you're fine. But I don't think you are really.'

'Thanks for the vote of confidence.'

'Well, you did ask.'

'You're right. I did.'

'Don't see a Freudian though. They're all really fucked up. See a Jungian.'

'Since when were you such an expert anyway? Have you seen a shrink?'

'Nah. George's sister has been doing the rounds for years, though.'

'Hasn't worked for her though, has it?'

Sarah-Jane ignores this comment. 'She said most of them are Freudians – they think everything is to do with fancying your parents or something.'

'Yuck.'

'Exactly. But she's seeing a Jungian guy now, whatever that means. It's supposed to be much more wholesome anyway. And they're really into dreams apparently. '

'Right.'

'I could get you his number.'

'No thanks.'

'Your call.'

'Right. So, more tea?'

SJ glances at her watch. 'Nah, I need to be getting home. George will be back soon.'

'Is tonight a shagging night?'

'Nope. That's Wednesdays and Sundays. Thursday is curry night.'

'You cook a curry every Thursday?'

'Me? Don't be daft. George picks up a takeaway on his way home. I have chicken biryani; George gets prawn madras.'

'Every Thursday?'

'Every Thursday. I can't help it. I love chicken biryani.'

Slowdown – Speedup

By Monday morning there remains only the vaguest sign of my literary mishap, a scar so tiny that an intentionally clumsy daub of spot-cover is enough to make it vanish entirely. I'm pretty certain that there will be no scar either as, being blessed with my mother's miracle skin, I have healed invisibly from far worse incidents.

My BlackBerry has been silent all weekend, but when I find that my inbox on the Mac is empty too, I phone Jerry, our IT man to check that everything is still working.

'Everyone is saying the same thing,' he informs me. 'Just send yourself an email and you'll see – it's all working fine.'

'You're right,' I say. 'Sorry to trouble you. It's just all a bit biz— spooky how quiet it is.'

'Spooky!' Jerry says, making me wish that I had gone with *bizarre*. As I hang up, I hear that he is singing the theme tune to *The Twilight Zone* into the receiver.

'Hello, beautiful,' Mark, standing just behind me says, making me jump.

'You're back!' I laugh, standing and hugging him. 'It's been biz—weird not having you around . . . Now you're not upstairs any more, well, when you're not at work either, I really miss you.'

'I missed you too,' he says. 'So what's going on here? It's like a ghost town!'

'I know. It's bad, huh? I was just phoning IT to check . . .'

'Yeah, I heard. I just went to see Stanton and he said that with the exception of Grunge!, everything's on hold.'

'Well, Grunge! is pretty much done now,' I say.

'You know that even Grunge! are thinking of pulling their ads, right?'

I frown. 'What do you mean, *pulling their ads*? They can't. They're already programmed.'

'Dunno. You'll have to talk to Peter, but he got a call when I was with him and that's what it sounded like.'

I shake my head. 'But they can't,' I say. 'Not till the end of the year, not till next summer in fact. It's all booked. It would cost them almost as much to cancel as to carry on.'

Mark shrugs. 'As I say, talk to Peter.'

'I will. So how was Scotland?'

'Wales.'

'I thought you were at Ian's.'

'At his sister's, near Cardiff. It was gorgeous. Amazing scenery. We see so little of Wales on the telly and stuff. It's a beautiful place.'

'But full of Welsh people.'

Mark frowns.

'Sorry. I had a bad experience once – couldn't get anything to eat because they thought I was English. Kind of put me off.'

'Oh right . . . I expect it depends where you go. I quite like them . . . Ian's sister and her husband are lovely anyway.'

'So, getting on with the in-laws! Nice.'

Mark nods. 'Yeah,' he says. 'It was ace. Really.'

'So why the long face?'

'I'm sorry?'

'You don't look like a man in love. A man in love who just got back from a week's holiday.'

'Oh it's just this place, freaking me out. I can't believe how dead it is.'

'Right.'

'Plus, you know how it is . . . When you get back from holidays and everything . . . I'd rather be in Wales shagging still.'

I laugh. 'Mona's law,' I say.

'Exactly,' Mark says. 'Seriously though, aren't you worried?'

'Worried?'

'Well, it can't carry on like this for long, can it?'

'No,' I say. 'No, I suppose it can't.'

In a meeting that lasts most of the afternoon Peter Stanton and I discuss the Grunge! account. He tells me that the slowdown is starting to hit retail hard – high street shops are announcing 70 per cent collapses in their sales volumes, and though initial returns from our campaign were good, overall sales in the sector are plummeting. Even Levi's have decided to scale back their US campaign for the jeans, and Harper & Baker are rumoured to be laying off a third of their workforce. Stanton doesn't need to tell me that unless something happens soon, the same thing will be happening here.

As soon as I get out of the meeting, I phone Tom in New York to check that he's OK. He tells me that, for now at least, any job losses are mere rumour.

Ironically, our own slowdown creates masses of work for me. It's a bit depressing, but any work is better than none.

On Thursday I have to phone Angelica Wayne's agent to cancel next month's photo shoot for the second new-year wave of the campaign, but before I can start to try to squirm my way out of it, he informs me that she has been taken ill and that it's unlikely she'll be able to honour her commitments for the next few months anyway. He seems reticent to explain what's wrong with her, which leaves me intrigued enough to head down to the gossip department, where I find Mark and Jude comparing a load of dairy adverts spread out across the table.

'Hello, gorgeous,' Mark says.

'God, I hope we get that contract,' I say. 'With all this work you're putting into it.'

'Yes, well, you make sure we do,' he says.

'Hey, I just had Peter McKintock on the phone, Wayne's agent.'

'I bet that was interesting,' Jude laughs.

I shake my head. 'You see, I knew you guys would be up on the gossip.'

Jude shrugs. 'Erm, *Hello!*' he says, reaching behind him for a magazine and skimming it across the table towards me.

I turn the magazine – this week's edition of *Hello!* – the right way up. The cover shows Angelica Wayne looking even skinnier than usual being led through a rabble of paparazzi into what looks like a clinic. *Anorexia beats Angelica*, the headline says.

I shake my head. 'How can I not know this?' I mutter, flicking through the magazine in search of the article.

'You're not reading the quality press,' Mark laughs.

'Yeah, well, you could have told me. You might have realised that losing our model is kind of important.'

'Hey, it only came out this morning. Anyway, next month's shoots have been cancelled, haven't they?'

I freeze theatrically and drop my jaw at him. 'And how the hell would you know that?'

Mark shrugs. 'VB's new policy of openness,' he says. 'Nowadays, if you buy her a soyaccino she'll tell you anything.'

'A soyaccino?'

'A cappuccino made of soya. She's gone vegan.'

I wrinkle my nose. 'Great! Just don't tell Cornish Cow,' I mumble, whilst skimming the few words squeezed on the page of photos of our ever-skinnier Angelica Wayne.

'You see,' Mark says, nodding at the page. 'I told you she was too thin.'

'Yeah. Well. No one could argue with you on that one now. It says here she's on a glucose drip!'

'Sexy,' Mark says.

'God, I suppose she'll put on weight now.'

'Probably come out looking like Britney.'

'God, I wish,' I say.

'Well, they reckon that fat is going to be the new thin,' Mark says. 'They reckon there's going to be a backlash against all these anorexic models.'

'Maybe my chance will come. Then again, they've been saying that for years. Poor lass though. It's this business. It gets them all in the end.'

'He's sexy though,' Jude says. 'Farmer Thexton.'

'Yeah. Farmer. And I'm a supermodel,' I laugh.

'I'm sorry?'

'He lives in Docklands in a thirty-thousand-foot glass apartment. All the dreadlocks and the ecology – it's just image. It's just bullshit.'

Mark shrugs. 'That's our business, sweetie. Bullshit is what we do.'

'What we did,' I say.

'Yeah,' Mark says knowingly. 'You could be right.'

As I close the magazine, Jude leaves the room, and Mark looks surreptitiously after him and then says, 'Did you know Darren's job might be on the line?'

I frown at him. 'No,' I say. 'And if it's the case, I really don't think that it's right that you should know that when I don't.'

He shrugs. 'Darren told me. Stanton hinted that if things don't pick up in October he might have to let him go.'

I grind my teeth. 'That's awful,' I say. 'Maybe I should talk to him. Stanton, I mean.'

'I don't think you should,' Mark says. 'He's not supposed to tell anyone. Stanton doesn't want the whole place freaking out.'

'Just Darren.'

'Well, he was just warning him, I think. So that he can think about other options.'

'Right. God, poor Darren. Well, I'll see if I can get Stanton to tell me . . . Is he OK?'

Mark shrugs. 'He's been a bit down lately anyway. I don't think this exactly helps.'

I spend the entire week struggling not to think about my underlying feeling that this crisis is more than just a blip . . . that in some way our western way of life is unravelling, and that along with the banks, advertising may be doomed. I study cancellation clauses and haggle with our own media department, advertising brokers, and occasionally the magazine owners themselves as I struggle to reduce the Grunge! advertising commitment in any reasonable way, but for the most part, it's a losing battle. In a recession it's every man for himself. By the time Friday night comes I have pulled half of their advertising but have only saved a quarter of the budget. I'm glad Stanton will be the one to announce the figures to them come Monday morning.

I'm Fine

'I don't know what to say really.'

'Anything. Or nothing. It really doesn't matter.'

'OK. I don't know why I'm here really.'

'No?'

'Though, I suppose everyone says that, don't they?'

'Not everyone.'

'No. But it's not like I'm depressed or anything. Well, I don't think I am, though you're the expert.'

'So would you say that you were happy?'

'Yes.'

'Good.'

'Well, happy might be overstating it a bit. But I'm OK. I'm fine.'

'Fine is good too.'

'My friend Sarah-Jane wanted me to come.'

'I see. Is she your partner?'

'No! No. Sorry. I don't have anything against . . . you know. But no. I'm single. And straight. SJ is just a friend.'

'And she wanted you to come here today?'

'Yes. Yeah, she's convinced I have issues . . . or one big issue about to swallow me up and leave me gabbling in a corner. It's mainly because I never cry. SJ is convinced everyone should blub regularly.'

'I see.'

'But I just don't feel the need. Does that make me crazy?'

'No. I don't think that does.'

'But you think I'm a bit mad anyway?'

'I have no opinion on you whatsoever.'

'No. I suppose not ... I thought you'd have lots of books and a big mahogany desk and stuff like they always do in films. But this is more IKEA isn't it?'

'Yes, some of it is IKEA.'

'Look, I don't think this is going to work.'

'Because the furniture came from IKEA?'

'No. Silly! No, I don't think I need this. I think I need something else.'

'What do you think you need?'

'More like a life coach. To sort my life out.'

'I see.'

'My problems are more, well, practical really.'

'Practical.'

'Yes. I need to reorganise my life. I mean, my life is fine. It's just that I want to change it all and I don't know where to start really. Because everything is linked to everything else, isn't it.'

'Things have a tendency to be like inter-linked, yes.'

'What I'd really like is to be living on a farm in Devon with some lovely bloke, growing veg.'

'I see. And how does that differ from your life now?'

'Well, I live in a flat here in London. And I'm single. And I work in advertising.'

'So it's very different.'

'Yes. But I don't want to do it on my own. So I really need to meet the bloke first.'

'I see.'

'But my life here fits perfectly. I mean, I have friends and a job and ... So I don't know how to start changing it all around.'

'No.'

'And I don't think you can help me with that sort of practical stuff, can you?'

'I don't know.'

'No. You see.'

'...'

'. . . I don't know what to say now.'

'I expect something will come.'

'Humm. I hope so. It's a bit expensive to sit in silence really, isn't it?'

'I suppose it is.'

'So do you think it's a problem?'

'What's that?'

'That I never cry.'

'I don't know.'

'No.'

'Do *you*? Think it's a problem?'

'Not really. I mean . . . I hate crying anyway. I think panda eyes are overrated, don't you? Sorry, but are you gay? Am I allowed to ask that?'

'You can say or ask anything that you wish. Do you think I'm gay?'

'No. Yes. Maybe . . . I mean, I have lots of gay friends, so it wouldn't be a problem.'

'I see.'

'And lots of them seem to have goatees and cargo pants at the moment. That's all.'

'I see.'

'I have a bit of a beard thing.'

'A beard thing.'

'Yeah, I hate beards.'

'I see.'

'Not yours, of course. But I hate kissing men with beards. God that sounds terrible. That sounds like I'm thinking about kissing you which of course I'm not. God, that sounds worse now. Just shut up, CC.'

'So would you rather I didn't have a beard?'

'No, not really. Seeing as kissing is off the agenda it doesn't worry me at all.'

'Good.'

'So . . .'

'So.'

'Change the subject, CC.'

'If you wish.'

'I haven't actually cried since Dad died.'

'Would you like to talk about it? Perhaps you'd like to tell me how he died?'

'No. Not really. I only thought of him because . . . never mind.'

'OK.'

'. . .'

'Did you cry a lot when he died?'

'Yeah. I couldn't stop. For days. Maybe a week.'

'I see.'

'But then you have to stop, don't you? At some point you just have to make a decision that the tears stop now. Because otherwise, it could go on forever.'

'I can see how it could feel that way, yes.'

'It was a heart attack, by the way. In a shopping centre.'

'I see.'

'It was horrible. He just collapsed on the escalator. Mum was hysterical. Which is understandable. But she kept hitting me.'

'Hitting you?'

'Yes. I was trying to, you know, resuscitate him. And she was hitting me round the head, telling me to leave him alone. I don't think she thought I knew what I was doing.'

'That must have been very traumatic.'

'Yeah. And I didn't really.'

'You didn't . . .?'

'Know. What I was doing. Well, I *did*. But I was too upset to do it properly.'

'Of course.'

'But I don't suppose it made any difference. I mean, I don't feel as if I killed him or anything like that.'

'Good.'

'But you always wonder don't you? If things had been different.'

'If you had done it properly.'

'Well, yes.'

'Don't you feel brave that you tried? Under the circumstances?'

'Yes, I do. That too. But they said it was massive anyway. The heart attack. I don't think there was much hope.'

'No.'

'But you always wonder.'

'Well, it's famously difficult to perform any kind of intervention on a family member. It's the reason doctors and surgeons never treat anyone they know. All anyone can do is their best.'

'Well that's what I think … Wow! Another ten minutes.'

'Yes. Does that seem like a long time?'

'It's just finding stuff to talk about.'

'Of course.'

'Because I'm done really.'

'So that's all you wanted to talk about? Your father's death?'

'Well yeah. No, I mean … I mean, I didn't really. Want to talk about it, that is.'

'OK.'

'So.'

'So.'

'Do we just sit here now and watch the hands go around?'

'If you want.'

'I don't know.'

'Well that's fine too.'

'Is it?'

'Yes.'

'Well, anyway. That's the last time I cried.'

'I see.'

'And then Waiine died two years later and SJ thinks I should have cried.'

'Waiine?'

'My brother. He died of Aids.'

'That must have been tough too.'

'Yes. I suppose so. I suppose he'd be saved today. I mean, they have all these drugs now, don't they.'

'Yes. Were you with him too? When he died?'

'No. I was at college. And he was in hospital for months. I came down to see him when I could, but … Well, I had exams and stuff. I couldn't be there all the time.'

'Of course not.'

'And no one knew when he would go, of course, so . . .'

'Of course.'

'So SJ thinks I'm abnormal for not crying.'

'This is Sarah-Jane, your friend?'

'Yes. And you? What do you think? Should I have cried?'

'I don't think there's any *should* about it.'

'No.'

'Do *you* think you should have?'

'Not really, no. I think it's fine. I didn't *want* to start crying again in case I never stopped.'

'Well that's a good reason.'

'Yeah.'

'OK.'

'So.'

'So, do you think that might really have happened?'

'What?'

'That you might really have not been able to stop crying?'

'No, not really. I was talking metaphorically.'

'I see.'

'Because you would have to stop at some point, wouldn't you.'

'Yes.'

'Otherwise you would end up rocking in the corner of a padded cell somewhere.'

'That sounds like a worrying idea.'

'Yes. So better not to start in the first place. Less risky.'

'I see.'

'But I *was* sad. Really sad. I'm not cold. And I miss him. Well, both of them. In different ways though.'

'How so?'

'Well Dad I miss because of who he *was*. I miss not having that funny, lovely man in my life.'

'Right.'

'And Waiine I miss more because of who he might have *become*. He was so young really. He wasn't really *done* yet, you know? So it's more of a fantasy about what might have been.'

'Of course.'

'It's sad though, isn't it? When someone, just . . . you know . . . ceases to be.'

'Yes. It's very sad.'

'But I think I have coped pretty well really. I mean, I'm still here, right?'

'Right.'

'Do you think I haven't? Coped that is. Because maybe I don't see myself clearly.'

'I don't really have an opinion. We each cope to the best of our abilities.'

'Right. Well. It's pretty much half past. Can I go now?'

'You have another three minutes, but it's really up to you.'

'Good. Thanks. Well, I think I'll be getting off then.'

'OK.'

'Is it up to me if I come again next week?'

'Everything is up to you really, isn't it. I mean, I have no way of physically constraining you to come here.'

'Good. Well, then, I'll, erm, let you know.'

'But when you booked I told you it was a minimum three sessions.'

'Right.'

'And you agreed. So your word is rather at stake.'

'I see.'

'So I'll see you next week hopefully.'

'Hopefully, yes.'

'Good. Well, goodbye then, Chelsea.'

'Good . . . I told you I hate being called Chelsea.'

'Yes, sorry. Why is it that you hate that?'

'Well, it's just such a chavvy name, isn't it?'

'It's *your* name though, isn't it?'

'Yes. Well I don't like it.'

'No.'

'OK, bye then.'

'Goodbye.'

Fun and Standards

Out on the street, I start to walk towards the taxi rank at Acton station, and try to work out how I'm feeling. The answer is: *pretty strange*.

I'm feeling inexplicably tense, somewhat irritated, incredibly tired, and just a tiny bit tearful. I feel like one of those snow-globes that has been shaken up. I feel like I won't really know how I feel until the snow has settled again.

When I was with Mr IKEA, other than a little irritation that I had made such an illogical decision as to go there in the first place, I felt little. But now I'm outside in the early evening air, I find myself with a sufficiently unfamiliar mix of emotions and feelings that I'm forced to admit that at least *something* has taken place. Only once all the flakiness has settled will I have any idea if that is a good or a bad thing.

The taxi rank at Acton station is empty, but there is no queue either so I stand at the head of the queuing zone and deliberate whether or not to cross to the tube station instead. I don't like the tube much at the best of times, but tonight, half an hour in the quiet sealed box of a taxi, alone with my thoughts, definitely strikes me as preferable.

Luckily, within a few minutes a taxi rolls into view. A big built guy in a dark suit squeezes himself from the rear of the taxi with a back pack and the proverbial laptop bag slung over his shoulder. He holds the door open for me, but as I start to duck to get in, he says, 'CC?'

I pause, and straighten to look up at him. 'Oh! Bro— Norman?'

'Huh, nearly got the name wrong,' he says, winking.

'No, I . . . never mind,' I say, scanning this new suited version of my speed date with approval. 'How have you been?'

'Good. Fine. And you?'

'Fine too.' I lean into the taxi briefly to ask him to wait, then straighten up again.

'You never called,' Norman says.

'No, well . . .' I say. 'After two cancellations I tend to give it up as a lost cause.'

'No tenacity,' he says, smiling.

'Maybe not.'

'Look, I'm sorry about that,' he says.

I shrug sweetly.

'Did you ever go back? To speed dating, I mean.'

'No. Never,' I say.

'I did, a couple of times, but . . . well, you know.'

'Sure,' I say, thinking that I have no idea what I'm supposed to know.

'So do you still fancy having that drink? Or maybe you met someone?'

I shake my head. 'No, I think I've given up on ever meeting anyone,' I say. 'I'm going to become a nun instead.'

Norman nods. 'Right,' he says. 'Well, I know how you feel. Not that I'm thinking of becoming a nun of course.'

'No,' I say.

A young creative type with dreadlocks pokes his head somewhat comically between Norman's shoulder and the cab. 'Are you taking this?' he asks, 'or just having a chat?'

I nod. 'Sorry, yes, I am. I have to get home.'

'And I have to get off anyway,' Norman says, nodding towards the station and glancing at his watch. 'I have a train to catch.'

'To Newcastle?' I laugh.

'No, just to Milton Keynes this time. I'm back tomorrow, though.'

'Right,' I say. 'Well, call me if you want. When you get back.

243

Do you still have my number?'

'Yeah, I think so,' he says.

The guy behind Norman is starting to irritate me by staring at me accusingly and hopping from one foot to the other as if he needs the toilet, so I throw Norman a smile and slide into the cab.

'Shall we?' the taxi driver asks, sarcastically.

'Sure,' I tell him. 'Primrose Hill.'

Norman slams the door and mimes holding a telephone, and I nod and smile and think, *Yeah, right.* Because of course Norman will never call. And if he does he will call twice. Once to make a date, and once to cancel it again.

As the cab accelerates out into the traffic the young Asian driver glances back at me, grinning and flashing beautiful white teeth. 'You should have given him your number,' he says.

'I'm sorry?'

'You should have given him your number again. Because now, if he doesn't call you'll never know, will you?'

I snort, a little outraged at his eavesdropping. 'I don't think that it's really . . .' But then intrigue gets the better of me. 'Never know what?'

'Well, if he couldn't find the number, or if he decided not to call,' he says, nodding and grinning at me.

'Right,' I say.

'Dating's a game,' he says. 'It's a real game. But you have to play by the rules if you want to win. One day I'll write a book . . . how to play the dating game or something.'

'Right,' I say.

'Like you make them wait,' he says.

'You make them wait?'

'Sure. If a lady gives you her number, you don't call for one week.'

'Right. Because otherwise?'

'Because otherwise she won't put out,' he says. 'Women are more slow than men. You have to give them time to think, time to imagine how good it's gonna be.'

I pull a face. 'Right, well, thanks for that.'

'And the ladies should never phone twice.'

I sigh and then despite myself ask him why.

'Because if a guy wants you he'll phone you back. One call is enough. You call twice, you scare him off.'

'Sure.'

'And never make the bed.'

'I'm sorry?' I ask, wondering how many of these he has.

'A guy should never make the bed. You go on a date, you leave the bed messy. Clean, but messy.'

'Right, and that's because?'

'Otherwise when he takes the lady home it's like he planned it all along. And the ladies like to think they make everything happen, not the guy. Rules of the game.'

'Well, in my experience it's not much fun. As games go.'

He glances back at me again. 'Well, you know what they say,' he laughs. 'You know the dating proverb.'

Again, caught between irritation at the conversation I'm reluctantly having with my twenty-something taxi driver and intrigue, I say drily, 'No, what's the dating proverb?'

'If you're not having enough fun, lower your standards.'

'If you're not having enough fun then lower your standards?' I repeat.

'Exactly,' he says, winking at me in the rear-view mirror. 'Because a good-looking lady like yourself – well, there's no reason for you to not be having fun, is there?'

I clear my throat and slither into the corner of my seat so that he can no longer see me.

'Well, thanks for that,' I say. 'Now if you could just . . . *drive*.' God, I nearly said, *take me home* . . . How would *that* have sounded?

When I get in I have two messages on my BT voicemail. The first is from my mother, simply asking me to call her. And the second, incredibly, is from Brown Eyes. He apologises for not being available this evening and leaves me his number, 'just in case'.

'So there was at least *some* point going all the way out to Acton,' I mutter.

But tonight I don't want to talk to my mother, or Brown Eyes, or anyone else for that matter. I don't want to think about dating, or Saddam, or Dad, or Waiine . . . In fact what I really want, over and above all else, is to think about *nothing at all*. So I make a cheese sandwich, pour myself a large glass of Gewurztraminer, and switch on *Big Brother*.

Of course none of the idiots in the house are ever doing anything vaguely interesting, and tonight is no exception. But at least thinking about them (if you can call this thinking) means that I'm not thinking about me.

Disposable One-liners

The rest of the week limps by in a state of continued minimalism. I have two meetings with Stanton about the Cornish Cow contract. It seems that Cornish Cow are dilly-dallying about signing a contract with us, and Stanton wants me to organise a trip to Plymouth (yes, Cornish Cow's offices are in Devon, not Cornwall) to, *work a little of my New York magic on them.*

'If we get this lined up we might just survive the downturn,' he tells me, gravely.

The only notable thing that happens all week comes as I head back from the second of these meetings on Friday afternoon. I call in to wish the Gay Team a good weekend.

The ambience in their usually effervescent office is decidedly low key. Mark is missing and Jude and Darren are both smoking with their feet on their desks.

'So you're not even *pretending* to smoke outside these days?' I say, pushing the door closed behind me and crossing to open the window.

Jude shrugs.

'Let them sack me,' Darren says. 'This week or next month . . . what's the difference?'

'Lord!' I say. 'Have you two forgotten to take your Prozac or something?'

Jude smiles weakly at me. 'Darren's right though. It *is* depressing,' he says. 'There's just nothing coming our way.'

'Stanton wants me to go and convince Cornish Cow,' I say. 'If we get that then you guys will have to put your thinking caps back on.'

'As I understand it, it's a few yogurt pots and a poster,' Darren says. 'It's hardly a game changer anyway.'

'Well we don't know that yet, do we?' I say, crossing the room to look out at the street below – it's only three-thirty but the light is fading fast. 'It all depends on what I manage to flog them,' I murmur, unconvincingly, and, in truth, unconvinced.

'Will you be going on your own?' Jude asks. 'Because I'd love a trip to Cornwall.'

'Devon,' I say. 'They're in Devon. In Plymouth to be precise. And I don't know. I expect it'll be just me.'

'We could all go,' Darren says. 'We could rent a bus. *Priscilla*-style.'

'I doubt Stanton will want it to become a company outing,' I say.

'Yeah but if I came I could photograph the cows and stuff,' Darren says.

Jude nods. 'He's not wrong.'

'Well, I'm quite handy with a camera myself,' I point out. 'But I'll see. If he lets me, I'll take you all. And Darren can come in drag and we can strap him to the top of the car with long flowing scarves.'

'Thanks.'

'Or perhaps a doggy mask.'

He frowns at me.

'Seriously though, have you actually got any work on at the moment?' Jude asks. 'Because we really are just sitting here twiddling our thumbs. It's a waste. Mark's gone home already.'

I wrinkle my nose and shake my head. 'Not a lot, to be honest. I think I'm going to go home early myself. Better to make up the hours when things pick up.'

'*If* things pick up,' Darren says.

'Yeah, well, I'm sure they will.'

'You doing anything nice this weekend?' he asks.

I shrug. 'Nothing planned really.'

'The forecast is awful,' Jude says. 'I'm supposed to be cycling from London to Birmingham, and . . .'

'You're cycling to *Birmingham*?'

'Yeah. It's only, like, a hundred miles or so.'

'God.'

'I need the endorphins. We're going along the Grand Union canal. But I'm really not sure I'm up to twelve hours of rain.'

'Well no. Personally I'm planning on watching every movie on Sky Box Office, and I find the idea of that quite tiring.'

'Lord. How brave of you,' Darren says.

'Yeah. Such exciting lives we live. Actually I bumped into that bloke from speed dating. I don't know if you remember, it was ages ago.'

'What, balloon boy?'

I laugh. 'No. The one who stood me up . . . well, cancelled. Twice. I may just attempt arranging a date with him again.'

Darren grimaces at me. 'I wouldn't bother,' he says. 'The hopeless ones always remain hopeless.'

'Well thanks, Mr Doom and Gloom,' I say. 'So what about you? Do you have any nice banisters lined up?'

'Banisters?' he repeats.

'Yeah. That's your new pastime isn't it? Being tied to people's banisters.'

He frowns slightly and shakes his head gently in apparent despair or disgust, I'm not sure which.

'Oh come on, I'm only having a laugh.'

Jude, beside him, gives me a wide-eyed look and subtly shakes his head.

Darren, for his part, stands, smoothly folds his MacBook into its carry-case and pulls his denim jacket from the coat-hook.

'Darren?' I say. 'You're not upset with . . .'

'Forget it,' he says, turning and heading for the door. 'I'm out of here.'

As the door closes behind him I look back at Jude. 'Jude?' I prompt.

'Leave him,' he says. 'He's been miserable as sin all week.'

'Right,' I say, thoughtfully. 'Look, I'll, erm, catch you later. Have a good weekend.'

By clip-clopping down the stairs as fast as my heels will allow, I manage to catch up with Darren in the lobby. I grab his shoulder just as he reaches the front door. 'Darren!' I say. 'Talk to me! What's wrong?'

He pauses, steps away from the door and turns to face me. 'You,' he says. 'You and everything and everyone.'

'Oh come on. We've been friends forever.'

He nods. 'Have we?' he says.

'Look, I'm sorry if I upset you,' I say. 'But of course we're friends.'

'Well you need to stop seeing your *friends* as disposable one-liners,' he says.

'Oh come on! That's not fair. You joke about this stuff all the time. You know you do.'

Darren nods slowly and stares at me. His eyes don't really look like they're focused on me at all. He looks like he's staring through me.

'Well,' he finally says, with almost robotic lack of intonation. 'Just because I joke about how pathetic my life is doesn't mean that *you* can.'

'Right,' I say.

'And just because I joke about it, it doesn't mean it's funny either.'

'No,' I say. 'I'm sorry. Look, why don't you come round? This weekend...'

'He shakes his head. 'Nah,' he says. 'I have banisters waiting.' And with that, he spins and walks from the building.

I linger in the lobby for a moment watching people stream by, and then I sigh, blow through my lips, and mutter, 'Brilliant! Excellent! Nice one, CC!' and then, finally, 'Enough!' I head back upstairs for my coat and bag.

As predicted, it starts to rain just as I get home.

I sit in my kitchen and watch water fall from the sky and

wonder if Jude is really going to cycle to Birmingham.

Personally, I can't summon the courage to step outside the front door. I'm feeling wintery and tired and vaguely depressed, and other than promising myself that I will phone both Mum and Brown Eyes before Monday morning, I plan nothing more than an overdose of carb, TV and wine.

Guinness – as dismayed by the weather as myself – seems most happy with my game plan, and pads from one end of the flat to the other as he follows me around. The second I sit anywhere he leaps onto my lap, turns around twice, and instantly falls asleep, and I'm stunningly grateful for the company.

I know it's considered the height of naffness to express one's feelings about a cat, but secretly I would have to admit that I love Guinness. Of course, other than the fact that my lap is warm, and that I know how to open tins of cat food, I have no idea whether Guinness has any equally deep appreciation of our relationship. But while the men in my life have come and gone, alternately promising ultimate happiness and then inducing months of misery, Guinness is still there, and he's still one-hundred-per-cent reliable: he comes home every night, if I want to watch TV, he's always willing to join me; he never complains about my choice of film, never criticises me about anything else either. And sometimes, like today, I wonder if I could cope with my life were Guinness *not* there waiting for me when I get home. For, crazy as it sounds, as long as he's there, I'm not quite alone. God, how sad is that? I'm turning into a cat-spinster.

On Saturday morning, Guinness and I watch a trashy romantic comedy involving Jennifer Aniston and a large dog. I say watch, but other than pointing his cross-eyes at the screen twice (when the dog barks), Guinness sleeps through most of the film. He is far more excited by my cooked brunch though, and ends up dragging the lion's share of two sausages across the carpet.

In the afternoon I watch a chick-lit number. The book wasn't fabulous so I have only the vaguest hopes for the film. This time we *both* doze through most of it.

And then, as per my weekend resolution, I steel myself, pick up the phone and dial the number. It rings twice, and then, surprisingly, *he* answers.

'Hello. Can I speak to . . . um . . . my mum, please?'

'Mum,' he repeats.

'Yeah. My mother.'

'Angela?'

'Yes. Is this, um, Saddam?'

'Yes,' he says. 'Saddam.'

'Well, um, good. Good to finally talk to you. So is she there?'

'Yes. I give you,' he says.

I grind my teeth as I wait for Mum to come to the phone.

After some muffled conversation and some scraping noises, she finally answers. 'Hello, darling. I was hoping you'd call.'

'Yeah. I got your message, so . . .'

'So . . .'

'So what's up?'

'Well, this has gone on long enough, really hasn't it?'

I pause for a moment, swallowing my pride and then say, 'Yeah. I suppose it has.'

'So you spoke to Saddam?'

'Yeah. I did. His English seems good.'

'Yes, it's getting better each trip. They learn so fast at that age.'

I swallow hard. I have been trying to blank the age thing from my mind. 'So how long is he over for?' I ask, trying to sound casual.

'Well he has to come and go for now. Because of the visa business.'

'Sure.'

'But he's been over for two weeks. He goes home on Sunday. Next Sunday, that is. Not tomorrow.'

'Right,' I say. 'So everything's still fine between you two.'

'Oh yes, dear. Better than fine.'

'Well, good.'

'That's why I called. I want you to come next weekend. Well, I wanted you to come *this* weekend really, but I expect it's too late now you've waited three days to call me back.'

'Yeah, sorry. I've been really busy. And I have to book a car and everything so it is probably, as you say, a bit late.'

'It's such a shame. That's why I phoned you three days ago.'

'Yes. But I've been really busy.'

'It only takes a second to pick up the phone.'

'Yes, I know.'

'So why can't you do that? Why can't you just call me back when I leave a message. It's not like I call you every day, is it?'

'No, Mum.'

'It shouldn't be too much to ask, should it?'

'Probably not.'

'*Probably* not?' she says, starting to sound outraged.

'Mum. Stop. It *is* too late now anyway.'

She sighs deeply. 'But I want you to meet him.'

'Yes.'

'And I've got some . . . never mind. That can wait.'

'What?'

'Nothing dear. But I want you two to meet. So that we can all move on with things.'

'Right,' I say, rubbing the bridge of my nose with my free hand.

'So can you come?'

'Before he leaves?'

'Well, yes. It would have to be Friday night.'

'But by the time I finish work . . .'

'Oh, of course you can come!'

'I'm not sure, Mum. I've got quite a lot on at the moment. Work-wise and stuff.'

'You said in your email that it was like a morgue.'

'Yeah. Um. Well, it was. But we've got this new contract. I have to go to Cornwall. Well, Devon anyway.'

'At the weekend?'

'Well no. Maybe. I mean, I don't know yet.'

'I wish you'd just say, yes. It's important to me.'

Behind her, I hear Saddam. He says it very quietly, but I hear him. He says, 'Leave. She doesn't matter. We don't need.'

253

And with the realisation that allowing myself to be relegated to *not needed* isn't going to increase my power to influence my mother one iota, I quickly re-evaluate my position. 'OK, Mum. Of course I will,' I say in my warmest tones. 'I'll have a word at work and juggle some dates around.'

'Excellent. Friday, after work?'

'Saturday. I'll book a car and be there by lunchtime, OK?'

'Friday would be so much better dear, because—'

'Mum, I can't.'

'Can't or won't?' she says. 'Because I really don't see . . .'

'Mum!' I interrupt. 'I'll come on Saturday. Or not at all. You choose.'

'Where did you get to be so stubborn?' she asks. 'It must come from your father, because you certainly don't get that from my side of the family.'

I pull a face and think that it's a good job we don't have video-phones yet. 'So I'll see you on Saturday?' I say.

She coughs. 'OK, Saturday then. But Saturday morning. And you'll stay the night?'

Again, I hear Saddam: 'No, not Saturday night. I must get to airport early on Sunday, remember.'

And I hear myself say, 'Yes, Mum. Of course I'll stay the night. We'll have all day Sunday to talk that way.'

After I hang up I sit and stare at the phone for a while and wish I still had a brother to discuss this all with. And then strangely, as if he hasn't been dead for nearly twenty years, I hear Waiine say, *'As long as she's happy, who cares?'*

And the answer is that *I* care.

On Sunday I bravely phone Norman as well.

He can't talk, he says, but offers to take me to dinner on Friday.

So as Guinness and I sit down to choose my third film of the weekend, I think, with dread and hope all mixed up, that whatever happens, at least next weekend isn't going to be like this one.

All I have to do is get through another week.

Test Drive

I get to Indian Zing ten minutes late. The second I enter the restaurant I see Brown Eyes seated against the far wall. He is suited again, but has removed his tie. He also has a newly sprouting beard.

'Hiya,' I say, trying not to look at his chin; trying to remember what he looks like without it. 'Sorry I'm late, but my taxi got stuck . . .'

'No problem,' Norman replies, half standing and then settling back into his seat as I hang my coat over the back of the chair and sit myself.

'So what's with the disguise?' I ask, unable to resist trying to find out if the beard is a permanent thing or not.

'Disguise? Oh, this?' Norman says, rubbing his beard and smiling. 'You like it?'

I shrug. 'Not sure,' I lie.

He shrugs. 'I thought maybe you weren't going to turn up. To get your own back on me for cancelling last time.'

'Not my style,' I say.

'Sorry about the work garb,' he says. 'But . . .'

'It's Friday night,' I say. 'I just came from work too.'

'Well you obviously make more effort with your work clothes than I do,' Norman says with a wink.

I'm wearing a French Connection ensemble. I smooth a hand across my skirt. 'Well, it's easier for guys, isn't it? It's jeans or a suit really. Or combats, I suppose.'

'Yeah, I suppose it is. So what work do you do again?'

'I work in advertising, well . . . if you can call it work.' Norman frowns so I continue, 'Oh, it's just so calm . . . nothing's really happening at the moment. It's quite worrying really.'

'The slowdown?'

'Yeah. It's hitting us hard. I spent most of this week reading the newspapers online. But that's depressing too.'

'It's hitting everyone hard. They're laying people off at my place too.'

'What is it you do again?'

'I'm in IT.'

'Right,' I say. And then I cock my head to one side. 'I thought you were in social services . . . Halfway houses or something.'

Norman purses his lips and shakes his head. 'No. IT,' he says, flatly.

'Weird.'

'Well, IT generally fails to impress the girls, so I tend to gloss over it.'

'Well, I know what you mean. Advertising doesn't always get the warmest reception.'

'No?'

'No. One guy told me it was about selling crap to people who don't need it.'

'A bit extreme,' Norman says.

'Well yes. And a bit true as well.'

'I guess.'

'It's really strange,' I say. 'I'm sure you said something about halfway houses.'

'Maybe I was configuring a network for one. There have been so many jobs since then I don't really remember. April, wasn't it?'

'Something like that, yes. March, I think.'

He licks his lips and then coughs. 'So the slowdown is really hitting you,' he says again.

'Yes.'

'Right.'

And then suddenly I can't think of anything else to say. My brain is perhaps too occupied analysing the meeting to come up with fresh subject matter.

There's a vague sense of expectation in the air, a little unease, partly caused by the new bearded face. But mainly, this doesn't, for some reason, feel much like a date. Maybe it's because it's just taken us too long to get this far.

A waitress crosses to our table and asks us if we're ready to order. 'Not quite yet,' I say, pulling a sheepish grimace and opening the menu. 'Have you eaten here before?' I ask Norman.

'Yeah. Quite a few times. The Kharphatla is lovely. Aubergine and prawns. And this chicken stew thing.' He leans towards me and points at the item on my menu. His beard is very close to my face. I can smell his cheap cologne.

'Right,' I say. 'Well, I have no idea really, so I'm happy to go with those two.'

'Good. Me too,' he laughs.

He waves the waitress over again and orders the dishes for both of us along with a bottle of house white. Being ordered for feels unfamiliar and vaguely quaint.

As we sip our wine and begin on the starters, I (because of my doubts) toss a few more questions at Norman about his job. But he answers so confidently that I decide I must have got the halfway-house thing from someone else. It's maybe a little shallow of me, but as he tells me about his (dull) job, he starts to become more of a Norman in my mind and far less of a Brown Eyes. I rather liked the idea that he did something social.

After the starter, which is really pretty sumptuous, Norman makes a trip to the loo. On his return, he hesitates, hovering awkwardly beside the table.

'Busy?' I ask.

'No, I erm . . . I'm regretting not doing something when you arrived. I'm regretting not giving you a peck. Because now I have to spend the whole evening trying to work out when I can slip that first kiss in.'

'There's a scene in a Woody Allen film about that.'

'Is there?'

'Yeah,' I say.

'How does it get resolved?'

'Um, they kiss.'

'Right,' he says.

I look up at his expectant smile and spot a tiny piece of bread lodged in his beard, and physically shiver.

I cough. 'Just sit down please,' I say.

Norman shrugs cutely like a schoolboy caught-out, and takes his seat. 'I'll take that as a "no" then shall I?'

I shrug back. 'Take it as "a maybe, but definitely not yet."'

'Right,' he says. 'Sorry. It's just that different people have such different rules about that stuff . . . It's hard to know *what* you're supposed to do these days.'

'No worries,' I say, a little impressed at his ability to express the situation so eloquently.

And then, for two whole minutes, silence reigns. I try to think of a subject, anything other than the weather, but momentarily my mind's a blank.

Eventually Norman speaks, 'Rubbish weather we've been having,' he says, and I almost laugh.

'Yes. Too much rain. Especially at the weekends.'

'Yeah.'

'I sometimes think I need to go and live somewhere sunny.'

'What, like abroad?'

'Yes. France, or Spain, or somewhere.'

Norman raises both eyebrows and nods slowly.

'Not your cup of tea then?'

'No,' he says. 'No, it wouldn't suit me.'

We sit again in awkward silence until Norman thinks of another subject. 'Weren't you going to some weird exhibition or something when we last met?'

I nod slowly. 'Good memory,' I say.

Norman smiles. 'Well, I have some failings, but bad memory isn't one of them.'

I decide that I rather like the way his eyes wrinkle when he smiles. It makes him look lived-in. If I can just keep my eyes away from his furry mouth . . . 'Yes, it turned out to be a *very* weird exhibition,' I tell him. 'A gay friend took me.'

He nods. 'So you're gay friendly,' he says. 'That's good.'

I frown. 'Is it? Why's that then?'

'Oh, no reason,' Norman says, pushing his lips out. 'My little brother is gay, that's all.'

I laugh. 'Well, as long as *you're* not . . .'

He looks at me questioningly, so I expound: 'I'm just a bit fed up with getting crushes on guys who are batting for the wrong team.'

Norman nods and then slips into a grin. 'No worries there,' he says. 'Feel free to crush away.'

I frown. 'I didn't mean . . .' I say.

'I'm teasing,' he laughs. 'Relax.'

'Right,' I say. 'Anyway . . .'

'The exhibition,' Norman prompts.

'Yes. Well. It was a Latin-American photographer. From Colombia. And the photos were a bit saucy really. They all had a bit of an S&M theme.'

Norman raises an eyebrow. 'Really,' he says.

'Men in harnesses and stuff.'

'Right. No women then?'

'A few. Oh, you mean the photos? No, well, the photographer – he's called Ricardo Escobar – he's gay as well I think, so . . .'

'Right.'

'The guy I went with – my friend from work – he ended up posing for him.'

'Really?'

'Yes, he tied him to the bottom of the stairs, made him wear a doggy mask, and did oil paintings of him.'

'Wow,' Norman says. 'So he paints too.'

I nod, a little surprised that the 'wow' was apparently prompted by Ricardo's artistic abilities rather than his pervy ways with models.

The main course arrives and the conversation stalls again, but this time for a good reason. The chicken 'stew,' which turns out to be a Kerala chicken curry, is absolutely sumptuous. 'Jesus, this is good!' I murmur.

He smiles and winks at me again. 'I may not know much, but I know about curry.'

'Do you cook as well then, or . . .?'

'Yeah. I love to cook,' he says. 'I don't do it so much these days because . . . well, for many reasons, really.'

'Being in Newcastle all the time?'

'Yeah,' he says. 'That kind of thing.'

I smile and fork another mouthful. 'The chicken is really juicy,' I say.

'Yeah. I always use organic chicken myself. That makes it even better. You get a much meatier taste.'

'Sure,' I say.

Despite his poor start with cancelled dates, dull-as-ditchwater job, and failed request for a beardy kiss, Norman is shifting back to becoming Brown Eyes again. He smiles a lot (which I'm a sucker for), he's reasonably self-effacing which I like, and he cooks to boot. With organic meat! And of course, best of all, he still has those brown eyes – big enough to skinny dip in.

As I lick my lips, now tingling from the curry, I almost regret refusing that kiss. Almost.

'So do you have a lot of gay friends, or just that one?' Norman asks, clearly casting around for a fresh subject of conversation. 'They usually come in groups.'

'You're right,' I say. 'They do.'

'What do you call a group of gay men? A troop?'

I laugh. 'A gander, maybe. A huddle?'

'A haggle perhaps. I must ask my brother.'

'But yes, I know a few,' I say. 'From work mainly. There's a lot of it about in advertising.'

'My brother's a film editor,' Norman says. 'He's really into cinema as well.'

'Well, there are lots of gay guys in media in general.'

'And hairdressing,' Norman laughs.

'Yes. That too.'

'Air stewards.'

'Yes. Actually the guy I was talking about – the one I went

to the exhibition with – he's got the hump with me at the moment. He hasn't spoken to me all week. Well, not except for 'yes' and 'no.' It's quite difficult really because I have to work with him.'

'Really,' Norman says, in the tone of someone struggling to sound interested. 'What's that about then?'

'Oh, nothing really. It's silly.'

'He presumably wouldn't agree with you on that one though . . .'

'No. No, he wouldn't. I just made a joke at work . . . about him being tied up. And he got all holier than thou about it.'

'Right.'

'He says that just because *he* jokes about his sex life doesn't mean that I can.'

'Oh. I see.'

I shrug.

'I suppose it's like your parents,' Norman says.

'My parents?'

'Everyone's parents. Or country.'

'Country?'

'Yeah. You can joke about your country all you like, but then if some foreigner joins in you get really offended. It's the same with family.'

I nod thoughtfully. 'Yes, I suppose it is,' I say, thinking, '*How perceptive. Two extra points.*'

'Still, all the same,' I say. 'If you're going to do weird shit like that, *and* tell everyone about it . . . Well, it's a bit hypocritical to then start pretending to be offended. I mean, I never thought he would be. And of course I apologised immediately.'

Brown Eyes shrugs. 'Well, people are into all kinds of weird shit really, aren't they? As long as no one gets hurt, I don't really give a damn what people get up to in their own bedrooms.'

'Or hallways,' I laugh. Wondering if I'm coming across as a prude I add, 'Well nor do I, I wasn't criticising him or anything.'

'Good,' Norman says. 'Broad minded is the way to be.'

I restrain a smile and squint at him. 'You're not into anything weird are you? Because I've had my share of nasty surprises ... fetish wise.'

'Tell me more!' Norman says.

'Erm, I'd rather not.'

'No, I'm not into anything weird,' he laughs. 'Though I would have to admit, for a moment there I *was* imagining you tied to the bottom of the stairs.'

I open my mouth to speak, but then close it again. His eyes are twinkling and I can't for the life of me decide if he's genuinely aroused by the idea or just winding me up.

'Well don't,' I finally say, trying to walk the fine line between sounding like a prig and stating clearly what isn't on the menu here. 'Don't imagine it, that is. Because it's not going to happen. Just because I don't disapprove of what Darren gets up to doesn't mean that I'm going to do the same things myself.'

'Sure,' he says, raising the palms of his hands at me in a surrender sign.

'Sorry, if you are into that, I wouldn't hold it against you either.'

'No?'

'No. But I'd rather you said straight out.'

He laughs. 'Honestly ...' he says. 'No, honestly I'm not ... But I am open minded.'

'Well as my friend Mark says: don't be so open minded that your brain falls out.'

He laughs. 'I like that. Yes. Very good. No, I just mean that I am into new things. I like the idea of spicing things up a bit anyway. But then I think anyone who has spent fifteen years with a frigid cow like Cathy would say the same thing.'

'Your ex?'

He shakes his head. 'My wife,' he says. 'Unfortunately.'

My mouth fills with saliva. I swallow. 'You're still *married*?'

He nods. 'Sadly, yes.'

'But separated presumably?'

'Not yet, no.'

I put down my glass and straighten my posture. 'I don't really understand,' I say. But I think that I probably *do* understand. I just daren't let it show. Not yet.

'Well, I'm looking,' he says. 'I'm waiting to meet the right person.'

'I see.'

He nods. 'Is that a problem?'

'Well . . .' I say. I think, *A problem? A problem?!*

He shrugs.

I cough. 'The thing is, Brian,' I say.

He frowns at me. 'Brian?'

'Sorry, *Norman*,' I correct myself, feeling suddenly sick. 'The thing is, that people usually do it the other way around.'

'Sorry, but who is Brian?' he asks.

None of your business, I think. 'Oh, nobody,' I say. 'An ex.'

Norman smiles. 'Should I take that as a good sign then?'

I screw my eyes up and tilt my head to one side. 'Erm . . . no. No, you probably shouldn't,' I say with exaggerated seriousness.

'OK. Anyway, don't get the wrong end of the stick, there. God, me and my big mouth! I will *leave* Cathy . . . just as soon as I meet the right person . . . when I, you know, have somewhere to go to.'

How lovely! I think. 'Right,' I say, flatly.

'Because obviously, we live together. So there are material issues too. I nearly left her at Christmas. I was seeing this girl . . . I thought it was going to work out. But then she dumped me.'

I nod and swallow hard again. 'So you were living with your wife and seeing someone else?'

'Well yeah,' he says. 'For a bit. Temporarily.'

I think, *What a slimeball.* I sigh deeply. 'And presumably your wife didn't know about this?'

He frowns. 'Well no. She'd make my life hell if she knew. I may like a bit of kink, but I'm not a masochist.'

'Right,' I say. 'So you had an affair. I mean . . . Well, really, *that's* what you're saying, isn't it?'

He frowns. 'Well no. I mean, not really. Because I would have left her. I was going to do it on Boxing Day. I didn't want to spoil Christmas, that's all.'

I nod. 'Right,' I say. I think, *Worm.*

'But women aren't cars,' I continue, starting to feel truly angry now. 'You can't just go around test driving them until you find a model that suits you better and then trade up.'

'No,' Norman says, thoughtfully. 'Well you sort of *can* actually,' he adds. 'I mean, don't get me wrong, of course women aren't cars, but as a bloke, well, you can't let them boss you . . .'

Mary, mother of Jesus!

'I need to pop to the loo,' I interrupt, pushing away from the table and grabbing my bag. I'm scared that if I let him finish that phrase I shall have to slap him.

'Me too,' Norman says, standing too. 'Too much tea at work.'

We head to the back of the restaurant side by side. I want to push him away from me. I have a little fantasy of him falling into the hot-pot at the big group table, sit-com style.

The ladies', as always, is occupied, so I wait and watch Norman disappear into the men's. As he vanishes behind the door, he winks at me again.

Cocky little shit, I think, as I fake a smile and give him a little wave.

And then I have an idea. I scoot back across the room and grab my coat from the seat-back, and not even taking the time to put it on, I stride to – and then out of – the door of the restaurant.

When I get outside it is drizzling lightly but there is nowhere really to hide. And so I literally jog – well, as close to jogging as heels will allow – to the first side street.

Once I have rounded the corner, I slow to a brisk walk until I manage to flag down a passing cab. The street is one way, so the taxi driver has no choice but to drive me back to the main road, and back past the restaurant.

I slump as low in the seat as I can; my heart is pounding. I feel like I have done something naughty and am about to be caught out. I feel the way I did when I went through my brief stint of shoplifting at thirteen. Adrenalin. Fight or flight.

I shake my head at my inability to ever pick a sane, normal, single, heterosexual male. Does such a person even exist any more?

I feel a wave of dismay at the fact that I have spent so very many months fantasising about this, entirely *pointless*, worm of a man.

And then I think of one of Darren's fabulous one-liners – *do I look like a side-dish for bored couples?* – and wish that I had used it.

For a moment I think about texting the line to Norman, but then I decide that picturing him waiting for me to return from the ladies' is going to be far more satisfying.

A Ghostly Presence

Because I have a car booked for nine, I have to set my alarm for seven. What with thinking about Norman, men, and my life in general, plus worrying about meeting Saddam, it's four a.m. before I finally drift off into the lightest of slumbers. What's more, I'm awakened a full fifteen minutes before the alarm by the dulcet tones of Guinness retching. I switch the light on just in time to see him vomit a prodigious quantity of semi-digested cat food over the pile of (until that moment, clean) washing I left on the armchair.

I groan, roll from the bed, scrape the worst of the brown gunge from a sweatshirt into the loo, and carry the entire pile of folded washing straight back to the washing machine.

I'm lacking so much sleep that I feel like I have been at an all-night party (when was the last time I did *that*?). So I dig out my trusted college-year remedy (vitamin C tabs) and make myself two double espressos and head for the shower. Vaguely aware that I'm trying to look younger but determined not to think about why, I dress in my trendiest pair of G-Star jeans and a French Connection sweatshirt, dump another pile of cat-food (a different brand this time) in Guinness' bowl, and head from the door.

It's a cold but sunny day, and I'm hugely grateful for this. Motorways in the rain have always given me the willies. For some reason I have always felt that I will probably die in a slithering pile-up on the M11.

At easyCar Euston, I learn that somebody has pranged my

Ford Ka, so I'm 'upgraded' to a diesel Mondeo, which, due mainly to tiredness, makes me disproportionately furious. I don't like big cars anyway but the Mondeo makes me feel like a long distance sales rep.

But once I get out of London and onto the M11 I forget about it and get entirely lost in my own thoughts which flip back and forth between yesterday evening's long-anticipated reunion with Norman (who this morning, I feel, probably should have received at least a slap) and nervous, sickly anticipation of meeting Saddam.

Thinking about Darren, Saddam, Charles, Brian and Norman, I decide that in fact men in general could do with a slap. In a vague fantasy world, I toy with the idea of becoming a lesbian. I imagine living with a woman instead of a man. I picture having her butch animal-rights friends around for a Sunday nut-roast. It actually all feels quite appealing until the movie in my mind reaches the obligatory sex-scene, upon which I pull a face and blank that entire thought process by thinking about Mum and Saddam again.

I wonder what he will be like. Mainly, when I try to picture him, my mind produces images of Saddam Hussein. Old and bearded, the day he was captured. *God! I hope he doesn't have a beard!* Not that I'm intending to kiss my mother's boyfriend of course, but all the same ... You don't want your stepfather – *stepfather!* now there's a thought! – being called Saddam, *and* looking like him. I remind myself that he's too young to look like Saddam Hussein, and force myself to imagine someone younger, but the image my mind's eye conjures up looks more like a twelve-year-old than a young man of twenty-three. And then I remind myself that I have already glimpsed him in Mum's photos so I try to recover that image. Interestingly enough that part of my data-bank is entirely blank.

As I hit the M25, thick grey cloud fills the sky, but the roads remain dry and the traffic is light, so I make good time. The radio in the Mondeo only seems to pick up soppy love songs which are *sooo* not where my brain is at this morning, so I end up switching it off and humming The Strokes instead. I pull onto Mum's drive at eleven o'clock precisely.

She appears from the side of the house, trotting across the gravel.

'I thought it might rain,' she says as I climb from the car. 'I'm so glad it didn't. I know how you hate driving in the wet.'

'Dry all the way,' I say, slamming the car door and hugging her perfunctorily as is our way.

'That's a big car for you,' she says.

'I know,' I say. 'They ran out of little ones. I wanted a Ka.'

Mum nods. 'Well . . . yes . . .' she says. 'Oh, a "*Ka*". That little blobby Ford thingy.'

'Yeah,' I say.

'Well come in,' she says, 'before it *does* rain.'

'Do you think it's going to?' I ask as I follow her to the house. I think, *Suspend judgement. Maybe he's nice.*

'Adam's out,' Mum throws over her shoulder, as if she's reading my thoughts. 'He's having a driving lesson.'

I smile and grimace at the same time. 'A driving lesson! Wow.'

I step into the hallway and Mum pushes the door closed behind me. 'Now don't be like that . . .'

'I'm not being like anything.'

'He can already drive. It's just he has to take his test again. They only give you twelve months on a Moroccan licence.'

'Right,' I say. 'Did you say *Adam*, or did I mishear you?'

'No, that's right. We've decided to re . . . what is it you advertising people say?'

'I don't know. Re-brand him?'

'Yes. That's it. We've decided to "*re-brand*" him.' I restrain a smirk as she makes speech-marks with both hands. 'The Saddam thing is turning out to be a bit . . . challenging . . . so . . .'

I briefly think of pointing out that Chelsea is a bit *challenging* as well. Especially when my birth certificate and passport say Chelsii. *Waiine, Chelsii, what was she thinking of?*

I decide, however, not to provoke her this early on. 'And he doesn't mind? Being called Adam?'

Mum shrugs. 'Why would he? Now come on in. A cup of tea?'

'Oh yes please,' I say, following her into the kitchen. 'I'm gasping.'

As she fills the kettle, I glance around the room trying to spot any signs of Saddam/Adam's presence, but other than a rather nice Adidas sweatshirt that I wouldn't mind myself, there are none.

'So how have you been?' I ask.

'Fine,' she says. 'Well, great really. You just get into the habit of saying fine, don't you? Yes, I spent the day gardening yesterday, sorting those rose-beds out.'

'That's good,' I say, '... keeping busy. Did Saddam help you?'

'Adam? No. Gardening's really not his thing.'

'Right. He could still give you a hand though, couldn't he?'

'Well I don't see why *you* would say that,' she says. 'I thought you'd be on his side.'

'I'm sorry?'

'Well *you* certainly never gave me a hand in the garden.'

'No,' I say. 'No, I suppose I didn't. But I help with other things.'

'Well so does Adam.'

'Fair enough.'

I hear the crunch of wheels on the drive, and then a car door opening and closing, but frustratingly the kitchen is at the rear of the house so I can't see him arrive. I would have liked to catch a glimpse of him before having to meet him face to face.

As I hear him put his key in the lock (so he has keys!) my heart starts to pound.

'That'll be Adam now,' Mum says checking her watch as if she might have different men coming at different times of the day.

And then he's there, standing in the doorway, jingling his keys. Our eyes meet for half a second, and then he averts his gaze and stares at the floor.

He's wearing jeans, a plain white shirt and Adidas trainers.

My first reaction – which I suppress – is to laugh. It's not that there's anything ridiculous about Saddam per se, it's just that if you were to fill a warehouse with photos of every single person on planet Earth, and ask someone to pick out a photo of my mother's partner, Saddam's photo would be, almost certainly, anyone's, *everyone's* last choice.

He is young (obviously). The white shirt somehow doesn't help this. It makes me think of school uniform. But he's also taller and darker than I imagined, almost black in fact, with frizzy, short, jet black hair. He has the largest, darkest eyes that I have ever seen, big cheekbones, and full, almost girlish lips. OK, OK, I admit it. He's *very* good looking. Almost too good looking – almost model-pretty.

'Hello!' I say with as much enthusiasm as I can muster, on reflection probably overdoing it a bit. I sound a bit like a Club Med guide.

He looks up at me and breaks into a big toothy smile – born more, I'm guessing, from embarrassment than pleasure. 'Hello,' he replies.

And then I decide that he reminds me of someone else, and realise that he looks like a younger, plumper version of President Obama. Obama with lip implants perhaps. I wonder if he's aware of the irony of being called Saddam and looking like Obama.

'How did the lesson go?' Mum asks, thankfully breaking the tension.

'It went good,' he says.

'Well,' my mother corrects him. 'It went *well*.'

'Well,' he says, unconvinced. He shuffles from one foot to another and takes a half step towards me. 'Should we ... embrace?' he says.

'Kiss,' Mum corrects him. 'Adam wants to kiss everyone. They're very French in Morocco.'

He lowers his gaze again and then steps back to the doorway.

'*Tu parles Français*?' I ask him.

'*Oui*,' he replies, briefly flicking his eyes at me.

'Not that it's much use here,' Mum says. 'And you're not to talk to each other in French, you hear? I'm not having you two forming some secret club.'

'*Non, Maman*,' I say, provoking another grin from Saddam.

'You make coffee?' he asks my mother.

'Yes. Do you want a cup?'

'Yes, and a sandwich. Cheese.'

I brace myself for Mum to explode and remind him of his manners, but she doesn't. She simply says, 'I'll bring it through.'

'So how did . . .' I say, turning back to the door. But he has already left the room.

'He'll have gone to watch TV,' Mum says. 'It's good for his English. He likes the American stuff best. He says it's easier to understand.'

'Well that'll be where, "it went good," comes from,' I say.

'Yes,' she says. 'Yes, I suppose so.'

'Staying and talking would probably do his English more good,' I point out.

She wrinkles her nose as she fills the cups. 'Yes, well, I expect he's a bit shy,' she says.

Once she has made my tea and his coffee and sandwich, I expect that we will head through to the lounge to join him, but in fact Mum delivers his snack-pack and returns to the kitchen.

'Shouldn't we . . .?' I say, nodding my head towards the lounge. People eating or drinking in separate rooms was always a no-no in my day.

'No, he's better just watching TV,' Mum says. 'So. What do you think?'

Following our three second exchange, it's entirely impossible to give an honest or educated reply, so I just say, 'Yes. He seems nice.'

That question – what do I think – remains impossible to answer as the day passes, for the simple reason that Saddam's presence in the house seems more like that of a timid lodger, or perhaps the ghost of a timid lodger than anything to do with my mother.

I catch glimpses of him from the corner of my eye, padding silently from one room to another. I hear the toilet flush and the TV go on and off, as if, perhaps, operated by an invisible, silent poltergeist. As I tour the garden with Mum, I glance up and catch a vague, somehow *transparent* glimpse of him upstairs, looking at us from behind the shiny windows of her bedroom – he instantly slips out of sight.

For the evening meal, Saddam momentarily occupies the same room as Mum and me. I'm reassured to be reminded that he is made of skin and bones. I was starting to feel a little spooked by his invisible presence.

Mum, for many years champion of the *British-Meat-And-Two-Veg* school of cooking, knocks up a surprisingly good lamb couscous, and once it's served and ready to roll, Saddam, summoned, joins us at the table.

He smiles at me, then lowers his gaze to the plate and starts to eat rapidly.

'So, Saddam . . .' I say. 'Sorry, should I call you Saddam or Adam?' I ask.

'Adam,' Mum replies.

Saddam flicks his eyes at me and smiles briefly. 'Adam is OK,' he says.

'So you're flying home tomorrow?' I say.

'Yes, he gets picked up by a shuttle tomorrow morning,' Mum answers. 'I hate driving these days.'

'So what do you do in Agadir?' I ask. 'It is Agadir, isn't it?'

'Well he's a guide, dear,' Mum says. 'You know that.'

I turn to my mother and smile tightly. 'I thought Adam might like to tell me about it *himself*,' I say, pointedly turning back to face him.

'Yes. A guide,' he says.

'So do you get to use your English when you're working as a guide?'

He nods and points at his mouth to indicate that it's full of food, and I wait for him to finish without glancing at my mother. But once he has finished, he just forks another lump of lamb into his mouth.

I glance back at Mum, a little consternated and she wrinkles her nose and mouths the word, 'Shy,' at me.

'You have brothers or sisters?' I ask, trying again.

'He has . . .'

'Mum!' I say, shooting her a glare which effectively silences her.

He raises four fingers in reply and continues to chew.

I wait until he swallows and ask, 'Brothers or sisters?'

'Three sisters. One brother,' he says with a vague French accent, before loading up with another forkful of couscous.

It would be easy to interpret these monosyllabic responses as rude or begrudging, but his body language, his facial expressions, his aura, his toothy grin, his wide eyes dropping to the plate at every available opportunity are anything but rude. In fact he emanates nothing but timidity and sweetness. He's a sweet, unsophisticated Moroccan boy who finds this whole situation rather uncomfortable, and – against all expectation – slightly more embarrassing than even I do.

At this point, I start to worry – not about Saddam fleecing Mum – but about *her* dominating and exploiting *him*.

I end up shovelling my food in a similar fashion to Saddam, just to get it over with. Immediately I have finished my plate, he stands, wipes his mouth, delicately folds the napkin, and says in a rigidly polite voice that is so quiet that I can barely hear him, 'Well, it was very good to meet you.'

'Thanks,' I say. 'You too.'

'And now I must sleep. Bus at six,' he says. 'Up at five.'

I nod. 'I understand,' I say. 'Sleep well.'

Nervously he shuffles towards me again, and this time I stand and reach out to hug him. But he just pecks me on both cheeks, swivels on the spot, robot like, and slides from the room. The overall impression is that of a polite child forced to give Mummy's guest a goodnight kiss.

I glance at Mum and she smiles and raises an eyebrow. 'It just makes you want to eat him up really, doesn't it!'

I force a smile and nod and sigh. 'Yes,' I say. 'Yes, right.' I clap my hands. 'So! Dishes.'

'I'll wash, you wipe,' she says, standing.

We wash and wipe in well-rehearsed fashion for a while and then, despite the fact that it's a bit risky, I try to start a proper conversation about Saddam. 'I still don't really understand . . .'

'Why I don't get a dishwasher?' she says. 'I know.'

I had been about to say, *'what your relationship with Saddam is all about.'*

'Well, no,' I say. 'It's easier. They say it's cheaper now than all that hot water anyway.'

'Yes, I know, dear,' she says. 'You always say it. But I like it. Washing-up and ironing. Now if someone could come up with a machine to do the hoovering or clean the windows, that would be a different matter.'

By ten, Mum has retired to bed as well, and though I am quite shattered myself, I can't quite face retiring to my old room, just two doors away from her and Saddam.

And so I sit in the lounge and watch, but don't actually listen to the TV, and wish again that Waiine was here to talk to.

'He's a doormat,' I would say. *'He's just a kid. She's stomping all over him.'*

And Waiine would reply, *'Other than a doormat, who could possibly put up with our mother?'*

Over the sound of *Have I Got News For You* I can hear a faint banging noise. It's not loud, but it's jolly regular and goes on for a very, very, very long time. I turn the TV up and pour myself a whisky and try not to think about where it's coming from.

Genetics

It always feels weird waking up in my old bed – there are always a few seconds when I'm not sure where I am, or more importantly *when* I am.

I glance at my alarm clock, its flip-over numerals tell me that it's 8:59, sometime after 1979 when I was given it for Christmas.

As I watch, it flips over to 9:00 a.m. with a satisfying *thrrup* sound, and I remember lying awake, waiting for 11:59 to change to 00:00 that first Christmas.

I roll onto my back and stare at the ceiling and wonder what, if anything, I want to say to my mother. And then, immediately fazed by the impossibility of resolving that one, I slip back into my memory banks and remember the sounds of my childhood – Waiine tearing around, Dad calling me down for breakfast of a Sunday morning in time for Mass. Both, of course, now gone.

Eventually I slip back to sleep and have a pleasant, if, on reflection somewhat unnerving, mini-dream about slotting together a Scalextric car track. In the dream there are three of us playing sweetly together: myself, Waiine and Saddam.

I find Mum in the kitchen nursing a cup of tea and the *Daily Telegraph*.

'Oh, hello, Sleepy-Head,' she says predictably. 'Tea's in the pot.'

'I always sleep so well here,' I say, moving to the counter and pouring myself a cup. 'I should take that bed back to London.'

'You'll do no such thing,' she says.

'So did he get off OK?'

'Yes. The shuttle was ten minutes late – so there was a moment of stress, wondering if it would come, but it all turned out OK. He sent me a *"text"* to say he was boarding.'

'Good,' I say, taking a seat opposite her. 'Do you miss him when he goes?'

She screws up her face and raises an eyebrow in disdain. 'Well of course I do,' she says. 'It's no fun rattling around here on my own.'

'No.'

'The financial crisis seems to be going from bad to worse,' she says, nodding at the paper. 'They make it sound like the end of civilisation as we know it.'

'Yes,' I say. 'I can't help but think they're exaggerating a bit, though. I suppose it sells more newspapers that way.'

'Well, I hope they make all these bankers pay for the mess they've made,' she says.

I pull a circumspect grimace. 'I think you can be pretty certain that they won't.'

'Well, no. No, I'm sure you're right.'

'They'll probably find some way to come out richer than before.'

'Yes,' Mum says. 'So.'

'So?'

'So. Go on. I'm sure you're just dying to tell me why I have it all wrong.'

'What? The financial crisis?'

'Saddam,' she says, then correcting herself, 'Adam.'

I sigh.

'I knew it,' she says. 'You had a face like a slapped arse all through dinner.'

I drop my mouth in outrage. 'I did not!'

'That's the one,' she says.

'Mum!'

'I'm joking! So come on. What did you think?'

I shrug. 'He seems . . . nice.'

'Ah. So you've decided to chicken out? To just tell me what I want to hear?'

I roll my eyes. 'Jeez, Mum. I can't really win with you.'

'You think he's too young, of course.'

'Well yes. Of course I think he's too young. He's a lad, Mum. He's a naïve young lad.'

'I had a two-year-old baby when I was his age. And a job. And a husband.'

I nod slowly. 'Yes, I suppose you did.'

'I was old enough to decide what I wanted. Why shouldn't Adam be?'

'Because of where he's from,' I say. 'He probably doesn't feel he has as many options as you did.'

'Options?'

'Well, yes.'

'What would you know about what options I had?'

'Yes, sure. But you know what I mean.'

'You *mean* he wouldn't be seen dead with a wrinkly old crone like me if he didn't need a ticket out.'

I frown. 'Well I wouldn't have put it quite like that,' I say.

Mum nods and pulls off her reading glasses. 'Well that's not it,' she says. 'He has a very nice life in Agadir. But he loves me.'

'Yes, but—'

'I haven't finished,' she says, sharply.

'Sorry . . .' I return to sipping my tea.

'And even if that were the reason,' she says. 'Even if Adam did want to be with me because he wants a better life, what would be so wrong with that?'

'Well, it would be . . .' I say. But the word on my lips is '*prostitution*' and I can't say that. I struggle to find another way to express what I want to say, but the words that come to mind this time are, '*economic slavery*' which clearly aren't helpful either.

'Why did Jenny Robinson leave Robert?' she asks me.

'Because being married to a man with a speech impediment – a man called Robert Robinson, or rather *Wobert Wobinson* – was just too silly for words?' I say.

'No,' she says, ignoring my rather witty retort. 'Because he couldn't hold down a job. Because he was always drunk.'

'And the *Wobinsons* are welevant because?'

'You stay with someone for a whole host of reasons. Because you find them attractive. Because they make you laugh. Because they have a good job. Because you think you'll have a nice life together.'

'Yes but that shouldn't be the principal reason,' I say. 'Surely.'

She shakes her head and looks out of the side window.

'What?' I say.

'I'm just wondering how you see me,' she says.

'How I *see you*?'

'Well yes. If you can't imagine anyone wanting to be with me.'

'Oh, Mum. I can! I love you. Dad loved you. But . . .'

'But Adam doesn't . . .'

'I just think it's . . . *confused*. Because of the age thing.'

'He *likes* older women, dear.'

Another not-useful word pops into my brain. *Gerontophile.* I think of a *Little Britain* sketch where the young man keeps *accidentally* touching-up the Gran.

'He likes older women,' she says again. 'He likes me particularly. He wants a better life. He sees he can have that with me . . .'

'And you? What's your end of the deal?'

'It's not *a deal*, dear.'

'You know what I mean.'

'I love it when he's here.'

'OK. Why?'

'Because having someone in my bed after twenty years of sleeping on my own is wonderful. Because having a bit of youth in the house makes me feel younger. Because I'm enjoying sex again.'

'Mum,' I say, pulling a face.

'Because I'm enjoying sex again,' she repeats pedantically, 'and I didn't think it was possible. Because having him around reminds me of when you and . . .'

'When Waiine was at home.'

Mum shrugs.

'But those aren't the right reasons,' I say. 'Surely you can see that those aren't the right reasons to go out with someone.

Because he reminds you of your daughter who has flown the nest and your dead son.'

'It's why people have relationships, dear,' she says. 'All those reasons are why people get together. Because it's bloody lonely and bloody boring being on your own.'

'I just don't think—'

'Why do you think you go around with so many homosexuals? We're all trying to replace what we have lost.'

'But I don't—'

'And who are you to judge anyway?' she asks, starting to get seriously hot under the collar. 'Who are you to tell me which are good reasons and which are bad? Since when did *you* become such a relationship expert?'

The comment stings me to the core. I'm lost for words.

'I didn't mean . . . I'm sorry,' she says.

I shrug.

'I'm sorry,' she says again.

'Right,' I say.

I stare out of the window at the grey day. I think of an Everything But The Girl song: 'Two Star', about not being able to judge the lives of others when your own is a mess.

'Right,' I say again.

'I'm sorry. I didn't mean to be . . . There are lots of reasons people marry, that's all I'm saying.'

'Marry,' I say.

'Well, live with, stay with, go out with, you know what I mean.'

'But you said *marry*.'

'I was talking hypothetically,' she says.

'So you're *not* going to get married?'

'No. Well . . . Oh, look . . . of course I am.'

'Of course you are?!'

'You've already worked that out anyway, haven't you? Let's not play games.'

And though that knowledge hadn't yet been acknowledged – though it was merely lurking at the back of my mind, she's right. I did know.

'And you don't approve.'

I shrug. 'No,' I say. 'You're right. Let's not play games. I don't approve. No.'

'Plus it's the only way to really sort out all this visa mess,' she says.

'So you get married, and he gets nationality?' I say. 'That's the deal?'

'There's no deal,' she says. 'Honestly, dear. But if we're going to be together, well, being married makes it all much easier. That's what Giles says anyway.'

I blink and shake my head in disbelief. 'This is Giles . . . Dad's old partner from the law firm?'

'Yes, Giles Anderton.'

'You're consulting Giles Anderton, Dad's partner . . . to work out the best way to get your twenty-year-old Moroccan lover into the country.'

Mum shakes her head. 'Darling. Whatever is wrong with you these days?'

'Do you think that's appropriate?' I ask.

Mum sighs deeply and shakes her head. She looks red-faced and angry, but also somehow slightly amused.

'What?' I prompt.

'Enough,' she says.

'Enough?'

'Yes. Time to change the subject.'

'Just, please don't rush into this. Just . . . give it time. There are legal implications and . . .'

She shakes her head again.

'What?' I say again.

'You remind me of my grandmother,' she says. 'Always very concerned about what was *"appropriate,"* Granny Stevens was. Lucky I didn't listen to her, or you wouldn't be sitting there today.'

I nod.

'I never thought you'd end up so stuffy. I suppose it's like hair colour.'

'Hair colour?'

'Yes. I suppose it can jump a generation. Anyway, I need a drink.' And at this she stands and struts from the room.

A drink! At ten a.m.! I sit at the kitchen table and think of *Absolutely Fabulous.*

'I have become Saffy,' I mutter morosely, 'and my mother has turned into Edina.'

But no, it's worse: my mother has turned into Patsy.

The Gift of Time

The first thing I do on Monday morning is to look up Giles
Anderton's number and call him. The fact that he is 'advising'
my mother has been playing on my mind and I need to talk to
him about it.

He picks up the phone on the third ring.

'Hello, Giles, it's CC, remember me?' I say.

'CC?'

'Yes, Angela's daughter.'

'*Oh, Chelsii* . . . sorry. So how are you? It's been ages, hasn't it?'

'It has. Really ages!'

'So what can I do for you?'

'Well, I expect you can work out why I'm calling.'

'I could hazard a guess, yes.'

'I'm really worried about her.'

'Of course.'

'She says you're advising her.'

'Well, advising is probably overstating it a bit. But I'm giving
her a helping hand.'

'With Saddam's immigration?'

'Well . . . Um . . . I'm sorry. It's a bit delicate. I, er . . . Well, I
can't really discuss a client's affairs. Not even with you.'

'Oh, of course. Silly me. Sorry.'

'No problem, it's just . . .'

'Sure. No worries. You retired, didn't you? When Dad . . .'

'Yes, that's right.'

'That would be the last time I saw you I think. At his funeral.'

'Yes.'

'Do you remember when he used to bring me into the office?'

'I do.'

'You used to let me use the typewriter.'

'That's right. I remember. You used to hit all the keys at once and jam it.'

'Yes. But you're retired now.'

'Yes.'

'So what's life like without clients?'

'Oh . . . rather nice really.'

'Right. So I suppose Mum's not really a client then, is she?'

'Well, no . . . I'm more giving her some advice. As a family friend.'

'Right. She's my mother.'

'I'm sorry?'

'Well, I'm part of that family.'

'Yes, of course.'

'All I want to know is if she's being careful, Uncle Giles.'

'Careful?'

'Yes. Has she, say, mentioned pre-nups to you?'

'Ahh! So you know then.'

'Well yes. She says you told her that marrying Saddam would make things easier.'

'In terms of his immigration, well, yes, it undeniably does.'

'It also makes it considerably easier for him to walk off with half of her estate. Half of our family estate.'

'Well, yes.'

'And seeing as I'm the only remaining family, that does rather affect me.'

'I suppose it does.'

'If Mum ends up destitute, she'll end up on my couch.'

'Well, I wouldn't think it will—'

'Or yours perhaps.'

'Yes, Chelsii. I get your point.'

'I don't want to be pushy, Uncle Giles, but . . . well . . . I want to know that we're singing from the same song sheet here.'

'I really do think that you need to discuss this with—'

'Oh, I will. Of course I will. But if she asks you, then you would obviously give her the same advice as me. Which is that a pre-nup is essential.'

'Yes, I suppose that is what I would say.'

'Good. I just wanted to check that you agree with me. Before I try to discuss it with her.'

'Yes, I do. Entirely. Of course. Anyway, do call in and see me next time you're over this way.'

'Are you still in . . .'

'Yes, still in Farnham. Still in the same house.'

'Great. Well, then I will. It will be a pleasure.'

'Oh, and Chelsii?'

'Yes.'

'Please don't phone me before ten. I am retired, you know.'

I glance at the clock on the wall (five past nine). 'God, I'm sorry. Did I wake you?'

'Not as such, but I only just got up so . . .'

'I'm so sorry.'

'No problem. Bye, pumpkin.'

When I hang up, my voicemail informs me that I have a message from Peter Stanton. He's asking to see me about Cornish Cow.

As they aren't yet clients of ours, and because they have, to date, ignored my suggestions of a visit, there doesn't seem to be much to discuss. In the end, Stanton simply wants to remind me how important a potential contract would be for the agency at this time.

'There's a rumour that Unibrand is going to buy them out,' he says. 'If that happens then their marketing budget could go sky high.'

I return to my desk and make a fresh attempt at calling their MD. I'm thoroughly convinced that his secretary will fob me off again, so I'm pretty surprised when she says, 'Oh yes. The meeting. Mister Niels suggested Thursday. Not this Thursday, that would be next

Thursday. Thursday the twenty-third. First thing.'

I phone Stanton to give him the news and then head straight up to Creative where I skip theatrically through the door.

'Hello!' I say to Mark, the only one present. 'Guess who has a meeting with Cornish Cow?'

Mark looks up at me and grins. 'Really? Hello!'

'Yep. Thursday week.'

'That's good news.'

'It is! Where is everyone?'

'Jude's getting . . .'

As he says this Jude pushes in through the door carrying two cups of coffee. 'Oh hiya. Did you want one?' he asks, handing Mark his cup, and hesitating with his own.

'No, I'm fine.'

'And Darren has taken the week off,' Mark continues.

'Sick, or . . .?'

'No, I think he's job hunting.'

'Job hunting? Wow! That's proactive. Stanton, hasn't said anything has he?'

'Well, you know he warned him,' Mark says.

'Yes, but nothing further?'

Mark shakes his head. 'No. But you don't have to be a genius to see what's happening . . . Or rather *not* happening. I think we should all be job hunting really. Hey, Jude. CC has a meeting with Cornish Cow.'

Jude smirks.

'What?' I ask him.

'Sorry, I just realised . . .' he says. 'CC? Cornish Cow?'

'Yes, very good,' I say.

'So when are you going?' he asks.

'Next Thursday,' Mark answers.

'Next Thursday,' I confirm.

'Apparently they're being bought by . . .'

'Unibrand,' I say. 'Yes, I heard the rumour. I don't think it's certain though.'

'So it might bring us some other work as well.'

'Well that's what we said about the Grunge!/Levi's deal,' I point out.

'Any news from the lovely Tom?' Mark asks.

I shake my head. 'Nothing much. It's the same as here. They're rushing around trying to pull ads to reduce their exposure until the slowdown speeds up or something.'

Jude crosses the room to put paper in the printer, and I notice that he's hobbling.

'God, you really went, didn't you?' I say.

He grins at me lopsidedly. 'If anyone ever invites you to cycle to Birmingham . . .' he says.

I laugh. 'That's an easy one. Just say "no".'

'It's not ten hours,' he says.

'No?'

'Twenty-two.'

'Jesus. In one go?'

'Well of course not,' he laughs. 'We stopped halfway.' He shakes his head as if ten hours cycling per day is somehow going to strike me as more feasible than twenty-two. 'So are you taking me to Devon with you?' he asks.

I shake my head. 'Stanton asked me to keep costs down for this first visit,' I say, which is a bit of a lie. Stanton did say that, but he was talking about hotels, not staff. But I have a couple of farmhouses I would like to look at on the way, and that's something I'd rather keep to myself. 'Is Darren all right?' I ask, suddenly. 'Because he was blanking me all last week.'

'Because of the banister business?' Jude asks.

'Well, presumably.'

'Banister business?' Mark repeats.

'Yeah, CC was ragging him about his modelling session,' Jude explains.

'I know it was a bit . . .' I say. 'But I did apologise.'

Jude shrugs. 'He's being an arse at the moment. I wouldn't worry about it.'

'Sure. But I hate it when there's an atmosphere. And especially because it's Darren.'

'Well, I'm sure he'll get over it.'

'Just buy him something nice for his birthday,' Mark says. 'He's a sucker for a pressie.'

'God! His birthday! I nearly forgot,' I say.

'Erm, hello! Party? Next Saturday?' Mark laughs.

'Of course,' I say.

'We have a DJ and everything,' he says. 'It's the eighties, so big hair and shoulder pads please.'

I nod. 'Eighties it is . . .' I say, wishing I had known before. I have boxes of eighties clothes in Mum's attic. 'OK, well, I suppose I had better get back and pretend to work.'

'You free for lunch?' Mark asks.

'Sure,' I say, happily. 'Twelve-thirty OK?'

'In the lobby?'

'In the lobby.'

The second we step out of the building, Mark links his arm through mine.

It's a crisp, sunny October day. 'I need to dig my winter coats out,' Mark says. 'They're lost in a pile of boxes somewhere.'

'Not finished unpacking yet then?' I ask as we cross the road.

'No. There are just not enough cupboards. So until we go cupboard shopping . . . and the way things are at work, I don't really want to go on a spending spree right now, so . . .'

'Right.'

'So how have you been?'

'Missing you, mainly,' I say.

'Yeah, right,' he laughs.

'No I do. It's horrible. Every time I remember that you're not upstairs, I feel sad.'

'Mister Patel hasn't replaced me yet then?'

I shake my head. 'It's too expensive. I phoned up, just in case. SJ and George are looking for a bigger place . . . they're trying for kids you see . . . but he wants three-ninety a week now.'

'Jesus!' Mark exclaims. 'I was paying two-ninety and I thought that was a lot. He'll never get that.'

'Especially not at the moment.'

'Where are we eating, by the way?' he asks, hesitating mid-pace. 'Ballantine's?'

'Suits me,' I say, following his change of direction. 'I just want a salad. *Waay* too many calories lately.'

'It's this winter weather. Me too.'

'So how's life in Tower Hamlets?'

'Lovely actually. I mean, it's an adjustment, isn't it? Because you end up changing all your routines. You end up eating half of your favourite food and half of his, and watching half of your TV and half of his . . . Which isn't always that easy when you've been single as long as I have.'

'But overall, it's a success story,' I say.

'Yeah,' he says thoughtfully. 'Yeah, it is. Because at the end of the day, I get into bed and there's this gorgeous cuddle-monster in the bed.'

'Right,' I say, as we step into the restaurant. 'Well, I'm very jealous.'

'So what about you?' Mark asks as we take our seats. 'Any love-news to share?'

I shake my head and shuck my coat. 'None,' I say. 'It's hopeless.'

Mark starts to remove his own lightweight jacket and then changes his mind and keeps it.

'You won't feel the benefit of it when you go back outside,' I say.

'My mother always says that,' he laughs. 'But I never believe it.'

'Nor me,' I agree. 'Oh, I did go and meet Brown Eyes. Do you remember Brown Eyes?'

Mark nods. 'A long time back. Norman or something?'

'That's it, Norman. What a memory!'

'And?'

'Erm: wanker; married; living with wife; just after a quicky, I think.'

'Oh.'

'Exactly. He says he's test-driving and that when he finds the right model he'll trade up.'

Mark pulls a face. 'Really? Did he actually say that?'

I wrinkle my nose. 'No, not quite. But that was the gist.'

'Eek!' Mark says. 'After all that waiting to meet him.'

'I know,' I say, shaking my head. 'But I got my vengeance. I walked out and left *him* waiting. He thought I was in the loo.'

'Nice one.'

'He's probably still there. But other than that, no . . . And nothing else even on the horizon,' I say.

'One day he'll come along. And he'll be big and strong. The man I love,' Mark croons.

'One day . . .' I laugh. *'When?!'*

Mark shrugs. 'Who knows,' he says. 'But it happens. You never know when. It's like that Abba song: 'The Day Before You Came'. One day you open the front door and everything changes.'

'Well I wish it would,' I say. 'I open my door and the only thing that happens is the postman hands me a final notice.'

'It'll come, sweetie. There's someone for everyone.'

'I told you about my mother marrying this twenty-year-old Moroccan lad, right?'

'She wants to *marry* him?'

'Yeah. That's what she says now . . .'

Our orders arrive – a salad for me and a roasted vegetable focaccia for Mark, but just as I raise my fork my BlackBerry rings.

'That'll be him now,' Mark laughs.

'Who?' I ask, answering the phone at the same time.

Mark sings, *'One day he'll come along,'* again, and having decoded the joke I roll my eyes at him. 'Yes?' I say, into the handset.

In fact it's the secretary at the gynaecology practice. She says she (finally) has my results, and wants to schedule a new appointment for me to discuss them with the doctor.

'So I have to have a consultation?' I say.

'Yes, Doctor Ynchausty said he would prefer to see you.'

'I'd rather see his colleague,' I say. 'I did tell him that.'

'OK, sure. That's not a problem. Though, I don't have anything until Thursday week.'

'The twenty-third? I'm away.'

'Then the Friday morning?' she says.

'Away again,' I say.

'Thursday the thirtieth?'

'God, are you sure there's nothing sooner?'

'No,' she says.

'And if I see Doctor . . .' As I don't want Mark to realise that I'm consulting Victor, I say, 'the other doctor. The one I saw before . . .'

'Doctor Ynchausty?'

'Yes.'

'I'm afraid it's worse. It would have to be Friday the thirty-first.'

'Can't I just pop in and get them?' I ask.

'Well normally, yes, but he said he wants to see you.'

I take a deep breath and think about this. 'Is something wrong then? Because if there is then maybe I should see someone sooner rather than later.'

'Hold the line please,' she says.

I smile sweetly at Mark and mouth the word *sorry*. 'Eat!' I murmur.

He shrugs sweetly and sinks his teeth into his lunch.

I nibble at my own as I wait for the secretary to return.

'Hello?'

'Yes, still here.'

'Look, we don't usually give this sort of information out over the phone . . .'

'No.'

'But everything's fine. I just got Doctor James to have a peek, and all your numbers are totally normal.'

'Oh, good. Thank God. So why do I have to come in?'

'I'm sorry, we don't know. And Doctor Ynchausty isn't here today, so . . . But I wouldn't worry. Doctor James doesn't seem to think it can be urgent.'

'Right,' I say. 'Well, maybe you can book me in for the Thursday the thirtieth appointment then. With Doctor James. That's a woman, right?'

'Doctor James? Yes.'

'Right.'

'OK, so, I'll book you in for the thirtieth, eleven-thirty in the morning, and then I'll check it with Doctor Ynchausty tomorrow. And if I've missed something, I'll call you, OK?'

'OK.'

'Great.'

'Thanks for being so helpful.'

'It's a pleasure.'

I put the BlackBerry down on the table and sigh as I fork a lump of tuna.

'Bad news?' Mark asks.

'No,' I reply. 'No, not at all. I had some blood tests, and in fact everything's fine.'

'But you don't feel fine?'

'Well, I do now,' I say, breaking into a smile.

'Can I ask . . . or is it personal?'

I take a mouthful of salad to give myself some thinking time. For now would be the perfect moment to start edging around the subject. I could tell Mark that I'm feeling broody and wanted to check that everything is OK. That would inevitably lead to a discussion about how best to father a child . . . And then . . .

But then I think that things are different now. Apparently everything is OK, and this means that I have time on my side . . . I swallow, and bat a hand at the air. 'No,' I say. 'Nothing important. Just girlie stuff.'

He nods and smiles.

'So have you and Mister Perfect finished decorating yet?'

The High

The second the taxi turns the corner, I can both see and hear the party.

In the middle of a darkened mews, the third house looks like an image from the fire of London, orange light spilling from every window. The windows of the taxi are rattling to the subsonic bass from the sound system.

'I take it this is the one,' the taxi driver, who looks surprisingly like Paul Newman, chuckles.

'Yes. Well, I hope so,' I say, handing him a twenty. 'I'll be gutted if my friends are all sitting in the dark next door.'

I step from the cab into the cold night, and as the cab speeds away, I appraise the house. My first thought is somewhat materialistic: how much did *that* cost? For the house, white stucco and glass brick and vast modern windows, and the location, a sweet mews tucked back from the street – well, you can just smell the money.

I adjust my orange leg-warmers, give my Kim Wilde hair a final poke, take a deep breath and step towards the front door. Seeing that it's ajar, and spotting Jude inside, I push the door open and walk straight in.

Mark spots me immediately and trots across the tiled floor to meet me. 'She's here!' he says with heart-warming enthusiasm, as if this were *my* party.

Jude also turns and smiles at me. 'Hello you!' he says.

'Shit, Mark!' I exclaim. 'You didn't tell me about this place!'

He flashes the whites of his eyes at me and grins. 'Nice, huh?'

As he helps me off with my coat, I say, 'But how? I thought you said he worked as a translator?'

'A big mortgage,' Mark says. 'Well, and a lot of help from his granny. She's loaded apparently.'

'You're telling me!' I say.

Jude steps forwards and kisses my cheek. 'Hello you,' he says.

'Hiya. How are the legs?'

'All better now,' he says.

'There's a bottle of vodka in there, and Darren's gift,' I tell Mark, pointing at my bag with one pink, trainer-clad foot.

'Great,' he says, pushing it beneath the hall table. 'Thanks. Let me show you around first.'

The house looks like something from *Grand Designs*. Everything is white sleek plaster or shiny, bluish glass. Mark shows me the two bedrooms on either side of the entrance, both of which have half a wall of glass brick separating them from the street. 'And this one's sort of the office and storage and, well, everything else . . .' he explains.

I look at a pile of boxes obscuring an entire wall. 'I can see why you couldn't find your coat,' I say.

'I know,' he laughs. 'I forgot to label them, so . . . I just borrowed one of Ian's in the end.'

'This must be lovely and bright during the day,' I say. 'With all this glass.'

'It is,' Mark says. 'A bit too bright really – *no* chance of a lie-in. I'll convince him to add curtains or blinds or something in the end.'

'Beautiful though,' I say.

'Yes.'

We move through to the vast central lounge. The rear wall of the room is a sliding glass partition opening onto a small enclosed garden. Just in front of it someone has set up a sound-system with proper mixing decks, huge speakers (they are taller than I am) and even some flashing lights and a glitter-ball. Outside four people are standing smoking and around them the garden twinkles like some rare precious stone with the light from a dozen huge garden candles that the boys have lit.

'Oh how beautiful!' I exclaim. 'God, Mark, you have really fallen on your feet here, haven't you?'

'I know!' he says, sheepishly. 'It's almost too much, isn't it?'

We turn back into the lounge and Mark launches into a round of rapid-fire introductions. 'CC, this is other-Mark, Peter, Joe, Jenny . . .'

'And Darren?'

'Not here yet.'

'And Ian?'

'Come,' Mark says, grabbing my hand and pulling me back towards the entrance.

As we pass the front door, the doorbell chimes, and Mark pauses to open the catch. 'Better just to leave it open,' he says, scooping my bag back up and handing it to me.

'CC, this is Dave, and Lucifer, and Jeremy . . .'

As he says this another group of five people appear behind them also grinning and holding bottles. 'Oh . . . time to give up on introductions,' Mark laughs. 'Come in!' he shouts. 'People, meet other people,' and with this he pulls me on towards the kitchen. 'I don't know who most of them are,' he says. 'Hopefully they're friends of Ian's.'

'Is that red-head guy's name really Lucifer?' I ask quietly.

'Nah, John. It's a nickname. And he's gay, so forget it.'

'I wasn't even . . .'

'Here he is!'

Ian is in the process of adding squares of smoked salmon to a plate filled with mini squares of toast. 'Hiya,' he says. He raises both hands like a surgeon, says, 'Fish-hands,' and leans in and pecks me on the cheek. 'Glad you could come. Love the hair.'

'I'm supposed to look like Kim Wilde,' I explain. 'Amazing place you have here.'

'I'm liking the leg-warmers,' Mark says, ladling punch from a bowl and handing me a glass.

'I know. They're back apparently,' I say. 'I thought they'd be really hard to find but they had them in River Island.'

'Leg warmers!' Mark laughs. 'Who would have thought it possible?'

'So you found the place OK?' Ian asks.

'I did,' I say. 'And now I have found it, just try keeping me away. I'm moving into that spare room on Monday.'

Ian glances up at me, I think to reassure himself that I am joking.

'Incredible house though,' I say.

'I know,' he laughs, concentrating on his hors d'oeuvres again. 'It's almost embarrassing, isn't it? But a friend of mine did some work on the place, pre-sale – those glass bricks, did you see them? And I saw it and fell in love with it. And then when Mum died Gran wanted to give me some money – some tax avoidance scam thing – so . . .'

'Well, I finally understand why you moved out anyway,' I tell Mark. 'You are officially forgiven.'

A slight woman with a bob haircut and a big smile pokes her head around the door. 'The guys who just arrived say it's horribly loud out front,' she says. 'Should I close the doors to the courtyard, do you think?'

'CC, Simone. She's our resident DJ tonight.'

We nod at each other. 'The cross,' I say, nodding at her crucifix. 'I wish I'd thought of that. I still have one somewhere from my Catholic days. Very eighties.'

'Yes, this is from my Madonna days,' she laughs. 'And . . .' she says, wiggling her fingers at me to show off her lace gloves.

'Very Material Girl,' I laugh.

She winks at me. 'Exactly.'

'Though I'm struggling to see what *you've* done,' I say, turning to Mark.

'I haven't changed yet,' he replies. '*He* has though.'

I frown at Ian who is wearing jeans and a T-shirt.

'Hey, these are snow-wash,' he says. 'What more do you want?'

'And he's tucked his T-shirt in,' Mark laughs. 'It's all in the detail. Anyway, I'm gonna go and change, so . . .'

'And the windows?' Simone asks.

Ian checks the kitchen clock. 'Well, I suppose it's getting on. Probably better close 'em.'

Abandoned by Mark, I offer to help with the food, and then, the offer refused, I ladle a refill of punch and return to the lounge to join Jude.

'So, any straight men here?' I ask him.

'I doubt it,' he says. 'Oh, actually, yeah. That old bloke outside in the shell suit could be.'

'And what about Darren?' I ask.

'No, he's definitely gay,' Jude laughs.

'Very good. I mean, where *is* he? I hope he's coming. I've got his present out there.'

'What did you get?'

'Oh, it's a surprise,' I laugh, wondering, for the umpteenth time if the chrome dog bowl, studded collar, and Supertramp box-set was such a good idea after all. It's very much kill-or-cure to our friendship.

'You want some of this?' Jude asks, proffering a joint.

'Nah, I'm just on punch tonight,' I say.

'Just say "no",' Jude says.

'Exactly.'

The room continues to fill and when Simone puts 'Pump Up The Jam' on her turntable, people really start to dance. I down my glass of punch and without really thinking about it move from grooving my hips to dancing myself.

'In fact, you look more like Olivia Newton-John,' Jude comments, prompting me to integrate some workout movements into my routine.

Mark reappears with red braces, red tie and a stripy shirt.

'That's such a good look,' I shout. 'You look gorgeous!'

He laughs. 'I have the whole suit. Got it from Oxfam. Big lapels and everything. It's too hot though.'

And it *is* getting hot. As the number of people in the room rises, so does the temperature, and by one a.m. there are so many people, whooping, grooving, wheeling, that I can feel the floorboards bouncing beneath our combined weight.

Ian appears behind Mark and slips his arms around his waist. Looking at the Cheshire grin of contentment that spreads across

Mark's face as he arches his back and pushes his neck against Ian's chin, I'm overcome by a surge of joy that Mark has finally found what he was looking for. For if truth be told, I would have been no more optimistic about his chances of meeting Mr Right than I am about my own predicament. His success somehow gives us all hope.

'Jennifer will be here soon,' Ian says. 'She just texted me.'

'His sister,' Mark shouts. 'They're driving from Cardiff.'

'They got held up because the babysitter cancelled,' Ian explains.

'Cardiff!' I say. 'They'll be knackered.'

'I'm sure I can find something to pep them up,' Ian laughs. 'Anyway, better get some more food out.'

'The host with the most,' I say, as he slips away.

'Isn't he lovely?' Mark says.

'He is,' I agree. Perhaps because of the heat, or maybe because of too much punch, I'm feeling a little flushed, so I push through the dancers and out between the sliding doors to join a small group of smokers in the garden. It's icy cold, but thankfully dry.

A guy in his mid fifties wearing shell-suit trousers and an *Amy Says Relapse* T-shirt looks up from his conversation and smiles at me, and I realise that he must be *that old bloke*, that Jude mentioned.

'Very good,' I laugh, nodding at the wording across his chest.

'I looked everywhere for a *Frankie Says Relax* one, but this was the closest I could find,' he says.

He's talking to a young woman with black trousers and sweatshirt and short orange hair. I'm not sure if she's disguised in eighties' Goth or if she's just a noughties' lesbian.

'It was all just about money anyway,' she says, apparently continuing their previous conversation. 'Nothing happened in the eighties except greed.'

I nod back at the lounge and say, 'The music was pretty good.'

'But even that was all flash and no substance,' she says.

'I don't think that's fair,' I say.

'What about all those left-wing comics?' the guy in the T-shirt says.

'Yeah, there was quite a counter-culture. Ben Elton, Rick Mayall...'

She wrinkles her nose. 'Rick Mayall?'

'Yeah, from the *Young Ones*? Swore a lot.'

'I suppose,' she says, pulling cigarettes from her pocket and then offering me one.

For old-times' sake and eighties' authenticity, I accept.

'But isn't the vehemence of the counter-culture just a symptom of the oppressive nature of the actual regime?' she says.

And I think, *OK. Lesbian, then.* The first puff of the cigarette makes my head turn. I'm already fairly drunk and the cigarette sends me over the edge.

'Sure,' shell-suit says. 'But a counter-culture still existed. Not everyone was a twat in the eighties. It wasn't a requirement. I was blockading Cruise missile convoys myself.'

'Were you?' she says. 'How cool! I would have loved to go to Greenham Common but I was too young.'

'I went,' I say. 'I got arrested for it and held in a cell overnight.'

Orange-hair turns and looks at me, then scans me from head to foot, and raises an eyebrow. 'Really?' she says, incredulous.

I nod. 'My parents were furious. They had to come and get me from the police station the next day.'

'I didn't mean... I mean, you just don't look the type,' she says.

'Well... I *am* in fancy dress,' I say, gesturing at my outfit. And then, before she can ask me what I do for a living, before I have to admit the horror of just how much some of us *have* sold out, I stub out the horrible cigarette, spin on the heel of a pink trainer, and head back in to the party.

Greenham Common to London advertising exec! There are moments when you suddenly remember who you used to be and there doesn't seem to be any possible way to get from there to here... to link that person to this one. Was that me? Or is this me? Or both? Or neither? I grab a fresh glass of punch from the kitchen, down it in one and try to blank out that thought.

As I head back through to the lounge, Grace Jones' 'Slave to the Rhythm' comes on. How I loved that song! Suddenly, from this huge sound system, it sounds so sumptuous I can barely believe it. It's as if someone has just patched the music straight into my brain.

I grin. My spine tingles. I push through the dancers to Simone's side and grin at her and start to copy her wiggle. 'I *love* this!' I shout grinning wildly.

And then I'm in the middle of the floor experiencing a full eighties flashback. Sister Sledge are singing 'We Are Family', and I'm convinced that it's the best record ever made. And then Lloyd Cole and the Commotions comes on, and I remember how to do the student chicken-wing shuffle and I can't decide whether maybe 'Perfect Skin' wasn't better still.

Jude is dancing beside me. 'Go easy on the punch, apparently someone slipped some MDMA in it,' he says.

I ask him what MDMA is and he says it's 'basically Ecstasy,' and I'm momentarily shocked – briefly outraged – and then I think, *well that explains this*, or *this explains that*, or whichever way around it is, but it feels great, it really does feel too good to care, and of course it's too late now anyway.

I hug him anyway for being lovely enough to warn me, and then I'm dancing with Mark and Jude and Ian and his sister, and Ian and his sister look like twins and dance the same way too which strikes me as a profoundly beautiful thing and I wish I could dance with my own brother and my eyes water as I think how beautiful that would be, how beautiful all the things we would do together would be and how much he would enjoy being at this party. And then someone is sliding an arm around my waist and it's Victor who I don't want to dance with because he's my bloody gynaecologist, *and* he has had his hands up my fanny, but he insists on dancing with me and then I *do* want to dance with him because he's beautiful and gentle and a kindred spirit who, like me wants to get back to nature, and he's an amazing dancer, and his groin is crushing against mine as we amazingly manage to salsa to 'Disco Inferno', and then I want to kiss him, and despite being gay, he lets me do this and laughs, and I see Mark laughing at us, and wonder if Victor has told Mark that I want a baby, and wonder if Mark has worked out that I want his sperm as well, and then Donna Summer comes on and I spin out of Victor's arms and dance with the orange-haired lesbian to 'I Feel Love', and she touches my breasts and I don't care at all, and then someone puts some electro on and I close my eyes and dance on my own, and then the record jumps and I'm somehow in a taxi going home and my phone is ringing, and though I can barely focus on the screen I see that it's Darren calling, Darren who will no doubt want me to go *back* to the party but I can't, I'm too out of it, and I feel a bit sick, so I drop the Blackberry back into my bag and sit and stare at London blurring by, and think how much I love Darren and regret not taking the call, but before I can dig the phone back out of my bag, I'm home and struggling to pay the cabby, and fiddling with locks, locks, bloody locks everywhere: locks on the cab door, and locks on the gate and locks on the front door.

And then the record skips again and I'm trying unsuccessfully to balance so that I can pull off my leg-warmers, and then lying in my bed *with* the leg-warmers on, and it doesn't matter because they feel nice anyway – they feel like being young again, and I'm looking at the ceiling and grinning and thinking how much I love Mark, and how much I love Victor, and how much I love Darren, and how much I loved Waiine, and even that, even the memory of Waiine tonight feels lovely, like a big woolly jumper I can wrap myself up in. And I think how much I love my life *just as it is*, and realise that *this* must be why they call the damned stuff Ecstasy.

Soup and Sympathy

It's just after midday when I wake up. I'm naked which means that at some point I have managed to remove the leg-warmers which I recall proved to be so problematic last night.

Dragging myself a little dizzily from the bed, I find one in the bathroom and one in the kitchen, prompting the vaguest of memories of a sleepy trip for rehydration.

I'm feeling pretty weird. My brain feels fuzzy, my eyesight a bit under-par as if someone has maybe attached a soft-focus lens to my head, and my balance is definitely out of kilter. I can only presume that these are the after-effects of the drug and wonder who was responsible for slipping it into the punch – surely not Mark or Ian?

I wouldn't deny for a second that I enjoyed myself last night, that it was, in fact, one of the best nights out I have spent in years, but that doesn't temper my feeling of outrage. For what if I had had five glasses of punch instead of three? What if I had suffered a reaction to the drug and keeled over in the middle of the dance-floor? Would anyone even have known that I had taken it?

Still, I finally got to try E – a suppressed desire since my twenties – and clearly, feeling outrage is preferable to suffering the guilt of knowingly having partaken.

As I cook breakfast and stare out at the dark shadows of my garden, I take stock of my hangover and decide that, all things considered, it doesn't feel too bad.

I cook and eat bangers, grilled tomatoes and fried eggs, and round upon round of toast – a crazy number of calories, but well, tough! I sit and sip cup upon cup of tea and review the party, remembering dancing (again) with the lovely Victor, letting orange-haired Carol fondle my breasts (albeit briefly) and hugging Mark and Ian in an attempt at absorbing a little of their new-found domestic bliss.

If only I could find that for myself . . . for how nice would it be to be sitting talking about last night instead of just remembering it? A reasonable-looking guy with a sense of humour to go to parties with: surely that's not too much to ask, is it? I mean, if Mark can find it, and Ian can find it, then shouldn't *I* be able to? Surely it should be easier for me if anything, as according to Mark, nine out of ten men are straight . . . But where are they? Where is he?

And then there's Victor. Beautiful Victor. Clever Victor. Dancing Victor. Kissing Victor. Victor who spent half an hour telling me about the bloody goat-farm he wants to buy in France. Victor who seemingly has been put on this earth to taunt me: So you think having gay friends is frustrating? Try this one! The perfect man. *Except.*

And how on Earth can *Victor* be single? What secret fault-line can Victor possibly be hiding that keeps all the guys around him at arm's length? For were I a bloke of the poofy persuasion I would snap him up. A weird fetish, perhaps? A tiny dick? Honestly, he could have a dick the size of a peanut and I'd manage to get over it. Perhaps Darren snapped him up last night. That would be sweet.

But of course, that wouldn't last either . . . Victor's dreams of muddy goat farms make him about as compatible with Darren as he is with me. And I suppose, in the end, that must be part of Victor's problem. Gay guys probably don't go for muddy farms in a big way. They probably aren't that turned on by the gynaecologist thing that much either, thinking about it. But it's a shame, and a waste . . . for looking at Darren from afar, he clearly needs a change – his life clearly isn't making him happy any more than mine is satisfying me. I wonder if he feels as stuck as I do?

Remembering his phone call, I hunt my BlackBerry from my

bag and check my voicemail. His call was at three-forty a.m. but he hasn't left a message – I had no idea that it was so late! I wonder if he found his birthday gift and I toy with the idea of phoning him. But realising that he'll almost certainly be out cold, I shrug and put the phone on to charge and carry Guinness through to the marginally less dingy lounge.

The day outside is suitably lacklustre that I don't have to feel any guilt about slobbing in front of the TV all day. I check the Sky guide and switch to Film Four and wait for *Speed II* to finish, and *Jane Eyre* to begin.

I wonder what Mark and Ian are doing, and feel another little wave of jealousy. I remember my brief snog with Victor. Honestly! I snogged my gay gynaecologist. What's that all about? And then I wonder if orange-haired Carol is sitting somewhere nursing a cup of tea and thinking the same thing about me. What it's about of course, is Ecstasy!

And then I flick the sound back on and pull a blanket over Guinness and me, and start to watch – and then doze in front of – *Jane Eyre*.

I'm awakened just after three by the chirrup of the landline. I peer blearily at the display and then at the titles rolling up the screen and then back at the handset, as I debate whether I have the energy to speak to Mark right now. My eyesight seems even more fuzzy than before, and I wonder if this is a side effect of the drug, and, thinking that I can ask Mark about this, I swipe the phone from the base.

'God, you weren't asleep, were you?' he asks. His voice sounds like ground-glass.

'No, well . . . sort of,' I say. 'Dozing in front of the TV.'

'OK, sorry,' he says. 'I was just about to give up, only . . .'

'Your voice!' I say. 'You don't sound like you at all. You sound like Marianne Faithful. You sound like I feel.'

'Yeah,' Mark says, quietly. 'CC, it's, um . . . I have some bad news.'

'Oh? Go on . . .'

'It's Darren.'

I shiver then, because I know exactly what Mark is going to say. I know it like I read it in yesterday's newspaper. And how can that be? My mouth fills with saliva. I swallow hard. 'Right,' I say.

'The police phoned . . . they, um, found his number in my . . . I mean *my* number in *his* mobile. I thought they might have called you too?'

'No,' I say. 'He's . . . is he . . .' And then, for a second, I decide that I'm being ridiculous; that I don't in fact know anything; that I'm in a drug-induced E-hole or something and that I'm assuming the worst when . . . 'Is he OK?' I ask.

'Well no. He's . . . Well, he's *dead*,' Mark says.

My vision glazes over entirely now. My mouth fills with an acidic taste. I raise a hand to my mouth and gasp, almost silently, 'God.'

'I know,' he says.

'And I knew it. Somehow, I knew it.'

'I'm sorry,' Mark says. 'I . . . I thought you should know.'

Guinness chooses this moment to squeeze from my grasp and I hate him for it.

'CC?' Mark prompts.

'I . . .' I say.

'I know,' he says.

'I . . . I knew . . . I should have . . .'

'He told me,' Mark says. 'He actually *told* me he was going to do it,' his voice quivers and cracks.

'Me too, Mark,' I say. 'He told me too.'

'I . . . I don't know what to do. You know?'

'No,' I say. 'I . . . I need some time. To take it in. Can I call you later?'

'Sure,' he says.

I listen to the line click dead and then lay the handset on the sofa as if any sudden movement might make it go off again, perhaps with *more* bad news. The room feels icy cold, so I stand and turn up the thermostat. My eyes are watery and I have a lump in my throat that is so big I can barely swallow.

Beyond the window, a child whizzes past on an electric-blue bicycle, laughing crazily. His father runs after him, and I want to shout at them to shut up, to stop laughing. And then I think of Darren's parents and think that Darren was a child once too – a carefree child on a bicycle. And now he is gone. And it's a waste. Because he should have stayed. He should have stayed and ridden a bicycle and laughed. It's as easy as that.

But Darren *wasn't* laughing, was he?

As the child cycles back the other way, still shrieking with joy, that thought strikes me as profound. For we all become so sophisticated, so cynical, that we forget how to 'en-joy' ourselves. But joy is easy. Joy doesn't need money or drugs . . . Joy just needs a wobbly push-bike. Somewhere along the way to becoming adults, we forget that simple fact.

And then as the father runs shouting back past the window, I think, *Well, those of us who don't have children forget it.*

I sit in shock, and stare at the world outside. A world that no longer contains Darren.

I remember him – it seems the least I can do.

I remember him at work, feet on the desk. I remember him sitting in my kitchen, perched on the counter-top . . . at the photography exhibition, at the salsa club . . .

And then, of course, I remember Waiine and Dad and wonder if they're all together somewhere (if Dad was right) or if, as my mother believes, that's it – they're just *gone.*

All these people who *were*, who had lives and possessions, and jobs and people around them who loved them, and then suddenly they are gone . . . For a while, their lives remain like an afterglow, that's the really strange thing. Darren's flat still contains Darren's clothes. Darren's iPod still contains Darren's favourite tracks. Darren's job, and Darren's desk, and Darren's friend CC . . .

A single tear slides down my cheek, because, yes, we all still exist, and all that arsehole had to do was stay, and continue to exist, here, with us. And it's all too fucking stupid for words.

At seven, I phone Mark back.

'How are you holding up?' he asks.

'I feel terrible,' I say. 'I feel like it's my fault.'

'He told everyone,' Mark says. 'Jude says he knew too. He told us all but we didn't believe him.'

'Only I think I did,' I say. 'Deep down, I think I did believe him. That's what's so stupid. God, I can't really take in that he . . . *isn't* . . . any more.'

'No,' Mark says. 'Tomorrow will be the worst. At work.'

'I know it's . . . How did he do it? I think I sort of need to know so that I can believe that he's . . .'

'Drugs,' Mark says. 'Ketamine. Masses of it.'

'The horse tranquilliser thing?'

'Yeah. He took enough to *kill* a horse apparently. Ian reckons he won't have suffered. He will have just slipped away.'

'But it was definitely . . . I mean, are we sure it wasn't an accident?'

'He left a note, apparently, for his mum. So no. Not an accident.'

'God, his mother. Imagine,' I say.

'Oh, CC,' Mark says, his voice cracking. 'I miss him so much already. I have this hole in my stomach . . .'

'I know, babe, me too.'

'If he'd have just come to the party. He could have seen how much . . .' Mark's voice trails off in a gasp.

'How much we loved him,' I say, my own voice gravelly.

'Yeah,' Mark says. 'I *did* too. That stupid boy.'

'It is . . .' I say. 'Stupid.'

'A waste . . . that's such a cliché, but it is,' he says. 'It's a waste. I just don't understand.'

'I know,' I say.

'Look, I have to go,' Mark says. 'Ian has made soup and is insisting I eat something.'

'I'll see you tomorrow,' I say.

'Call me if you need to,' Mark says.

'Sure.'

. . .

I put the phone back in the charger and sit and wrap my arms around myself and think that it's certainly stupid and definitely a waste. But it's also entirely understandable.

Because being single can be desperately hard. Being alone can sometimes be *unbearable*.

And my nose runs, and my lip trembles, and I feel desolate and desperate, but not now for Darren – for myself.

Because right now, at this moment in my life, the one thing, the only thing that could possibly help, the only thing which might possibly ease my pain would be if someone – any one human being on this entire stupid bloody planet – cared enough about me to bring *me* a bowl of soup.

But that person doesn't exist.

And that's why I understand far better than I care to admit, that Darren didn't want to exist any longer either.

Surprise Visit

'So this is a bit unexpected.'

'Yes. I'm sorry about that.'

'It's fine. You're lucky I had a cancellation though. I can't usually fit people in at such short notice.'

'Yes. I'm sorry. Really. As I said, I didn't think I wanted to come back. And then something happened, and . . . well, I've been feeling a bit stuck.'

'Stuck.'

'Yeah. I couldn't face going to work this morning, because, well, Darren won't be there.'

'Who won't be there?'

'Darren. The guy who died. On Saturday night.'

'This is someone you worked with.'

'Yes, a friend. From work. I used to see him outside work sometimes too.'

'I see.'

'He killed himself. On Saturday. He took an overdose.'

'That's very sad.'

'Yeah. Well, that's the thing really. I mean, I understand.'

'You understand.'

'Yes, I understand why he did it. I almost think he's . . . he was . . . right. I mean, I'd rather he were still here, of course. But that's more for me than for him. Being dead doesn't matter to him, does it?'

'I'm not sure I follow.'

'Well he's dead. It's awful for his mum, and for us. But for him, well . . . he's not feeling anything, is he? Does that make any sense, what I'm saying?'

'I suppose it does in a way, yes.'

'I feel guilty too. I mean, I know everyone says that whenever anyone dies. But he warned me, so . . .'

'He told you he was going to commit suicide?'

'Yes. He even said he was going to do it on his birthday. He couldn't stand being single any more. Which I understand. But I didn't take it seriously.'

'Was there ever any romantic . . .'

'Darren's gay. He *was* gay. So no.'

'OK. And why do you feel guilty? Do you think you could have stopped him?'

'Well, maybe . . . I think I could have done more. I mean, to start with I might have cared a bit more when he didn't turn up at the party. But someone had put something in the punch, so I was off my head.'

'The punch was drugged?'

'Yeah. Liquid ecstasy or something.'

'MDMA?'

'Yes, that's it. I'm not a junky or anything. I don't do drugs. But someone slipped it in the punch. So I sort of noticed he wasn't there, but in a way didn't notice either.'

'I see.'

'Plus there was this trip to Cornwall. Well, Devon. And Darren wanted to come. And I sort of think that maybe if I had let him, well, he would have had something to look forward to next week. I'm not making much sense really, am I?'

'You think that if you had invited your friend to Cornwall with you he might not have killed himself?'

'Yeah, but that's stupid, isn't it?'

'I'm not sure. What do you think? Does that sound likely?'

'No. Not really. I think it's overestimating my importance a bit. I mean, he liked me, but . . .'

'Right.'

'And I didn't cry again.'

'I'm sorry?'

'When Mark told me. I didn't cry. I mean I got choked up, but . . .'

'I see.'

'When he told me . . . Mark . . . that Darren was, you know . . . dead. Well, it was weird because it was like I already knew. I wasn't surprised at all.'

'Because he had warned you, yes.'

'Maybe. But it was more of a feeling of, *that's what happens . . .*'

'That's what happens?'

'With men.'

'With men?'

'They die.'

'I see. So you weren't surprised.'

'Well no. And then yes, in a way. Because Darren was always so happy-go-lucky. Well, he wasn't really. Clearly. And especially not lately. But that's how he came across. But it's all just an act, really, isn't it? We're all pretending that we're fine, and deep down we aren't, are we? Deep down we're all so lonely we could die. And so in a way, I wasn't surprised either.'

'Because you empathise with him.'

'Yes. I suppose.'

'And you – have you ever contemplated suicide?'

'No, never. Well, not as such. I mean, sometimes I think that it would be easier.'

'Easier?'

'Than putting on a brave face. Than pretending to be fine all the time. Because really life is just a big string of let-downs, isn't it?'

'You feel your life is a string of disappointments?'

'Well, a bit. Yes. I . . .'

'Yes?'

'Look, I was watching a kid on a push-bike . . . he was learning to ride it, tearing up and down laughing. And I thought that Darren *was* that kid once. And so was Waiine. And so was I. And I remember how easy it all seemed. You learned to ride a bike and you fell in love, and lived happily ever after. That's how all the bedtime stories went, anyway.'

'Innocence.'

'Exactly. Whereas in real life you fall in love with a boy who never even notices you exist, and then you settle for someone who seems nice enough, but who would rather write down train numbers than a message on a birthday card or even better just get drunk and watch TV, and then he starts slapping you when he's drunk, and then even *he* dumps you. And so you wait around, and one day you have a big love affair, only it turns out that this one is shagging someone else, and then he makes you have an abortion and then dumps you to live with the other woman ... and ... so it goes on. That's what *real* life's like. Men are disappointing, or unfaithful. Or they die. And no one tells you that when you're a kid. Otherwise it wouldn't come as such a shock.'

'*They* die ...'

'Well yeah. Some do.'

'Some? Your father, your brother ...'

'And now Waiine.'

'Darren?'

'Yes, Darren.'

'You said Waiine.'

'No, I said Darren.'

'You said Waiine.'

'Did I? Sorry. That's weird. Isn't it? *Is* it? I'm sure you're reading all sorts of things into that.'

'It's interesting, but ... who knows. *Was* Darren like your brother? Or perhaps like *a* brother to you?'

'Not really, no.'

'I see. So *men die* ...'

'Some don't. Some dump you.'

'I see.'

'You don't sound convinced, but I'm not making anything up here.'

'I didn't think for a second you were.'

'Dad died, Waiine died. Darren died...'

'Yes, yes... I can see how you might link those together.'

'And I can't go back to work. I can't face seeing that empty chair.'

'That's understandable. You probably need some time off to come to terms with it.'

'Yes. Maybe I should take some time off...'

'It's a shock. It's perfectly normal.'

'Yes. A shock. But somehow not entirely unexpected... as I say. Not like when Dad died.'

'Because?'

'Well, that was *really* sudden. I mean, Waiine, well, you knew... we knew... not exactly when it would happen, but we knew. And Darren, well, as I say, in a weird way, I knew.'

'So how did you feel when your father died?'

'Shocked. Devastated.'

'And you cried?'

'Yes. For weeks.'

'Do you remember how that felt?'

'Awful.'

'Can you describe how it felt?'

'Well... awful.'

'Can you describe further?'

'Sickening. Numbing, I suppose. From the trauma mainly.'

'The trauma?'

'Of *seeing* him die. Of actually being there. I think that kind of overshadowed the loss – the grief. It was mainly shock to start with. From the event itself.'

'Can you describe the event to me?'

'I'd rather not.'

'I think it would be useful.'

'As I say, I'd rather not.'

'I'm sure. I can only say what I think would be useful to you. In the end, like coming here, it's all up to you.'

'Is that IKEA? That red chair? Because I really like it.'

'No. It's Roche Bobois.'

'Oh. No wonder. I wish I liked cheap stuff. It would make life so much ... well, so much cheaper.'

'So?'

'So ...'

'So. Your father.'

'I can try, I suppose.'

'Good.'

'We were shopping. For Waiine's Christmas present.'

'So Waiine wasn't with you?'

'No. It was just the three of us. Mum, Dad, and me. We were in the shopping centre in Camberley. We had lunch somewhere ... probably BHS, Mum liked the BHS canteen in those days. And Dad said he had indigestion, which is a classic sign of course – yes it was definitely BHS – but no one thought anything of it. Of his indigestion, that is. You know what? I really don't want to ...'

'Please carry on, you were doing really well.'

'Right. OK. So, then we were on this escalator, and Mum and Dad were in front. And I was looking at this punk guy going down the other way ... he was kind of cute ... and then halfway up he just sort of slumped sideways. Dad, that is ... he crumpled. And Mum and I held him upright to the top, and then we couldn't hold his weight and he just slid to the floor. And that's it really.'

'But you tried to resuscitate him?'

'Yeah. We thought he had fainted so Mum slapped him. But then somehow I realised ... I don't know why ... but I took his pulse, and couldn't find it ... And that was it – he was dead.'

'That must have been very traumatic. For a ... how old were you?'

'Seventeen. I was seventeen. I ... I was doing my A levels.'

'So what happened then?'

'Some guy came out of John Lewis ... and he ran off back into the store to call an ambulance. And I did CPR.'

'CPR.'

'You know, two breaths, thirty pumps. We learnt it in Guides. Only I couldn't remember the numbers, how many of each, so

I'm not sure if I did it right.'

'Well, it was a very stressful situation.'

'Yes. And Mum started trying to pull me off . . . and slapping me around the head. She thought I might hurt him, I think . . . She didn't realise he was . . . Well, it all got very . . . And then the ambulance arrived, and I had to stop. And even then I thought they would just magically bring him back to life . . . I thought I was keeping him going till they could bring him back to life with electric shocks or something . . . but . . . then . . . I just stood there and watched, and they didn't. I suppose they thought it had been too long or something. It was quite a long time . . . They faked it . . . trying to resuscitate him. I saw them faking it . . . Mum doesn't know that.'

'That must have been very hard.'

'It was the feel of his mouth. That was the worst thing. That's what I remembered . . . over and over. The feel of my mouth on his, like a kiss . . . but, obviously not a kiss . . . Because he was dead of course. And every time I remembered it, it made me cry, so I tried to blank them out, those final . . . But they kept coming back. And every time it made me fall apart all over again.'

'You're crying now.'

'Well, my eyes are watering a bit.'

'No, you're crying.'

'Am I? A bit maybe. Do you have a tis— thanks. No, I don't really cry properly anymore. This is as spectacular as it gets.'

'But you *are* crying now. Your chin is wet.'

'Is it? A bit, I suppose.'

'Quite a lot.'

'Yes.'

'You say it was like a kiss. Didn't you mention kissing last time? I'm trying to find it here in my notes, but . . .'

'No, I don't think so.'

'No? Oh. OK . . . No . . . yes, here it is . . . *beards.*'

'Oh right. Yeah, I said that I don't like beards.'

'Did your father have a beard?'

'Oh.'

'Did he?'

'Sorry, is this some Freudian thing? Because there was nothing...'

'Not at all. But did he? Have a beard? Just for the record.'

'Yes. But that's not ... is it?'

'Not what?'

'The beard thing? Is that why?'

'Your biggest life trauma involved you giving mouth-to-mouth to your dead father. Who had ...'

'Yes ... stop. I feel sick.'

'What do you think?'

'No. I don't. I don't think so.'

'Another tissue perhaps?'

'Thanks.'

What He Would
Have Wanted

I end up taking an entire week of annual leave. I'm feeling tired and a little depressed, but more than anything, I simply can't face walking into the office and seeing Darren's empty chair. I'm hoping that the funeral, organised on Thursday, will make this easier come Monday morning. That is, after all, what funerals are for.

It's a strange week though, slithering unnoticeably by in a sort of monochrome bubble of numb sadness.

The weather is cold but sunny, so I take walks through a frosted Hyde Park and think, in an unfocused, unproductive way about Darren, and Dad, and Waiine, and my own life. Talking to the shrink has shaken everything up again, and there's too much really to even start to think about it all, but it drifts around at the back of my mind. Hopefully at some point it will drift into some useful shape.

I'm so lost in the freezing fog of my thoughts that the slightest of tasks – getting food in, finding a florist, reheeling my funeral shoes, or rescheduling the Cornish Cow visit, or, in ricochet, my gynaecology appointment – seem to take an entire day.

On Friday morning, as I step down onto the platform of Plumpton station (*a short platform, please disembark from the front three coaches only*), I feel ready for the closure that the service will provide . . . eager, almost, to move on to whatever comes next.

For thinking about Darren's life has convinced me at least of one thing: that if your life isn't working for you, you have to grab it by the throat and shake it up and down until it does. Because the alternative clearly doesn't bear thinking about.

As I leave the station I see two separate couples of good-looking (no doubt gay) men. All four are suitably dressed in black suits and white shirts. I follow them down the main road, assuming that they will lead me to the funeral. After about thirty yards though, one of the men pauses, turns to face me and asks, 'Excuse me, but do you know where the church is here?'

I shiver. He looks uncannily like Darren. I shake my head and pull my collar a little higher against the chill wind. 'I'm sorry,' I explain. 'I was following you.'

A van pulls up beside us wanting to cross the pavement to enter a property on the right. I step back to let it do so and as it crawls past I ask the man driving for directions. And then with my black-clad entourage I carry on down the road. I feel a little like Madonna – out and about with bodyguards.

'I take it you're going to the funeral?' the Darren lookalike asks.

'Yes,' I say. 'Darren Langston?'

'Dan,' he says, holding out a hand. 'The brother.'

He doesn't introduce the other three men, and none of them even acknowledge my existence, so I simply nod, smile weakly and say, 'Of course. You look alike. I'm so sorry. I'm CC. I worked with Darren.'

'Right,' he says. 'Good to meet you. It's a waste. A terrible thing. So many of us are struggling to stay alive, and then you get someone like Darren . . . anyway . . .'

'Yes,' I say, repeating Mark's words. 'It's a cliché, but that's the only way to describe it. A terrible waste.'

And then, there, on the left, is the little church. A perfect parish church, surrounded by a weathered stone wall, and a shabby green lawn. None of the pomp or circumstance of Catholicism here.

I spot Mark and Ian just beyond the gate and, giving a

restrained nod and a tiny wave to Darren's brother, I step off the path to join them.

'Hello,' Ian says. 'God that bloke looks exactly like . . .'

'That's his brother,' I say quietly. 'I met him on the way here.'

'Wow, he really looks like him – were they twins?'

'Nah, he's two years older,' Mark says. 'It's good to see your friendly face, Miss CC.'

I hug each of the two men and then turn to look at the two distinct groups forming in front of the church. 'Don't you know *any* of these people?' I ask Mark.

He shrugs. 'I know a couple of the faces – from night-clubs and stuff. But no, not really. And those people over there are his family.' Nodding at a wiry ashen-faced woman he adds, 'That's his mother.'

'Gosh,' I say. 'Imagine. The poor woman. Have you met her before?'

'Once . . .' Mark says. 'Once was enough. Beware. She isn't very gay friendly.'

I frown at Mark, wondering whether to take this apparent honorary membership of the gay club as a compliment or a wake-up call.

'A lovely day for it,' Ian says, his Scottish accent, suddenly strong. I wonder if it's like my own Irish one, stronger in moments of stress.

'Yes,' I say. 'Cold wind though. So has it been quiet?'

Mark pulls a face indicating non-comprehension.

'At work?'

'Oh, I've been off,' he says. 'Didn't you even notice?'

'Oh, no . . .' I say. 'No, I've been off too. I took the whole week off.'

'Ahh, OK. I just thought you were off that day I phoned you about the funeral. Stanton didn't say . . .'

'No. So how come she invited this lot?' I ask. 'If she's not gay friendly.'

Mark shrugs. 'He left a list apparently.'

'And a note,' Ian says.

'Notes,' Mark corrects. 'Multiple notes. One to be read out today.'

'Jesus,' I mutter. 'Dramatic to the last.'

'Indeed.'

'No sign of Victor then,' Mark says, giving me a calculated wink.

'Please don't,' I say. 'I'm embarrassed enough.'

'No,' Ian says. 'And it's hardly appropriate.'

'Were he and Darren . . .?' I start to ask.

'Oh yeah,' Mark says. 'Yes, they were really close.'

Which doesn't really answer my question.

'God, is Victor really coming?' I ask. 'I'm so embarrassed.'

'Why?' Mark says.

I roll my eyes at him.

'I don't think he'll make it,' Ian says. 'He's on a really tough schedule . . . His colleague is off sick.'

'With bird flu,' Mark says.

'Swine flu,' Ian corrects.

'Well, with whatever . . . I can't keep up with them,' Mark says. 'There's a new phantom killer virus every year, and nothing ever happens. It's all bollocks, if you ask me. The powers that be keeping us scared.'

'And never doing anything about HIV which does exist,' Ian says.

'Well, they don't care – it mostly kills poofs,' Mark says, a favourite subject of his.

'Has she really got swine flu?' I ask. 'That's not good for a gynaecologist. No pregnant woman is going to want to see *her*.'

'No,' Ian agrees, pointedly looking at Mark. 'That's why it's supposed to be a secret.'

A movement catches my eye, and I turn to see that everyone is moving, not as expected into the church, but towards the rear.

'Hey ho,' Mark says. 'Looks like we're on the move.'

We circle the church and join the others gathered around the graveside, strictly respecting the family/friends grouping.

The vicar, a balding, bumbling, charming man, explains the unusual order of the day.

'Darren Langston was not a religious man but he did have fond memories of this church from his childhood. These, it has to be said, were probably more of hiding amongst the gravestones than attending services, but before he died he wrote me a letter asking very specifically to be buried here. He also specified who should be invited, and how the service, if one can call it that, should proceed.'

'That boy was such a control freak,' I whisper to Mark.

'Exactly what I was thinking,' he says.

I turn to see one of Darren's young men glaring at me, eyes glistening, and I pull a guilty face and lower my gaze to the casket in front of us.

'Now Darren didn't want sermons, and he didn't want hymns, but he did permit me, in his largesse, to say a brief word, so I shall try to keep it short. Darren Langston was a lovely child who I remember well. He grew up, I'm told, to be an equally charming man who helped anyone and everyone whenever he could. He will be sorely missed by those left behind, and I pray that he is now in heaven with Our Father bringing as much humour and wit to those around him in the afterlife as he did to everyone present today.

'Now, I believe that Darren's brother, Daniel, would like to read a specific text that Darren prepared for this moment.'

'God this is freaky,' Mark whispers. 'Darren's double reading his . . .'

I see Ian nudge him, cutting him short.

Dan steps forward, and pulls an envelope from his hand. 'Hi, um, yes. Those of you who know the family will know that Daz and I weren't exactly close,' he says, his breath rising in steam-train puffs. 'That's a bit of an understatement really. I couldn't begin to tell you what that was all about, but of course, it all feels pretty stupid and petty now. But it's too late to put anything right. That's what . . .'

His voice is breaking, and emotion is jumping across the gap between us. I run a hand across my mouth and bite my lip.

'That's what's so hard . . .' he says, 'about what he's done . . . Anyway, Darren wanted me to read this here . . . I, um, don't know what it's about. Knowing him, it's probably a surprise . . . so you, you'll, um, have to bear with me.'

Here he licks his lips and glances at his mother so we all turn our attention to her.

Her eyes are bulging and her cheekbones are so pronounced, they look as though, if she pulls her mouth any tighter, they might rip through her papery flesh.

'Right,' Dan says . . . waving the letter. 'OK . . .' His face is swelling, seemingly doubling in size. A deep red stain is rising from his collar. 'I'm sorry, this is . . . well . . . hard,' he says, pulling the pages from the envelope.

He unfolds the letter and stares at it. The pages are blown shut by the wind, so he has to pocket the envelope and open them again with both hands.

'So . . .' he says, his voice cracking again. He glances at his mother again, and she rolls her eyes and shakes her head.

'Dan,' she says. 'Stop it. I told you.'

'But it's what he wanted,' he replies.

The vicar steps forward, clears his throat, and says, 'If you wish, I could read it. If that would make things easier.'

'Knowing Darren, I hardly think that would be appropriate,' the mother says. 'Give it here.'

Her voice is so cold, so hard, and suddenly the only thing I want in the whole world is for this woman *not* to be the one to read Darren's parting words.

'I can read it if you want,' I hear myself say. 'Please . . . I'd like to.'

Dan glances at his mother, who shrugs. A tear rolls down his cheek as he reaches over the casket to hand me the letter.

I look at the first page, and remembering that handwriting from so many notes at work, my own eyesight goes watery; my own voice fails.

'So . . .' I say, my voice no stronger than Dan's.

I cough and clear my throat.

'So this is it,' I start. 'As they say in all the best movies, if you're reading this it's because I'm now . . .' I have to swallow before continuing, 'I'm now dead.'

I glance up at Mark opposite and realise as I do so that this is a mistake, because his own tears set off my own. I wipe my eyes, apologise, and start again, my voice now flat and controlled. 'So this is it. As they say in all the best movies, if you're reading this it's because I'm now dead. Well, it was me. I did it. Not Colonel Mustard . . . not Professor Plum. No . . . it was no one's fault but my own.

'When we were kids we used to listen to the *Hitchhiker's Guide to the Galaxy* on the radio. Do you remember that, Dan? Do you remember the bit about the dolphins, and how man always thought he was cleverer because whilst he ran around like crazy building bypasses and bridges and sending men to the moon, all the dolphins ever did was swim around eating fish and playing with balls. And the dolphins knew that in fact they were the clever ones, for precisely the same reason?'

'What *is* this rubbish?' Darren's mother mutters, causing me to pause and look up. I look at Dan and he shrugs. I glance at Mark who tearfully nods that I should continue.

'. . . the same reason . . . um, and, I would have liked to have been like the dolphins. To know how to just swim around and be happy. But I wasn't built that way. I was never satisfied. Never. And sometimes that made me a perfectionist, and sometimes, mostly, it just made me unhappy.

'I've had moments of friendship, and I have had some great holidays, and I have had some great sex, probably more than most . . .'

The word *sex* produces a gasp of pious disapproval from Darren's mother, but this time I do my best to ignore it and simply carry on.

'But it was never enough. And that feeling of *never enough* has become unbearable for me. Because I know it will never end. And I don't know how to feel satisfied with what I've got. And I don't know how to fix my life so that I *am* satisfied.'

'But the good bits were good, and everyone here contributed to that. So thanks to you. Thanks to you, my family, and you my framily. And if you don't know what framily is, you're missing out, so ask my friend CC. And don't feel sad, or guilty, just feel proud that your bit was one of the good bits.'

'But there is one thing I have to say . . . specifically to Dan, and to Mum. And you both know what's coming next. Because there's one aspect of our relationship that really didn't help me – it really didn't work for me at all.'

I can see from the corner of my eye that Darren's mother is moving through the mourners around to my side of the grave.

'Some of you were never that comfortable with the fact that I'm gay . . .' I continue, more rapidly. 'In fact . . .'

And then the pages are ripped from my hands.

'That's enough, thank you,' Darren's mother says, her voice now flat and controlled. 'I'm sorry, but this isn't how I want to remember my son,' she continues, stuffing the pages into her pocket.

'But those are his words . . . you can't—' I start.

'Gay, gay, gay . . . it's all he ever talked about when he was alive. And it's all illness and depression and . . . and there's nothing gay about it. So enough. But thank you very much, whoever you are,' she says. 'You read very well.'

'CC,' I say, drying my eyes and having a vague fantasy of rugby-tackling her for the letter. 'I'm framily. He mentioned me in—'

'Yes, I'm sure,' she says. 'Now if anyone else has anything they'd like to say about Darren that isn't to do with his sex-life?'

Mark steps forward. 'Yes,' he says, red-faced, tears streaming down his cheeks. 'I do. Goodbye, Darren. From all your friends, *gay* and straight. We loved you. And we wish you had stayed around. Goodbye.'

Ian says, 'Yes, goodbye.'

A hubbub of goodbyes come from the people standing around him.

'Thankyou,' the mother says. 'Now, perhaps those of you who

aren't family could give us a moment to bury my son in a quiet appropriate way.'

I open my mouth to say something, I have no idea what yet, but thankfully (because it wasn't going to be something appropriate) Ian links his arm through mine and tugs me gently away. 'Come on,' he says. 'It's not worth it.'

And as we and twenty or so other people turn away, we hear the mother say, 'Could you say a prayer please?'

'That was awful,' Mark says when we reach the gate.

'Yes,' I say. 'I'm sorry.'

'No,' he says, 'not you. You were perfect. Bloody religion. It's always the Christians casting the first stone.'

'I shouldn't have let her . . .'

'There was nothing you could do,' Ian says.

'That woman though!' Mark says.

'We have no idea what those poor people are going through,' Ian points out.

'No,' I agree. 'Losing a brother. Losing a child. They're things you just never get over.'

When we reach the street, I pause. 'I take it we're not invited to the wake or anything.'

'No,' Mark says. 'I don't think I would want to go even if we were.'

A man pushing past us through the gate pauses and looks at me watery-eyed. 'Thanks,' he says in an American accent. 'You people were great.'

I nod and shrug. 'It didn't go quite how I would have hoped, but . . .'

'We're going to the pub over there,' he says, nodding at a building just up the road. 'It would be nice if, well, if we all went together.'

Ian and I turn to Mark, and he nods. 'Yeah,' he says. 'We'll have our own mini-wake. Fuck 'em.'

Icy Water

It's amazing how a funeral can provide a sense of closure, incredible how the atmosphere can change in the forty minutes it takes to remember, say goodbye, and bury someone.

At my own father's funeral I was too young, or perhaps too traumatised to understand that process. In fact, the chatter and merriment of the wake made me hysterical with rage. I remember, still, feeling that I would explode, or implode, or at least slap someone if I remained in that room, surrounded by cucumber sandwiches and cheese on sticks and stupid irritating grins. I had run off instead to hide alone in a copse of trees at the end of our road, where I surveilled the drive until the last of the drinking, laughing guests zigzagged their way from our house.

Today though, a drink is exactly what I need, and as I'm not driving, and don't have to work I can't see any reason to deprive myself.

In the end there are seven of us in the pub: myself, Mark and Ian, two men who I deduce are ex-tricks-become-friends of Darren's, a colleague from Darren's previous job and his boyfriend. We take a table in a corner of the pub and eat fish and chips and drink San Miguel – Darren's favourite beer – and ponder what else was in the unfinished note.

As tradition requires, we relate our favourite stories about Darren. I can't help but wonder if he is watching us, and if he approves. Perhaps he would say, 'Just because I joke about my life doesn't mean that you can.'

Or perhaps he would now see the funny side. Maybe he would

now see how stupid giving up on life was, when all he had to do was join us in laughing at the absurd pointlessness of it all.

Afterwards, Mark and Ian head off to Cardiff and I take a train to London. As I tipsily watch the rolling Sussex countryside slide past, dappled with winter sunlight, I think again about Darren and with alcohol-induced simplicity wonder why he didn't just take some Prozac. I know he was *against* antidepressants. The crazy universal reliance on anti-depressants was a subject we agreed on. But that now strikes me as an absurd hypocritical position to have taken. Darren, after all, took coke to get going, E to get high, dope to mellow out, and Valium to come down. What the hell was stopping him taking a few Prozac to stay alive?

Myself, if I have an infection I take antibiotics, if I have a headache I take an aspirin. If I felt so sad I couldn't see the point of carrying on, why on Earth wouldn't I take an antidepressant?

I think about an article I read in the *Sunday Times* about how they test these wonder-drugs. Apparently they make rats swim in icy water and time how long it takes before they give up and resign themselves to drowning. The longer they struggle to stay alive, the better the pill has worked. And I think that though that struck me as a stupid, cruel and obscene way to test a pill, that must have been exactly how Darren felt. Icy water, and no way out. And I realise that I have been feeling pretty much that way myself. The last few years, since Brian left at any rate, have felt like slowly drowning in icy water. And so, as I sit on that train, watching farmhouses and hamlets whizz past, I decide that I will give myself until Christmas to put together a realistic escape plan. I will allow myself nine weeks to turn everything around. And if I haven't managed it by then I shall go to the doctor and get a prescription for something to keep me afloat.

I spend Saturday in a *my-head-may-be-a-mess-but-look-at-my-house* cleaning spree. Guinness, who hates the hoover, watches me from the garden. He looks thoroughly irritated by my burst of cleanliness.

Sunday, I walk to the Asian supermarket where I buy proper ingredients and cook myself a real chicken Korma, and then spend the afternoon browsing potential properties to visit during my Devon trip.

By Monday morning, as I brace myself for the freshly chilled water of Spot On, I'm feeling quietly optimistic that, at least until Wednesday night when I head off to Devon, I can stay afloat.

Deciding that if I put it off, the shadow will hang over me all day, the first thing I do is march into Creative. Mark and Jude are sitting at their desks but clearly staring into the middle distance.

'Morning, chaps,' I say brightly.

Both men look at me as though I have just murdered their mothers, so I feel obliged to explain myself. 'Listen, guys,' I say. 'I'm sorry if this offends anyone, but I can't do this any more. I spent all last week feeling guilty. I went to the funeral. I felt like shit all weekend. But if it carries on any longer I swear I shall end up taking an overdose myself.'

Mark smiles weakly at me and says, 'I feel exactly the same. But . . .' He shrugs and nods at Darren's empty desk.

'Right,' I say, leaving and heading for the storeroom.

I return with two empty boxes and start to scoop everything from Darren's desk into the boxes.

'What are you doing?' Jude asks.

'This desk has to go,' I say, 'and it has to go now. You're the boss here. You should have done this before Mark arrived.'

He stands and crosses the room. He raises one hand. 'A minute,' he says. 'Just one minute.'

He stands and stares at the desk, and I realise that without having attended the funeral, he needs a symbolic moment.

I pause and after a few seconds start to feel emotional again, but then, thankfully, Jude says, 'OK. You're right. Let's do it.'

As we clear the desk, then carry both the table and the chair to the storeroom, the energy in the room changes. You can almost feel the oxygen flooding back in.

Afterwards I head up to Peter Stanton's office. He is with Victoria Barclay (who, to my relief, fails to hug me). They both look miserable as sin, so I explain to them what I have done. 'There's only so much misery people can take,' I tell them, 'and things haven't exactly been optimistic lately here anyway. The funeral is over, and I really think we all need to make an effort to pep things up again.'

And then I tell Peter that if he doesn't give me some work to do soon, I shall just go home and start redecorating my lounge.

'What about Tom?' VB suggests. 'Don't they have anything they need help with in New York?'

I shake my head. 'I called. And no. Nothing.'

'Cornish Cow?' Peter Stanton asks hopefully.

'I'm going down Wednesday night. But the pre-pitch is all ready.'

'There's only one thing I can think of,' Peter says. 'But I don't think you're going to want to do it.'

And that is how I end up tasked with taking two American, rather good looking, slightly shiny-faced, very well dressed Levi's account executives out on the town.

Why We Need Prozac

Peter Faulks and Michael Faegan are both in their early forties. Peter looks vaguely like an older version of Justin Timberlake, and Michael could probably pass, on a good day, for Colin Farrell. They are both from Levi's accounts division in Delaware and are both exquisitely dressed in sheer business suits (one grey, one black), white shirts and sober ties. Both have wedding rings.

I feel a bit like I'm stepping out with the glamour department of the Mormons – if they had such a thing. I am wearing the Girbaud outfit I bought in New York, and a pair of stilt-like Jimmy Choos. This is just as well as both guys are pretty tall.

As we step out of the lobby I catch a glimpse of us in the window opposite and think, *Wow!* and wonder if Peter Stanton was taking the mickey when he said that I wouldn't want to do this. Because right at this moment in time I can't think of anything more likely to distract me than an expenses-paid night out on the town with two, young, good looking, heterosexual men.

To ease us into our evening together, I take them to The French Bar in Covent Garden. The two men clearly know each other well, are friends even, which eases considerably the task of entertaining them. In fact, as discussion of work is basically off-limits (their reasons for visiting Spot On are top secret, though I hope to interrogate them once drunk), my role is reduced to listening to their happy banter and laughing appropriately. And even that's not too hard. These are, as it turns out, two pretty funny guys.

The French Bar does exactly what it says on the tin. It's a perfect replica of a French brasserie along with marble tables, waistcoated waiters and po-faced service.

I match the men's double whiskies one-for-one with gin and tonics (singles). I will have to slow down later, but for now I know that, for outings like these, alcohol is the oil that makes the wheels turn.

After two whiskies the men loosen their ties and start to laugh more honestly as they tell me some well-rehearsed stories from previous trips abroad. I attempt to find out more about what they do by asking why they were in Hong Kong, but Mike just says, 'On business, as always,' and simply winks at me.

They tell me about a trip to Paris and how Mike bet he could run to the top of the Eiffel Tower and needed a paramedic after doing so.

'But other than that, and maybe that big museum with the pyramid thing . . .'

'The Louvre?'

'Yeah, other than that, Paris was kinda boring.'

'Like here,' Mike says.

'Yeah, like here.'

Clearly my signal to move things along.

The three of us stride towards Soho where I have booked a table at Little Italy, the best Italian restaurant I know around here.

Darren of course, is lingering around in the shadows, waiting to trip me up, so I talk a little maniacally, and laugh a little too loudly, determined to fill the centre stage enough to keep him in the wings. And the strategy works. It feels good. As I walk along, dressed to the nines, a beautiful young man on each side, I wonder if in some parallel universe Chelsii strides out on the town like this every night. I suppose that if it's true, then there surely exists another one where she never gets to do it at all, and decide, in line with my new policy of positive thinking, to be grateful for small mercies and simply enjoy every second of it. Which for now involves downing another half a bottle of wine with my Tortellini del Mare. Between them, the guys polish off another bottle and a half.

Outside the restaurant my chaperones decide they require a *normal* English pub, so I lead them along Compton Street towards the Coach and Horses.

As we walk past Comptons, Pete says, 'Hey what about this one? This place looks busy.'

'Yes,' I say, pausing, and pulling an embarrassed face. 'Actually, it's not *quite* a normal English pub . . . It's gay.' Pete grins, and for a second I think he is going to reveal, like Tom in New York before him, that Comptons suits them both just fine.

Instead, Mike laughs, pushes Pete towards the entrance and grabs my arm. Shouting, 'You go explore your feminine side, boy, I'll look after CC here,' he drags me off down the road.

Pete runs to catch up with us and takes my other arm. 'Oh no you don't,' he laughs. 'You think I'd leave this lovely lady alone with a monster like you?'

I know I should unlink my arms from theirs . . . I know that it's unprofessional . . . But what can I say? It feels lovely.

Inside the Coach and Horses, the crowd is already thick. The men adventurously demand pints of 'English' beer, and then, these pushed to one side, settle for pints of lager. I myself move, discreetly, from G&T to simple 'T'.

The TV is showing American football, prompting a spirited if incomprehensible debate about NFL and NCAA rules. I smile demurely throughout.

As the crowd swells we're inevitably pushed closer together, and again, I can only admit that it still feels lovely. The men are elegant, good looking, fit, well dressed, funny . . . and sexy. In fact, at such close proximity, they're maybe a bit *too* sexy. It might just be the temperature within the pub, but by ten-thirty I'm starting to feel a little flushed.

When I suggest that we move on, however, Mike smiles amiably and insists that he's fine. He too is looking a little red-cheeked.

'So, CC,' he asks me, whilst Pete is in the loo, 'how come you don't have one of these?' He flashes his wedding ring at me.

I shrug. 'Divorced. You know how it is.'

'How anyone could divorce you,' he says. Then to Pete, who has apparently reappeared behind me, he says, 'Eh, Pete! This one isn't married! What do you think of that?'

Pete lightly places one hand on each of my hips and grooves a little to the music – The Sugababes.

I gently push his left hand from my waist, and then transfer my glass to the other so that I can repeat the action on the other side. 'I hope I don't need to remind you that you both *do* have rings,' I say, tilting my head away from Pete's chin and pointing at Mike's hand.

He shrugs and steps forwards, and with a devilish grin he removes his wedding ring and drops it into his top pocket.

'Nice,' I say. 'And who says romance is dead?'

I realise that Pete is pressing against my back now, indeed Mike is so close I can feel his breath on my lips. Suddenly, very suddenly, things have got out of hand.

I shift my head to the left to escape Pete's mouth against my ear as he whispers, perfectly calmly, 'Hey, no offence, but you don't fancy showing us back to our hotel, do you? I'm not sure we can find it on our own.'

I break away, squeezing sideways from between the two men. 'Hey! Boys!' I say with a perfectly faked laugh. 'Calm down. It's *not* going to happen. I need to go to the ladies', so in the meantime I suggest you boys find yourselves a fresh target to seduce. Preferably one you don't have to work with tomorrow morning.'

As I queue for the ladies' I realise that I'm trembling. Of course, a come-on from two guys, from two work colleagues, is stressful. I have handled it well.

I have to admit to myself, though, that I'm not *only* trembling from stress – I'm trembling from arousal too. It's a good job humans can't read each other's thoughts, because just at the moment I said, 'Hey! Boys!' an image had slipped through my mind, an image I would never share with anyone. I saw myself, with my dress slipping to the floor, and with Pete/Justin Timberlake behind me, nibbling my ear, and Mike/Colin Farrell cupping my breasts from the front, caressing them gently with his smooth hands. In my imagination I even felt the silky sensation of Pete's erection pressing against my buttocks. No wonder I'm feeling flushed.

And then, a moment later, I'm not sure if I *did* imagine that, or if I'm only now realising that that is what just happened. Because Pete was pressed against my back. For a moment, just for maybe ten seconds, I let myself stay with that reverie. And then I think, *Out of hand! Go home!*

Apparently I think this thought out loud because the woman in front (she looks like Anne Robinson or Esther Rantzen – it's hard to tell them apart these days) turns to me and says, 'Exactly what *I* was thinking.'

As I head back through the bar I'm still feeling a little flattered by the attention, but I have also re-centred myself. I know exactly where I'm going from here: home.

At the bar I find that the men have already found themselves a new target: they are standing either side of a tall blonde woman. She's pretty, if perhaps what my mother would call *brassy*. I nod a warm, 'hi,' to show her I'm not a competitor, and say, 'Hey, boys. I'm gonna have to go now.'

'Sure,' Mike says, placing a hand on my back. 'I hope we haven't vexed you. Pete was only horsing around, weren't you, Pete?'

'Sure,' Pete says, winking at me.

'Not at all,' I say. 'But I have a long day tomorrow and I don't think . . . anyway, I just need to get home now.'

Pete lurches and pecks me on the cheek. 'Thanks for an awesome night out,' he says. And then Mike does the same thing, and repeats, 'Yeah. Awesome.'

'Can you find your way back to the hotel?' I ask.

'Without you?'

'Seriously, guys.'

'We just get a cab and say the Hyatt, right?' Mike asks.

'The Regent's Park Hyatt,' I say. 'There are a few Hyatts and you don't want to go the wrong one.'

'OK. Regent Park Hyatt. You got that, Pete?'

'Yes, sir,' he laughs.

'Don't worry, I'll make sure they get back OK,' the blonde woman says.

I bet you will, I think. For some reason a scene from the Almodovar film *High Heels* flashes through my mind. And then with a little wave, I turn and start to squeeze my way through the crowd towards the door.

As I walk, something about that film registers though, so I pause and glance back at the threesome to check. Sure enough, Blondie is marginally taller than either of the guys, at least six foot two, and sure enough, when I peer at her feet, I see that she isn't wearing high heels – she's wearing flats. I wonder if the guys aren't going to be in a for a little surprise when they get back to their hotel.

As I put one hand on the doorknob to push out into the street, someone grabs my arm. I turn back to see a guy with a red face staring at me. 'Excuse me,' he says excitedly, droplets of spittle spraying from his mouth. 'But my mate really likes you. Can we, um, buy you a drink?'

'I'm sorry,' I say. 'But I'm just on my way...' And then I see the friend.

Wow! Colin Farrell, Justin Timberlake *and* a Colin Firth lookalike in the same evening?

I hesitate just long enough for him to reach us through the crowd. He's rolling his eyes in embarrassment, which I find rather cute.

When he reaches his friend he knocks his sweaty paw from my arm. I'm somewhat grateful for this. Then he glances at me, smiles vaguely, and says, 'Sorry about that, love,' and yanks his friend back into the crowd.

I watch their backs for a moment, and then shrug and step outside. It has started to rain.

Just as the door closes behind me, I hear the fat guy say, '*What?* You said...' And unfortunately, I also hear the Colin Firth lookalike reply, 'Not *her*, you prick. The *other* one. The brunette with the tits over there.'

The noise of the pub vanishes as if sucked out of an airlock as the door finally closes behind me. I stand and look at the newly wet streets and think that, yes, *this* is why we need Prozac. For whose ego could possibly stand up to this kind of battering without chemical help?

Office Minimalism

I never see or hear of Peter Faulks or Michael Faegan again. Which is a shame if only because I never get to find out if they did in fact end up taking a six-foot tranny back to their hotel.

I take Wednesday morning off to pack for Devon and phone a few estate agents, and in the afternoon I head down to easyCar and pick up another grey-and-orange Mondeo.

It's another cold sunny day and as I head down the M4 and then onto the M25, I wonder, naughtily, whether global warming might mean that this is now what British winters will look like. I know that's a bad thing to dream of, but I'm sure we would need far less Prozac as a nation if every day looked like today.

Unlike my mother, I love driving. It sends me into a meditative trance where I perhaps don't think about driving as much as I possibly should, but where I find the space and time to drift around and sift through my thoughts in a way that doesn't happen to me at any other time. And with four hours' driving ahead of me, I don't even need to schedule my thoughts . . . there's room for everyone.

I think about Pete and Mike to start with. Both apparently married, both apparently determined to find some business-trip excitement. I wonder what their wives are like. I wonder if they could ever imagine their two husbands either side of a six foot blonde. And I wonder, almost jealously, what that might have felt like for her. Quite a result, I would imagine.

I remember the Colin Firth lookalike who fancied the 'Brunette with the tits,' and wonder again what that makes me.

The brunette *without* the tits? I glance down at my chest. I've had some slap-downs in my time, but no one has ever implied I was lacking in the bust department.

It's a tough assignment, but I'm determined not to reach the obvious conclusion that all men are cheating, sexist arseholes. Because that thought doesn't do me any good; that thought removes hope. And life without hope leaves nothing but a basin of icy water.

I think about Darren too, of course, and for the first time I imagine the actual act of his suicide. And I realise that of course it won't have been a single act. He will have got rid of his collection of porn, cleaned up or perhaps deleted his email account . . . He will have written the note, and visited his dealer for Ketamine. Maybe he cleaned the flat. Perhaps he thought about which room he preferred to be found in, in what position, by whom . . . I had imagined it as a sudden act of desperation, but I realise now that of course, it wasn't. He had been planning this for years.

At Andover the sun begins to set. The twilight is tough on my eyes, so I pull over into a Little Chef and take a table at the window where I can watch as the sky flames red, and then glimmers and dims. Other than the big plate-glass window, there is not one feature of the Little Chef that pleases me, and I'm sure that any of the pubs I passed would have had better food and more comfortable chairs, but there's something to do with the anonymity of the place that makes it less uncomfortable to eat alone . . . something to do with the fact that everyone here is like me, simply pausing on their way to somewhere else.

After a reasonable if somewhat predictable lasagne and a Diet Coke, I head on along the A303 towards Plymouth.

As I pass Salisbury I think about my shrink and admit to myself that it might be doing me some good. I couldn't, for now, say exactly what form that good is taking, for other than raking over the past, I don't seem to be achieving anything . . . But then maybe that's it – maybe to rake over the past is the whole point. After all, the stuff I have been discussing – it's actually more of a monologue than a discussion – is stuff I have simply never vocalised to anyone. For who else could I possibly have told? For anyone who knew Dad or Waiine it would be way too painful. And for anyone who didn't, way too *personal*. And I suppose that in the end, that's what a shrink is. A friend who is paid to listen to things that are too painful or too personal for anyone else.

Just as I park the car in the hotel car park, my phone rings but seeing that it's Mum's landline I decide to ignore the call and phone her back after check-in.

Ten minutes later I open a beer from the mini-bar, kick off my shoes, and hurl myself onto the bed. I dial her number and lie back and close my eyes. They feel, after my night drive, as if they have been pickled in vinegar.

'Hi, Mum, it's me,' I say, when she answers. 'I was driving when you phoned, so . . .'

'Driving?'

'Yeah, I'm in Plymouth.'

'What are you doing there?'

'Oh, work stuff. I'm seeing a client tomorrow. So what's up?'

'Your father and I went to Plymouth once. Stayed in a very nice hotel.'

'Well this is just your basic Premier Inn, I'm afraid. Cost-cutting measures and all that.'

'What a shame.'

'Oh it's fine. I don't really care to be honest, Mum. As long as it's clean. And it is. Anyway, you called me on my mobile. What's up?'

'Nothing really. But I need to see you.'

'OK. Why?'

'I need some daughterly advice.'

'Daughterly advice?'

'Well yes. Don't sound so surprised.'

'Well . . . when did you ever ask my advice?'

'If you're going to be . . .'

'Sorry, Mum, I won't. What's wrong?'

But she won't tell me. It's something, she says, to do with Saddam. It's something we need to discuss face to face. Which means either that she and Saddam are having problems, or that they want to move forward with the marriage thing. I can only pray that it's the former.

I click the phone off and glance out at the Victorian façade of the building opposite. And then I close my gritty eyes for a moment's rest before heading out to explore Plymouth.

When I open them again the bedside clock says 00:02 and my first thought is that there has been a momentary power cut and that the clock has reverted to zero. But when I check my BlackBerry, it turns out that it's my body-clock that has gone haywire. I have been asleep for four hours, not, as I'm convinced, ten minutes.

And so, too lazy even to remove my make-up or clean my teeth, I wriggle out of my clothes and slip between the crisp white sheets.

The meeting with Roger Niels at Cornish Cow is so low-key it's an embarrassment. I'm just glad that no one is here to witness it.

I obviously didn't expect (even if I secretly hoped) to meet Niels in the middle of a cowshed, but all the same . . . looking around the two spartan rooms they have rented in this serviced office complex it's hard to spot a single visual clue that they are in the dairy business. Indeed Niels himself couldn't be further from the ruddy-faced west-country bumpkin I had imagined. He's a young (late thirties) wiry man wearing cords, brogues and a white open-necked shirt. He looks like a banker on his day off.

It quickly becomes evident that not only has he not given much thought to marketing, but he's not quite sure who I am or why I am here either.

All of this I explain patiently between multiple phone calls he seems unable to resist answering.

When I produce a folder of roughs that the boys in Creative have knocked up, he seems more confused than impressed. 'I'm sorry,' he says. 'But do we have a contract with you people?

Because I haven't seen a single budget entry for any of this work.'

I explain that we don't yet have a signed contract but that because we see Cornish Cow as a strategic diversification of our agency portfolio we have decided to stun them with our enthusiasm.

But Niels is having none of my silver tongued ad-speak. 'Yes, I'm sure,' he says. 'The slowdown is hurting everyone.' He flicks through the mock-ups and comments coldly that none of it looks 'very organic.'

'I didn't know Cornish Cow *was* organic,' I say, making him laugh out loud.

'That doesn't mean it shouldn't *look* organic,' he says.

The only other comment he makes before flipping the portfolio closed and handing it back is that the cartoon cow drinking from a straw on the final sheet is 'cute.'

'Yes, Darren did that,' I say. 'He's good isn't he . . .' And then I frown, and think about reformulating the phrase with a past tense, and then decide that it's best not to go there. Not for sales purposes, and not for myself.

Within forty minutes of meeting him, I'm back on the street, the folder under my arm.

I drink a cappuccino in Starbucks to gather my thoughts, and consider phoning the office, but decide that in the interest of at least creating an illusion of a fruitful meeting it's better to wait until this afternoon. Not that I think that this rudely summary meeting has been a wasted journey. I know from experience that business heads like Niels are famously difficult to impress with creative stuff. But at some point, a flick of his pen will send their marketing budget this way or that, and often an inauspicious meeting like today's will end up being what influences in whose direction his pen will flick.

I walk briskly along the rather splendid seafront, inhaling the iodine air, and then, spotting clouds forming to the west, I double back to the hotel to drop off the folder and change into jeans and trainers.

Rather excited, if still unsure whether this will turn out to be the first act in a new chapter or a simple fantasy, I pull my list of properties from my suitcase and grab the car keys from the bedside table.

Body Double

I have worked out that my flat in Primrose Hill is worth the obscene sum of three-hundred and eighty thousand (though apparently in the process of plummeting because of the crisis) so I have listed only cottages below two-eighty (to give myself a little financial cushion) and with enough land to have at least a large kitchen garden if not cows or goats.

I have four properties on my list, though sadly, I have left the second page concerning property number four behind, so I have nothing but a photo and the name of the town to go on. Still, I'm hopeful that this will suffice. If the place looks anything like the picture I should be able to see it for miles around.

I haven't booked viewings with any of the estate agents for the simple reason that I can't even convince *myself* that I'm a serious buyer, let alone anyone else. I have a job and a life and a flat in London, and no realistic plan whatsoever how I might earn a living here. For the moment this is just about daydreams. But if I find the right kind of place at the right kind of price, well, who knows? Daydreams can sometimes become reality, right?

As I drive along the A38 I look out over the moors and start to smile. I wonder if it could really be this simple. Could human happiness be as basic as a glimpse of green? Could this sensation of focusing in the distance, focusing, for once, on infinity . . . could that be all I really need?

Finding the house in Liskeard should be easy. The address turns out to be on the main road into the town, and yet, when I reach the town centre, I realise that I have somehow missed it.

After a few repetitions of the roundabout at one end, and a few three-point turns at the other, I finally realise that it can only be the house behind the wall of thirty-foot Leylandii. I bump the car up the kerb, climb out, and surreptitiously edge towards the gate wondering if in addition to the trees-from-hell a clone of Mrs P is living next door.

The first surprise is that the place is so small, and so close to the road. Comparing it with the printout, I realise that my brain has assumed the windows to be of a certain size – about five-foot-square, whereas in fact then are more like three-by-three. The house around them is therefore correspondingly smaller – minute in fact. Still, it's a pretty cottage – grey stone walls, a white painted outhouse, and it even has roses around the door, albeit straggly ones. But the main road is a whooshing, roaring presence that even an impenetrable wall of Leylandii can't temper. And the lawn, in complete shade from the monster trees, is in the same, sorry, sun-starved state as my own.

I shrug and return to the car. I never expected to find my dream-house today anyway. At least looking is turning out to be fun.

The house in Bodmin is far harder to find, because each of the houses on the lane are set at the end of their own track, and half of these are entirely hidden by trees or hedgerows. This leaves me hugely optimistic though – clearly traffic noise isn't going to be a problem here.

I park the car at the entrance to a farmer's field and climb back out. Incredibly the temperature has dropped at least five degrees since Liskeard ten minutes ago, and I can see that the cloud cover is about to obscure the sun. The air smells like rain. I remember this smell from my childhood and I think how the air in London never really smells of anything except perhaps traffic pollution.

I edge as far down each of the tracks as I dare, enough to see that the house is not the one I'm looking for. They are all incredibly small though, as if built for a race of tiny people. I wonder what they would make of my mother's cavernous house in Surrey.

After forty minutes I have only covered a third of the lane, so when I cross paths with an old man walking a dog I show him the sheet and ask him if he knows it.

He peers at the house and then says, in a Farmer-Jack voice worthy of children's TV, 'Arrr yes, tha'll be ole Margaret's place, tha'll be. Come on, I'll show you. I'm only walking Boris anyway, so . . .'

He walks incredibly fast for an oldie – the tempo apparently dictated by the dog. I myself am virtually jogging to keep up.

'So looking to move to Bodmin, are we?' he asks.

Hyper aware that I don't want to slot into the cliché of London professional moving to the moors, I slip into my thickest Irish lilt. 'I am so,' I say. 'I think it's beautiful down here. Though I'm just really having a mosey around today. Having a peek to see what's on the market.'

'It's all become royt pricey,' he says, yanking at Boris' training collar. 'All these strangers buying everywhere for holiday homes. A crime it is. No offence meant.'

'Well if we do buy here, it won't be a holiday home, that's for sure,' I say, grimacing inwardly at my invention of a 'we.' And then I think of Guinness, and decide that I haven't lied after all.

'They're building houses all over now, but it doesn't stop the prices going up, oh no.'

We round a huge privet and the house in the photo appears, complete with for-sale sign. It's a pretty, white-painted bungalow. Again, it's much smaller than I thought.

'This is the one isn't it?' the man says, glancing at my printout, and forging on.

'Yes,' I say. 'Yes, this is it.'

Spotting a woman at the rear of the property, I pause and try to grab my guide's arm to bring him to a halt. 'This is fine,' I say. 'I only wanted to have a peek.'

'Nonsense,' he says, already waving. 'Maggie? Maggie!'

The woman stands and places a hand in the small of her back, that universal gardening gesture, then shades her eyes and waves. The dog barks and when the man releases the lead it tears around the house and jumps up, putting its paws on her shoulders.

As we near the house, I see that it has a fairly extensive vegetable patch at the rear – not much growing right now, but clearly these rows of cloches and bean-poles are Maggie's pride and joy.

As for the house, though, despite its supposed three bedrooms, the entire thing can't be much bigger than my flat.

Just as the dog-man says, 'I found this lassie out in the lane. She wants to buy your house,' I raise my eyesight and look beyond the end of the garden and see that I don't want to buy it, I really *don't*. Just beyond the furthest limit of Maggie's garden is a parked bulldozer, and beyond that, at far as the eye can see, the hillside has been divided into swathes of tiny plots. At the top of the hill, on the horizon, Barrett are building hundreds of tiny, red brick houses. And as the red corrugated tubes poking from the earth reveal, they are clearly heading this way.

'Hello,' Maggie says, removing a gardening glove and holding out a hand. 'The agency usually calls before visits – there must have been a mix-up.'

For half an hour I pretend out of politeness to be interested in Maggie's pretty little house, a pretty little house soon to be surrounded by a hundred Brookside Closes, a pretty little house with ceilings so low that if I were to put on a pair of Jimmy Choos – I know, I know, there would be little call for them here – but if I did put on a pair, I would only be able to pace up and down lengthwise between the beams. Walking across the room would require either a shoe change, or a stoop.

I wave goodbye to the dog-walker and slump into my car.

I know about house-hunting, of course. I know from experience that nothing ever lives up to unreasonable expectation, and that finding the right house is as much about slowly tapering that expectation as anything else . . . But even with that knowledge, those first visits, that initial realisation that it's going to have to be smaller, and uglier, and more remote or if not, noisier than imagined . . . well, it's always just a tiny bit soul-destroying.

I sit in the car and watch the hill to my right as it turns a deep, dark grey, and figure I can make out a slanting texture in the light that indicates that it's already raining up there. I wonder, for a moment, if I could really imagine myself living here? And the only answer I can honestly give myself is, 'No.'

I glance back at my list of properties and decide that number three in Tregony is a bit too far for today, and settle for a final peek at number four, the house on the hill, if I can find it.

Ten minutes later, I'm just driving past the *Welcome to Bolventor* sign, and I can already see the house to my left. It's not immediately obvious how to reach the lane that leads to it, but as I drive around in ever decreasing circles, I start to become seriously excited. For this house is in a completely different category from the others.

'So where's the problem?' I mumble, as I park the car in a siding a hundred yards below the house and climb out.

The sky is now blackening and a chill wind is humming vaguely in my ears. I wish I had brought a hat.

I look up at the house. It's big – at least three bedrooms I'm guessing, though of course I don't have the details with me.

It's another white painted farmhouse, though this time with two storeys and a slate roof. It dominates the landscape in all directions, and I wonder if someone is already watching me from behind one of the blackened windows. A VW van is parked on the gravel drive and smoke is drifting from the chimney. For some reason I decide that the presence of a VW hippy bus rather than the classic Land-Rover Freelander implies a far nicer class of person inside.

As I start to walk past the wooden fence separating the land from the lane, the sun suddenly dips below the cloud-line, bathing the side of the house in a warm, pink glow, and I think, *God! How beautiful!*

I stride nonchalantly past the house as if on a mission to somewhere else, though I doubt anyone would be convinced . . . the lane clearly doesn't *go* anywhere else.

As I pass the big bay window, despite feeling something of a voyeur, I peer into the uncurtained lounge. The right-hand wall is entirely covered with book-cases and a man of regular build in jeans and a simple grey hoodie is standing with his back to me, staring, I think, at the flames from the log fire. The walls of the room flicker and jump as the light shimmers.

And then a woman appears in the doorway opposite holding two cups and says something to the man, and then frowns and nods at me, and he turns, still grinning from some previous remark, and I snap my head back to where I'm headed and hurry on down the lane.

My heart is racing, but not from being caught out . . . My heart is racing because that house is *my* house. That house is exactly the house I imagined. In fact, it's more my house than I ever imagined, only I couldn't know that until I had seen it. And the woman – that woman holding her cups of tea, or soup, or hot chocolate, or whatever it was – was my height, and my age. Other than her pregnant belly, she looked *just like me.* And the guy in the hoody, the man with the easy stance and the wry smile looked exactly as I always imagined the missing boyfriend would be. Just for a moment, I feel like an impostor has stolen my life.

I walk briskly for a few hundred yards, and then, when the first drop of rain strikes my forehead, I spin around and walk back the other way, debating what to say if the woman from the house comes out to ask me why I'm there, or if the guy comes out to offer assistance to this lost, non-pregnant double of his wife.

But the curtains are now drawn so I take a deep breath of the fragrant wood-smoke and, imagining this other-me inside my house, settling in front of my log fire, with my baby inside, and my smiling boyfriend *be*side, I walk briskly, and then as rain starts to fall from the sky, run, *alone*, to my car.

The Matrix

As I head back to Plymouth, and then on homeward, I wonder what choices I have made to bring my life to this point . . . I wonder, more specifically, what might have happened if I had moved to, say, Plymouth or Bournemouth instead of London, how different my life might have been. For the first time ever, I wonder if my fragmented, catastrophic love-life might not be a symptom not of what I do, but of where I live . . . if it might not be the trade-off for having chosen the excitement of the capital over the stability and relative calm of a smaller, more rural place. After all, somewhere along the line, there has to be a reason my body-double ended up with the baby and the log fire and farmhouse and the lover, whilst I ended up with the career and the gay friends, and the parties on E and a wardrobe full of Jimmy Choos. Without a doubt part of the cause is me. But maybe, just maybe, part of it is geographical as well.

I remember Darren telling me that waiting to do things until the right person came along was a mug's game, and I wonder if perhaps *he* should had gone to live somewhere else instead of quitting the planet entirely. Might he not have found a better way of living in Cambridge or Edinburgh or France even – one which he found more satisfying? In Darren's memory, perhaps I should now find out? Because if London really *is* the problem, then I need to find out now. A couple more years in this rut and my options, both marriage and baby, and career-wise will have narrowed to *none-at-all*.

As I come out of Exeter, I realise that I have taken a wrong turn, but recognising the town of Brampford Speke signposted ahead as one of the Cornish Cow sites, and figuring that a few photos of cows will add to the illusion of a busy, fruitful business trip, I carry on up the A377.

After a few miles and a few turns I find the sign: *Cornish Cow: Brampford Speke*, and turn onto what is little more than a farm-track.

It's only as I park the car in front of a vast grey steel barn that it crosses my mind that not only are there no cows in the fields but that again, we aren't in Cornwall here . . . Brampford Speke is well within Devon. Is there, I wonder, anything Cornish about Cornish Cow?

I grab my camera and the portfolio and cross the muddy car park to the only visible door, dwarfed in the middle of the vast grey frontage.

There are no signposts, no secretaries, no farmers and most notably, no cows. For a moment I wonder if this isn't a factory or depot rather than a farm, but then the wind changes and the stench of slurry hits me, and the sound of a cow, and then cows plural, reaches my ears.

I open the door and step into a hallway. It stretches the length of the building with a doorway every thirty yards or so. And then a door a few hundred yards to my left opens and a farmer appears wearing overalls and wellington boots. He looks at me, pauses for a moment, blinks as if he maybe can't believe his eyes, and then starts to stride towards me.

'Hello?' he says, his voice rising at the end of the word. His frown looks more like *What the fuck are you doing there?* than anything else.

'Hello,' I say. 'My name's CC Kelly.' I offer him a hand but he just frowns a little more and ignores it. 'I work for an advertising agency and we're preparing a brief for Cornish Cow,' I say. 'I met Roger Niels this morning in Plymouth, and I was just driving past and I saw—'

'Sorry, you're telling me this because?' he says, his aggression thinly veiled.

'Well, because I met Mister Niels in the offices I couldn't get any photos of the cows. So I was just wondering...'

'I'm sorry,' he says, 'but no. I don't know you from Adam, and this is a sterile unit. You'll have to come back another time with proper authorisation.'

I nod and fake a smile and move to his side as I open the portfolio, more intrigued now than ever to see behind those doors. Something about this guy's demeanour is profoundly unsettling.

'Here, have a look,' I say, starting to leaf through the mock-ups. The man folds his arms across his chest, and I think, *This really isn't going to work.* But then he uncrosses his arms and reaches out to stop me turning the page. 'That one's cute,' he says, nodding at Darren's cartoon cow with a milkshake. The man is almost smiling. Breakthrough!

'Ah, OK! You like that one?' I say. 'That's useful. A few people have said they like that one best, but it's good to get the opinion of someone in the business,' I add, flattering him intentionally.

I leaf through the remaining images and then say my parting shot, 'So surely you could let me take just a couple of shots? Just something for the guys in Creative to work with?'

He looks at me sour-faced.

'I'll be less than five minutes. Less than *two* minutes? Oh go on ... Please?' I bat my eyelashes at maximum speed. *'Pretty please?'*

The man snorts and caves in. 'OK,' he says, glancing at his watch. 'But you need to be out before four because there's a shift-change then, and I don't want to get into trouble.'

'Brilliant,' I say, winking at him.

'Of course,' he says, leading me to one of the doors, 'if you want cows in fields, you'd be better going to the show farm in Gwennap.'

'The show farm?'

'Yes. They have a smallholding in Gwennap. Because this place is just a ZG unit.'

'Of course,' I say as knowledgeably as I can manage. I'm

suddenly feeling more like an undercover detective than an advertising exec. We pause in front of a shelf of wellington boots, and the guy nods at my feet.

'You'll need to take those off I'm afraid,' he says. 'As I said, it's a sterile unit.'

'For diseases and things,' I say.

'Exactly.'

I remove my trainers and put on a pair of oversize wellingtons and follow the man through a foul-smelling foot-bath, and then we push through a scratched heavy plastic curtain, and I freeze with the shock of the sight before me.

For this cowshed is truly vast. In fact, the term cow *shed* really doesn't do it justice. I look around as I slowly take in the details: cows as far as the eye can see, cows in perfect rows, packed in, side by side – cows on concrete, cows in four inches of their own excrement.

'God!' I say. 'How many are there?'

'About four hundred,' he says. 'Three hundred and seventy, to be precise. Thirty are in the calving pen.'

'Of course,' I say.

'But they'll be back tomorrow,' he says.

'Tomorrow? Right. And the babies? Sorry, the *calves*. I can't see any here.'

'The heifers will be reared for here in a different unit. And the bull-calves go to Europe.'

'They go to Europe?'

'Yeah, for veal. There's no call for veal here.'

'Right.'

'So?' he prompts, nodding at my camera.

'Yes,' I say, heading for the closest cow. As I approach its rump, I see that its head, which is poking through a metal frame to a feeding tray, is loosely tethered there. Oh, that won't work . . . he can't turn round . . .' I say. 'I wanted him looking back at me.'

'No, *she* can't,' the man says.

I pull a face. 'She! God, how embarrassing. Of course. God I feel like such a twit.'

The man really smiles for the first time. 'Here, come round to the feeding alley,' he says, beckoning with his head.

I circle the cow and follow his lead climbing over a small wall into a distinct concrete alley between two rows of cows facing each other head to head. The alley is filled with a grey powder which smells almost as rank as the slurry.

'Is this food?' I ask, looking at the cows unenthusiastically chewing the dust beneath my feet.

'Yeah,' he says.

'What is it? It looks like concrete.' *And smells like shit*, I think.

He shrugs. 'It's high protein dairy feed,' he says. 'Soya and stuff.'

Looking down at the two rows of cows, maybe a hundred heads all turned to face me, each with two huge yellow tags through the left ear, the industrial scale and nature of the operation really hits me for the first time.

I crouch down to take a close-up shot of the first cow. Now it might just be me projecting, but as I look into her eyes I can't help but frown in dismay – for I can sense nothing but sadness here. The contrast with Darren's cartoon cow couldn't be more pronounced.

'You don't look very happy,' I murmur, and I swear that cow stares straight into my eyes, and zaps a reply straight into my brain. 'Look around,' she says. 'Just look around.'

I sigh and straighten up and smile at the technician. 'Are there any at all outside I could take pictures of?'

He shrugs. 'Not here,' he says. 'It's ZG here.'

'ZG? Sorry . . . we city girls,' I say.

'Zero-Grazing.'

'Right,' I say, taking this in. 'So they just . . . what, *stay here*?'

'Well, yeah,' he says, a little incredulous at my stupidity.

'All the time.'

'All the time.'

'They *never* go outside?'

'Well no. It's ZG. As I say, if you want to see cows in fields you need to go to the Cornish show farm. That's what it's for.'

I nod. 'And how many cows are in the show farm?'

He shrugs again. 'Ten, maybe fifteen.'

'And here, four hundred.'

He shrugs. 'Yep.'

'So do they get any exercise at all?'

'We take them for milking three times a day.'

'OK,' I say with some relief. 'Where's that?'

He nods to indicate the far corner of the cavernous steel shed where twenty or thirty cows are tethered into different, rotary stocks with tubes from the vacuum pumping devices attached to their udders.

I feel suddenly sick. Actual bile rises into my throat and I have to swallow it back down. It could just be the smell, for the mix of odours rising from the grey powdered feed and the slurry the cows are standing in, and the smell of milk and udders, is far from a happy one. But it isn't that; it's out and out disgust, revulsion even, that humans could invent and build something so . . . obscenely *in*human. For this system, cows tethered in stocks in a dingy smelly barn, cows who can't turn around, cows standing in shit, cows who have their offspring ripped from them apparently on the day of birth so that *we* can have their milk instead, this *is* obscene. This place is Auschwitz for cows and it's quite literally making me puke. It's like something from *The Matrix*, only with one major difference. These cows know *exactly* what's happening to them.

I think about the boss saying that our drawings didn't look very organic, and ask, 'Just out of interest. Do they farm organic cows in the same way?'

He shrugs. 'I don't think so,' he says. 'I don't think the rules allow it, but I don't know much about it, I'm afraid. You'd have to ask a farmer.'

'You're not a farmer?'

'No, I'm a production technician.'

Then because my *production technician* is starting to frown suspiciously at me again, I snap three of the miserable beasts from a variety of angles and then pretending to fiddle with the camera controls, blindly take two random snaps of the whole disgraceful vista without him realising. And then I thank him profusely, and head as quickly as I can from that awful, awful place.

My trip just gained an entirely new purpose. It's no longer about gaining a contract, it's about convincing Peter Stanton that we don't want the contract. We don't want it *at all*.

I stand outside looking at the empty fields around me, and I wonder why on earth anyone would decide to farm this way? How many pennies do we save on a pint of milk by inflicting such abject misery on so many creatures?

No, we will not advertise for Cornish Cow. I haven't felt so determined about anything since I sat in front of those Cruise Missile convoys all those years ago.

Choreographed
Compromise

Despite a freshly filled litter tray, a salad bowl of cat-munchies, and two full tins of Whiskas, Guinness is furious by the time I get home at ten. He screeches at me discordantly and then sits in front of the back door, his tail thwacking irritatingly against the tiles.

'You really have no idea how lucky you are,' I tell him, thinking of the cows. I try to stroke him but he's having none of it so I simply open the door and release him, before heating and eating a bowl of macaroni cheese that's been sitting in the fridge, and then collapsing into my bed.

The discussion with Peter Stanton on Monday morning is of course, lively. 'I hardly think that the current economic climate is the time to get picky about which clients we are going to take on, do you?' he says.

I push my photos back across the desk at him. 'Please,' I say. 'Just *look* at them.'

He sighs and fingers the photos. 'Did you ask them if they're unhappy?' he says. 'Do you even know if a cow *can* be unhappy?'

'Any living thing can suffer,' I say. 'And this place . . . this place is a concentration camp for cows. Honestly, Peter, just the stench . . . I couldn't even put milk in my tea this morning.'

'I'm sure,' he says, then with another sigh he continues, 'Look, we haven't got the contract anyway. So let's just wait and see what happens, eh? But if they do choose us, well, the future of quite a few jobs here could depend on it. And that would be a hard thing to refuse over mere principles.'

I nearly challenge him on the concept of *mere principles*, but think better of it. 'Well, look . . . I'm sorry, Peter, but I can't be clearer on this. *I* won't work with them. I just can't.'

'Right, well, if push comes to shove Victoria can do it. As long as *she* doesn't visit the farm we should be OK.'

'Victoria won't want to run the whole caboodle,' I point out. 'She won't want to liaise with Creative and Media and . . . Anyway, the last I heard she's gone vegan.'

'If she has to she will. And as you know full well, if Spot On don't do this then one of our competitors will.'

'I expect that's what the men who built Auschwitz said,' I say, remembering one of my favourite student arguments.

'I expect they did,' Peter says. 'And I expect like Hugo Boss, and Siemens, and Mercedes Benz, they all got bloody rich.'

'Nice,' I say.

'Indeed. Now, if you don't mind, I need to get off to a meeting.'

Mark and Jude are thankfully more understanding of my point of view. 'If we do have to do it, we'll do it really badly,' Mark tells me.

'I'll make sure they get the worst advertising campaign Spot On has ever produced,' Jude agrees.

Even if we all know that this wouldn't truly be an option, it's sweet of them to say so. I can only hope that we never do get that contract.

· · ·

On Saturday morning I head up to Waterloo to meet my mother.

She starts complaining about South West Trains even before she reaches the ticket barrier. 'Guess how much this cost,' she says, shouting and waving her ticket at me over the head of an old lady between us. 'Go on, guess.'

'Hi, Mum,' I say. 'Well, at least you didn't have to drive. You usually arrive fuming about the traffic.'

'Twenty-nine pounds twenty,' she says. 'From Camberley! Can you imagine? I could drive to Scotland for that.'

'I don't think you could actually, but—'

'Completely full, and bubblegum all over the seat. I had to ask a man for a page from his newspaper, and now I expect I have newsprint all over my bum. Honestly. And they wonder why no one uses the train.'

'You said it was full,' I point out, hugging her briefly.

'Only because the one before was so late everyone got on ours,' she says. 'Anyway . . .'

'Yes, forget it now. You're here. And I'm taking you for a lovely lunch in Covent Garden.'

As we head across the concourse towards the taxi rank, I wonder if I can ask her straight off what the visit is about. I'm feeling a little sick about our impending discussion. 'So,' I say, steeling myself to pop the question.

'So,' Mum replies, 'how was your trip to Portsmouth? You drove, you said?'

'Yes. Horrible. Well professionally, it was horrible.'

'I really liked the place myself, but I suppose that was a long time ago.'

'Oh, I liked the towns, and the countryside down there is beautiful. It's just I had to go to this farm – our client is a dairy company: milkshakes and yogurts and stuff – but it was the most awful place, Mum, honestly you wouldn't believe it. A factory farm I suppose they call it. All the cows were tied up in rows. They never turn around, and they never go outside. They never even see a blade of grass. Not ever.'

'Really,' she says, flatly. It's exactly the voice she used when I was sixteen and ranting about Thatcher or the miners or nuclear power.

'Yes. I don't think I'll ever buy non-organic dairy stuff again.'

'Do you think it tastes better?' she asks, apparently missing the point entirely.

'Yes,' I lie. 'Much better.'

The man in front of us is wearing Grunge! carpenter pants. I nudge her and whisper, 'Grunge! We did the advertising for those. They're everywhere now.'

The guy in front overhears me and turns around. 'They're great,' he says. 'I love these trousers.'

Mum smiles. 'You must be very proud,' she says, unconvincingly.

And I think, *Am I?* For in the end, despite the fact that we have convinced millions of men that they need two zips instead of one, the world clearly hasn't shifted on its axis.

'Yeah,' I say, vaguely.

By the time we climb into our cab it has started to rain.

'Does it always rain in London?' Mum says. 'Because it was lovely in Surrey when I left.'

'It was lovely here too, Mum. The weather's changing today – they said so on TV. It's back to winter now.'

As (with the recent exception of couscous) Mum's tastes rarely stretch to anything more exotic than French, I take her to a lovely little bistro in William Street: Terroirs. It's a choice that thankfully meets with her immediate approval.

'Gosh how lovely,' she says. 'Exactly like being in Paris.'

We both order leek soup followed by steak tartare for Mum and, because I don't think I'll be able to do beef or dairy for a while, fish for me.

And then, served with two jolly generous glasses of red wine, we sit and stare alternately at each other and at people hurrying past outside, and prepare ourselves for whatever is to come.

'So other than the cow thing, you had a nice trip,' Mum says.

'Yes, I loved Cornwall. I even looked at a few properties down there, just to see.'

'You wouldn't move to Cornwall!' she laughs.

'Why not?'

'How could you? With your job and your friends and . . .'

'I'm not sure London's working for me,' I say. 'I'm not sure it's making me happy. Not deep down.'

Mum raises an eyebrow. 'You've taken a while to work that one out, haven't you?'

'Yes,' I agree. 'Yes. Far too long.'

'But Cornwall!' she says. 'It's just so far!'

'From you?' I say. 'From Surrey?'

'From everywhere.'

'It's not far from Devon,' I point out facetiously.

Mum frowns. 'What's in Devon?'

'Well nothing. I just mean far from where? Far from what?'

'The outer Hebrides aren't far from the outer Hebrides,' Mum says. 'But it doesn't mean that I'm going to move there anytime soon.'

'That was my second choice actually,' I say. 'How did you guess?'

'Yes, dear. Well don't forget to send me a postcard.'

'So what about you?' I ask. 'What's happening?'

'Oh everything's fine.'

'But you wanted to talk about something.'

'Yes.'

'Daughterly advice, you said.'

'Yes, that's right.'

At that moment our soup arrives.

Once the waiter has retreated, I sip my soup and prompt her again. 'So?'

'This is very buttery. It's good, but very buttery.'

'Yes. So?'

'I'm quite scared of you actually,' she says. 'Isn't that strange?'

'Scared of me?'

'Yes. I feel like a child. I suppose I know you're going to shout at me and get all irate, and I just don't know if . . .'

'Oh, Mum!' I say, reaching to touch her hand, a hand she instantly withdraws. 'I won't. I'm just concerned about you, that's all.' I make a note to myself that I now really must not get irate.

'Well you know what it's about, I expect,' she says.

'Saddam,' I say. 'Adam.'

'Yes.'

'Is everything OK?'

'Perfect,' she says. 'Better than ever.'

'Then it's about what . . . marriage again?'

Mum slurps her soup and then clears her throat. 'Well yes. It's the only practical solution to the problem.'

'But you don't marry someone as a practical—'

'But I want to as well. I know you don't believe that, but I do.'

'Actually I do believe it,' I say. 'I'm just not sure that it's—'

'And he does too. And I know you think that he just sees me as a ticket, as a passport or something and I'm not stupid, I think that maybe that's part of it too – probably, in fact. But I don't care. It suits me.'

'Right.'

'So the question is, do we do a big proper wedding in spring, in, say March? Or a quick registry office thing with just the two of us in November.'

'This November? I mean, it's November *next week*,' I point out.

'Yes. But in December I'm off to Agadir for the winter. So it'll be too late.'

I frown. 'But if you're off to Agadir then there's no hurry anyway. There's no problem to be solved, is there?'

'So you think do it properly, in March.'

'Mum, seriously . . . I don't want to . . .'

'No go on,' she says.

'Well . . . Look . . . I don't . . . I'm not . . . particularly thrilled about it, you know that.'

'Yes.'

'But if you *are* going to get married, I can't see how you *can* have a big wedding anyway. For one, he's Muslim, isn't he?'

'Yes. Oh, I don't mean a *church* wedding. I just mean with a guest list, and a reception afterwards.'

I realise that by providing me with two options, Mum has effectively circumvented any discussion about the desirability of the marriage itself. And I know her well enough to know that this will have been an entirely choreographed move.

'Look . . . Are you *sure* you want to marry him?'

'Please don't . . .' she says.

I point the palms of my hands at her in a gesture of submission.

'Hey, I'm just asking the question,' I say. 'It's a question that needs to be asked.'

'OK, then yes. I am.'

'Why? Other than the visa business.'

'Because I don't want to lose him.'

'Why don't you want to lose him?'

'Because . . . because I've been rattling around on my own for twenty years, and because, to use your words, it hasn't been working for me.'

'Right.'

'Adam makes me happy,' she says with a shrug. 'And I didn't think that could happen again . . . not really.'

'Right,' I say.

'And we can't live together unless we get married. And I'm worried that if we don't he'll . . . you know . . .'

'Leave you? Find someone else?'

'Well, yes. Unless I move to Morocco permanently. But I don't want to do that.'

'*I* don't want you to do that.'

By the end of lunch, by gently pointing out that the only people Mum could invite to a wedding would all also be friends of Dad's, and that, human nature being what it is, most of them would be fairly uncomfortable about her new choice of partner, and by reminding her how chronically shy Saddam is, I have convinced her not only that a small private wedding is the way to go, but that there's no reason why it can't wait until spring.

But just as when I was a child I would cry for an ice cream for half an hour, and Mum would finally give in and say I could have a boiled sweet, and then proceed to produce one from her pocket, I can't help but feel that I have been hoodwinked. I can't help but feel that my negotiated compromise is exactly what she planned all along. She's clever that way, my mum.

Nothing Gay About It

Before I have even closed the door of the surgery behind me, the secretary exclaims, 'Oh, CC Kelly. Oh God! I was supposed to phone you.'

I push the door shut, and cross the marble floor to her desk. 'Hello,' I say. 'I'm sorry?'

'Hello. Oh please don't have a go at me, I'm having such a bad day. But I was meant to call you, wasn't I? You wanted to see Doctor James.'

'Yes.'

'She's off sick, I'm afraid. I should have phoned. God Vic . . . Doctor Ynchausty is so gonna . . .'

And then the door to Victor's office opens. 'Yes? I'm going to what?' he asks.

'I'm so sorry, doctor,' she says. She sounds like she might cry. 'I was supposed to reschedule Ms Kelly to see Doctor James, and I did, but now you're standing in, and . . .'

'Well,' Victor says, clearly irritated. He looks at me and shrugs and forces a smile. 'Actually I only need to go through the blood tests with you anyway. What do you think?'

I shrug and nod. 'Yeah. Might as well. Now I'm here.'

'I'm really sorry,' the secretary says as Victor ushers me into his office.

'It's fine,' I say, giving her a sly wink.

I take a seat in front of his desk and Victor closes the door. 'She is bloody useless though,' he says.

'Oh it's fine,' I say.

'But it has all been very hectic. Moira has the flu and...'

'Swine flu?' I say.

'Ah, you heard about that.'

'Yes,' I say. 'Actually, thinking about that, I think I'd rather see *you*.'

'Flattery indeed,' Victor says taking his seat. 'So how have you been? I hear you were at the funeral.'

'Yes,' I say. 'Well... Miserable with it all.'

'Yes it's awful. I never would have imagined he'd... Anyway. I missed it... the funeral that is. Things have been such a mess here... there are only two of us, so...'

'Sure.'

'But I made the wake.'

'Oh!' I say, surprised. 'How was it?'

'Fine. Sad. And happy. Wakes are strange.'

'They are. And Darren's mum?'

'Fine. Upset.'

'Sure,' I say, a little shocked that she didn't turn Victor away with the rest of us.

'She can seem very hard... but she's just suffering,' Victor says. 'She has a lot on her plate. More than you could know.'

'Right,' I say. 'You knew him well then? Darren?'

'Oh yes, forever. Since we were kids. He was pretty much the first friend I made when we moved over here.'

'Right.'

'And the funeral? How was that?'

I think about it and decide to lie. There's no point adding any extra pain if he wasn't there to witness it. 'Nice,' I say. 'Well, obviously not *nice*... It was...'

'Appropriate?' Victor says, fingering a chrome cube paper-weight.

'Yes, I suppose so.'

'Anyway, enough, huh?'

'Yes.'

'I have to force myself to think about other things, otherwise...'

'I'm the same.'

'So . . . Onto happier things. Your results,' he says, unfolding three pages pulled from a folder. 'These are all fine.'

'Everything's normal?'

'Yes.'

'So no explanation for the irregularity . . .'

'None. I would guess it's just a blip. Have you been feeling stressed? Or run down? Or depressed?'

'A little.'

'Well that's probably it.'

'So I'm not menopausal.'

'No, as far as we can see, not at all.'

'Good. Well, that's a relief anyway.'

'Yes. I'm sure.' Victor slides one of the pages towards me across the desk and points at one of the figures. 'You see that: AMH?'

'Yes.'

'Well, it's more and more accepted that it's a pretty good indicator . . . it drops off considerably a few years before the final period.'

'And mine's fine?'

'Yes, absolutely normal.'

'So I have a few years.'

'Yes. Well, probably. I have to tell you that it's a little controversial to use it as an indicator. Because it's quite recent science. And because it's not one hundred per cent, as an indicator.'

'I see.'

'But generally speaking, yes. Generally speaking that would seem to indicate that you have at least five years fertility before you.'

'Five years.' I can barely contain my grin.

'But beware . . . these things can be wrong. So the advice, if you want to have a baby, is obviously . . .'

'Don't hang around forever.'

'Exactly. Because all of this hocus-pocus just comes down to probability in the end. You're playing poker here and every year that goes by, the risk of your being called out increases. This shows that the *probability* that it will happen tomorrow is low. But it's not impossible. And the odds clearly aren't improving.'

'OK, well, that's clear, at least. Thanks.'

'Have you advanced in your project?'

'My project? Oh! Not really.'

'Do you have a donor lined up? Because if not, I can give you some addresses.'

'I . . .'

'Perhaps you don't want to discuss that with me. That's fine, of course. I've done my bit here really, so . . .'

'No, it's fine. I have an idea, who I'm going to ask. But I haven't . . .'

'You know it's not quite as simple as sticking the stuff in a turkey baster.'

'I haven't really looked into it that much yet.'

'There are many things you need to think about and discuss, if not with me then with someone else.'

'Yes.'

'There are legal implications – without a disclaimer, for instance, you could go after the father for child support for instance . . . so *that* all needs to be clear.'

'Yes, I know that.'

'And there are health implications . . . screening for genetic diseases, and sexually transmissible diseases like hepatitis, syphilis and HIV.'

'Of course . . . Look . . . I *don't* really want to discuss it. If that's all right. It does feel a bit weird. Because, well, I know you, and you know people *I* know and . . .'

'Yes. Of course. Well. Look. I know this is delicate of course. So tell me to butt out if . . .'

'Yes.'

I think but don't say, *Yes, butt out.*

'It's just that, well . . . it's not Mark, is it?'

'I'm sorry?'

'Actually don't tell me. But if you were thinking about asking Mark, then please don't.'

'I . . .' But the conversation is so bizarre that words fail me.

'It's just that he can't. I know that. And I shouldn't tell you this, so of course it's in the strictest confidence. But he can't. Someone already asked him, a while back, and he was terribly upset that he couldn't. And he's so upset about Darren at the moment . . . it just wouldn't be . . .'

'Well it wasn't Mark,' I lie. 'It's someone you don't know, so . . .'

'Oh good. Then I'm sorry. And please forget I ever said anything. I don't know why I thought . . . I'm sorry.'

'It's fine.'

'And please don't say anything to Mark.'

'No, of course.'

'Good. Thanks.'

'So . . . I suppose I don't need another appointment, do I? Seeing as everything is normal.'

'No, sadly you don't.'

'Sadly?'

'Oh, I just mean, with Darren gone, I'm not likely to bump into you again, am I?'

'No,' I say. 'Maybe through Mark?'

Victor wrinkles his nose. 'No, Darren was my, you know, contact with that little group.'

'OK,' I say.

'So if you ever want to talk, or salsa a little . . .'

'Right.'

'You have my number.'

'I do.'

'Good, well . . .'

'OK then.' I cough and stand. 'I pay the secretary, right?'

Victor wrinkles his nose. 'Um, no charge for this one. The lab will probably mail you a bill though for the blood work.'

'Right.'

'Well, good luck then.'

'Yes, thanks.'

• • •

Out on the street I'm feeling a swirl of conflicting emotions amidst a cacophony of different thoughts.

I'm stunningly relieved that everything's OK, and, provisos apart, that I have maybe five years in which I can still conceive. And I'm worried about Mark, for the obvious reason he wouldn't be able to donate sperm is HIV, but could he really be positive without my knowing? I suppose the answer is that of *course* he could, and of course he wouldn't tell me. So I'm a little shocked to learn that despite having lived next door to him for five years and despite having worked with him for seven, I really don't know him at all. But then, perhaps, like Darren announcing his imminent suicide, Mark *has* told me. Perhaps I just don't listen.

And then I think about the bizarre tension as I left Victor's office. It was almost like a date, almost like the lingering goodbye on a doorstep when you're waiting to be invited to stay the night.

I suppose that, to Victor, I'm one of the remaining ripples from Darren's life, and saying goodbye to me is saying goodbye to yet another sign that Darren once existed.

Perhaps I should have arranged to have a drink with him. But in truth I'm exhausted with thinking about Darren. And what else could we have talked about?

I reach the taxi rank and join the queue and pray that Norman won't pop his head out of one of the taxis, which of course he doesn't.

No, I don't want to talk to Victor, and I don't want to think about Darren, and I don't even particularly want to face Mark at work. I think I must be all gayed out. In fact, right now, secretly, I would have to agree with Darren's mother. There's nothing gay about it.

Dodgy Equipment

Against all expectation, I have a busy week at work.

Grunge!, apparently advised that the recession may be shorter than initially thought, request that I budget for re-purchasing a small number of their now cancelled magazine ads, and because I have been so bored recently I hoard the work for myself and only inform the media department on Wednesday when everything is finished.

Victoria Barclay swings by my desk on Thursday morning and urges me to, 'Think very carefully about the implications of refusing work.' Her raised eyebrows and menacing leer confirm my impression that she is now entirely back to normal after her breakdown.

On Friday I field calls from two small dairy companies in Cornwall. One of these is organic and both are on the edge of bankruptcy. They have mysteriously heard that we might be doing some work for Cornish Cow and want to know if I honestly think that strategically placed advertising might help them survive the downturn, so I spend the rest of the day hunting for statistics on the internet to support this unlikely hypothesis. Clearly some strategically placed advertising would help *us* survive the downturn.

By keeping busy all week, it's Friday night by the time the myriad of thoughts lingering in the shadowy recesses of my brain manage to elbow their way to the fore.

I pour myself a large glass of wine and retire to the lounge with Guinness and think about Victoria Barclay's thinly disguised threat of redundancy, and for once, everything seems clear to me: I don't want to work for Peter Stanton any more with his 'mere principles' and I don't want to work with VB with her venomous ways . . . I don't want to repackage the Cornish concentration-camp-cow as a happy-go-lucky milkshake-sipping cartoon beast either, and despite my sterling efforts I don't even really want to take money from two struggling dairy companies unless, as I doubt, we really *can* help them. Most surprisingly, I have even lost my desire to work with my old allies in Creative as well.

And without that, what, if anything, is keeping me in London?

I log onto some property sites on the internet and recalculate the value of my flat, again reaching the conclusion that it's worth somewhere around three hundred and eighty thousand.

I then hunt down the sheets I took to Cornwall and look again at the properties I visited, saving till last, relishing even, a fresh peek at my house on the hill. For today, what seems obvious is that I need to let Spot On make me redundant, and I need to sell this place, and then I need to go and build an entirely new life in my house on the hill before it's too late. From the spectacularly simplified viewpoint my brain has produced today, it seems evident that if it worked for my body-double, there's no reason why it shouldn't work for me.

It takes me some time to hunt down the house on the hill again, and there's a devastating reason for this. For some reason it no longer appears in the two hundred to four hundred thousand bracket. Today, it is in the six to seven hundred thousand slot.

The shock of realising that, on my own, this house, or any house like it, is way beyond my means, saddens me so much it feels like an actual body-blow.

I close the laptop with an angry thud, and murmur to Guinness that it's a shame because he would have liked it, and then I slop more Chianti into my glass.

As I place the bottle on the table, I jolt with the shock of seeing a face pressed against my lounge window. Because it's dark outside I can't initially see who it is, but then Mark gives his little signature wave, so with a mixture of relief and a vague sensation that no matter how much you try to change your life, the old one always hunts you down, I head to the front door.

'Are you avoiding me?' Mark asks the second I open the door.

'No, sweety,' I say. 'Why would I be avoiding you?'

'I haven't seen you all week,' he says, stepping past me into the hallway.

'I've been busy,' I say.

'Busy!' he repeats, mockingly.

I roll my eyes, close the front door and follow him into the hall.

'Lounge or kitchen?' he asks.

'That depends. Tea or wine?'

'Oh wine,' he says. 'Every time.'

'Lounge then,' I say. 'I'll just get another glass.'

When I return, Mark is perched on the edge of the sofa. He looks distinctly uncomfortable. 'You look upset,' I comment. 'What's wrong?'

'No,' he says, shaking his head vigorously. 'Nope, not upset.'

'So why are you slumming it in Primrose Hill?' I ask.

'I wanted to check in on you,' he says. 'You've been hiding all week.'

'I soo haven't, Mark,' I say with a laugh which sounds false, even to me.

As I slop wine into his glass, he looks up at me circumspectly. 'You so have,' he says.

I sigh. 'I know. But look, it's not *you*, though. It's just the whole Darren thing. I've been trying not to think about it.'

'Join the club,' Mark says.

'I just feel so guilty,' I tell him. 'And sad too. But mainly guilty.'

Mark sips his wine, then places it thoughtfully on the coffee table. 'I told you. Everyone feels that way. We all do.'

'Yes,' I say.

'He told everyone what he was going to do. So the responsibility is everyone's. But mainly, in the end, it was just his.'

'Right,' I say. 'Except that he phoned *me*.'

As I say this I think how amazing it is that I had forgotten this. I had wiped it entirely from my memory until now. But now that it has resurfaced, the fact of it swamps me with guilt. It feels like someone has dumped a donkey-yoke around my shoulders. 'Please don't tell anyone else this,' I say, my throat suddenly constricting. 'But he phoned me. The night he did it. I could have saved his life. Only I didn't take the call.'

Mark's mouth drops. 'He phoned and you didn't *answer*?' he asks incredulously.

'No, I . . . yes . . . I saw it was him, and I filtered the call. And I should have known. So yes, he told everyone, but he phoned *me*.' My voice wobbles as I say 'me.'

Mark puts his glass down and moves to my side. He rests a hand across my back. 'Why didn't you tell me?' he asks.

'I forgot,' I tell him. 'I honestly forgot. I think I wiped it out.'

'And what did he say?'

'I didn't . . .'

'No, the message.'

'Oh, he didn't leave one.'

'God.'

'But I was so drunk . . . and I thought he would ask me to go back to the party, and I was completely out of it on that bloody drugged punch.'

'When was this?' Mark says frowning.

I frown back at him. 'What do you mean, *when* was this? It was after the party. When I was on my way home.'

'Well then it wasn't him,' Mark says.

'What do you mean, it wasn't him?'

'The call. It wasn't Darren. It can't have been. It was probably the police. They went through all the numbers in his mobile trying to contact his family. He was already gone by then.'

'Are you sure?'

'Yeah. The policeman found him at twelve, and they said he must have died about eleven.'

'A *policeman* found him? Where?'

'At home. He sent them an email. To the police station. He thought it would take them a while to respond, and it did . . . not that long, but, well, long enough.'

'God!' I say. 'You're sure about this? That it was at midnight?'

'Certain,' Mark says. 'They called me as well, but I didn't hear it. I phoned him back the next morning, and the police answered, and that's when they told me, and that's when I called you.'

I stare at the ceiling and struggle to catch my breath. 'God it wasn't him.'

'Nope,' Mark says, rubbing my shoulder in little circular movements.

'God, I've been feeling so sick about that,' I say. 'Especially after what he said about me treating him as a one-line joke.'

'A one-line joke?'

'Yeah. We had an argument. And he said I treat my friends as one-line jokes.'

'I didn't know about that,' Mark says. 'But he was awful that last week. The depression, I suppose. He gave us all a hard time.'

'But it was true too,' I say. 'I didn't listen enough. I didn't give him enough time. We're all so wrapped up in our own shit. It's like you.'

'Me?'

'Well, you've got your own problems too, haven't you? And I should be there more for people. I need to be less selfish. I wonder that no one tells me stuff, but I'm not really listening.'

Mark removes his hand from my back and looks at me strangely.

'What's up?' I ask.

'Well, you're not selfish . . . anything but. But more to the point, what problems have I got?'

I shrug. 'Oh nothing, I just mean we all have our problems,' I say, backtracking as fast as I can.

Mark's brow wrinkles. He stands. 'Loo,' he says. 'But this is to be continued.'

I slosh the remaining Chianti into my glass and then fetch a fresh bottle from the kitchen, rinsing my face as I pass the kitchen sink.

When I return, Mark is sitting with the same suspicious face as before. I had hoped he would have forgotten and moved onto something else.

'Has Stanton said something?' he asks. 'Am I losing my job?'

'No,' I say. 'Don't be silly.'

'Have you seen Ian out with someone? Because I know what he's like.'

'No,' I say. 'Mark. Stop.'

'Then?'

'Jesus, there isn't . . .'

'I know you,' he says.

'Jesus, Mark!'

'Tell me.'

'There's nothing to tell.'

'I think there is,' Mark says, looking at his watch. 'I have all night. Ian's at the opera tonight, and lord knows I hate opera.'

'You're being silly.'

'You're not being straight with me.'

'*I'm* not being straight.'

'You see. There you go. I have no idea what you're talking about.'

I sigh. 'God, Mark!'

'Tell me what you know. What you *think* you know.'

'I can't. I promised,' I say.

Mark shakes his head unamused. 'Now I know there's something,' he says. 'And you know me well enough to know that I'm not going to . . .'

'OK. I know, all right? About your health issues.'

'My health issues?'

'Yes.'

'What, you saw the meds?'

'Meds?'

'In the bathroom?'

'No I didn't,' I say. And then I wish I had replied in the affirmative. It would have been a great alibi.

'So what . . . someone told you something? Just tell me the truth.'

'Look, you virtually just said it yourself, Mark. Why don't *you* just tell me?'

'You think I have HIV, right?'

'Well yes.'

'OK. So now I really need to know why. Because I don't. Have it, that is.'

'You don't?'

'No.'

'But the meds. You just said yourself . . .'

'The meds you saw . . . sorry, didn't see, were Ian's.'

'Right.'

'So what did you hear?'

I gasp in exasperation. 'I . . . I'm sorry. I mean, I'm glad you don't, but I'm sorry. I must have got the wrong end of the stick.'

'OK. What stick? Whose stick?'

'Jesus. Victor,' I say. 'Happy?'

'Victor,' Mark says. 'Why would Victor tell you that?'

'He didn't. He said you couldn't father children, and it was me . . . I just assumed.'

'Curiouser and curiouser,' Mark says. 'So why exactly would you and Victor have been talking about my ability to . . .'

'He's my gynaecologist, OK? And I was talking about options for having a child.'

'A child.'

'Yes. I really want a baby, and you know . . .' My voice is wobbling and my eyes are watering. 'There are time limits for a woman on that stuff.'

'Oh, sweetie.'

'And he thought I was going to ask you for a donation . . . and so he warned me off. Happy now?'

Mark massages his brow with his left hand and sips at his wine using the right. 'Can I smoke?' he asks.

'Sure,' I say, reaching to my right for an ashtray and sliding it onto the table. 'As long as you give me one.'

'Were you?' he asks pulling the packet from the pocket of his jacket.

'What? Was I what?' I ask, taking a cigarette.

'Were you going to ask me?'

'I don't . . . no.'

'Oh,' he says.

'Yes,' I say, suddenly not sure what the least hurtful answer would be here. 'Yes. I hadn't decided if I was going to go that route exactly, but yes, I did think about asking you.'

Mark snorts.

'What?'

'Well, it's ironic,' he says. 'Here's me gagging for a kid, and people *keep* asking me – you're the third person to want my spunk . . . Crazy shit life throws at you, huh?'

'But it's true? That you can't?'

'I should be flattered, I suppose,' Mark says. 'And no . . . in answer to your question, no, I can't. I have zero viable sperm, for some reason. They don't know why.'

'God, I'm sorry.'

'I know.'

'And that's why he didn't want me to ask you. That's the only reason Victor told me – because he knew it would upset you. That's why he warned me off.'

'Sure,' Mark says. 'Fair enough.'

'And you definitely can't?'

'No. We did all the tests. Nothing but blanks. And it really is ironic, because nothing would please me more, but I was never able to . . . not with a woman, and now I can't even . . .' His eyes are glistening with tears. He makes a clicking noise and nods his head. 'Yep,' he says. 'Ironic is the word.'

'I'm sorry, Mark,' I say. 'I understand. Because I do too. Want a kid. I know what that feels like.'

'Right,' he says. 'God. And so you deduced that I have HIV. It's logical enough, I suppose.'

'Yes, I don't know why I thought that.'

'Oh it's an easy enough conclusion to jump to. Darren had it, Ian has it . . . everyone seems to have HIV these days. It does my head in.'

'Darren had it?'

'Sure,' Mark says. 'Why do you think the idiot was so depressed?

Well, one of the reasons. His meds stopped working, and so they were trying different things . . . anyway, it was all very wearing.'

'God,' I say. 'He didn't tell me.'

'No, well . . . maybe . . .'

'Yes?'

'Never mind.'

'No, what?'

'Really. Please. Nothing. You know that Dan, his brother has it too, right?'

'Dan?!'

'Darren's brother. Dan. It's the reason they didn't get on. And one of the reasons the mother's so uptight as well.'

'Is he gay as well then? I had no idea.'

'No. He got it from a blood transfusion I think,' Mark says. 'He's had it for years. It's why he doesn't get on with Darren. Because he always goes on about being one of the innocent victims, so by implication . . .'

'Innocent?'

'Exactly,' Mark says. 'If Darren got it, then according to Dan, it's his own fault.'

'And Ian too?' I say. 'I'm so sorry, sweetie. I had no idea.'

'Ian's had it forever. It's why his face is so marked. Did you never notice that? It's the treatment that does that. But he got it at the beginning, in eighty-three. So at least he has the excuse of not having known, I guess.'

'And how are you with that?'

'It's OK. We're careful. I mean, I wouldn't say it's a plus or anything, but you get used to it.'

'I can't believe that I didn't know any of this. Maybe I haven't been such a good friend. Maybe I've been too wrapped up in my own stuff.'

Mark shrugs, which I take as confirmation that he doesn't entirely disagree.

'I'm sorry,' I say.

He shrugs again. 'It's fine,' he says. 'We're all dealing with our own shit.'

'You won't say anything to Victor, will you? I really think that he meant well.'

Mark shrugs. 'No,' he says. 'Anyway, I'll probably never see Victor again.'

'Oh please don't be like that.'

'No, that's not what I mean. It's just that he's not really a friend. He was Darren's mate and then when Jenna wanted a baby, she asked me, and we went to him for the tests. But mainly he just put up with the rest of us for Darren's sake.'

'He went to the wake,' I say. 'I'm surprised they let him in.'

'Well, he's an old family friend. He went to school with him.'

'Were he and Darren ever . . . you know?'

Mark laughs. 'No!' he says. 'Don't be daft.'

'Why is that daft?'

'Well . . .' Mark laughs. 'Though of course, who knows what those boarding school boys get up to. But no. I doubt it! And what about you?'

'Me?'

'Yeah, did you ever?'

'With Darren?'

'With Victor! Honestly!'

'Now *you're* being silly,' I say.

'Because he's your gynaecologist?'

'Just because we had a drugged-up kiss at a party,' I say.

'I thought that might go somewhere,' Mark says. 'I was rather disappointed in you not seizing the moment on that one.'

'Well . . .' I say. 'He's not . . . you know, is he?'

'Not what?'

'He's not bisexual, is he?'

Mark laughs. 'Not that I know of . . .' His face slips into a deep frown. 'Why? Do you . . . You don't think that Victor is . . .?'

And as he says this, I say, 'You're not saying that Victor is . . .?'

'Gay?' Mark says.

'Straight?'

'Huh!' Mark laughs.

'Is he? No, he's gay. Tell me he's gay.'

'Is he?' Mark says.

'Surely he is. Oh stop winding me up. You! You're terrible.'

Mark starts to snigger uncontrollably now. 'Honestly, CC, you're unbelievable.'

'Victor is straight? That's what you want me to believe now, is it?'

'He's a gynaecologist, sweetie.'

'This much I know.'

'So he spends his life putting his . . .'

'Enough. I know what a gynaecologist does, Mark.'

'So how many gay men do you think grow up dreaming of doing *that* all day long?'

'Stop,' I say.

'Sorry, I forgot, you've been there. Or rather Victor has.'

'Stop, I said.'

'Well!' Mark laughs. 'You really have some dodgy equipment, don't you?'

'Dodgy equipment?'

'Yes! You so need to get your gaydar retuned, honey.'

'I don't believe you,' I say, even though I'm starting to believe him.

'He's been cruising you since he first met you, you silly bitch.'

'He has *not.*'

'Smiles, drinks, salsa . . . what did you think that was all about?'

'I thought he was just another gay man in search of a fag hag,' I say.

'Right,' Mark says, his mirth fading for a moment.

'Joke, Mark,' I say.

'Yes,' Mark says. He isn't laughing.

'I'm sorry, I didn't mean . . .' I say, grimacing as I belatedly realise how demeaning those words might sound.

'Thanks for that one.'

'That's not . . . You know what I meant.'

'Sadly, I do.'

'I'm sorry. Really I am.'

'It's fine. Anyway . . .'

I sigh and stroke his arm and then continue, 'Anyway, we all danced salsa.'

'With each other! Victor was the one rubbing groins with *you*.'

'God. No! Really?'

Mark nods.

'How amazing. I missed that one entirely.'

'Looks that way,' Mark says.

'So why is he always with you guys? I mean, you can see how I thought . . . Are you *sure* you're not winding me up?'

Mark raises a hand to his heart. 'Honest to God,' he says. 'He's as straight as Ian's willy, and that's pretty straight, believe me. And he's been bleating on about you since you first met in March or whenever it was.'

'And why didn't you tell me?'

'I thought I had. And, well, I just assumed you had dipped your toe in the water, and not liked the temperature or something.'

'I do not *dip my toe in*. I'm not that kind of girl.'

'Well clearly not.'

'Anyway, he's a gynaecologist,' I point out. 'That's a real turn-off for a girl.'

'It's pretty icky if you're a boy,' Mark says. 'More so, probably. Anyway, he won't be for much longer.'

'Won't be what?'

'Well he's retiring, isn't he.'

'Retiring? How can he be?'

'Well, not retiring exactly. But he's off to France, isn't he? To set up a farm or something.'

'Is he really doing that?'

'Yeah. I think so. His parents left him a place and he's been buying up extra land around it.'

'Shame. He's cute. I finally find out he's straight just when he's leaving.'

'I bet you're wishing he was staying in gynaecology now, aren't you?'

'Why?'

'Well, be serious.'

'I don't get you.'

'Well, otherwise you could go for it. I mean, I can't imagine you tripping around in the mud in your Manolo Blahniks.'

'You're getting me confused with Carrie Bradshaw, dear. I can't afford Manolo anything.'

'Or your Jimmy shoes or whatever.'

'Jimmy *Choos*. God, you really don't know me at all, do you?'

'Huh!' Mark laughs.

'Huh?'

'Well if I don't, whose fault would that be?'

Mark and I down the two bottles of wine between us and then I slurringly, gigglingly order pizzas and then open a third bottle whilst waiting for the delivery.

Mark phones Ian and informs him that he won't be home, and we sit and drink and eat and drink some more until the first signs of daylight appear in the east.

Mark tells me about Ian and his illness and how he, Mark, is struggling to come to terms with the open relationship that Ian has imposed. He tells me that it's not his thing, but that he's determined to make things work, because despite everything, he's simply never been happier.

For my part I tell him for the first time about my dad, and Brian, and Waiine, and wanting a baby, and thinking of leaving Spot On for a new life somewhere far away from London.

As the evening progresses, I feel like a weight is being lifted from my shoulders, and realise that I have made considerable efforts these last years to keep those around me at a distance. In the end though, all of this stuff is better out than in, and it strikes me that if I hadn't spent so much energy keeping things to myself, perhaps I wouldn't have needed a shrink in the first place. Certainly, if I had expressed how I felt about Victor to Mark, my life could, it seems, have been very different. I just wish I had found the time to talk to Darren like this. Perhaps that's all it would have taken.

Short-Sighted Date

I look around the restaurant and check my watch. I wish I had had the nerve to organise this myself, because I'm now realising that letting Mark set it all up has just added an extra layer of embarrassment to the whole thing.

I straighten my top and check my watch. A quarter past twelve. I sigh, and think that letting Mark organise things has also increased the possibility of a complete cock-up.

I pull my BlackBerry from my pocket and phone him to check that I am waiting in the right restaurant, but there's no answer, so I pull Victor's card from my purse, and sigh and start to type the number in.

But then he's there in the doorway, the low November sun streaming around him.

He crosses the restaurant and pulls a face. 'I'm so sorry,' he says.

'I was just about to phone to check that Mark hadn't given us two different addresses,' I say. 'Just for a laugh. That would be *so* his style.'

Victor removes his suit jacket and slides into the seat.

'Nice jumper,' I say. 'Not sure about the stubble though.'

He laughs. 'Oh this is just two days. When I grow a proper beard I look like one of ZZ Top. I *am* sorry I'm late though. I had an appointment at the surgery and it went on far longer than expected. I would have called but I don't have your number, so . . .'

'It's fine really. I only got here five minutes ago myself,' I lie.

'God, it's posh here isn't it?' Victor says looking around. 'When he said Indian I imagined some little side-street place.'

'Yes. I've never been here either.'

'So, what's this about?'

I feel a rash of heat rise instantly from my collar. 'Mark didn't say?'

Victor frowns. 'No. He just said you needed to talk to me.'

'Jesus!' I say.

'Is that a blush?' Victor asks, apparently amused.

'It might be,' I say. 'I just . . . I just thought he would have said something.'

Victor pouts and shakes his head. 'Nada,' he says.

I rub my brow and fiddle with the menu. 'Oh God,' I say.

'So hazarding a guess, it's something embarrassing?' Victor says.

'A little, yes.'

'Is it professional? To do with your project to—'

'No,' I interrupt. 'No it really isn't to do with that.'

'How are you getting on with that? Have you . . .? Oh. You're not going to ask me to . . .'

'No!' I say. 'No, I *said*, it's nothing to do with that.'

'Right,' Victor says, frowning now. 'Is it something to do with Darren?'

I shake my head. 'No, it's . . . God this is awful!'

Victor shrugs. 'Just . . .' he says with a shrug. 'I don't know, say it. How bad can it be?'

'It's Mark. He thought . . . he *thinks* that we might get on.'

'We might get on . . .' Victor repeats.

'Jesus,' I say. 'Can we just forget it? Can we just have lunch?'

Victor nods, and then, clearly trying to restrain a smirk, he says, 'Sorry, but, when you say, *get on,* is this, like, a blind date or something?'

I cough.

Victor's face is distorted with mirth. 'Oh my God, it is!'

'Well, it's not exactly blind, is it? Perhaps a bit short-sighted . . .' I laugh weakly.

Victor nods and says, 'God!'

'Look, if you want to forget this, we can just . . .' I say, reaching vaguely for my coat.

Victor extends an arm across the table and touches my shoulder gently. 'No, please,' he says. 'Let's have lunch as planned.'

I relax back into my seat and fan myself with the menu. 'I told you it was embarrassing,' I say. 'It's Mark's fault. He was convinced that you're keen or something. Stupid boy.'

'Keen,' Victor repeats, laughing.

'Look,' I say. 'If you're just going to . . .'

Victor shakes his head. He thinks this is all so funny his eyes are glistening with tears. 'CC,' he says, shaking his head. 'I . . . I really . . . keen doesn't really begin to describe how I felt about you.'

That past tense feels like a razor-blade slicing right across my jugular.

'But . . . God, your timing is bad,' he continues.

'My timing,' I repeat, quietly, wondering if it would be really hysterical of me to just stand and sprint from this restaurant right now. Because all I want to do is lock myself in my flat and close the curtains. 'Look, this is turning out to be excruciating for me,' I say. 'Maybe we *should* just go separate ways and pretend that this never happened.'

'It's not that . . . Look,' Victor says. 'Look, I really *do* like you, CC, don't get me wrong. I am keen. But I'm just not . . . well, I'm not available for that sort of thing now. And why now anyway? Why suddenly me, now? Were you seeing someone before?'

'No.'

'Then . . .' he shakes his head and shrugs.

'I thought you were gay,' I say in a whisper.

'You thought I was *gay*?' Victor repeats incredulously.

'Yes. Well you were always with Darren and Mark, and . . .'

Victor's face cracks into a grin again.

'Oh, don't laugh at me,' I say. 'I'm sorry. But yes. I thought you were gay.'

'Hey, no need to be sorry,' he says. 'Darren is . . . was . . . my best friend. But I can see how . . . and you're not the first and I don't suppose you'll be the last. And I don't mind in the slightest. In fact I'm rather flattered. My girlfriends were always saying how much better looking gay men are.'

'Yes, well, now you know,' I say.

'The thing is, CC,' he says.

'That you're not available,' I say. 'Yes, don't worry. I got that.'

And then I realise why. Of course. I'm too late. I would be. Victor has met someone else. At that second, I am so disgusted with my own stupidity I could throw myself off a cliff there and then . . . well, except that there isn't a cliff in the restaurant of course. But really, I could. For this guy, this gorgeous, smiling, clever, beautiful guy has been asking me out for nine months . . . *nine months!* And all the while I have been hunting high and low . . . I have been to speed dating, I have followed random perverts to Nice, and he was here; Victor was here in front of my very eyes from the start. Only I was too goddamned stupid to see it.

'You've met someone else,' I say. 'Of course.'

Victor frowns. 'What ever happened to women's intuition?' he asks.

'I'm sorry?'

'Never mind . . . No. Look, that's not it at all. It's just that I'm leaving.'

'For France.'

'Mark told you?'

'Yes.'

'So you know,' Victor says with a shrug. 'I just don't see . . . unless . . . Are you one of those hopeless cases who never grabs at anything until it isn't available any more? Is *that* why this is happening now? Because it's bloody irritating.'

And he has me almost convinced. For a minute I think, *Maybe yes. Maybe that's my problem.* 'I . . .'

'Sorry, that was rude,' Victor says, laying his right hand over mine. 'But it's just so . . .' he shrugs.

'I really thought you were gay,' I say. 'I'm sorry. Otherwise I would have . . .'

'You could have just asked me,' Victor says.

'I just assumed.'

'Anyway, yes. The timing's . . . well, impossible really. Because I'm going to France. As soon as the sale of my share of the practice is signed. I'm hoping in a couple of weeks, or at worst by the end of the year. I've been dreaming of this forever, and, when Darren died . . . well, it makes you think about things, something like that; it makes you want to get on with things.'

I pull my hand away. 'I understand entirely.' I consider telling him about my own dreams of another life, but realise that it will come across as cloying. He could only end up thinking that the real reason I'm approaching him now is because, like Saddam, I see him as a ticket to a new life; because I want to hitchhike a lift on the back of his adventure.

I sigh deeply. 'Look, I'm so sorry, can we please try to forget all that and just have lunch?'

Victor nods. 'Sure,' he says. 'That would be sweet.'

'So tell me about your farm.'

'Well it's not really a farm. Not yet,' Victor says.

And so he tells me all about it. He tells me of the tumbledown farmhouse he has bought and all the work that needs doing on it. He tells me of the land he has bought from the ageing neighbours. He tells how he's been to visit a friend's smallholding in the Lake District to learn how to rear goats and make cheese.

I half listen, merging in my mind's eye Victor's dreams with my own. And with the other half of my brain, I desperately search for a way to salvage this stupid silly missed opportunity. But his departure is too soon, and everything has happened the wrong way around, and the one phrase that is pulsing through my brain like tribal drums is the one phrase that I can't say, the one phrase that on a first date would make *any* man run a mile. And so, as I watch him waving his hands around as he describes the shape of the outbuildings, as I watch his gleaming eyes, his face ever more youthful as he explains the project with a crazy level of excitement, it is all I can do to stop that internal chant spilling out from between my lips. *Take me with you. Take me with you*, it goes.

Seize the Day

By the time I get back to Primrose Hill, I'm feeling thoroughly desolate.

I dump my bag on the kitchen table and head through to the lounge and hurl myself onto the couch. I feel swollen like a balloon, as if the pressure of my unexpressed desires, of the words that pride and reason would not let me pronounce has made me swell and stretch to bursting point. *Take me with you. Take me with you. Take me with you.* I can still feel them, lodged in my throat, suffocating me. But of course there was no way to say them without sounding desperate, or needy, or indeed, utterly, utterly crazy.

And now there is nothing left to do except sit on this sofa and wait, like Tom Hanks on a beach, for the tide to bring something else, another chance meeting with Victor, or another Victor perhaps, and hope that, just maybe, next time, I won't be so stupid.

But being honest with myself, what are the chances of either now?

I hear my BlackBerry ringing but ignore it. Without even looking, I know it will be Mark enquiring after my lunch-date.

I sit, numbly, my hands folded on my lap, and my eyes start to water and then my throat constricts and I blink, and tears start to dribble down my cheeks. I hear the voice of the shrink saying, 'That *is* crying,' and think, *Some victory.*

I hear the mobile ring again in the other room but ignore it. Then my body shudders and with a juddering gasp – even though

I'm not entirely convinced that I shall ever get back out again – I let go of the ropes and allow myself to fall into the pit. I weep for Victor and then Dad and Waiine, and Darren, and for every aspect of my stupid, stupid fucked-up life.

I cry self-indulgently for an hour or so and then, a little surprised, note that the flood has abated, and that the stock of tears was, apparently, finite after all. But I'm left feeling emptied and numb – not better at all.

I blow my nose and return to the kitchen and wash my face at the kitchen sink. The tap water seems to dance with an unusual sparkle, and I realise that a square of sunlight is illuminating one corner of the sink. It only covers a couple of square feet, but it's been years since I have seen direct sunlight in my kitchen. I peer out at the Leylandii and see that the branches are drooping unusually, and that some of the lower branches even look a little brown, and I remember Darren offering to kill it for me, and remember jokingly saying yes, and wonder . . .

I shake my head and glance back at the shimmering tap, at the light glancing off the BlackBerry's screen.

I pick it up and listen to my messages.

The first is from Mark saying that Victor is asking him for my number and asking if he can give it. 'Why on Earth didn't *you* give him your number?' he says. 'You're useless. You're completely useless.'

The second is from SJ asking me to call her back. 'I have some news,' she says, simply.

As I position my finger over the button to call her back, I hear a knock at the door, and thinking, 'Mark! The tenacious bugger,' I sigh and cross the hallway to turn him – as gently as possible – away.

When I open the door, however, it's not Mark that I find on the doorstep but Victor. He looks serious. Stressed even.

'Victor?' I say.

'Sorry, I'm disturbing you,' he says.

'Are you OK? You look funny,' I say.

'You look worse,' he says.

'Shit,' I say, rubbing at what I don't doubt are my panda eyes. 'Bloody mascara,' I say.

'Are you OK, CC?' he asks, reaching out to touch my shoulder. 'Because you look like you've been . . .'

And then my face collapses anew, and my body shudders. Victor steps forward and first rubs my shoulders tentatively and then, as I continue to sob, wraps his arms around me, and I think, *Nice one CC. That'll seduce him.*

'Hey. Hey!' Victor says.

'I never cry,' I gasp.

'No. I can see that,' he says. He just sounds embarrassed.

'It's just . . . bloody . . . everything. I'm just so useless. I'm completely useless.'

'You're not,' he says, rubbing my back and pressing the side of his head against my wet cheek. 'You're beautiful and funny and smart, and a surprisingly good salsa dancer.'

I manage to merge a laugh and a gasp into an entirely convincing but not very seductive piggy noise.

Victor steps back and looks into my eyes with wry amusement, then, glancing behind me, leads me into my lounge.

'I'm so sorry,' I say. 'It's just been such an awful few weeks. With work, and stuff with my mother, and Darren, and now today . . .'

He sits me on the sofa, reaches for the box of tissues and then crouches in front of me. 'Here,' he says, proffering the tissue.

'I'm not like this,' I snivel. 'Honestly I'm not.'

'I know,' he says. 'I've seen you being not-like-this, remember? But shit gets us all down sometimes.'

I blow my nose. 'Sorry. Jesus! So . . . what? How come you're here? Did Mark give you my address?

'I called him, but he wanted to ask you first. He's loyal that one.'

'He is.'

'So no. I called the office and got it from your file. Are you OK now?' he asks. 'Is there something . . .'

'No, I'm fine. I'll be fine, really. It must just be hormones or something. I'm all over the place at the moment.'

'OK. Sure. Well . . . maybe now's not the time.'

'For what? Why are you here?'

'I just didn't want to . . . well, to leave things like that.'

'Meaning?'

'I . . . Well. I really like you, CC. A lot. I always did. And it's stupid, I mean, just because I'm moving . . . I . . . I don't know what you think, but maybe . . . I just thought, perhaps we could stay in touch. Maybe you could even visit me . . . and if, say, suppose you like it down there . . . . Oh, I don't know. This sounds stupid now.'

I'm aware that I'm grimacing, my teeth clenched against a stupid smile and/or a new flood of tears. And then, I can hold them no longer, and a fresh batch of them rolls down my cheeks.

Through my blurred vision, I see Victor look confused, and then disappointed. 'I'm sorry,' he says. 'I knew it was stupid even before I came here. I sound like a bunny-boiler. I should go.'

But as he stands, something in me shifts. I think, *No, not this time.* I hear Darren, his voice clear as a bell. It sounds like he's in the room. 'If you do know what you want, then seize the day, CC,' he says.

'No,' I say quietly.

'No?'

I stand and throw my arms around him. 'No,' I say, again, my tears now wetting his cheek.

'CC?' he asks, trying to pull away to look at me. 'You're freaking me out now.'

'I can't let you do that,' I say. I lean back and look at him and start to smile.

'You can't?' he says

'No,' I say. 'I can't.'

And then, bracing myself for the prickle of his stubble, I do it. I kiss him.

The kiss is my first ever sober kiss with Victor, but amazingly I remember the feel of his lips, I still remember the physical sensation of the last time at Mark's party, and it feels comfortable, it feels like home.

Victor laughs and then brushes his nose against mine, and then I slightly part my lips and lean into him again, taking his bottom lip gently between my own.

'God,' he groans.

I pull away and smile at him, and we look deeply into each other's eyes.

'I *am* going, though,' he says, after a few seconds.

'I'm sorry?'

'I am going. To France. Whatever happens, you can't expect me not to go.'

'I know,' I say.

'If we do . . . *do* this, you can't then ask me not to go. I've been planning it for years.'

I shrug. 'Maybe I don't care,' I say.

'You say that now, but once I'm in the Alps and you're in . . .'

I raise a finger to his lips to silence him. 'Shush . . .' I say. 'Maybe I need a change too.'

Victor frowns at me, then raises one eyebrow. 'Really?' he says.

I nod. 'Really,' I say.

'Well then that's something we can work with,' Victor says.

'It is,' I agree.

And then he grins, and leans towards me again. 'In the meantime,' he murmurs, putting one hand behind my head and reeling me in.

The Day Before You Came

An hour later, once Victor has gone, I sit on my sofa and think about phoning SJ but decide that I can't call her without telling her what's happened, and that it's premature to tell her what *has* happened. I need to wait at least until I see if he returns.

I look around the room.

With the exception of Victor's scarf which he has forgotten, nothing in my lounge has changed. And yet, everything looks different. The scarf changes the entire room, in fact, *I* feel like a completely different person.

I am CC Kelly who seizes the day. I am CC Kelly who, incredibly, unbelievably would appear to have a new boyfriend: a beautiful, wonderful man with dreams of farms, and plans to make those dreams come true. A beautiful man with olive skin and a stubbly chin (*just* within acceptable limits, it turns out) who is coming back in two hours' time for dinner, and who, if I have anything to do with it, will be staying the night.

As I shower and change, and fix my face, I can hardly believe it's true. When did that happen?

It was Brian who taught me that nothing is permanent, and of course, Victor could still panic and change his mind. He could still phone and inexplicably cancel. He could still decide that it's all a bit too heavy, and do a runner.

But as I rummage in the freezer for something for dinner and hesitate with the thought that perhaps I shouldn't defrost two tuna steaks until he returns, I decide that no, this *will* happen. The act of putting the two steaks out to defrost, of laying the table

for two, of cooking courgette gratin for two feels superstitious –
it feels in fact like black magic.

Once everything is ready I lean back against the counter-top
and dare to look at the kitchen clock. It's five past eight. He
should be here by now.

And at that instant, there's a knock at the front door. I cross
the hall and open it.

Yes, it was Brian who taught me that everything can change
in an instant, Brian who taught me that no matter how good
things are, all it takes is a gust of wind and the whole shebang
comes toppling down.

I should have known this time around. I really ought to have
realised.

I should have understood that it works both ways.

I should have believed Mark when he said that, like that Abba
song, no matter how bad things are, everything can change in
an instant.

And one day, against all expectation, you open the front door,
and there he is. The missing boyfriend is missing no more –
he's right there on the doorstep, clutching a bottle of wine and
grinning cutely and rubbing his chin.

'Better?' he says.

I laugh and point at my own face. 'Better?' I ask.

'You said you weren't so keen on the stubble so . . .'

'No. Weird shit. I'll tell you all about it one day,' I say, 'but not
now. It might scare you off.'

I take Victor's coat and hang it in the hall, and then turn
towards the kitchen, but he reaches out and touches my shoulder
from behind and says, 'Hey.'

When I turn back to face him, he kisses me.

It's not a big passionate kiss. It's nothing more, in fact, than a
peck, a peck that says, simply, 'I can do this.' But that peck, well,
it's a peck that promises a thousand future kisses.

'You!' I say, smiling, and taking his hand to pull him through
to the kitchen. 'Oh, can you just give me one minute,' I say. 'I have
to call Sarah-Jane. She left a message on my voicemail earlier on.'

'Sarah-Jane Dennis?' he asks.

'Yes.'

'Then you should definitely call her,' he says.

'She says she has some news.'

'Yes, she does.'

I frown at him. 'How would *you* know?'

Victor shrugs mysteriously.

'Is it good news?'

Victor grins. 'You'll have to call her yourself, won't you?'

I grab my BlackBerry and head through to the lounge. 'I'll be one minute, honestly,' I say as I leave the room.

'Something smells good,' Victor calls behind me.

'Well I hope so,' I shout back. 'I hope it all turns out OK.'

But for the first time in ages, I know it will.

For the first time in ages, I know that everything, for once, will turn out OK.

THE END

Turn the page
for a preview of

SLEIGHT OF HAND

Paradise Lost

It was the incident with the dog that did it. We were sitting having a drink at Max's – a scruffy wooden bar at the edge of the national park. It had become a ritual of ours, a Friday night mojito, sometimes two – our attempt at marking the beginning of the weekend – at marking the passage of time. Neither Ricardo's random callouts as a doctor, nor my occasional translation work, nor the weird, season-less weather of Colombia provided much clue as to where you might be in the week, the year, in life. Our stay here so far felt, somehow, out-of-time – as if contained within brackets.

Max's was a perfect beach-bar and (in season) a sometimes-restaurant: a wooden shack built on stilts with the dense forest of the national park to the west, the occasionally raging Caribbean to the north, and a dusty/muddy car park everywhere else.

It was a twenty minute walk along the coast from our house and often, outside the tourist season, we, along with the effervescent, whistling Max, were the only people there. Occasionally there would be a couple of gamekeepers playing draughts in a corner, and of course for those few months of the year when Europeans and Americans take their brief holidays, the place would look more like Club Med than a lost corner of the Caribbean. But generally the only noise was the endless salsa drifting from Max's thankfully weedy transistor radio, and, depending on the direction of the wind, the sound of the waves.

Before the *corronchos* arrived it had all felt pretty perfect. The late afternoon sun was warm, the mojitos were cool enough for condensation to be trickling down the outside of the glass, and Max's radio had, rather superbly, run out of batteries. Not only had I finally finished and emailed my fifty-thousand word drudgery on EEC agricultural policy, but Ricardo's so often absent colleague was, for once, on-call: a whole weekend to ourselves.

Ricardo drew a circle in the dew on the side of his glass, looked up and smiled at me. "You know, Chupa Chups, there are moments when this place really is pa . . ." he said, and then paused, distracted by the sound of a car.

Like all nick-names *Chupa Chups* came about by accident. I had asked him what the lollypop brand name meant, and Ricardo had translated it as, *"Sucky Suck."* For weeks, I had been unable to see or hear those words without cracking up laughing, and the name had stuck. It still made me grin, even though I was mortified when from time to time, he accidentally used it in public.

We both turned to watch as a Porsche Cayenne appeared from the forest track. It stopped at the edge of the car park in a cloud of dust, and four young men in Miami-Vice suits got out – one of the guys actually had his jacket sleeves pushed up.

Ricardo sighed and looked back out to sea, and I copied him and did likewise, for there are men that you don't watch in Colombia – men, often enough, with Porsche Cayennes.

The four men lingered by the car talking energetically or maybe arguing. With the distance and their accents, and over the salsa music drifting from the car, I couldn't understand a word. Their over-loud voices sounded, though, like a challenge. The main thing they seemed to be saying, was, *"Look at us. Look over here. Aren't we something?"* And that was when the dog appeared.

It was irritating, it's true – a mangy, skinny half-breed sniffing around the edges of the terrace, pissing in a corner, pushing under tables and around chairs in its hunt for crumbs, and then around our feet, and finally out into the car park, and over towards the Porsche.

It snuffled its way around the rear of the car, and then fatally, and I mean, *fatally,* pissed on one of the tyres. One of the Porsche boys – the fat one with pocked skin, gave it an ineffectual kick and it yelped before starting somewhat lazily, to bark.

I became aware that my stress levels were rising. My skin was prickling and my throat felt suddenly dry, and I wondered briefly if I was being paranoid, or if I was channeling some future catastrophe, or if Ricardo, so calmly looking out to sea, was, as often, radiating his own specifically Colombian understanding of the situation.

One of the guys shouted over and asked, "¿Es éste tu perro?" – *is it your dog?* and Ricardo glanced over and simply shook his head in reply. To me, as an aside, he murmured, "No contestes." – *don't reply.* From the fact that he had chosen to speak in Spanish I knew I wasn't imagining *anything:* the only reason Ricardo ever used Spanish with me, was to avoid drawing attention to my status as a non-Colombian. I held my breath, and we both turned and looked back out to sea.

Nothing happened for a minute or so and despite the tension provoked by *not*-looking, I managed to start to breath again.

And then I heard the boot open and one of the guys laughed, and another cheered, and as cover, I raised my glass for a sip and glanced over just in time to see the fat guy pull an AK47 from the boot of the car and raise it to his hip. I opened my mouth to warn Ricardo but he kicked me hard, so I turned back out to sea and remained, like he, stoic, merely imagining the dog's dancing body as the rounds of gunfire let rip and hoping that there, that day, the dog would be the only one to die.

In the year since we had been living here, there had been other events of course: the disappearance of the Swedish girl last summer, the stabbing at a party we attended, the minicab murders . . . And even if Ricardo found reassurance variously in the fact that the Swedish girl had been found (with apparent amnesia) and the stab victim had survived (with a scar), and the minicab murders had all happened more than two-hundred kilometres away, for me these were all straws on a camel's back, drops of water in a proverbial French vase.

But the tipping point, the moment I specifically thought, *"No, I don't want to live here. I want to go home,"* was when they shot that dog. Because that's when I realised that these guys in suits in Porsche Cayennes have machine guns stored next to the wheel-jack. And that's when I saw that Ricardo sighed. As my own body jerked at each fired round, Ricardo *sighed* – he had become used to this. And I didn't *want* to get used to it.

I had assumed that the guys would now come to the bar, but once no more amusement was to be found in filling the dog with bullets, the gun was put back in the trunk, and the four guys simply climbed back into their 4x4 and accelerated off in a cloud of dust and fading salsa rhythms.

With a *whachagonnado* shrug and a raised eyebrow Max descended leisurely to the car park, and scooped the corpse of the dog into a bin-bag. When he had done this, his hands still bloodied, he leant against the fence and rolled himself a cigarette.

I said automatically, "I want to go home," and Ricardo, assuming that I meant to Federico's beach-house, downed the last of his drink and, with a nod and a weak smile, stood up. I chose, for the time being, not to explain further.

Ricardo took the coastal path back to the house and I didn't argue. The route through the forest was shorter but felt, if you were in a particular kind of mood, more menacing.

The path was pretty narrow, so I followed him – a little numb from the adrenalin aftershock – watching his buttocks move up and down, his shirt slowly sticking to his back, and then glancing left at the brochure-perfect beaches and right into the long shadows of the forest, and back again at the perfect beach. I thought about the contrasts of Colombia, so beautiful, so friendly. And yet . . .

Ricardo only turned once to speak to me during the walk. "I'm sorry about that," he said, as if it had somehow been his fault. But I knew what he meant. It was his country. He had brought me here. I knew how he took such things personally.

As we walked, I wondered if this feeling – that I had had it with Colombia – was a new permanent state of being or simply a momentary reaction to danger, and I decided that I needed a trip back to Europe to find out. I hadn't been back since we moved here over a year ago. It was time.

But if I told him how I felt, would it damage our relationship? That would be the last thing I would want.

Faithful, good natured, straightforward Ricardo – the man I thought I would never meet.

A part of him, the Colombian part, will always remain alien to me. It's hard to explain what the essence of that difference is . . . Perhaps a coldness that enables him to sigh as someone machine-guns a dog to smithereens is what best sums it up. Maybe a lightness of being that means that these things don't get to him the way they do to me – an optimism that is entirely unaffected by murder, rape or natural disaster. I know that all sounds contradictory, and really that's the whole point. The fact that I can't decide whether to describe it as solid and unshakable, or courageously optimistic, or cold and unfeeling, says it all: alien. Simply.

But other than this undefinable otherness, we are the most perfect fit I have ever found.

Back at the house, Ricardo said, "You just relax Chupy and watch the sunset and I'll make dinner," and I knew that the business of the machine gun and the dog – the most violent thing I had ever witnessed – was now over for him. For Ricardo it required no further discussion.

I checked my email to make sure my translation had reached its destination (it had), and was just about to shut down the computer for the evening when a rare email from Jenny popped up. Her mother had died, she said. She felt incredibly sad and alone, she said.

And my first thought, my very first shameful thought, was that *here* was the perfect excuse for a trip home. And then, I thought, *"And you reckon Ricardo is the cold one?"*